The Family
Business

The Family Business

Carl Weber

with Eric Pete

www.urbanbooks.net

Urban Books, LLC
97 N 18th Street
Wyandanch, NY 11798

ISBN 13: 978-1-60162-709-4
ISBN 10: 1-60162-709-2

First Mass Market Printing August 2013
First Hardcover Printing February 2012
First Paperback Printing September 2012
Printed in the United States of America

10 9 8 7 6 5 4

Distributed by Kensington Publishing Corp.
Submit Wholesale Orders to:
Kensington Publishing Corp.
C/O Penguin Group (USA) Inc.
Attention: Order Processing
405 Murray Hill Parkway
East Rutherford, NJ 07073-2316
Phone: 1-800-526-0275
Fax: 1-800-227-9604

Acknowledgments

First off, I'd like to thank my co-author, Eric Pete, for the phenomenal job he did molding this story. It's not an easy thing to take someone else's dream and make it your own, but you did, by breathing life into the Duncans. My thanks, Eric. I look forward to working with you on our many future projects.

To my adopted family, the Ds. If you look inside yourself, I'm sure you'll see one of these characters. I hope you take it as a compliment and a testament of my love for you and yours. Thank you for a lifetime worth of memories.

My thanks to Miss Martha for all the help and support you give me. As Chippy would say, "I hope you know which side your bread is buttered." And I do.

And last but not least, my thanks to Portia Cannon for her help in putting this whole thing together. Without you, this whole thing wouldn't have come together.

—Carl

Acknowledgments

A hearty welcome to all the readers out there who make this possible. And thanks to God, who makes it all possible.

I see you got your hands on The Family Business, the first collaboration between me and the big dawg, Carl Weber, who was Lookin' for Luv back in the day when I was just finding out Someone's In the Kitchen. Get it? If not, you Gets No Love. But enough of that, let's give thanks.

Marsha, thank you for putting up with me. Couldn't think of another person to keep my head above water with, making waves when we can. Best believe, we're gonna make tsunamis one day. Just . . . not . . . the . . . harmful ones, okay?

Chelsea, damn proud of the lovely, intelligent young lady you've become. Remember . . . Do great. Be great. (Couldn't let her have my motto now, could I?) I see ya with ya guns up. Now go wreck 'em, kid.

To all my friends and family, God has blessed me way more than I deserve with all of you in my life.

Couldn't do it on this book, but appreciate all my ghost readers over the years—Jacqueline, Shontea, Jackie, Jamie, Judith, Carmel, Natalie, Tommy, Nicole, Demetrius, Angela, Bob, Shelia, and Lisa. Your feedback and criticism is invaluable.

Carl Weber, glad we were able to come together on this project. Thanks for that tap on the shoulder. We did the damn thing, huh?

Portia Cannon, thank you for your tireless efforts on my behalf.

To all my fellow authors, I am honored and humbled to be counted among you Hey, in this business, ya just never know. Let's keep it going.

In closing, if this is your first time hearing of me, WTF? (I kid. Maybe.) Hope you kick the tires and take some of my other works, such as Piano in the Dark, Reality Check, Crushed Ice, Sticks and Stones or the upcoming Frostbite, for a spin. If you've been rolling, may you continue to roll.

As before, as now, as always,
Can't stop. Won't stop. Believe that.

—Eric

Drops mike.

Dedication

This book is dedicated to LC and Chip. You were like second parents to me, and I look forward to seeing you again someday.

—Carl

Paris

1

"Okay, Paris, let's go over this one more time. What exactly did the man who shot Councilman Sims's son look like?"

It was late, almost three in the morning, and standing in front of me was an obnoxious New York City homicide detective with bad breath and a Brooklyn accent. He and his partner, a homely brown-skinned woman who needed to do something with her ugly-ass weave, had me sitting in a small, dimly lit room somewhere in a police station in Brooklyn. This was the fifth time he'd asked me the same damn question, and there was no doubt in my mind that he was going to ask it again, because I wasn't saying shit.

You see, less than two hours before, I'd witnessed the shooting of my date, Trevor Sims, son of New York City councilman and congressional candidate Ronald Sims. Regrettably, Trevor didn't make it. He died five minutes after he was shot, right in my arms, which was why I was covered in his blood from head to toe. To say I was having a bad night was an understatement. I was having a terrible fucking night.

"Trevor, dammit! His name is Trevor! Stop calling him the councilman's son. He has a name," I corrected him as tears welled up in my eyes. I would have paid a million dollars to be anywhere but where I was right then.

"Correction, Paris. Had. He had a name," the bad-weave bitch stressed. "Trevor's no longer with us, because he's dead, and we're trying to figure out who did it. Now, I hate to break this to you, but you're the only witness we got to his shooting, so we're going to go over what you saw again. And, Paris, this time I want some fucking answers."

"Look, I told you I ain't got nothing to say. I just wanna go home. Look at me." I spread my arms apart so that they could see my blood-soaked DKNY dress.

The dog-breath detective laughed. "You're not going anywhere until we get some answers, Paris. We've got a congressional candidate's son in the morgue. Do you have any idea what that means?" He paused only for a second and then answered his own question. "That means the newspapers and media are going to be crawling all over this. Which means the chief of detectives is gonna be crawling up my lieutenant's ass, wanting some answers. Which means my lieutenant's gonna be crawling up my ass, looking for those answers. So, until I get them, I'm gonna be crawling up your ass."

"You can crawl wherever the hell you want to," I said flatly, folding my arms in defiance. "I ain't got shit to say."

I stared at the cop and wondered, if Trevor's dad were a garbageman or the janitor at Jamaica High School instead of a councilman running for Congress, would we even be going over this so thoroughly? My fellow clubgoers were being questioned all over the precinct about other victims of tonight's shootings, but Trevor's death was drawing the most attention because of his father's political connections and the fact that it was the only shooting outside the club, not inside. I was sure the mayor would have something to say about it in the morning. I just hoped they left me and my family out of it. God, my dad was gonna kill me just for being there.

"Why don't you have shit to say? Because of some stupid 'no snitching' code of the streets?" the female cop snapped. "Is that it? You got some stupid moral code?"

I stared at her briefly, then exploded in anger. "Are you for real? Do I look like I'm worried about some moral code of the streets? Bitch, I'm wearing a ladies' Rolex that's worth more than both your damn salaries combined." I flashed my wrist in front of her face. "Look, I'm a party girl, not a gangbanger. I've got Kim Kardashian on speed dial, not Lil' Kim. But maybe you don't know who I am, so let me introduce myself. My name is Paris Duncan, daughter of LC Duncan, the owner of Duncan Motors, the largest African American—owned car dealership chain in the tristate area. He donated almost a million dollars to the PBA last year, so why y'all hassling me? Maybe you need to make a few calls and find out just who the fuck I am and where I come from."

"We already know who you are," she replied irately, "and personally, I'm not impressed with you or your nigger-rich daddy. I just—"

I sprang to my feet, pointing my finger up in her face. "Don't be talking about my father, bitch. You don't know him!"

"I don't need to know him! And I'll talk about whoever I damn well please. Now, get your finger out my face and sit your ass down before I break it and you."

"I'd like to see you try." I was about to step around the desk and show her just who she was fucking with. Good thing for her that her partner cut me off.

"Paris, please sit down. Don't pay attention to her. She's not going to do anything to you. Just have a seat so we can talk, please. This is about

Trevor, not you and her. Let's focus." He guided me to my seat, then turned to his partner. "Anderson, sit your ass down!"

Would you believe that hooker with a badge did exactly as she was told? I turned my attention to her partner, who pulled his chair up next to me, gently encouraging me to sit down, like he was on my side. I gave that heifer a smirk that said I knew who had the real power in that partnership.

"Okay," he said. "So, if it's not some code, then why won't you cooperate? We're not the enemy here. We're just trying to find out who killed your boyfriend, so why won't you help us?"

"He's not my boyfriend. He was just a good friend. We just started dating." What I really meant was that he was a friend I never should have gone out with. "And the reason I ain't talking is because my lawyer's not here . . . yet," I replied. "I know my rights."

"You ain't got no rights," his partner barked.

"Anderson, will you please shut the hell up?" he snapped so I didn't have to. He turned to me, speaking so nonchalantly I almost felt like he meant it. "Paris, you're not under arrest, so what do you need a lawyer for?"

They were playing one hell of a game of good cop/bad cop, and I bet all those fools they interrogated fell for it—but not me.

"Yeah, famous last words. I'm not trying to cause any trouble. I'm just protecting my rights. Y'all ain't gonna get me caught up in no shit. My father told me about how cops play games and set people up, and he also told me to never say a word until I had a lawyer present." I sat back cozily, as if I were on a piece of designer furniture at home instead of this rickety old piece of shit in a police station.

"Look, we're not trying to play games or entrap you. You're a party girl . . . a celebutante," he said, making air quotes with his fingers. "I get that. But the longer we're playing around here, the longer your boyfriend's killer goes free. Don't you want justice?"

"He's not my boyfriend. How many times do I have to tell you that? And of course I want justice, but I also want to be alive to see it. Those dudes that killed Trevor are still on the street. I'm not getting involved with you so that they can come knocking on my door." I mumbled, "I'm not stupid. I watch Criminal Minds and Law and Order."

"Look, Paris, we can protect you. And we've got a pretty good idea who these guys are, but we just need a witness—someone who can identify at least one of them—and I know you saw who did this, didn't you?"

I didn't answer him, but couldn't restrain a nod in the affirmative.

He smiled, then said, "He was a big, dark-skinned black guy with a bald head, wasn't he? He was the one who shot Trevor, wasn't he?" I gave him a half nod, and he turned toward his partner with a nod of his own. "Look, Paris, all I need you to do is write down what you saw and look at a few pictures, and then you can get on out of here."

"That's it?" The thought of escaping that place had me lifting my head, but I wasn't convinced by a long shot. "That's all you want from me?"

"Yep, that's it," he said. "So, are you ready to go on the record with that? Write this down for us? Please." He picked up a legal pad and a pen. "You write this statement and I can have you out of here in a half hour, tops."

"I can have her out of here right now, and she doesn't have to write down a thing."

I cut a smile as my brother-in-law, Harris, stepped into the room, followed by a balding white man in a bad suit. Harris was the husband of my older sister, London. He was one of the best attorneys in New York and worked exclusively for our family business, Duncan Motors.

"What he said," I added, suddenly perking up.

"Who the hell are you?" Anderson asked.

"I'm her lawyer, and unless she's being arrested for something, I'm taking her home." He held out a hand to help me up out of the cheap-ass chair. "Come on, Paris."

"Lieutenant, she knows who the killer is," Officer Unbe-weave-able whined to the white guy who'd come in with Harris.

He just shrugged. "Cut her loose."

"Bye, guys," I said as I snatched my purse from the table. Walking to the door, I turned to Brooklyn's ugly-ass partner and smiled. "You impressed now, bitch?"

I almost skipped past Harris and the lieutenant, grinning from ear to ear, until I saw the imposing figure standing in the corridor outside the door.

"Uh-oh." I nearly let go of my bladder and peed on myself. Just the sight of my father, LC Duncan, standing there with his trademark fedora, tailor-fitted overcoat, and gray scarf draped over each shoulder scared the crap out of me. A huge part of me would rather have gone back in the room and faced the cops than dealt with the scowl on my father's face.

"Daddy, I didn't do anything. I swear."

LC
2

Eight hours earlier . . .

I walked into the large conference room of Duncan Motors for our annual year-end board of directors meeting, followed by my wife, Charlotte, who I called Chippy. Already seated at the table was Orlando, our tall, slim, brown-skinned third son. He had a phone to his ear as he worked an iPad like it was a piece of him. He didn't say much, other than to acknowledge his mother with a wave as we took our seats. Orlando wasn't being rude or anything; he was engaged in a phone conversation with one of our distributors about a shipment of pre-owned Bentleys for one of our six high-end pre-owned car dealerships.

Like myself, Orlando was a workaholic. He ran a tight ship, for which the devil was in the details. He was the company's chief operating officer, in charge of running the day-to-day operations of our dealerships. Only thirty-three years old, he was turning into one hell of a man, if I did say so myself. Of course, like everyone, he had his flaws of a sort. He had no idea I knew anything about it, but we were going to have to address it in the very near future.

"We're good, Pop. They turned the cars over to our guys in Maryland, and the shipment will be delivered sometime tomorrow," Orlando called out to me with a thumbs-up before continuing his conversation. In addition to our pre-owned car dealerships, we also owned three Toyota dealerships, which made us one of the largest African American dealers of cars in America, as per Black Enterprise magazine.

Chippy shook her head. "Will that boy ever learn to slow down?"

"Somebody has to pull the load around here," I replied, wishing the rest of my children had what Orlando possessed. They all contributed to the family business, but none of them had his work ethic. He was the first one in the office every morning and the last one out every night.

"I heard that," my youngest and more defiant son, Rio, chimed in as he walked into the conference room and took his seat. Rio was wearing a bright yellow paisley shirt that could be seen halfway across Queens.

He glanced over at Orlando, who had just finished up his conversation. "No offense, bro, but I bust my ass around here just as much as you. You're not the only one who makes a lot of money for this family. I don't hear anybody complaining when the money from the clubs gets deposited on Monday morning, or about the two BMW 650 convertibles DJ Two-Tone bought on my recommendation last week."

Rio spearheaded the marketing and promotions aspects of Duncan Motors, a creative endeavor he came up with himself. He paired the two things celebrities loved most: exotic cars and parties. Where there were celebrities, there were fans willing to buy everything their idols purchased. I wouldn't admit it to him, but his brainchild was a brilliant, unquestionable success that had only served to expand the family's reach in ways I didn't think possible.

Orlando nodded, acknowledging his brother's work, but I took a different path, rolling my eyes in my youngest son's direction. "Do you call going out to a club all night and sleeping until three and four in the afternoon busting your ass?"

"Nope," Rio huffed, meeting my gaze with one of his own. "I call it the night shift. When you're sleeping, I'm working. Why can't you understand that? Is this because I'm gay?" Rio pulled his sunglasses down, peering over them as he struck a very feminine pose.

"Don't mess with your father, Rio. Not tonight, all right?" Chippy warned, with a look that said she meant business.

Rio shrugged his shoulders and gave her an angelic smile. Of all our children, he was the closest to Chippy. She loved and accepted him as is—no exceptions. I, on the other hand, loved my son but just couldn't accept his lifestyle. I just couldn't wrap my head around the fact that my son was a homosexual. I didn't think I ever would. His sexual preference disgusted me.

"I'm not messing with him, Momma. I'm just trying to make a point. I bring business into this company too." Rio sat back in his chair and folded his arms. "I just think a little recognition would be nice."

"Are you finished?" I asked. The look on my face said everything that didn't come across my lips.

With a final glance from his mother, Rio softened his demeanor and nodded. "Yeah, Pop, I'm finished."

I turned my attention away from Rio just as a cute little bundle of energy came into the room, scurrying around the conference table and chairs as if they were her own personal playground. That little bundle of joy was my granddaughter, Mariah, and with her mother on her heels, she bolted just out of reach behind me and her grandmother.

"Mariah! What did I tell you about running in here?" her mother shouted.

Mariah's mother, my eldest daughter and fourth child, London Duncan Grant, was a tall, classy, butter almond–colored woman, the spitting image of her mother when she was the same age.

"It's okay, London," I said, handing my only granddaughter one of the lollipops I carried in my suit pocket just for such occasions. She was the apple of my eye. I loved my children, but my granddaughter stole my heart from the moment I set eyes on her. As far as I was concerned, I would lay the world at her feet. "Let her be. She has just as much right to be here as the rest of us. One day this will all belong to her, anyway."

Mariah took the lollipop out of my hand and gave me an affectionate kiss on the cheek before taking off again. When she passed my eldest son, Junior, he caught her with one arm and deposited her in his lap as he took his seat. She giggled at her uncle's sudden display of strength. If she were older, she wouldn't have questioned it at all, because Junior was six feet five inches tall and a solid 270 pounds of pure muscle.

As big as he was, Junior could be as gentle as a lamb—unless provoked. He was in charge of our car carrier and transportation fleet of trucks, along with overseeing our service mechanics. He wasn't involved much with the financial end of our company, but he could drive and fix anything with an engine, which in our business made him very valuable indeed.

"Humph. Daddy, you'd let that girl get away with murder if you could. I don't recall you ever saying anything like that to us when we were growing up," London said with a slight attitude as she took a seat beside her husband, Harris Grant. He and my daughter had met while she attended George Washington University in Washington, D.C., and Harris was attending Georgetown University Law School.

Harris was always thinking, and that keen mind of his had allowed him to graduate magna cum laude from Georgetown. In the years since he and London got married, Harris had become an integral part of all our business affairs and was now the company's in-house legal counsel. This allowed London to happily relinquish her duties as sales manager and focus on being a loving mother and devoted wife, something she took very seriously and sometimes to extremes.

"Y'all were my kids. It was my job to raise you right. Mariah's my granddaughter, and it's our job to spoil her." I smiled at my daughter, then lifted my hand to my wife, who gave me a high five.

"Well, that ain't making my job any easier. That girl is just as spoiled as can be."

"Ha! That's what the fuck I'm talkin' about, Mariah," Paris, Rio's twin and perhaps the most attractive of our children, blurted out inappropriately as she walked in with some man I didn't know behind her. "Let them spoil you, girl. You gonna be just like your aunt Paris, aren't you?

Kiss the boys and make them motherfuckers cry!" Paris laughed, but no one in the room—other than Rio—joined in.

London glanced at her younger sister and rolled her eyes. "Could you please stop cursing in front of my daughter? What is wrong with you?"

"Stop tripping, London. She hears much worse than that just sitting out in the service area with Junior and them."

"Well, I haven't heard that, but I heard you—"

Harris gently took his wife's arm and mumbled, "London, it's not worth it."

London glanced at me and my wife and then at her husband before she sat back in her chair obediently. "This is some bull. They'd never let me get away with this."

"Daddy," Paris said in this gushing voice that customarily rose in pitch when she was seeking my approval. It usually worked, too, except when it had to do with men. Yes, she was a daddy's girl; there was no question about that. I didn't know why, but I had a weakness for my youngest daughter, despite the fact that she always seemed to be getting herself in some kind of trouble I had to bail her out of. "Daddy, I'd like you to meet Trevor. Trevor, this is my father, Lavernius Duncan Sr."

"Pleased to meet you, sir. Ma'am," he said, greeting Chippy as well. "You have a wonderful daughter."

"Uh-huh," I said. Still holding the young man's hand in mine, I turned to Paris, who was smiling like she'd won the lottery. "So, in what hole did you find this one, Paris? Please tell me you didn't buy the suit he's wearing, like you did the last one." I spoke loudly to be sure the young man understood I didn't care if he heard my insult.

"Daddy!" Paris shrieked. Her pretty, high yellow face turned beet red from embarrassment. I loved Paris dearly, but I never was one to mask my disappointment in her, especially in her choice of men.

"We met at Antun's catering hall in Queens Village, sir, and it's not like that at all. The suit's mine," Paris's date asserted, to my surprise. The rest of the family was taken aback, too, from the looks on their faces. Most of Paris's little male friends were, unfortunately, bad boys, thugs, or sheep, and were intimidated by me. Surprisingly, this one wasn't.

"Oh, really? Tell me how it is, son," I urged, my curiosity piqued by the nature of the stranger in our midst.

"We were having a fund-raiser for my father's election campaign when I met Paris, sir. Nothing improper. I believe your wife was there also."

I glanced over at Chippy, who nodded.

"His dad is Councilman Sims," Paris added, trying to take back control of the conversation.

"Ronald Sims? He's running for Congress, isn't he?" I was keenly aware of New York's political landscape and the players in all five boroughs, especially Queens. Ronald Sims was definitely a player who was on the rise.

"Yes, he is." Trevor smiled.

I was sure he was hoping for a quick thaw between us, but he'd forgotten one thing: Paris was my daughter, and I knew his only objective was to get her into bed. He was going to have to show his face around here a hell of a lot more, and preferably on days I wasn't conducting a board of directors meeting, if he expected me to thaw.

"So, no, I don't need anyone to buy me a suit—but my father could really use your support in his reelection campaign," he added.

I let out a hearty chuckle that filled the room, and then glanced over at Orlando and Harris, who both nodded their heads and discreetly began to type into their iPads. "You know what, young man? I admire your moxie—or rather your swagger, as it's called these days. I've always been one to preach involvement in family endeavors to my children. Good to see your father is of a like mind. We'll have to see what we can do for our future congressman."

I nodded at Paris, who seemed pleased as she placed her arm in Trevor's and led him toward the door. While not quite up to the level of her sister, perhaps there was some hope, after all, when it came to Paris's choice in men.

Chippy leaned over and whispered in my ear, "Dear Lord, LC, has Paris lost her mind and invited that man to sit in on one of our board meetings?" I glanced back over toward the door and, to my dismay, watched Paris and her new friend take two empty seats by the entrance. Why the hell she would have that man sit in at one of our board meetings was beyond my comprehension. Perhaps Chippy was right; she'd lost her damn mind.

"Uh-huh, that's exactly what she's doing." I took a deep breath, trying to calm my nerves, because I was known to have a very explosive temper. Why couldn't that girl be more like her brothers and sister and just use common sense? Ain't no way London or any of the others would be stupid enough to invite a stranger to one of our private business meetings. I was about to storm over there when Chippy took hold of my wrist.

"She's only doing this to impress you. You know she usually doesn't date guys like him. She wants you to see she can pick a smart man like London," Chippy mouthed softly. "We might not be able to speak as candidly as we'd like with him in the room, but let's see how it goes. The kids all know better than to discuss anything beyond the basics in front of a stranger, so it won't matter. We can always ask him to step out of the room if we get on a topic that's not for his ears. The rest we can discuss tomorrow in private."

I glanced over at Paris, who was leaning up against the boy, with her head on his shoulder. She really didn't have a clue, and that scared me.

"Besides, Trevor . . . and his father could be useful to us one day."

I looked over at my wife, a little shocked by her response. "You sure about this?"

"Yes, I'm sure you can handle it. You always do. Now, let's go get us a plate so we can get started." Chippy smiled that prideful smile she sometimes gave me, admiring my ability to always think on my feet and adapt. It was one of the many qualities she said attracted her to me those many years past. Back then, she knew I was a man with drive and a certain "moxie" myself—moxie that rescued her from the cursed path upon which she once strode.

Once everyone was seated, I stood and cleared my throat to get everyone's attention. They turned to me, looking eager for whatever I had to say, probably because they knew the year-end meeting was when I thanked everyone for their individual contributions and handed out rather substantial bonus checks. The only one who seemed to sense something awry in my demeanor was Orlando. He exchanged looks with his mother but came away with nothing.

"First of all, I want to tell you all that your mother and I are blessed to have everybody together tonight, including our new guest," I said, with a nod to Paris's friend Trevor.

I couldn't help but notice how the acknowledgment chafed Harris, the last outsider to become something more within the family and the business. I could see he had already begun assessing whether the young man was a potential threat.

I continued, "As I do at the end of every year, I have called all of us together for a brief slowdown from the crazy pace we set for ourselves. This moment is to reflect and to thank you for your hard work. You're all very special to me and your mother, and not just for your value as part of what we've built here, but as a family. It's not my normal demeanor to be so emotional, but I do love all of you, despite some of our differences. I'm proud of you all." I purposely glanced in Rio's direction. Chippy patted my leg approvingly under the table.

"Damn, Pops!" Rio exclaimed, a mischievous grin forming on his lips. "You tryin' to break a brother down or what? You acting like you got cancer or somethin'." He wiped fake tears.

"Rio!" Chippy scolded.

"Oops. Sorry, Momma."

Rather than burning Rio with my gaze, I said, "Let him be, Chippy." This unusual action got everyone's attention. London shushed Mariah, who was now seated on her lap. Paris stopped fidgeting with her hair for Trevor's benefit. Junior sat with his mouth agape. "Right now, each one of you owns three percent of the company, for a total of eighteen percent. Your mother and I are giving each one of you five percent more."

"Dad, what's up? You and Momma okay?" Orlando asked.

With a glance at Chippy, I spoke, my deep growl diminishing with each successive word, to where it was almost a whisper at the end. "Yes, son. We're okay, but your mother and I will be ending our hand in the day-to-day business operations."

The room was silent, until Paris stood, ready to take on the world to protect me.

"Why, Daddy? Did something happen? 'Cause don't nobody mess with the Duncans. 'Cause—" Paris cut herself off, glancing down at her date. I was sure she would have loved to say more, but Trevor's presence kind of hindered that.

"No, princess. Nothing happened other than old age. All of you are grown now, and your mother and I aren't getting any younger. We'll be retiring to the house on Fisher Island soon, so we wanted to give you all time to adjust to the changes ahead."

"Retiring," Harris blurted out. I guess my right-hand man was caught more off guard than anyone. He looked hurt, too, probably because Chippy and I had kept this announcement very close to the vest, and he was used to being in the know. I was sorry for that, but he'd have to get over it, because it was already done.

"So if you're retiring, who's going to be in charge? Who's going to be you while you're in Florida?" I was sure Junior was simply seeking clarity. Although he was the oldest and possessed unquestionable loyalty to the family, nothing in his makeup said leader.

The room fell silent again as they all waited for my answer.

"I'm glad you asked, Junior. Your mother and I thought long and hard about this," I replied, sure to make eye contact with each of them. "First of all, technically nothing changes. Your mother and I are still the majority shareholders, but someone has to make decisions in our absence, and ultimately . . . we decided the person best suited for the job is Orlando."

All eyes turned to Orlando, and as they studied him, I studied them. They had no idea what the future would bring, and neither did I, but I knew something wasn't right, and that was why I was stepping down so that I could prepare.

Orlando

3

Every eye in the room was upon me the second my name slipped out of my father's mouth. I scanned the room, looking each of my siblings in the eye as I tried my damnedest to hold back a smile. Yes, my father had chosen me to lead them, and I was sure there was going to be some resistance, but he had to choose me. It was the most obvious choice. Who else would he have chosen to lead us—Harris, Junior, or Rio? I don't think so. I mean, Rio didn't have a chance, and although Harris was smart and close to the old man, he still wasn't blood, and everyone knew Junior didn't want the responsibility. Besides, I'd worked my ass off for this business, for this family, so why wouldn't they appoint me its new leader? I just wished Pop had told me ahead of time so that I could have come up with something inspirational to say.

No matter. I'd think of something when the time was right.

I hadn't even gotten a chance to let things sink in before my pain-in-the-ass little sister Paris stood up, pointing her finger at me and shouting with her usual lack of tact, killing the moment. "Daddy, why him? Why would you choose Orlando to be in charge?"

My father's head swiveled in her direction. "You wanna know why? Because I said so, that's why."

Paris's spoiled nature, along with the fact that she was my father's unquestionable favorite, allowed her leeway in most situations, but the look in the old man's eyes was all that was needed to remind her to sit down and not question him any further.

It was obvious to us all that he wanted to say more to my sister but held his tongue due to her guest, the politician's kid. Why the hell would she bring someone she barely knew to a business function like this, anyway? All she was really doing was trying to seek brownie points with the old man. Maybe if she were more focused on business, like the rest of us, instead of partying and men, she'd have his attention the way she wanted it.

Foolishly, she mumbled something to my brother Rio, and my father looked even more pissed.

"What was that?" he snapped, his eyes shifting back and forth between Paris and Rio. "You two got something to say?"

Rio slumped back in his chair, but Paris boldly stood up again and said, "I'm sorry, Daddy, but I gotta say this. What about Vegas? How you gonna put Orlando in charge and pass by Vegas?"

Once again the room fell silent, and this time all eyes, including mine, were on LC. Heck, now that she'd mentioned it, I wished I had asked that question myself. Vegas was my older brother, between Junior and me. He'd been away for almost three years, but everyone in the family, including me, knew he'd been groomed to be the heir apparent since we were little. He was the only one in my family, other than the old man, I'd have no problem taking a backseat to.

Pop glanced knowingly at my mother, as if this had been the subject of many conversations between them. He sighed, then glanced at each one of us. "Your mother already spoke to Vegas about this, and he's one hundred percent behind our decision to have Orlando run the business. As you all know, he's got other things he's taking care of right now."

Yeah, but what's going to happen when he comes back? I thought as I watched Paris take her seat. My little sister and I were going to have a long talk in the near future, because there were going to be some changes around here now that I would be in charge. Her spoiled behind wouldn't like the changes one bit, but she was going to have to deal with it.

"Are you sure about this?" I asked before adding, "Um . . . about the retirement?" Couldn't let them think I was unprepared for the announcement—even if I was.

"Mm-hmm. We're sure about our retirement, son, just as we are about you leading this family." The look he gave me almost dared me to refuse. Of course, he knew I wouldn't, even though it was not going to be easy to deal with my siblings—and Harris. But life isn't about knowing everything, especially in our business. It's about how you handle the unknown; how you stare it in the eye, laugh in its face, and conquer it.

"Is this something immediate, LC?" Harris asked. I knew he hoped it wouldn't be, because that would give him time to manipulate things to his benefit. Despite the fact that my brother-in-law and I worked well together, it didn't mean I trusted him completely. Maybe it was our matching ambition and intensity that put us naturally at odds.

Harris had made us all a lot of money over the years, but I still questioned my father's reliance on this dude. He hadn't done anything to betray the family, and I didn't have any clear-cut reason to distrust him, so it probably just rubbed off on me from Vegas. He had never trusted Harris, and wasn't shy about his feelings, despite Harris's hard work and apparent loyalty to our family. Vegas never told me what his beef with Harris was, but I was pretty sure it had something to do with our sister London.

"No, Harris. We'll have time before Chippy and I wash our hands entirely of the business, but I felt it was time to let you all know. That way those who may need to step up and pull their weight will have the opportunity to do so. You don't have anything to worry about, Harris. Orlando may be sitting in my chair, but yours will remain next to it. He's going to need your advice and counsel."

"I see. That's good to know," Harris replied, adjusting his suit jacket. It had been established that there was still a need for him, and I was sure he'd do all he could to exploit that. Still, my father had made his decision, and the decision was me. I didn't think it could have been any clearer.

"Congrats, bro," Junior succinctly uttered. He'd have my back in this. He was too easygoing to want to deal with this leadership shit. As good-natured and gentle as he was, that was what Junior did so well—the not-so-gentle stuff.

"You okay with this, bro?" I whispered. I really didn't want him to feel as if I were taking him for granted.

"Yeah, you know me," he said, as expected. "Can't say the same about the rest of them, though. With them you're going to have to prove yourself. Maybe even knock a few heads, if you know what I mean." He let out a chuckle and looked around the room at my other siblings and my brother-in-law.

I already knew where Paris stood in all this. She'd made her position clear, but the rest were riddles, sure not to talk about or reveal their true feelings in front of Momma, Pop, or the outsider at the table. All I had were my assumptions, as Rio, Harris, and London took turns sizing me up the rest of the night.

While they did that, I tried digesting what it was going to mean to head an organization created by the great LC Duncan. What would I do differently once given complete free rein? What I did know was that I had to continue to build the empire my father had worked so hard to establish.

Finally, Harris walked over, extending his hand. "Congratulations, O. How about we sit down at the house with a cocktail and go over your vision for the future? I've got some great ideas for expanding in the South and Midwest."

I wasn't sure what he was up to, but if he was extending an olive branch, I was going to take it. "Sure, Harris, I'd like that. We're going to take this family to the next level. You wait and see."

"We sure are." He gave me a smile that almost looked like a smirk as he walked back over to my sister. "See you back at the house in, say, an hour?"

"I'll be there." I slipped my BlackBerry from my pocket when I felt it vibrate. I'd received a text.

Just got some new shit in right off the boat. You were the first one that came to mind. You interested?

I lifted my head from the phone, then glanced left and right to make sure no one was within eyesight of my BlackBerry screen.

I glanced over at Harris, who was guiding my sister and niece toward the door, then replied to the text.

Damn right I'm interested. I was just given a big promotion at work and have a lot to celebrate. Give me about an hour to slip away.

The return text read, Congratulations. I'll have my sister set everything up for the exchange.

I glanced over at Harris again. Sorry, Harris, but our little meeting may have to wait until morning.

Paris

4

I'm sorry, but I couldn't get with the Kumbaya after hearing Daddy was leaving us—leaving me—for palm trees and sunshine. So, with Trevor in tow, I bolted out of there right after Daddy adjourned the meeting, so I could fucking breathe. There was nothing else to talk about, anyway. At least nothing left for me to talk about.

I'm sure King Orlando had a lot to say after Trevor and I were in the wind. I just didn't understand what the hell Momma and Daddy were thinking about by leaving Orlando in charge, anyway. I swear, I loved my brother, but if he tried to put me on an allowance, I was gonna kill his ass.

"You have quite a family," Trevor said as he drove me away from the dealership.

I guess he didn't notice that I wasn't in the mood for small talk. And what the fuck did he mean by "quite a family"? I wasn't sure if he meant that shit as a compliment or sideways-ass insult. Right about now, I didn't give a damn what he meant by it. I just wished he would shut the fuck up and drive. I needed a drink and some good music, and perhaps, if he was lucky, some dick, so I told him to head to the Jackie Robinson Parkway and good old Brooklyn.

Orlando in charge? Orlando? I could see Vegas, but all Orlando cared about were his reports and numbers. He couldn't see the big picture, my picture. Pompous ass. He already thought he ran things, walking around like he owned the dealerships, telling me what I could and couldn't do. Luckily, Daddy was always there to set him straight. But now? Now it was gonna end, because basically Daddy had confirmed what Orlando had always thought: that he was the king of the world—or the Duncans, anyway. Well, we'd see how much of a king he was when Vegas came home. If he ever came home.

I rolled my eyes in Trevor's direction as I opened my phone to read a text that had just come through: You ain't had to say bye, heifer. Despite how angry I was about everything that went down, I had to laugh at my twin brother's text. He and Vegas always knew how to bring a smile to my face.

Sorry, bro. Had to get outta there. Going to BK for some drinks and music. Wanna meet us there? I replied.

Can't. Got to work the club, or big bad O may fire me. LOL.

He ain't gonna do shit! I replied.

I know. Just messin' with you. So what's up with your boy Trevor? Thought we were into bad boys.

I know, right? Shit, I'm still trying to decide if he's on your team or mine.

Don't get it twisted, sister. He ain't on my team. If he was, I would know and would have let you know when he first walked in. I wish he was, though. He's cute, in a preppy kinda way.

He's kinda boring. That's what he is. The things I do for Daddy. Listen, we need to talk about O when you get home.

"Paris?" Trevor called just as I hit send. From the tone of his voice, you would have thought he read my text.

"Huh?" I turned to him.

Dammit, if somebody had told me there was going to be an announcement tonight, I would have never brought Trevor's preppy ass to the meeting. He made me look like a fool in front of Daddy and the rest of the family. Without him around, Daddy never would have snapped at me and probably would have answered my question.

Not that I gave a shit about Trevor. Sure, he was cute, and I was a little curious about what he was packing under the Ivy League suit, but he was as boring as watching snow melt. Nah, to be truthful, I think I'd rather watch snow melt than listen to his boring ass. All he ever talked about was his father's election and what graduate school he planned on attending. God, if he told me one more time about how hard it was to choose between Harvard Law and Princeton, I was going to throw up in my mouth. Why the hell couldn't he talk to me about something important, like when the hell he was gonna fuck me? This was the third time I'd been out with his ass, and he ain't even tried to sniff the pussy. I'd basically written him off. Only reason I dragged his ass along today was so I could show Daddy that I could attract the same kind of boring-ass man as London if I wanted to.

"Why aren't you talking?" he asked as we entered the Jackie Robinson Parkway.

"I'm sorry. My brother was texting me," I answered just as Rio's reply came in.

We sure do. Knock on my door when you get home.

I gave Trevor a fake smile, then texted, K, gotta go. Mr. Boring wants to talk. LOL.

"Your father surprised you, huh? Mine does that to me all the time, always springing a change in campaign strategy or unscheduled appearances. I know a car dealership—"

"Ships. Dealerships. Plural. We own many," I said, correcting him as I held one hand aloft. He was starting to bug me more with each passing minute. Why couldn't he just sit there and look cute?

"Oh. Sorry. What I was saying was that car dealerships are different than politics, but some things are the same."

"It's all politics, Trevor." I swooshed my hand and stared out the window.

"Yeah. You're right," he agreed. "I should've learned that when I attended Harvard. . . . You know, I never asked you this. Where did you go to school, Paris?"

Damn. Now it was twenty fuckin' questions. "I didn't. After high school I attended a very special finishing school in Europe, and then I came home and got involved in the family business."

"Oh, wow. I never knew you didn't go to college."

"Why? Is it a problem?" I snapped back with attitude. I knew he wasn't about to talk shit about my upbringing!

"No, no, not at all. I just assumed you went, is all. Most people our age who have family like yours have gone to college." This SOB sounded genuinely disappointed that I hadn't experienced the richness of an Ivy League life like he had. "Ever thought about college?"

Blah. Blah. Blah. "Too busy for college."

"Too busy? Too busy doing what?"

"Stuff for my dad. I'm the company trouble-shooter. I handle collections."

"Collections, huh?" he scoffed. "Sounds like your dad just made up a job for you. You trust fund babies got it made. But I'm not mad at you."

"Huh? What the fuck is that supposed to mean? Nigga, for your information, ain't nothing I do for my father made up. I work for a living, and I probably make more than you and your daddy combined, so what the fuck I need with college?" As I pierced him with my eyes, I prayed that he didn't call me out for lying. The truth was that although I did have a job with the company, I wouldn't know where to send the check if Orlando handed me my American Express bill.

"Hey, I'm sorry. I always heard about you and your brother Rio at parties and clubs and stuff. I figured you were living off of some inheritance. I never knew you worked a real job. Poor assumption on my part."

That was the problem with men: they could ruin their chance of getting a good piece of ass by opening up their mouths and letting some dumb shit come out.

"Yeah. Poor assumption, all right. You have no clue, no clue at all how hard I work," I muttered, looking at my reflection in the car window.

He changed the subject. "I hope you don't mind me asking, but I couldn't help but notice that you and your siblings are all named after cities. What's that all about?"

I wanted to say, "None of your fucking business, and why the fuck do you keep asking me all these dumb-ass questions?" but instead I answered with plenty of attitude, "My mother was real poor when she was growing up, and she always wanted to travel. So, after they named my brother Junior after my father, she named the rest of us after cities she wanted to see. I hope you don't have a problem with the fact that she was poor."

"No, no, I think it's interesting, really. Truth is, my mom was kinda poor until she met my dad also," he said, like I was supposed to care. "So, has she had the chance to go to any of those places?"

"Every damn one of them, and so have I."

"Oh yeah? What did you think of Rio? I went down there as part of this National Geographic photography program when I was in high school."

"Jesus Christ, can this motherfucker get any more boring?" I muttered under my breath.

He leaned over in my direction. "I'm sorry. Did you say something?"

"Yeah," I replied, reaching over into his lap. "I said you're boring me, and I hate to be bored, so let's try something a little more interesting. You drive while I suck." I unhooked my seat belt and leaned my head over into his lap to give him a blow job. Shit, maybe if I was lucky, this would finally shut him the fuck up.

London

5

After my dad's announcement, Harris, Mariah, and I were the first ones headed home to the family compound in Far Rockaway, where my immediate family, my parents, and my siblings lived—or in some cases, kept rooms to appease my mother. I still couldn't believe how childish Paris had been, bitching and moaning about Daddy and Momma's decision. Not only that, but what was she thinking by bringing that boy to our board meeting? If that was me, Daddy would have wrung my neck without giving it a second thought. Well, thank God that Orlando was going to be in charge now; he'd make sure she wouldn't get away with anything like that in the future. I just hoped he'd let Harris have a free hand in things like Daddy did, so my husband wouldn't lose his mind.

It was pretty evident from his reaction that, like Paris, Harris was concerned about Orlando being in control. Personally, I didn't understand what the big deal was. We were all going to get rich no matter who called the shots. Why the heck was everyone so obsessed with the power structure? Besides, none of this was even going to matter if Vegas ever decided to come home.

I glanced over at Harris, who was fiddling with his phone while he was driving. "Honey, stop texting while you're driving. It's dangerous. You could have an accident, and Mariah's in the car."

"Yeah, I know," he said but still continued what he was doing. He finally slipped the phone on his hip, giving me a fake smile. "Sorry, sweetheart. I was just texting Orlando back. He said he has something to do and can't meet with me at the house like we'd planned. He wants to meet after breakfast."

"So meet with him after breakfast. It's not like the company's going to fall apart between now and the time the two of you eat your Raisin Bran."

"I guess, but if I'd known that, I could have met with your father. Damn, what could he possibly have to do right now?"

"I don't know, Harris."

He glanced back and forth between the road and me like I had some hidden answer.

"I bet you he's going to meet with some of the boys in the office, or even with Uncle Lou." He sighed. "This could be bad for us, London. This whole situation could be very bad for us. Did you know anything about this before tonight? Did your mother tell you this was going to happen?" Harris asked, cutting a glance from the road to me. "And stop slouching. It's not ladylike. What type of example are you setting for my daughter?" He shook his head.

I sat up in my seat to appease him, because I hated when he took that tone. I hoped this mood didn't last too long. I hadn't seen him this uptight since before my father asked him to work for the company full-time right after I got pregnant with Mariah. I guess he was really hurt by Daddy choosing Orlando over him to run the business. He did seem to fancy himself Daddy's son, despite the fact that he was only a son-in-law. As much as I loved him, he just didn't get it. He was family, but he wasn't blood, and to LC Duncan, that meant everything.

"What about your father? Did he say anything about this?"

"Honey, we both know you spend more time with him these days than me," I replied, stifling a yawn as I watched the streetlights roll past. "Home and kids, remember? Suzy Homemaker, that's me. You make it; I spend it."

"And that's the way you like it. Remember?" he shot back. "Time to shop, do lunch with your girlfriends, get your nails done, and do charity work with your mother. No more worries about the business, which used to stress you out. You got everything you ever wanted, and we only have one kid so far."

"But no stress over that, right?" I sighed. "Except when you bring it up."

"What do you want from me, London? I come from a big family."

I rolled my eyes but kept my mouth shut. I did not want to fight with him. I wasn't in that type of mood. I'd had a few drinks earlier, and all I really wanted was to get home, put my daughter to bed, and have my husband make love to me. That would be a perfect end to the evening.

"Well, maybe if we had sex a little more often, we'd have another child." I tried my best to sound encouraging, but there was a lot of frustration behind my words. "We could work on that tonight, when we get home, if you'd like." I ran my index finger up the side of his thigh. "What do you think? Wanna make a baby?"

Harris's BlackBerry interrupted us before he could reply. I watched him slide it out of its holster and glance at it. Rather than answer it, he did something he rarely ever did: he hit the ignore button.

"Don't you need to take that call?" I asked.

"Nah. We're talking," he said, but that didn't make sense, because he always answered his phone. "Now, what were you saying about working on expanding our family?" He gave me this bullshit grin that just screamed guilty. The question was, guilty of what?

"Honey, let me see your phone for a second, please?" I didn't get indignant. In fact, I asked nicely, like the lady I was.

"Huh?" He placed both hands on the steering wheel.

"Don't huh me, Harris. Now, can I please see your phone?" I calmly repeated to my suddenly deaf husband.

There was a pause before he answered me. "London, please don't start."

"Sweetheart," I said coyly, "I'm not trying to start. I just want to see your phone." I stuck out my left hand and waited.

"Why?" he asked, now determined to pay more attention to the road than me.

"Because I'm not stupid, Harris, that's why. I think we both know I'm a highly educated woman. Now, may I please see your phone?" I moved my hand closer to him.

"You're barking up the wrong tree on this, London. That phone call was business."

"I'm sure it was. Now, why don't you let me see your phone, and this will all be over." I was trying to remain cool. My daughter was sleeping in the backseat, and the last thing I wanted was for her to wake up to her parents arguing.

"No, it's business. You're not in the family business anymore, so there is no need for you to see it. Now, I think it's time to change the subject, before I'm the one who gets mad." He reached down and turned on the radio.

Well, if he wasn't going to give me his phone on his own accord, then I was going to have to take matters into my own hands. I reached for his holster where his phone was hooked, but before my hand got within six inches of his phone, his hand came out of nowhere and he slapped me in the face.

I'd been hit harder, but this wasn't a love tap, either, and my head went flying up against my window. I instinctively raised both hands to stop the next two blows.

"Why are you always pushing me?" he shouted, both hands back on the wheel. "I told you it was a business call, but you always have to push me, don't you, London?"

I was massaging my cheek and lip where the first blow had landed. "Why'd you hit me? I didn't deserve that." Although I tried, I couldn't hold back the tears.

"Yes, you did. You need to learn your place and stop questioning me. You are not your mother, London, and I am not your father. I am not going to put up with your shit. How many times do I have to tell you that? Next time I'm not going to be so nice."

Orlando

6

I entered the two-bedroom condo I kept in Port Washington, out on Long Island, and tossed my coat over the back of a chair. This place was my sanctuary, my home away from home that no one in my family knew about. It was fully furnished from top to bottom with every gadget a man could desire: a water bed, a fully stocked bar and fridge, and a hot tub on the balcony, which overlooked Hempstead Harbor. I came here once or twice a week, when I needed to unwind and indulge in the only vice that truly gave me pleasure.

"Maria," I called out before plopping my six-foot-one frame down on the sofa. I picked up the remote control to turn on the TV.

I knew she had already arrived when I spotted the open bottle of wine on the kitchen table. If I knew Maria, she was probably in my bedroom, preparing everything for tonight's little party. I'd been dealing with Maria and her brother Remy for a little more than two years now because of their discreet business practices and the high quality of their merchandise. Very rarely had I been disappointed, and on the rare occasion that I was, Remy quickly made it up to me with something even better.

"Hola, Orlando," Maria replied from the direction of the bedroom.

I turned toward the voice, and there stood Maria Lopez, a drop-dead gorgeous Dominican beauty with a long, flowing weave, a perfectly made-up face, and a surgically enhanced figure that would have put any Playboy model to shame. She was wearing a tight-fitting gold dress that cut off just below her perfectly round hips, and a pair of six-inch gold heels that accented her supermodel legs. I swear she looked like some kind of hyped-up mythological goddess who was put on this earth for one reason and one reason only—fucking.

"Hey," I replied as she walked over and gave me a gentle peck on the lips. Her lips were so soft and inviting that the thought entered my mind to slide my tongue in her mouth. Thank God I caught myself before I did it, because that would have cost me. To Maria, everything had a price, including something as simple as a French kiss, and she was way too expensive for my taste. A kiss like that probably would have cost me somewhere in the neighborhood of five hundred dollars. Don't get me wrong; I was willing to pay to play, but not quite that much for a kiss. Besides, Maria and I had gone down that road once before, and it almost turned out to be a disaster.

You see, Maria wasn't my girlfriend, or even a woman I dated. She was a high-class call girl who, along with her brother Remy, ran a business called R and S Fulfillment Services, LLC, one of the most exclusive escort services in the country. They specialized in discretion and had the unusual ability to fulfill almost any request or fetish their wealthy, high-profile clients desired. They were by far the best there was at what they did. If Tiger Woods and Governor Spitzer had been their clients, they would both still be married and on top of their game right now. Crazy-ass Remy would kill a bitch if she opened her mouth about one of his clients.

"My brother tells me you have reason to celebrate," she purred in her seductive Latin accent.

"You could say that," I answered proudly. "I was named president of the company today."

"Congrats. Now, that is something to celebrate. You should have requested a night with me. I would have made it a very memorable night, just like I did on your birthday, yes?" She gave me this look that made my manhood leap.

There was no doubt about how good she was at her profession. Old girl had put it on me that night like no one I'd ever been with. She was the first woman in years who actually made me feel like we had some kind of connection between us; that is, until we were finished and she turned off the affection and reminded me that it was all business. That was when she asked me for payment and told me just how much our night of erotic bliss had cost me. Well, I refused to pay, which prompted her brother to show up at the dealership with a nine millimeter, looking for his money.

"Yes, it was memorable, all right, and I'm sure you would show me the time of my life." I shook my head to clear the erotic memories before they could tempt me to take her up on the offer. "But you're a little too pricey for me. As good as the sex was, the one thing I remember most about my birthday was how much it cost. I should have asked the price before I went down that road. Nobody's pussy is worth ten grand a night."

"I have a pretty long client list that would disagree." She gave me a confident smile. "But, Orlando, you're in the car business. You know what they say: when you go to buy a Rolls-Royce, if you have to ask how much it costs, then you couldn't afford it in the first place."

I let out a chuckle. "Well, I guess you're right about that. My older brother Vegas always used to say a man has to know his limitations. I guess when it comes to pussy, I'm just a BMW and Mercedes man, 'cause I got to know the price before I spend my money."

"And there is nothing in the world wrong with a BMW or Mercedes. They will both give you a damn good ride, but no matter how much you sugarcoat it, we both know they are not a Rolls-Royce." She laughed and I joined in. "Don't worry, though. I think I have just what you need. My girl Ruby is a Mercedes sports car if I've ever seen one." She turned to the bedroom and called, "Ruby!"

It took a few moments, but when Ruby finally walked out, I had to catch my breath. She was stunning. She didn't have that commercial beauty like Maria. No, Ruby had natural beauty you could almost call wholesome. I had this thing for dark-skinned women, and her skin was the color of dark chocolate and smooth as a baby's ass. Her hair was shoulder length but natural. I liked that a lot. There was something special about a black woman that wore her hair natural. That was sexy to me. Not to mention the fact that I loved to bury my hands in a woman's hair while I was riding her from the back.

"Ruby, this is Orlando. Orlando, I'd like you to meet Ruby. She's just come to this country from the island of Jamaica."

Ruby had these huge dimples in each cheek that brightened her face as she smiled at me.

"Nice to meet you, Ruby," I said, giving her firm body the once-over.

"The pleasure is all mine, Mr. Orlando," she said softly in a strong Caribbean accent that almost melted me on the spot. Maria and Remy had outdone themselves this time. I had only a few requests when it came to the women I dealt with from their agency. Two were mandatory, and the other three were a wish list of sorts. Ruby had already satisfied number one on my wish list, because she was not American born. Their country of origin wasn't important, and even race didn't matter that much, as long as the women they brought me had some kind of accent. That was so damn sexy to me.

Ruby turned to Maria and spoke to her as if I weren't even in the room. "I did not expect him to be so handsome and fit." Remy had told me once before that most of his clients were older, overweight white guys, so the girls appreciated the time spent with someone as youthful and in shape as I was.

"Yes," Maria said, "Orlando is quite handsome and very capable in the bedroom. I can assure you that there is no better man to cut your teeth on in this industry. Sometimes I think we should be paying him, but we must not forget this is business. Nonetheless, I'm sure he will make you scream like he did me. Just don't expect to see him again, because he only sees each girl once."

I tried to contain it, but I was sure I was blushing. I mean, you couldn't get a bigger compliment than to have a woman who charged ten grand for a roll in the hay say she should have paid you.

"Sooo," I said, changing the subject, "I'm starved. Ruby, what do you plan on making for dinner?"

"I was going to whip up some jerk chicken, cabbage, and rice and peas. Do you like spicy foods?"

I loved it when women cooked their native cuisine for me.

"I love spicy foods. And for the record, I can't wait to taste you. I hope you're hot and spicy." I licked my lips, and my eyes didn't leave hers until I saw both her dimples twinkling back at me. I glanced at Maria and winked, letting her know that she had done a great job.

"Well then," Maria interrupted. "Why don't I leave you two lovebirds alone? Ruby, the car service will be here to pick you up around seven-thirty tomorrow morning. That work for you, Orlando?"

Both Ruby and I nodded, prompting Maria to walk to the door. "You two have fun. And don't do anything I wouldn't do. Ruby, enjoy it while you can, girl. He's one of the special ones."

I watched Maria leave, then turned toward Ruby, who was now in the kitchen, searching for the cookware she needed. Neither of us said a word as I sat on the stool that faced the center island she was working on. She tried to be nonchalant and ignore me as she prepared the food, but I caught her sneaking a glimpse at me every few seconds.

Finally, about five minutes later, her eyes shifted in my direction. "Is it true what she says?"

"Is what true?"

"That you only see the girls one time?" she asked.

"Yes." I nodded without going into detail. "Why? Do you plan on changing that?"

One of my mandatory requirements was that Maria and Remy never bring me the same woman twice. I worked better when I didn't have the distraction of a woman in my life. Don't get me wrong; I loved women and I loved sex, but when I was in a relationship, I lived and breathed that relationship, and it usually took away from something else in my life—namely, my work. That was okay when Vegas was around, because he picked up the slack, but when he left two years ago, I made a conscious decision to step into his shoes. I cut off all the women I'd been seeing in order to concentrate on business. The problem was my dick didn't agree and wanted no part of leaving women alone. Most women weren't interested in skipping the romance and commitment for a roll in the hay—at least not unless they were getting paid, and that still didn't guarantee I would be drama free.

That was when I came up with idea of using escorts and found Remy and Maria's service. For me, these nights of pleasure were like mini vacations from the world of LC Duncan and Duncan Motors; and well, nobody wants to go to the same place twice if they have the chance to see something new, right? Of course, some people would argue that there's no place like home, but I hadn't found anything that felt like home yet, and I wasn't sure if I ever would.

"Mr. Orlando, I must tell you, this is my first time doing anything like this for money. If you don't want to see these other girls who are experienced, what chance do I have of making you happy? And Mr. Remy made it very clear that I am to do whatever it takes to make you happy. I'm so afraid I'm going to mess up."

"You're not going to mess up," I said, getting up from my stool and walking around to where she was. I placed my hands on her hips. "That's why they brought you to me. I love first timers." I lowered my head and my lips met hers in a polite peck that turned into a passionate kiss.

I turned off the stove. The food could wait until later. It was time to sample the dessert.

LC

7

I'd been pacing around the dealership for the better part of an hour, contemplating the future of our business and family. Despite her protests, I'd finally sent Chippy home after all the children had gone their separate ways. I wanted her to ride home with Harris and London, but she'd complained so much that I relented, letting her stick around another half hour as I went over paperwork. She needed her rest, though. She'd been suffering from a bad cold that didn't seem to want to go away, and it wouldn't get any better with her staying out in the street with me till all hours of the night. It wasn't like we were twenty-five anymore.

Besides, I needed time to think. I always thought best late at night, when I walked the showroom floor. No one but me could see it, but times were changing, perhaps for the worse, and it had nothing to do with me appointing Orlando to lead the family. What I was concerned about was the unknown competition I'd been hearing about through the grapevine, and the sudden tightening of shipments from our distributors. Someone was trying to muscle in on our territory and discredit us with our distributors. I couldn't share what I had heard or felt with my family in front of Paris's date, but it was important that we were all on the same page and that I flushed out our hidden enemy before the shit hit the fan.

"You're doing the right thing, LC. Retirement's the only way you can make sure this family survives. You've got to make them think the family's weak, while you work from behind the scenes, like Vegas used to," I spoke aloud to myself.

I chuckled. Listen to me. Heaven help me if I was turning into a paranoid old man. And heaven help everyone else if I was right and they came after my family or business, because paranoia and power are a dangerous combination.

"You talking to yourself, Pop?"

I looked up and saw Junior walking out of the service area. He was carrying a toolbox. "Yeah, son, I guess I am. Why are you still here?"

"I'm here because you're here," Junior replied calmly as he approached from across the darkened showroom floor. He began pacing the tiled floor around me, as if on guard for some unseen threat. Ever since he was little, Junior always thought he had to protect me. "Why didn't you go home with Momma?"

"I needed to think," I replied, adjusting the brim of my hat. "The silence does me good."

I glanced at the dealer invoice on the passenger window of the 2006 Maybach, thinking back to how much I'd paid for my first used car. My younger self would've died on the spot . . . or would've been thrown out from a place such as this. But time changes a lot of things. It makes some men wiser and others more foolish. I'd like to think I was one of the wiser ones.

My hand was still on the car window. I removed it, noticing the fingerprints left behind. Again, my mind went back to that younger man, to a time when my fingerprints were recorded by the NYPD for cause. I swore I would never be locked up again, and thank God I'd delivered on that promise and many more on my way to this point. I had to admit, it wasn't easy as a black man trying to make it in America, but I'd made it with Chippy's help.

"Sooo, any hard feelings that I didn't pick you to run things? You are the eldest." I was hoping he'd give me a truthful answer. Knowing where he stood would go a long way to helping me transition Orlando into leadership.

He shook his head. "Nah. Orlando's the smart one. He's a lot like you and Vegas."

"You're saying that as if you're not smart. All my children are smart," I said confidently.

"You know what I mean, Pops. O plans for things. When something goes wrong, he has a backup plan. Me, I'm not a planning guy. I'm good with my hands. I know that, and I'm all right with it." I nodded my understanding. "Like Vegas always said, a man has got to know his limitations. I know mine."

It made me feel good to know my son was comfortable with who he was. Junior was a good boy, a good son. He wasn't as bright as the other boys, but he was a hundred times more loyal, and he cared about this family—perhaps even more than Chippy and myself. In many ways, he was the heart of our family, while Vegas was the soul.

"So you're completely fine with this? No hard feelings at all?"

"None whatsoever, but—" His face became very serious and he folded his massive arms over his chest as he leaned back against the car. "I do have a question, and I'll keep it just between you and me."

"Of course. You can ask me anything."

"Okay, well, I'm not knocking Orlando at all, but what I wanna know is, why didn't you choose Vegas? If you wanted him home, all you'd have to do is pick up the damn phone."

I sucked in a bit of air as I studied my oldest son. For the child who wasn't supposed to be so bright, he'd asked a damn good question. Funny thing was, it was a question I'd asked myself a thousand times.

"I didn't choose Vegas because he doesn't need this." My eyes traveled around the show-room. "Vegas can build an empire anytime he wants. He's smarter than all of us."

I took off my glasses and wiped my eyes. Vegas had been away almost three years, and I missed him dearly. Everyone who met him just seemed to love him. I never thought a child could teach a parent, but then there was Vegas. He'd taught me more about being a man and about sacrifice than anyone I'd ever met. "And to be honest with you, Junior, I don't think he's ready to come home yet."

"You might be right." Junior walked over and placed a comforting hand on my shoulder. "You really miss him, don't you, Pop?"

I tried to clear the frog in my throat. "More than I'd miss my right arm if you cut it off. What about you, son? Do you miss him?"

"Of course I miss him. Vegas wasn't just my brother. He was my best friend."

A smile crept up on my face, and a laugh escaped. "I feel the same way. I feel the very same way."

"You know, it's gonna be strange not having you around here," Junior said.

"Not half as strange as it's gonna be for me."

My son wrapped his arm around my shoulders as we walked toward my office. I stopped, turned around, and took a last look at the showroom. "I've spent the better part of my adult life putting this place together."

"So why you leaving? You don't have to go to Florida. O's got everything here under control, and you and Momma can travel anytime you want. You guys can be snowbirds."

"Well, son, it's a little more complicated than you think, and there are a few things your mother and I haven't told you kids."

He clearly wanted to ask for more details, but our conversation was interrupted by a reggae-style ringtone. He glanced down at his phone, then raised his wrist to check his watch. "It's my guys driving the truck with those Bentleys we won at auction. I told them to check in before they went to bed."

"Go ahead and answer it. We'll talk when you finish." I stepped away from him, gathering my composure as he took the phone call. I can't say I didn't understand my kids' confusion. This whole thing would have been a lot easier if Vegas were here. I wouldn't have even had to make an announcement. Chippy and I could have just slipped off to Florida, because it would have been understood that Vegas was in charge.

My own cell phone began to vibrate. I smiled when I saw the overseas phone number. "Hello?"

"Mr. Duncan, this is Lee Sumyo. I'm sorry to call so late." Lee handled most of our business in Japan and the Far East. He'd been my connection in Asia for almost twenty years.

"No problem, Lee. How you doing? We're looking forward to that shipment you're sending us next week. I have a customer who has prepaid for that fully loaded Lexus LFA you promised us."

"Mr. Duncan, that is why I am calling." I didn't like the sound of that. "There is not going to be a shipment next week." Suddenly my knees got weak.

"Excuse me? Lee, we've already paid for that shipment. I've got customers lined up. I've made commitments."

"I know, Mr. Duncan. I am very sorry, and I can assure you your money will be returned via wire in the morning."

"I don't want my money back, Lee. I want my cars. I want that LFA." I usually tried to handle Lee with a little more finesse, but this called for the direct approach. He needed to know how important that shipment was to my business.

"Mr. Duncan, there is nothing I can do. It is above my head."

"Above your head? Was it above your head when we stopped dealing with Detroit and went with you exclusively back in ninety-one? I burned a lot of bridges to deal with you and your people, Lee. I expect some loyalty."

"I know this, Mr. Duncan, but many things have changed since the tsunami and earthquake. I am truly sorry." He sounded sincere in his apology, so I tried to calm down, but that didn't mean I was willing to accept what he was telling me.

"Lee, I need that shipment. Without it I might as well go out of business."

"I understand. Perhaps you can speak with another distributor."

I could detect something in Lee's tone, as if he already knew that speaking with another distributor would be useless. It was starting to feel like the rumors were true. Someone was trying to destroy my relationship with my overseas distributors.

"Lee, my friend, I must ask you a question."

"Certainly. Please ask me anything."

"Am I being blackballed? Is someone trying to take my franchise with you?"

There was hesitance on the line, and that gave me the answer I sought.

Finally, Lee admitted, "Mr. Duncan, I am not sure what is going on, but it is bigger than both of us, and they are using the tsunami and earthquake to their advantage. I was lucky to get you your last shipment. Things are very difficult here, and there is much bureaucracy and government intervention when it comes to your name. Someone is throwing a lot of money around. So, while I cannot say for sure, you may be right."

"I thank you for your honesty, my friend. One more question. Who is throwing all this money around?"

"I am not sure, but the first place I would look is to your west."

"Yes, I think you may be right." I sighed. "Lee, it's been a pleasure working with you. I hope this will not be the last time we do business."

"Yes, I feel this way also. May I make a suggestion that may help you?"

"Please."

"If I were you, Mr. Duncan, I would watch my back."

I chuckled. "That may end up being the best advice you've given me in years."

I hung up and turned toward Junior, who had just finished his call. "Junior, I need you to do something for me."

London

8

I was putting Mariah to bed when I heard voices coming from the foyer, letting me know someone was home from the dealership. It definitely wasn't Harris's polished, deliberate male tones. Who knows where he'd run off to once we got home; probably somewhere to call that no-good home wrecker he didn't want me to know about. Lord help her if I ever found out who she was, because the lady in me was going right out the window. I'd already proven once before that I'd do whatever it took to protect my marriage and keep my man, so doing it again would be that much easier.

What I didn't understand was why these whores had to chase after married men instead of finding men of their own. Well, you know what they say: competition only makes you stronger. So, when my husband came to bed, I was going to remind him just why he married me. He needed to know that I could still be his lady in the streets and his freak in the sheets.

With that thought in mind, I kissed my slumbering baby's forehead and went in search of whatever family members had just arrived home. When I approached the top of the stairs and looked down, I saw my mother taking off her coat. She was pale and didn't look so good.

"You okay, Momma?"

She glanced up at me as she handed off her coat and gloves to Iris, our housekeeper. Although she smiled warmly, I could tell she was trying to hold back another coughing fit. She hadn't been feeling very well the past few months, and I worried about her declining health. I was sure it had contributed to my father's decision to move down to Florida. Our parents' love for one another was an example to us all, especially me in my marriage to Harris.

"I'm fine. Just a little tired is all. It is rather late."

"Where's Daddy?" I was surprised she'd come home alone. If I had known, I would have insisted she ride home with Harris and me.

I didn't expect Paris or Rio, or even Orlando, after Harris mentioned he'd canceled their meeting, but I figured my father would have at least accompanied my mother home. Then again, who knew? Maybe he and Orlando had stayed back at the office to strategize and discuss the transfer of power between them.

Oh, who was I fooling? If I knew my father and brother, this had probably been worked out months ago, and they'd been keeping the rest of us in the dark all along. Dammit, I scolded myself for even entertaining that thought. I hated it when I caught myself thinking like Harris, the king of conspiracy theories. Sometimes I wondered what made him so damn paranoid.

"You know your father. He's still over there at the dealership," she answered. "But don't worry. Junior's there with him. He'll make sure he gets home safely."

"What about Orlando? He over there too?" I was going to be so mad at my brother if she said yes. Harris had offered him an olive branch, and if he'd blown off my husband to sit in the office with Daddy, it would be such an insult.

"No, he said he had some business to take care of out on Long Island. You know that boy can't stop working. I wish he'd find a woman and settle down."

Momma gestured for me to come downstairs. I quickly descended the staircase and gave her a hug and a kiss. She hooked her arm into mine and guided me toward the living room, where we sat side by side on a love seat.

"Awfully quiet around here. Everybody asleep?" She looked around our unusually silent home.

"Mariah is. As you know, Rio and Paris won't be home until the wee hours, if at all, but Harris is around here somewhere." I gave my mother a somber look as I decided to defend my husband's honor. "I don't know if you or Daddy realized it, but your news stunned him tonight. I think his feelings are a little hurt."

Momma gave me an "are you for real?" look. "His feelings are hurt? About what?"

"Well, to be honest, your announcement of Orlando being in charge was kind of a hard pill to swallow for a man who's usually in the loop, y'know. You could have at least told us you planned on picking Orlando to run the business."

My mother cut her eyes at me. There was something behind the look, but she quickly composed herself and held back whatever it was she'd been thinking. Instead, she took the diplomatic approach.

"Baby, I want both you and Harris to know we weren't trying to hurt anyone's feelings. You know how your father feels about your husband. We didn't even tell Orlando about our decision until we announced it to you all. Why? Do you have any problems or doubts about his ability to lead?"

"No, no, I don't have anything against Orlando. I think he's a good choice, but, I mean, Harris does have a law degree, and he is Daddy's right-hand man. I mean, you can make an argument—"

My mother cut me off quickly. "An argument for what? London, is this about Orlando being the right man for the job or the fact that Harris wasn't chosen?"

"Both. I love my husband and my brother, but I just wanna make sure my husband got a fair shake. He's a very bright man, Momma."

"To be honest, we gave Harris considerable thought, but in the end we thought Orlando was the right one for the job. Truth is, he's the only one of you, other than Vegas, who's got the stomach to get his hands dirty—except maybe Paris, and she's too young and impulsive right now to assume a true leadership position."

"Too stupid is more like it," I spat, rolling my eyes at the sideways compliment my mother gave my little sister.

Of course, my mother stared me down like I'd done something wrong. "Despite her impetuousness, Paris is the best at what she does for us, London. She never questions LC whenever he tells her to do something. She just gets it done. And she'll continue to do that for Orlando once we're gone."

"Oh please, Momma. Only reason the little slut doesn't question Daddy is because she's afraid he'd cut her off."

My mother slapped my leg like I was a child. "London, why do you hate her so much? The two of you are sisters. Why do you have to be at odds?"

"Humph. Ask her," I replied snidely.

My mother's expression hardened. "I have, and she tells me it's nothing. I don't believe her any more than I believe you. What the hell happened between you two?"

I shrugged. "Just leave it alone, Momma, please. It's not worth it. Paris is just childish, and she doesn't know how to keep her legs closed. You know that."

"Maybe so, but she's still your sister."

"That was by design, not by choice. Believe me when I say it. Paris is going to tear this family apart one day. Mark my words. She just does not know how to avoid trouble."

"She'll grow out of it, baby." She reached out and touched my face, looking at me with concern. "Speaking of marks, what happened here?" She gently massaged the place where Harris had slapped me.

"Nothing." I pulled away from her. Jesus Christ, please tell me Harris didn't bruise my face. If Daddy saw that mark and figured out that Harris had done it, he'd throw him out of the business or, worse, kill him with his bare hands.

"That ain't nothing. You've got a bruise on your face," my mother stated. "How did that get there?"

"Oh, that?" I touched it gently. "It's nothing. Mariah kicked me when I was putting her to bed."

My mother hesitated before speaking, staring at me as if she could read my thoughts. "Oh, really? Is that so?" I was sure she didn't believe a word I said. It was time to get as far away from her as possible so I wouldn't have to lie to her anymore.

"Y'know . . . I think I'm going to find my husband. Good night, Momma."

"Good night, London. I love you."

"I love you too." I could feel her eyes on me as I walked away.

Paris

9

Mmm. Now, that's what I'm talking about, I thought as Trevor's leg went over mine and he began kissing the side of my neck. I sat back on the plush sofa in the VIP section of the Nightlife Café with a margarita in hand, content for the first time since I'd walked out of the board meeting. Just as I predicted when I left the dealership, this was just what I needed—good song, good drink, and the possibility of some good dick.

I'd finally gotten Trevor's stiff ass to loosen up after giving him a blow job on the way over here, then filling him up with shots of tequila right after we hit the door. He still wouldn't shut the fuck up with all that Ivy League crap, but that was okay, because I could barely hear a word he was saying with the loud-ass bass being pumped out of the club's speakers, anyway.

I let out a slight murmur when his hand slid its way up my DKNY dress so that his fingers could gently rub the thin material of my thong. He wasn't talking now; he was attempting to handle his business, and in public no less, but we'd see how far he was willing to go with that in a minute. I turned to him, and his lips found mine as I leaned forward, placing the margarita on the table in front of us. I had to give his Ivy League upbringing some credit, though, 'cause the boy had some skills. I hadn't messed with a dude in a long time that could do what he was doing with his fingers. He had my pussy dripping like a faucet.

Two jealous-ass bitches I'd seen giving Trevor the eye earlier walked by, staring, and I gave them the finger with one hand while massaging his dick with the other. Mine, bitches, all mine.

One thing I was grateful for was that Trevor's parents sure didn't short him in the dick department. I will tell you the man was blessed with a small baseball bat, and I couldn't wait to get it inside me. I let go of his dick, then broke our kiss, reluctantly removing his hand from underneath my dress. He said something, looking disappointed, but I couldn't hear what he said, nor did I care.

I took hold of his tie, then stood up, giving him no choice but to stand up with me. Still holding his tie, I led him past the VIP bar and into the unisex bathroom, where two women, one cute and the other one very butch, were doing coke. It was pretty obvious they had some kind of a relationship going on there.

"You wanna bump?" the butch one asked as she damn near shoved the small spoon up the other one's nose.

"Nah. Thanks, but I'm after an entirely different high." I turned to Trevor and pulled him closer to me. I locked my lips on his and sucked on his tongue as I gently pushed him into one of the stalls. "Sit," I ordered.

He hesitated for a few seconds, but then relented when I took hold of his belt and began to undo his pants. I admired the size of his dick for a brief moment as I kicked the stall door shut. I'm not going to lie; I was more than a little concerned about taking all that meat, but a girl had to try.

I stepped out of my thong, sucking in an anticipatory breath as I took hold of his dick and straddled him. I rubbed the head against my clit, and without even thinking about a condom, I slid down on him, savoring every single thick-ass inch. I couldn't believe it. I'd never been so completely full in my entire life, and I'd been fucking on the regular since I was fifteen.

As good as it was just sitting on his dick, Trevor didn't give me a chance to savor the moment at all. He grabbed my hips and started lifting me up and down, pumping that thing in me like there wasn't going to be no tomorrow. It felt so damn good, all I could do was encourage him.

"Oh my God. Oh, God. Please don't . . . please don't stop! A little harder. Yeah, right there. Oh yeah!"

My foot almost slipped off the toilet from the sheer force of his upstrokes. The boy couldn't dance a lick and his conversation was boring as hell, but he had a big old dick that he sure as hell knew how to use. He was fucking me so good, I was contemplating putting up with his boring ass on a regular basis. Especially if it kept Daddy happy.

"Got-damn, you got some good-ass pussy! So wet and tight, makes a nigga wanna scream," Trevor grunted as his dick ran deep in me, all signs of civility gone to the wind. My pussy had him forgetting his private school upbringing and takin' it to the streets faster than he could drop his creased slacks to the floor. "Shit!" he screamed.

"Uh-huh, go ahead and scream, baby. Let the world know Momma's shit is the damn bomb!" I was not shy about admitting my sexual skills, either. Better men than he had lost themselves between these legs.

"Da-yum! I want some of that," one of the coked-out dykes said a little too loud. I guess she must have been bisexual or something. Her friend shoved her against the wall, asking her if she knew who I was and telling her that she needed to shut up.

That's right, bitch, I thought. Glad my reputation precedes me.

"Don't stop, baby. Don't stop," I gasped, and Trevor obeyed, gripping my hips tighter with his strong fingers as he redoubled his efforts. The next thing I felt was an aura of ecstasy that swept over my body like a monsoon. I rocked my hips in rhythm with the driving 808 bass from Ciara's new song echoing outside the restroom, until my flows of ecstasy coated his dick. I came so hard, I could barely breathe.

I couldn't be sure, because I was still in quite a fog from my orgasm, but I could have sworn I heard the rat-a-tat-tat of gunfire right before a sudden silence replaced the thumping beat outside the bathroom door. Before I could even react, the bathroom door seemed to explode. The lesbians screamed at the top of their lungs and someone shouted, "Freeze, bitches! This is a fuckin' robbery!"

Ain't that some shit? A motherfuckin' robbery! I should have known better. Rio warned me about all the shit going down in Brooklyn lately. Dammit, why the hell didn't I ever listen? I glanced down at Trevor, who looked like he was gonna shit on himself. From the space under the stall, I could see two sets of legs. I placed my finger on my lips, signaling for him to stay quiet and not move. Maybe, just maybe, if we were lucky, they wouldn't realize that we were in the stall.

My wish came true as the robbers forced the two girls out of the restroom without even a glance under the stalls. Talk about it being our lucky day. Trevor helped me down from the toilet with trembling hands.

"I'll get us outta here. Just . . . just stay close," he uttered, up close in my face. He was talking a good game, but I could see he was scared to death. He unlocked the stall and peeked out.

"Let's get the fuck outta here." I pushed homeboy to hurry the fuck up. All I wanted to do was get back home to Queens, but he stopped me.

"Keep your voice down and relax. We don't know what's going on out there," he warned, looking toward the door. We could hear the melee on the other side.

Trevor crept over to the bathroom door and opened it slightly, but then shut it quickly. "Oh my God."

"What? What'd you see?" I was about to push his ass out of the way and look for myself.

"There's a whole bunch of dudes out there with machine guns, and they're making everyone take off all their clothes. Half the people out there are naked, and the rest are stripping off their clothes. I'm not going to lie, Paris. This doesn't look good, and I'm scared." He looked like he was about to cry. "Jesus Christ, what the fuck did you get me into bringing me down here? I'm not some homeboy from the hood. I live in Forest Hills."

I rolled my eyes at him. Forget what I got him into. What the hell did I get myself into, going on a date with such a little bitch? He was definitely not the dude you'd wanna be with in a fucked-up situation like this.

Orlando

10

"Right here? Right now on the counter?" Ruby asked me in an almost bashful manner. "But I—"

My tongue ate up her words, and that was not all it desired to eat up. It was hard to tell our tongues were strangers as they surveyed every corner of each other's mouths, knowing exactly where to go. Although our mouths were like magnets, I could feel her hands resting on my chest almost unwillingly as she attempted to push me away.

"Is something wrong with the kitchen?" I asked. There was a sudden pause in the action, allowing me time to imagine myself throwing her ass up on the countertop, my dick surveying every corner of her pussy with the same familiarity as my tongue had just shown her mouth.

"No, no. Not if that's where you want it, Mr. Orlando," she replied, looking everywhere but directly in my eyes. I wasn't quite sure yet whether she was that intimidated by me, or if it was all part of a coy little act she was putting on. For some reason, I sensed this was no act. Regardless, it only made my dick harder.

"But?" I asked, sensing there was more she wanted to say.

"But I didn't know we would . . . you know . . . so soon." She looked at me—briefly—giving me the pleasure of gazing into those eyes that hummed to a silent Caribbean beat. Then her eyes darted off elsewhere again. "Not that I don't want to do it now." This time she rested her hands on my chest to comfort me. "Not that I didn't want to do it the minute I laid eyes on you. It's just that, you know, I had this all planned out in my mind I'd prepare you a nice dinner, we'd eat, talk a little, and then—"

"Let me guess. Cuddle?" I laughed. I could tell it angered her by the slight push I felt against my chest before she placed her hands on her hips. I wondered how long she'd been in the States and how long it had taken for the sisters to get to her. If she started snapping her neck and pointing her finger, I was going to request her birth certificate.

"No, not cuddle," she said with her sexy-ass accent.

"Talk," we both said in unison. I was being sarcastic again; she was dead serious. I couldn't help it. Maybe this was an act. I mean, for real, a paid escort really thinking she was going to get paid to talk?

"Yes, talk. But then, you know, ease into things." She wrapped her arms around herself as if she were already buck naked and had caught a chill. "I told you this was my first time doing something like this."

She dropped her arms in defeat and turned to face me. "Look, you sure you don't want someone else? Someone more experienced? From what I can tell—from what I've heard—you deserve the best. Although it would be too good to be true for my first time doing something like this to be with someone like you, I'd totally understand if you've changed your mind."

Damn, damn, and damn! Those eyes were starting to hum again, and I swear to God I thought I even heard them sing a note this time.

"It's okay," I told her, now dead serious. It wasn't a laughing matter anymore. Perhaps the best pussy I might have ever experienced in my life was about to walk away. "Look, I was just joshing around. I thought joking around might loosen you up a little bit, not hurt your feelings."

She didn't say a word. She just stood there, looking like she was debating whether to respond.

She finally spoke. "You didn't upset me." I exhaled, but before my breath could barely hit the air, she added, "But you did hurt my feelings a little bit." Her eyes stopped humming, singing, or whatever they'd been doing—though they were still smiling.

"Look, I didn't call you over so I could hurt you."

Her eyes smiled wider. "Is that your way of apologizing, Mr. Orlando?"

I walked closer to her. "It's my way of saying let's start over. Let's do things your way." Instead of laying another passionate kiss on her, I placed a soft, gentle one on her forehead, turned the stove back on, then headed out of the kitchen before calling over my shoulder, "I'll be waiting in the living room."

We played the game her way. Yeah, I was on home court, but it never hurt to let the visitor call the shots every now and then. I retreated to the living room while she prepared the meal. Once it was done, she appeared in the doorway and summoned me to the kitchen. I followed the scent, both hers and the meal, into the kitchen, where she had a nice setting for two laid out.

She served me and made sure I had everything I needed before she even sat down to join me. The meal was exquisite. I hoped she could cook in the bed like she could in the kitchen. Hell, even half as good would have gotten me off. When it came to women, seconds were usually a no-no, but I already knew that rule would be null and void when it came to this delicious Caribbean meal.

***

"You have something on your mouth," Ruby stated after she'd cleared the table and joined me back in the living room. She nestled in beside me on the couch, wiping the corner of my mouth with her thumb.

I didn't know if something was really there, but I liked her touch. Maybe this was what she meant by leading into things. Funny how I'd just been promoted to lead the family, yet here I was, willing, ready, and able to be a follower.

Not only was Ruby a good cook, but she was a good talker as well. I was actually impressed by how much she knew about cars. Then again, Maria could have had her do her homework in that aspect. Nonetheless, I appreciated the effort, and that, like pretty much everything else Ruby did, made my dick hard.

After a while it became difficult for us to concentrate on a conversation because the sexual tension was building. She excused herself to go to the bathroom. Knowing that was her cue, I gladly directed her to the master bath adjoining the bedroom.

As she walked away, I couldn't take my eyes off that ass. Her eyes hummed, sang, and all kinds of other shit, while her ass made me think of the sound of ocean waves hitting the shore. No, it didn't really make a sound, but if it could, that was the sound it would have made.

"Aaahh!"

The shrill sound coming from the bathroom caused me to leap from the couch and run to Ruby's aid. "You all right? What's wrong?" I wondered if I should grab the protection I kept in the nightstand drawer, but I didn't want to scare Ruby and make her think she was fuckin' with some gangster or something.

"Oh my goodness. A Jacuzzi? A big, huge Jacuzzi?" she said in excitement. Or shock. Or both.

"Are you serious?" I asked, trying to watch my tone. I usually wouldn't have given a fuck about walking on eggshells around a broad, but my dick would never forgive me if I allowed this one to get away without tapping that ass. "You've never seen a Jacuzzi before?" I decided to make a quick save. "Then again, it is pretty big."

"I've not only never seen one this big, but I've never seen one at all. I've heard about them, but have never seen one live and in person." Her smile was beautiful. I hadn't noticed until just now.

It was definitely time to move things along. I walked over to her. "Then I guess you've never made love in a Jacuzzi before, either."

She looked up at me, and no words needed to be spoken at that point. I turned the water on at a nice warm temperature, and as if on cue, both

Ruby and I began removing our clothes, staring each other down the entire time.

When her succulent breasts fell out of her bra, I thought my shit was gonna shoot right then and there, but I kept it together. It was that bare-shaved triangle that had my ass scooping up a buck naked Ruby and setting her feet down gently in the tub as if I were carrying her across the threshold.

I stepped in after her, and we stood, my rock hard manhood pressed against her, resuming the passionate kissing that we'd left off at earlier in the kitchen. My tongue reached depths down her throat that made my penis jump for joy in anticipation of its chance to experience her deep throat.

"You know, I honestly never imagined myself doing something like this," Ruby confessed. "But since I am, I'm so glad it's with you. I can see it now. I want to see it. I want to see it all." With that being said, she bent over and rested her hands on the edge of the tub, facing the mirror. "I want to see," she repeated, "everything."

"Oh shit," I moaned as her chocolate moon stared up at me. I spread her open wide to shoot for the pink stars. I entered her, and it was like falling into a pool, though her body hadn't even been in the water yet. She was wet for me. She'd wanted me all along. She'd wanted this all along. Well, now she was about to get it.

"Mmmm, Mr. Orlando," she crooned, her ass up against me, watching my every move through the mirror.

I stared back at her as long as I could before I got in too deep, way too fucking deep, as I thrust in and out of her. Out farther and then back in deep. Hard. She threw it back like the pro she said she wasn't.

The smacking, the wetness, they were sounds my ears had never heard. It was like a real live Caribbean band was right there in the bathroom, serenading the moment. I'd screwed, fucked, boned, smashed, made love—whatever else you wanted to call it—but I'd never, ever made music.

If I hadn't watched the shit in the mirror, I wouldn't have believed she did it, but Ruby threw her leg up backward and managed to twirl around on a brotha's dick until she was facing me. I was speechless, and it was a good thing, too, because the "talking" part of the night was long done and over with.

We sank down into the water without missing a beat. She rode me like she knew me. What the fuck was up with that? Up, down, fast, then slow. She teased; she tormented; she pleasured. Bells and whistles, sirens, fireworks, and all kinds of shit started going off. I even thought I heard some ringing.

Fuck! I did hear some ringing. My phone was ringing. Ruby fucked, pounded, and pounced. The phone rang and rang and rang. Whoever was calling really needed to talk to me, but I really needed to finish what I'd started with Ruby, and I wasn't about to ruin the moment, the ecstasy of it all, with a rushed orgasm. I decided to let the phone keep going to voice mail. Five more minutes—I'd return the call then. What more could happen in five minutes?

The phone began its shrill ringing again.

Fuck! Nothing more would happen if that phone kept ringing and messing up my groove.

"Damn," I cursed under my breath.

"No, no, no. Not now," Ruby practically begged. "I was just about to do my special little trick."

"Yeah, well, I want to be able to enjoy your special little trick, and I can't with that fucking phone ringing nonstop."

Thank God I was in great shape. I was able to lift my body and reach for my pants with Ruby still on top of me. I got a grip on them and pulled them near. Just as I got the phone out of the pocket, I saw the moon, stars, heaven, and earth. I didn't know what the fuck she did, how she did it, how she moved to make her pussy pop off on me like it did, but she'd done it, and before I knew it, I'd exploded deep inside of her.

The ringing phone would have to wait—indefinitely, considering that it was now resting at the bottom of the Jacuzzi, while an exhausted Ruby rested her head on my chest.

"So, Mr. Orlando, is it really true that you never see the same girl twice?" Ruby asked, knowing she'd put it on me.

"Never," I replied without even a second thought. I couldn't give her room to doubt me.

She slowly lifted her head and stared at me. "Really?" There was a sadness about her now. Still, I stuck to my guns.

"Really."

She looked down, then back up at me again. "Oh well." Her lips split into a smile. "Guess I better make the best of it now, then."

Paris

11

"What are we supposed to do, Paris? I can't believe you brought me to a ghetto place like this!"

Trevor's girly reaction was starting to piss me off more than the fact that there was a robbery happening right outside the bathroom door. I couldn't take it anymore; I went off on him. "What? You punk-ass motherfucker. You weren't complaining about this joint when you was fucking me in that stall a few minutes ago. Now, man the fuck up and get us outta here."

Suddenly, we heard three loud shots and plenty of screaming.

I was scared about our situation, but Trevor looked terrified, and there was no doubt in my mind that he was holding back tears. "Look," he said, "maybe we should just go out there. If they catch us in here, they might kill us."

"Fuck that. I ain't going out there." I reached inside my bag and pulled out the little semiautomatic .22 Junior had given me a few years back.

I pulled back the hammer and let a bullet slide into the chamber.

Trevor was staring at me with more fear than he had for the men outside committing the robbery.

"What?" I snarled.

"You have a gun?"

"Ah, yeah," I said sarcastically. "This is New York City we live in, not Disneyland. My sister was almost raped ten years ago. I don't go anywhere unless I'm strapped."

Bang! Bang! Bang! Three more shots. Poor Trevor started shaking so bad, I thought he was about to have a nervous breakdown.

"Oh God, they're gonna kill us," he whispered. "They are going to kill us."

With my free hand I reached into my bag for my cell phone and started dialing.

"Who you calling? The police?" He looked relieved, but that didn't stop his tears from falling.

"Hell no. You can call the police. I'm calling my brother." Sure, I talked a lot of shit about Orlando leading the family, but when the chips were down, he was the one who always got my ass out of the fire. I just hoped he could get me out of this.

The phone rang six times and then was answered by Orlando's voice mail. I didn't even give it time to finish playing the full message before I hung up and dialed Junior's number. I probably should have called my father, but the last thing I wanted him to know was that I was out at a club and had gotten myself into a situation I couldn't handle.

"Hello."

"Junior, I'm in trouble. Big trouble."

"What do you mean, you're in trouble?"

"I'm at that spot on Sterling Place, the Nightlife Café, and some dudes just busted in the club and are robbing the place. Me and Trevor are in the bathroom, but it's not gonna be long before one of them figures out that we're in here."

I could hear him sigh, but then he flipped on me. "Didn't Orlando tell you to keep your ass out of Brooklyn?" he yelled.

"Yeah, Junior, but Orlando ain't my—" I stopped myself, remembering what my father had told me about thinking things through before I spoke. Now was not the time to be starting a fight with my brother when I needed his help. "Yeah," I started again with a more respectful tone. "He did, and I should have listened, but that ain't gonna help me right now. I need you to tell me what to do."

He sighed again. "You on the first floor or second floor?"

"First floor."

"Is there a window?"

I looked around. "Yeah, but it's small."

"See if it will open, and then get your asses outta there."

Damn, with everything happening so fast, I didn't even think about looking for a window, and obviously neither did Trevor.

I pulled the phone from my ear and turned to Trevor, who'd just ended a call. "Trevor, see if that window will open."

He ran over to the window and pulled it, but it opened only halfway, probably to prevent people from sneaking in. "It won't open all the way. We won't fit."

I studied the window. "You won't fit, but I will."

He looked at the small opening, then at me. "You really going out that window?"

"Yep, if you give me a boost."

For a quick second, he looked pissed, like I was deserting him, but then he finally manned up, cupping his hands for me to step into them.

"I'll call you when I'm outside," I promised.

He took a deep breath. "All right, you go ahead. I'll be okay. The cops are on their way. I'll meet you at the car when this is all over."

"Nah. My people are on the way—and trust me, you don't wanna be here when my brother shows up. He's not gonna be a happy camper, and he's gonna blame it all on you."

"But—"

"Time to go." I threw my bag out the window. "Bye, Trevor." I gave him a soft kiss on the cheek. "I had fun."

"Paris, please. I had a good time. I know I'm a little bit nerdy by your standards, but I like you. I don't give a damn what your brother thinks." His eyes refused to meet mine, and hurt registered on his furrowed brow. He probably wanted to continue what we began in the club. Maybe the "nice guy" in him wanted more. I know it sounds lame, but part of me kind of wanted that too, despite the little-bitch way he was acting just a few minutes ago. Hell, with a wife beater, some baggy jeans, and a couple of tattoos, I might be able to pass him off as a thug. Besides, good dick was hard to find, and so was a guy who Daddy would approve of.

"Okay, Trevor, I'll meet you at the car. Here, take this." I handed him my gun, then kissed him again. "All you have to do if anyone comes in here is point and squeeze the trigger. The safety is off, and I already have a round in the chamber."

"See you outside." He smiled and handed me his keys.

He cupped his hands again, and I stepped up and out the window. A few seconds later, I was on the ground outside the club, picking up my purse. I had a few scrapes from my fall, and my stockings and dress were ruined, but I was no worse for the wear. Now all I had to do was call Junior and let him know I was okay.

LC

12

I checked my watch, shaking my head as I walked down the hall to Harris and London's bedroom. The last thing I wanted to do was disturb my daughter and son-in-law so late at night, but unfortunately, as Harris was the family's lawyer, I needed to talk to him about a problem that just couldn't wait until morning.

I raised my arm to knock but stopped myself when I heard noises coming from behind the door. I was a little embarrassed to admit it, but they were the kind of noises that would make any father uncomfortable, despite the fact that my daughter had been married for five years and had her own child. I thought momentarily about leaving them alone and returning to my bedroom, but I had no choice. This situation needed immediate attention. I knocked on the door twice. Thankfully, the noise stopped and was replaced by whispering.

"Mariah . . . honey, is that you?" London called.

"Ah, no, London," I replied. "It's me. Is Harris awake? I really need to speak with him. It's important."

There was more whispering, and then London said, "Yeah, Daddy. Just a minute. He has to find his robe." I was sure she was as embarrassed as I was.

Harris opened the door, wearing his robe, slippers, and an irritated look on his face. I wished there was something I could say to him to smooth things over, but what do you say to a man who was screwing your daughter less than five minutes ago?

"What's up, LC? Everything all right?"

"No. I need you to get dressed. We've got work to do."

"What's going on?"

I lifted my head and shifted my eyes toward his bedroom door to signal that I didn't want London to hear us. "I'll tell you in the car. Meet me downstairs in ten minutes. I'm gonna try and reach Orlando."

He nodded his understanding, then headed back into his bedroom to get dressed.

As I waited for Harris, I tried to call Orlando again. This was probably the twentieth time I'd called him since we found out the shipment from Asia would not be delivered, and the twentieth time I'd reached his voice mail. He'd better have a damn good reason for not answering my calls, because if he wasn't dead or seriously injured, I was going to kill him myself.

It wasn't long before Harris came downstairs, retrieved his coat, and followed me to the front door. He looked tired, but then again, so did I.

"So what's going on?" he asked.

"It's Paris," I told him as we headed for the BMW I'd driven home from the dealership. "She's being detained at the Fifty-first Precinct in Brooklyn."

"Son of a bitch! What is wrong with that girl?" Harris didn't mask his frustration. I was sure he was sick of leaving his family in the wee hours of the night to retrieve her. "What are they holding her for now?"

I stopped in my tracks and told him, "Harris, that boy she brought to our board meeting to-night is dead."

Shock registered on his face. "Get the fuck out of here! The councilman's son? You're kidding, right?"

"I only wish I was." If he was half asleep be-fore, he sure as hell was awake now. "Here, you drive."

"Jesus Christ, did she do it?" Harris asked as he slid into the driver's seat.

I wasn't surprised to hear him ask that ques-tion. I didn't want to believe she did it, but the possibility had crossed my mind as well. I loved Paris, but we both knew that she had a lot of issues to work through and a lot of growing up to do. She had been known to make impulsive decisions that got her into trouble ever since she was Mariah's age. Not only that, but she had a temper that only I could control—probably because she'd gotten it from me in the first place. Unfortunately, this wasn't the first time she'd been held by the police and needed to be rescued. Usually, it was for fighting some woman over a man. One time it was for something as stupid as someone looking at her wrong, but not this time. This time it was because someone was dead, and we both had to wonder if Paris could have done it.

"No, I don't think she did it," I replied.

"Has she been charged?"

"From what the desk sergeant told me, she's being held as a material witness. She was there when the boy got shot."

"Well, that's a good thing." He placed the car in gear, and we headed down Rockaway Boulevard. "LC, this is what I'm here for. Don't worry. We'll get this cleared up quickly and have Paris home in no time. What did Orlando have to say?"

"Nothing. I haven't been able to reach him."

Harris tried to play it cool, but I could see it caught him off guard. "That's unlike him. I hope he's okay. Last thing we need is for him to show up missing."

"Look, Harris, I don't need anything else to worry about right now, okay? Let's just focus on getting Paris away from the police. Orlando is a big boy. He can take care of himself."

"Point taken," he said, but that didn't stop me from worrying about my son. Harris was right; this wasn't like Orlando at all. If he wasn't home when I got there, I was going to have to make a few calls.

Silence took over the car for a while as we were both lost in our thoughts about this latest situation.

After a while, Harris said, "Can I ask you a question?"

"Sure." I already knew what it was going to be about.

"It's about Orlando."

Yep, I should probably have my own psychic network the way I could read his mind.

"What about him?"

"You sure this whole leadership thing hasn't gone to his head? I mean, he should be here or with Junior. . . . Look, I know he's your son and the man works hard for the company, but—"

"But what?" I leaned back in my seat and gave him a hard stare. Yes, he was my son-in-law and he did a lot for our company, but Harris was treading on thin ice talking about my son.

"Don't get me wrong. He's bright, but he still has a lot to learn about the business." He gave me a sideways glance, and the confidence left his tone. "I mean, not that what I have to say matters. You've already made your decision. I just hope it's the right one for the family. Personally, me and a few members of the family aren't so sure."

"Is that so? Which family members?" I was putting him on the spot because I knew there could be only one family member he'd spoken to, and that was his wife. I studied his face for a reaction. It looked like he was struggling to keep a poker face, but all his tension was evident in the way he was gripping the steering wheel.

"Hey, you know me. I'm a lawyer. I'm not going to throw anyone else under the bus. I could have kept this all to myself, but like you're always telling me, you pay me for my opinion, so I'm giving it to you. But I'm not the only one with concerns."

"Okay, so if you were in my shoes, how would you have handled it?"

He took his eyes off the road for a second so we could make eye contact. "Well, if I were you," he began cautiously, "I would have named a temporary leader. That way if Vegas comes home, he can just take over, and if he doesn't and the temp does a good job, you could make him permanent—or if Orlando is ready by then, you could put him in charge."

"Sounds to me like you have this all worked out. So, who would you appoint temporary leader?" I asked, as if I didn't already know who he would say.

He relaxed his grip on the steering wheel and placed one hand on his chest in a falsely humble gesture. "Hey, look, I don't want to sound self-righteous, but I would have appointed me." Oh, he sounded self-righteous, all right. "I already know the ins and outs of the businesses as well as you. I have a law degree, which, I might add, comes in mighty handy, and I have the respect of most of our employees. I could have done a great job. I would have made you proud."

"And you don't think Orlando will?" I asked, pushing.

"No, sir, I don't."

I sighed out of sheer exhaustion. Why did it seem like everyone in my family was determined to try my patience tonight? "Harris, if you'd like, once we get Paris home and I get some sleep, I will explain to you in detail why I chose Orlando over you. From what you said here, you've made a good case for yourself. I'd like you to listen to the case that was presented against you. Would you like that?"

He turned to me and smiled. "Yes, sir, I would, as long as I get a chance to redirect and defend myself."

"I wouldn't have it any other way."

Harris

13

Once again I came through like a champ, saving the Duncans' asses and doing it with style. It took me less than fifteen minutes to get Paris out of police custody, a feat I was sure impressed LC. She'd still have to come back in a few days and answer the cops' questions, but hopefully by then this whole thing would calm down so I could sit down with the right people to have it all swept under the rug. LC had made it very clear to me that he did not want Paris or the Duncan name attached to this case in the media in any way. Of course, that was a tall order, but doable considering how greedy both cops and reporters were these days. I'd already made some inroads with the lieutenant on the case, so I wasn't concerned about the police, and thankfully, it was already too late for the story to make the morning papers or TV news.

Now all I had to do was get Paris home. That, of course, was if LC didn't kill her first, because when I walked out into the hallway, the two of them were staring each other down like gun-fighters at the O.K. Corral.

"Daddy, I didn't do anything. I swear," Paris pleaded, taking a step back so she was out of his reach—which was probably smart, because LC did look like he might smack the shit out of her.

"Shut up," he said angrily, pointing his finger in her face as he closed the gap between the two of them. "Just shut up. Don't you say another word."

"But, Daddy—" That damn Paris just didn't know when to be quiet. She was always trying to explain her way out of things, when the smart thing to do would be to just shut her mouth. This time, though, she must have sensed the level of her father's anger, because she cut her sentence short.

I watched as LC closed his hand into a fist. I had no doubt what his next action would be, so I acted fast. "This is not the time or place," I reminded him through clenched jaws. He shifted his eyes in my direction, and I saw that cold stare he got when he was about to explode. "Remember where you are," I continued calmly. "This is a police station."

He glanced around, then nodded as if I'd brought him out of a hypnotic trance. Paris had just dodged a bullet, and I was not even sure she knew it.

"Paris, why do the ones I love the most always disappoint me so?" he asked. They continued their staring contest for a few more seconds, and surprisingly, Paris didn't have anything to say. Without another word, LC turned and walked toward the exit.

His reaction must have stung more than any slap in the face. Paris looked like she wanted to break down and cry, which was not something I saw often from her. I walked over and wrapped my arm around her shoulders, but she pushed me away.

"I'm a'ight," she said, following behind her father but giving him some distance.

When we first arrived, LC and I had come in the back door of the precinct, in case the press was camped out in front of the building. I decided that it was best we left the same way, considering the lieutenant told me that Trevor's family was on their way.

Once we were safely outside, I didn't waste any time getting Paris in the car and putting some distance between us and that police station. It would be daylight in a few hours, and I couldn't wait to get to my bed, where, if I was lucky, London might want to finish what we'd started before LC interrupted us.

"Harris, I got to give it to you, brother-in-law. You was gangsta in there with that law shit. I thought those cops were going to crap on them-selves when you told me I could leave," Paris said with her version of affection. She stretched across the black leather seat, stifling a yawn, as if this were just another night out at the club for her. It appeared she'd forgotten about her little confrontation with LC just that quick. He, on the other hand, was obviously still stewing.

"Anytime, sis, but let's try not make this a hab-it," I replied, wishing this could be the last time I had to do something like this—but knowing that in all likelihood, it wouldn't be. I preferred the corporate side of the law when working on behalf of the Duncan family interests; that was the side that made me lots and lots of cash.

"Paris, I'm gonna ask you this one time and one time only." LC spoke in a calm, nonthreaten-ing voice. The proud, defining lines on his face barely shifted, despite the tension at hand. "Did you have anything to do with that boy's death?"

I didn't know what he expected her answer to be, but I certainly expected her to say no. The longer she remained silent, though, the more nervous I became. I felt my stomach twist into a tight knot when I heard her answer.

"Yes, Daddy, I did have something to do with it."

I slammed my foot on the brakes so hard, the car came to a screeching halt. Thank goodness for seat belt laws, because without them, LC and I would have gone through the windshield. I said a quick prayer of thanks for the simple fact that there had been no other cars on the road to crash into us from behind.

"Tell me I didn't hear what I think I just heard," I said, turning to LC. "Please tell me she didn't just admit to killing that boy."

"I'm sorry, son, but you heard right. We both heard right," he growled. "I spent almost half a million dollars sending her to special schools in France and Asia so that they could refine her, teach her discipline, so she would act like a lady, and all they did was send me home a cold-blooded murderer. Little girl, I don't know what I'm gonna do with you. I'm about ready to give up."

"Wait a minute! Hold on! What the hell are y'all talking about? I didn't murder him or anything like that."

"You didn't?" LC and I said in unison, turning toward the backseat.

"No, but I might as well have pulled the trigger myself by bringing him to that club. He didn't deserve this, Daddy. He didn't even wanna go to the club, but I insisted. If it wasn't for me, he'd be alive right now." I almost thought I saw a tear in her eye. This night just kept getting more and more bizarre.

Her sudden sentimental attitude was not something we were used to seeing, but I, for one, was willing to brush it off as shock from the incident. I took my foot off the brakes and started driving again. I would need to know more details before she went back to answer questions at the precinct, but for now, I was happy to accept her words at face value and head home.

As we crossed the Brooklyn-Queens line, I glanced back at her as she looked out the passenger-side window with misty eyes. Her mind was probably still somewhere back in Brooklyn, rewinding Trevor's death over and over again. I have to admit I felt sorry for her, and I think LC did too.

"Honey, these types of things happen in life. That's why Harris, your brothers, and me are so hard on you. You can't do everything you want to just because you know we're going to bail you out of it. There's an order of things in this family. You are going to have to start taking responsibility for your actions."

"I am. I will . . . I'm gonna do better, Daddy. I promise."

He turned around fully in his seat to face Paris. "I hope so, because I won't be up here to help bail you out much longer. Once Orlando's in charge, he's not going to be putting up with this like I do." LC straightened in the seat, looking through the windshield again, and announced, "You are staying home the rest of the week. I don't want you bumping into any reporters or cops by accident. Then, Monday, you're coming in to work, and I don't want to hear a negative, trifling word out of you."

My eyes met Paris's in the rearview mirror. She knew silence was best on her part. It was no time to test her father. Besides, now that she was safe, his mind had probably already moved on to Orlando.

London

14

Thanks to Paris, there would not be a late-night romp with my husband or much sleep, for that matter. Not with Harris running out in the middle of the night with Daddy for yet another emergency involving Paris—which, of course, they didn't have time to discuss with me. Shutting me out was becoming more and more of a habit for them ever since I stopped working.

The only reason I even had the little bit of information I did was because I ran downstairs and confronted Junior as soon as I heard his loud-behind car pulling in the driveway. He looked like he was carrying the weight of the world on his shoulders. He obviously wasn't in the mood to talk about it, but when I asked him where Daddy and Harris were, he mentioned something about Paris and the police. That little wench couldn't stand the idea of Orlando having the spotlight. I guess she had to go and do something stupid to get Daddy's attention.

I turned on the back lights and went for a walk in Momma's garden as I waited for Daddy and Harris to return home. I could only hope the tranquillity of its beauty and the small pond would calm my nerves. Instead, it just left me on simmer, so I returned to the house. I had just reached the top of the stairs when I heard car doors shutting.

I ran to the catwalk overlooking the foyer and living room and quietly watched Harris, Daddy, and Paris enter through the front door. None of them seemed very talkative, though if Paris really was in trouble with the police, I could assume there had been quite a bit of discussion in the car on the way home. I'd heard plenty of Daddy's lectures in my day, back when I was more involved in the business, and I remembered them as if they were yesterday. Daddy always called them his "teaching moments."

Daddy said something quietly to both of them before excusing himself and walking into the living room, where Junior was sitting. Harris said a few words to Paris, and she reached out to hug him. From my point of view, the hug was way too long, her hand was way too close to his ass, and I was way too distrustful to let it go—especially since her newest cry for attention had interrupted some of the best loving my husband had given me in a long, long time. Now she was hugging my husband, playing for more sympathy . . . or who knows what else. Oh, no, I wasn't having that. I raced down the stairs and cleared my throat to make my presence known.

Paris jumped in surprise as she realized I was only several feet away and had witnessed the entire thing. Harris was equally startled and quickly backed out of my sister's embrace.

"Well, don't you two look cozy," I sneered.

"Oh, please, London. I was just thanking him," she replied, her bravado returning quickly to replace her surprised look.

"Thanking him for what? What did you do this time, Paris?" I snapped. "What did you do that had you in the custody of the police? Another bar fight with some sister-girl's man?"

"Da-yum. You all up in my business. Shouldn't you be asleep?" She waved her hand dismissively, as if she were shooing me back to bed. I was not about to budge, but I'd be damned if Harris didn't take up for her!

"London, let it go," he said. "We worked it all out. Everything is taken care of."

"Is that what you were doing just now? Taking care of it? Or were you working it out?" My sister had such a superior smirk on her face that a thought suddenly entered my mind. "Was it Paris who called you last night on your phone?" I asked.

"Oh my God!" He rolled his eyes up toward the ceiling. "Now you're sounding silly, babe. I think you must be sleep deprived."

"Is that what I am, silly and sleep deprived? Well, maybe I need to sleep in the guest room for the next couple of nights."

"Look, honey, there's no need to take this to another level. Paris was just thanking me for my services. Isn't that right, Paris?"

"Mm-hmm, and I appreciate your services." Harris couldn't see it, but the smirk on her face told me exactly what services she was trying to imply. Yeah, maybe I was tired and a little cranky, but I was not going to take that shit.

I lunged at her to lay a slap on her face. Harris tried to get between us, but he was too slow. Still, when my open hand arrived, Paris had already sidestepped it with the grace of a ballerina. Nothing was left in front of me but open space. My momentum carried me onto the floor where I fell, my robe spilling open. "What kind of services, you little hooker?"

"Law services, you stupid bitch." Paris mocked me with another smirk. "Don't nobody want no man that belongs to you."

Harris was quick enough this time, folding me in his arms to prevent any further violence. As I struggled to close my robe, I shoved my husband's arms away.

"What about Jesse?" I screamed. "You sure as hell wanted him, didn't you?"

As if I had cracked open a hard-boiled egg to reveal the soft inside, Paris's angry face softened and her voice wavered as she spoke. "Damn, you still on that Jesse crap? How many times I gotta tell you I'm sorry? You wouldn't even be with Harris if I hadn't helped you to break up with that loser."

She was right. I wouldn't have even met Harris if it weren't for her, but that didn't change a damn thing. She could say she was sorry a million times, but it would still never be enough. Not after what she did. Not after she broke the sacred rule and our sisterly bond. The pain of her betrayal still stung as if it had happened only a day ago.

It had happened at the beginning of my senior year at George Washington University, when I invited Paris down for the weekend before she went off to private school in Europe. We were four years apart and had a fairly close relationship. Paris actually seemed to look up to me back then, probably because I knew what it was like to be a teenage girl in a household with LC for a father and three well-known, overbearing older brothers. My parents wanted me to talk to her about the trouble she'd been in and why she needed to stay focused on her studies while she was in Europe.

"So, you ready for Europe?" We were sitting on the grass outside my dorm the day she arrived. I wasn't an ugly duckling, but it was amazing to see all the guys checking her out as they walked by. I have to admit I was a little jealous of my eighteen-year-old sister's knack for attracting male attention and making it seem so effortless.

"I guess, if that's what Daddy wants," she said, pouting.

"It's not what he wants, Paris," I said. "It's what he thinks is best. You have to admit you do have some anger issues. It's your senior year, you've only been back to school two weeks, and you've already been in two fights. What do you want Daddy to do? They expelled you."

"He could have backed me up. Okay, maybe I was wrong for hitting Lisa Jackson, but that bitch Trina . . . she deserved it."

I shook my head and laughed. "She caught you giving her boyfriend head under the bleachers. What would you have done?"

"I would have whipped my ass. But obviously, she can't whip my ass. That's why her jaw's wired shut now and I'm still looking as flawless as ever."

I couldn't help but laugh. I know I shouldn't have encouraged her, but the things she said were so funny sometimes. God knows I loved her, but Paris definitely did not see reality the way most people did.

"Nonetheless, your only other choice is to get a GED, and you know LC ain't having that. From what Momma told me, this school is going to help you to hone that aggression you have inside you. Make a lady out of you."

"Hone my ass! All they're gonna do is try to change me, London, and that ain't gonna happen. You can take the girl out of Queens, but you can't take Queens out of the girl." She folded her arms, posing in a B-boy stance. "Southside! Jamaica!" She started throwing her hands up in the air, not caring who walked by and saw her doing it. Back then I wished I had half of her confidence.

"You know what? I'm glad you came here before you left. I missed my little sister."

"Missed you too, London."

I pulled two apples out of my bag and tossed one to her. She caught it, then took a bite.

"So, you thinking about college when you come home? If so, I have nothing but good things to say about GW," I offered.

"I hear you, but I doubt it. I wanna work for Daddy, like Junior, Vegas, and Orlando. He said that when I get finished with these two years in Europe, I'll have a job waiting for me," my sister said, grinning as if eager to prove herself.

"Don't be in such a rush," I admonished her. "Trust me about that. Junior and Vegas have told me stories. When it comes to the family business, enjoy your youth. Have fun, sis. I'm only telling you this out of love."

"Hey, London. You ready to go?" I turned to the familiar voice belonging to the tall, dark-haired, olive-skinned man with a backpack. He wrapped his arm around me and planted a kiss on my lips.

"Paris, this is Jesse," I said, offering introductions. "Jesse, this is my sister, Paris."

From her expression, I could see she was surprised. I'd been going with Jesse for almost two years. He was my first and only lover, but I hadn't told anyone in the family other than Vegas about him, and Vegas was sworn to secrecy.

"Hey. What up, Paris? I heard a lot about you," he said jovially, with that preppy swagger that I thought was so hot. He stuck out his hand, and when Paris reached to shake it, he took hers and kissed it. She started blushing from ear to ear.

"Well now, I guess I showed up at the wrong time. If you two have plans, I can find something to do until you get back," she said.

I waved my hand. "Nonsense. You're my little sis. I've missed you." I turned to face my boyfriend. "Jesse, is it all right if Paris hangs with us tonight?"

"Of course it is. Does she dig poetry?" he asked, reaching out and taking a bite of my apple.

"Cool. You mean like a Poetry Slam Jam?" she asked.

"Uh . . . no." Jesse looked at me and winked. "She's cute, London." He turned back to my sister and explained, "More like the classics. Robert Frost, Shakespeare, Kipling, Wordsworth, T. S. Eliot . . . But you may hear a little Langston Hughes. Don't get out much, do we?"

"No, I don't, but I'm trying to make up for lost time."

Jesse glanced at me for an explanation, but I just shrugged. My little sister was trying to act grown. Little did I know how far she was about to take things.

"Look, Jesse, there are two things I need before I leave D.C., and my sister doesn't seem to know how to help me with either."

"Okay, little sis," he said, chuckling. "What do you need?"

"Number one, I need some weed, dude."

I lowered my head in embarrassment. She had been asking me about getting some ever since she got off the train, but I had no idea she would bring it up so casually to someone she just met.

"Number two, I'm about to go to Europe for two years on Monday, so one of the things I promised myself before I left was that I was gonna get me some college dick. So, if you got some friends, hook a sister up."

I threw my hands up in the air. "Paris, I can't believe you just said that to him."

"You said you were going to treat me to a good time. If I can get those two things accomplished, I will have officially had a good time. No doubt about it."

I turned to Jesse. "Baby, I'm sorry. She's a little bit . . . high strung."

"Don't worry. I won't hold that against her." He laughed, but Paris didn't—until he said, "Don't worry, little sis. We're gonna make sure all your dreams come true this weekend."

God, if my father had had any idea what I was letting my sister get into, he'd have killed me.

We went to the poetry reading at a small club off of Fourteenth Street. It was a chance for the three of us to get acquainted and loosen up. Afterward, we stopped at Burger King before retreating back to Jesse's place, a sparse student apartment just off campus in what tourists would call "a dangerous part of town."

Jesse brought out a bottle of MD 20/20, better known as Mad Dog around campus. It was cheap and sweet, but we college kids loved it because we could get drunk on a budget.

"Damn, this some good shit," Paris said with surprise as she sucked down half the bottle of blue raspberry Mad Dog. "They don't sell this in New York."

"Oh, they sell it, but not in your neighborhood," Jesse teased. "London, you might wanna slow your sister down, or she's gonna have quite a headache in the morning. That Mad Dog has quite a kick."

Jesse lit the bong he'd been filling. Paris had nagged him all night about rounding up a bag, until he relented, calling up one of his people before we went to his place. I'd hesitated to let her drink or smoke at first, until my little sister reminded me of a few wild parties Orlando and I had held at the house when our parents were away. I couldn't argue when she pointed out that she was already older than I'd been when those parties took place.

I laughed, then took the bottle from Paris to finish it off. "Well, she's my responsibility, so if she's gonna have a headache, I might as well have one too."

When I turned back toward my sister, she was taking a hit from the bong. She tried to brag, saying, "New York's shit is better, but this ain't b—" but she was overtaken by a coughing fit. She was still a kid, after all, only eighteen.

Both of us laughed at her as the thick, sweet odor filled the room.

"Don't hog it all," I called out, yanking the bong from her fingers.

"Anybody want something else to drink?" Jesse asked.

"Yeah. I'm kinda thirsty," I said, only now aware of the time. I knew I would most likely be late to class the next day, but with the way I was feeling, I didn't give a damn.

"Me too. Some more of that Mad Dog—and can you bring the rest of that weed, too, please?" Paris asked.

Jesse flashed a smile at the two of us sitting on the floor, slumped over one another; then he walked back to the kitchenette.

"Girl, maybe you right about this college stuff. I might have to rethink working for Daddy," she said.

"Paris, I am having so much fun tonight," I said with a giggle.

Paris left my side and crawled over beside the television. A Cosby Show rerun was airing, and it wasn't long before I was mouthing along with the classic Huxtable family lip-sync routine to Ray Charles's "Night Time Is the Right Time."

"So, are you serious about this dude?" Paris whispered to me as she began fishing through Jesse's movie collection.

"Yeah, I think I am," I answered with a big grin.

She glanced toward the kitchenette. "Yeah, he's cute, no doubt about that. But do you think

Daddy would approve of him? I mean, damn, London, he's white."

"I have eyes, Paris. And no, Daddy won't approve, but I don't really care. I don't live for his fucking ass." Whatever was in the weed had me too relaxed for my own good.

Paris leaned back, looking surprised by my words. "Excuse me. Who are you, and what did you do with my sister, London? 'Cause you're obviously not her."

"London is right here. And she is her own woman, who does what she wants, where she wants. I'm not LC Duncan's slave or his property. If I want to date someone outside my race, then that's what I'm gonna do," I said, full of a confidence I never would have had without drugs and alcohol.

"Easy to say when he's not standing in front of you. You know he's expecting you to bring home a black doctor or lawyer. Your boy Jesse ain't no doctor or lawyer, and he damn sure ain't black."

"If he wants a doctor or a lawyer, black or white, let his ass find one for himself. I'm sticking with Jesse."

Paris wasn't buying into my bravado for one second. "But what you gonna say when he finds out about Mr. Tall, White, and Handsome over there and cuts you off?"

"I dunno. Get married, maybe start a little family, and lead a nice quiet life somewhere far away from Queens. We been talking about going to California, maybe the Napa Valley. Jesse's really into nature."

"So y'all can grow old and broke and watch porn together?" she joked, holding up one of Jesse's DVDs that she'd discovered.

"Girl, put that back!" I squealed, embarrassed that Rudy and Vanessa and Claire and Cliff and Theo—oh, and Denise—could see the name of the video being waved in front of them: Big Tits 12. I could have sworn they stopped singing on the TV. What the hell was in that weed, anyway?

Paris swiftly put it back where she found it, just before Jesse returned with our drinks in his best plastic cups.

"What have the two of you been talking about?" he asked as Paris crawled back toward me.

"Fairy tales," my sister answered. "Speaking of which, when are you going to call that friend so I can get some dick?"

He handed us our cups and a refilled bong, then picked up his cell and walked to the bedroom.

"I hope his friends are cute," Paris said.

"They are. Especially Andre. If I wasn't with Jesse, I'd do him myself. But if you're really gonna do this, Paris, make sure you use a condom." Last thing I wanted was for my sister to get pregnant—or even worse, get a disease from my boyfriend's friend while she was visiting me.

"Oh, no doubt. No glove, no love," she said as she sucked on the bong.

Jesse returned a few minutes later, smiling. "My friend Andre's coming over, but he wanted to know one thing." He turned to me. "Is she over eighteen?"

"Yeah, she's over eighteen. Her birthday was last month," I said, though I was starting to wish I'd never let things get this far.

"Okay, little sis. Me and London are going in the room for a while, but when Andre comes, give us a shout." Jesse stretched out his hand for me and pulled me up.

"You gonna be all right?" I asked.

"I'm gonna be fine. Just leave the weed."

"It's right over there on the table." Jesse pointed with a laugh as he guided me to the bedroom.

Jesse quickly undressed me, and we made love like two animals in heat. I was so high and drunk that I passed out as soon as it was over. I awakened some hours later to the worst hangover in my life.

I could feel Jesse's leg next to mine. I tried to open my eyes, but the light from the TV in his room hurt my eyes so badly that I immediately closed them again. I tried sitting up, but my whole body ached, so I just lay back down. My stomach was knotted up, and it was difficult getting my body to move like I wanted it to. I had never felt like this after smoking weed. It must have been the Mad Dog.

Once I got the pounding in my head under control, I got brave and opened my eyes again. Once again, the light hurt my eyes, but I refused to turn away, especially after I heard the moans. I knew it wasn't Jesse, because I could hear him snoring.

It took me a minute to get my bearings and realize the moaning was coming from the TV. I looked at the screen, only to see a big ass covered in a fishnet bodysuit, bouncing on an equally big dick. It was Jesse's porn tape. Somebody had placed it in the DVD player.

I forced myself to get up and walk over to turn it off. That was when I realized Jesse and I weren't alone in the bed. Paris was under the covers right next to him.

He wouldn't. She wouldn't, I thought as a horrifying possibility entered my mind. I reached down and pulled the covers off of the two of them, and had to hold back the bile that lurched up into my throat as my worst fears were realized. Tears welled up in my eyes at the sight of Jesse's nude body next to my naked sister. A condom still covered his limp penis, and that just solidified the truth for me. I'd been using birth control pills for the last four months.

I didn't even wake them. I just got dressed and left. The note that I left for Paris said that I would never forgive her and her ass could take a train home. Jesse's note just said, Leave me the fuck alone.

As fate would have it, I met Harris in a Starbucks that afternoon, and he turned out to be the man of my dreams and the lawyer my father always wanted me to marry.

"Who the hell is Jesse?" Harris yelled, snapping me out of my horrific trip down memory lane. I was so pissed that Paris had even taken my thoughts there that I almost lunged at her again. Now I was going to have to listen to Harris question me for the next three days.

"Nobody," I said dismissively, glaring at my sister. I would now also be forced to address the lies I'd told my husband about being a virgin when we met. I had made him wait until our wedding day before we consummated our relationship.

"Look, London, I fucked up. I was drunk and high that night. I wish I could take it back, but I can't," Paris argued. "Hey, look on the bright side. If I hadn't done that stupid shit, you wouldn't even have Mariah."

"What is she talking about, London?" Harris asked angrily.

"Nothing, Harris," I snapped, pointing a finger at Paris. "And you leave my baby out of this, and stay the fuck away from my husband. You've been warned." I turned to walk away, only to see my father standing in the foyer entrance, with Junior standing behind him.

"What's going on in here? Y'all gonna wake your mother," he chastised.

"I'm already up," my mother said from the first-floor hallway that led to her bedroom. "They were making enough noise in here to wake the dead."

"Paris," my father said, "what's going on in here?"

"Nothing, Daddy. Just a little disagreement between us girls about something that happened back in the day. Nothing to worry about. It's already over."

Paris played with the truth so much that Daddy didn't even want to believe her now. He turned toward me for an explanation.

"Is that true, London?"

Well, technically it wasn't a lie, so I nodded my head, looking for a quick exit. "I'm tired. I'm going to bed."

"I know that's right," Paris said. "I'm going to bed too."

"No, you're not," Daddy said, blocking her way. "As soon as Rio gets here, I want everyone but London headed to the office for a very important business meeting. It's time all of you understood what's on the line here."

"What about Orlando?" Junior asked.

"What about him?" Daddy replied.

When I glanced in Harris's direction, he didn't even try to hold back a smile. Thank goodness his mind was on something other than me and Jesse.

Orlando

15

I pulled into my parking space at the dealership at about eight o'clock. It had been a long time since I'd slept in past seven, but I had to admit it was worth it. After a wonderful evening highlighted by some of the best sex I'd had in a long time, I'd fallen asleep. When I woke, Ruby made me this bangin' Jamaican breakfast of salt fish, ackee, eggs, bammy, and plantains. My mom could really cook, but I swear Ruby's breakfast was better than anything I'd ever eaten. We topped breakfast off with another round of sex that literally had us falling asleep in each other's arms.

It was a good thing I met Ruby through Maria and Remy, because a woman like her was dangerous. If it wasn't for that car service driver banging on the door and waking us up, I might have lain up with her the rest of the day—and I couldn't have that. Sure, she was good at what she did, but I had to remember that when it all came down to it, she was a whore, a woman paid for her services, and nothing more. Whores came, they did what they got paid to do, and then they left. That was the deal. Laying up? Hanging around? That was for wives and girlfriends—and I don't need to reiterate my feelings about girlfriends. No, there was no reason to even go there. Just the thought was starting to give me a headache.

I got out of my car, briefly stopping to look at Rio's Ninja ZX motorcycle, which was parked in his spot. It confused me a little, because Rio was like a vampire; he never came out during the day, especially not in the morning. Then again, the old man did hand out bonus checks last night. I wouldn't put it past him and Paris to sign out some dealer plates and take one of the nicer sports cars to the Tanger outlet on Long Island for a very expensive shopping spree. Jeez, what a waste of time and money. I guess I couldn't judge them but so much, though, because it wasn't like Junior, Vegas, and I didn't blow a few bonus checks of our own back in the day. Only difference was that we'd spend our money at Foxwoods or Atlantic City for a night of whoring and gambling.

I'd barely gotten my butt in the building when I was met at the door by Junior, who looked irate. "Where the hell have you been? We've been calling you all night."

I raised my palm to stop him from taking his rant further. "Will you relax? Can't a brother go out and get laid? Junior, you should have seen this smoking-ass Jamaic—"

"Shhhh!" He nodded his head in the direction of the catwalk that overlooked the showroom floor. I looked up at my father, who was leaning against the railing in front of his office. He did not look like a happy camper.

"Don't let Pop hear you saying that. Not if you want your head on your shoulders. He's pissed."

"Pissed about what?"

"Orlando!"

I looked up and saw the old man point at me and then at his office. Without saying another word, he disappeared through the glass doors into his office.

I turned to Junior. "What happened? What's going on around here?"

"Man, what hasn't happened?" he said as we climbed the stairs to the second floor. "Let's just say you should have answered your phone last night."

Junior was being purposely evasive, but there was no doubt in my mind that I would soon find out for myself.

When I walked into my father's office, I saw Harris, Paris, and Rio. They were all staring at my father, who was seated behind his desk. I could tell by everyone's expressions, especially Rio's, that it wasn't a happy occasion that had them all at the office at this time of morning.

"What's everyone doing sitting around here at"—I looked down at my watch—"eight o'clock in the morning?"

"Well, at least we know his watch works," Paris shot off. "Too bad we can't say the same thing about his phone."

I ignored Paris, which wasn't hard to do. I'd been ignoring her for years. But there was more to this; I could sense it. Suddenly, I felt like I had a rock in my stomach. Jesus Christ, where the hell was my mother? She'd been a lot sicker than anyone wanted to acknowledge lately.

I turned my attention to the only person I knew who would give me a straight answer. "What's going on, Pop? Why's everyone look so somber—"

"Well, for starters . . . ," Harris interrupted.

I wanted to say, "For starters, nobody was talking to your ass," but I let him finish.

"Your little sister here had a mishap with the police and had to spend the better part of the night being interrogated." He nodded toward Paris.

"Yeah, and where were you when I called, Mr. I'm-the-New-Head-of-the-Family?" Paris snapped off again.

"That's none of your business." If my father wanted to know where I was, that would be different, but I was not going to entertain Paris. "But this little gathering looks like it's for more than you getting arrested."

Honestly, it looked like a lynch mob, and I felt like I was the one about to get lynched. I guess they'd had a chance to mull over the idea of me being their leader. Paris and Rio weren't smart enough to orchestrate something like this so fast, so I had no doubt Harris was the ringleader.

"Almost getting arrested," Paris corrected, rolling her eyes. "Lucky for me, my brother-in-law was around last night—unlike you—or there's no telling what could have happened to me."

It was time to start ignoring her again.

"Anyway . . ." I turned to Harris. "This isn't the first time you've had to bail her out. You're the lawyer. What did you need me for?"

"He wasn't the one who was looking for you." The old man finally spoke up. He didn't sound very pleased, and his expression matched his serious tone. "I was. Now, where the hell were you, and what were you doing that was so important you couldn't return my call?"

"I . . . I was out on Long Island, spending some time with a friend," I tried to explain.

"Likely story," Paris shouted.

I shifted my eyes in her direction. I swear, if she said one more fucking word . . .

My father spoke up again. "They lose cell phone service out there on Long Island? 'Cause I must have left you twenty messages myself."

Despite being all business all the time, I was entitled to be human every now and then, right? I could have a little fun. It wasn't a crime to get laid, was it? These were the thoughts that ran through my head, but somehow, I still felt like I'd let him down.

"It fell in the water." I dug it out of my pocket and held it up, like that would mean something to him, or anyone else, for that matter.

LC stepped toward me. "If you're going to lead this family"—he stepped even closer—"then lead. Being a leader means you're available twenty-four fucking hours a day."

He made a good point, and there wasn't much I could say, so I allowed him to continue his reprimand without interruption.

"Get your shit together, Orlando, 'cause if you can't handle being in the big chair, there are other people willing to do the job."

He glanced over at Harris, who smoothed out his mustache in an attempt to hide a smirk. I was sure Harris had scored every single point he could the night before, when I couldn't be reached. I wanted to scream at all of them to cut me some slack, but I knew how immature it would make me look.

I still couldn't understand why everyone was acting so over the top about this. I mean, sure, I should have been reachable, but it wasn't as if my brief absence was the beginning of the end for the Duncans. Besides, I wasn't even the leader yet. In truth, LC was still in charge.

"So that's it? Paris has another minor mishap with the law and you're all sitting around here like it's the end of the world? Pop, why are you making a mountain out of a molehill? You're acting like somebody died or something." In the corner of my eye, I could see Junior waving his hand at his neck as if to signal me to shut up, but I saw it too late.

The old man cut his eyes toward me and stood up. Harris and Rio sat back in their chairs as if they were about to watch a fireworks show. What the hell was I missing?

"What the hell did you just say? You know what, Orlando?" LC said in this soft but still menacing voice. I recognized it as the tone he used when we were kids and he was about to put his foot in our asses. "Yes, somebody did die. And from what I hear, if you had answered your goddamn phone when Paris called, you might have been able to prevent it. So, you tell me. Is it a mountain or a fucking molehill?"

I had the right to remain silent, so that was exactly what I was planning on doing . . . but I had to know. "Who died?" I asked in a much less confident voice.

LC didn't answer me. He just sat there simmering.

Harris broke the silence. "That kid Trevor, the one Paris brought to the meeting, took two to the chest."

No wonder they were all so upset with me. This was a beehive falling on our heads if I'd ever seen one. I shifted my eyes to Paris with one question in my mind: Did she do it? We all knew she carried a gun. No, no, I decided quickly, she obviously didn't do it. Harris was good, but it would have taken him a lot longer to get her out of there if she had a murder charge.

"Sorry, sis," I said. "He seemed like a nice guy."

"Like you fucking care." She flipped me the bird.

"Paris, not the time," my brother Rio shouted, and she fell back in line.

"Don't worry about it, O. I've got this under control. You've got much bigger fish to fry," Harris said.

"Huh? What bigger fish to fry?" I turned to my father. "Pop, what's going on?"

"I got a call from Lee last night. His people have pulled our distribution arrangement. . . ." My father's words faded, as if he was trying to keep his voice from cracking. He couldn't mask the hurt and anger in his eyes, though. I hadn't seen that look since he caught Rio in bed with another guy. My father had worked so hard to get us to this point. For it all to be taken away with just a phone call didn't seem right.

"They can't do that, can they? We spend millions with them every year," I said.

"Seems to me that they already have," Harris replied, and the old man nodded his agreement.

"But why? Thing are going so well. We haven't reneged on any payments or caused them any trouble."

"I don't know why, Orlando, but I suspect we're being blackballed."

"So what are we going to do? We've got less than two months' inventory."

LC stood up again. "I'll tell you what we're going to do. We're going to find a new distributor, which is why I'm sending you to Detroit to see if you can negotiate a deal with the folks up in Dearborn and Flint. If we're lucky, maybe Richard Coleman and the cooperative won't hold it against us that we've ignored them over the past fifteen years."

I was surprised the old man didn't want to go himself, but maybe he hadn't lost faith in me after all. I decided to throw Harris a bone, since he was going to be my right-hand man— whether I wanted him or not. "Why don't I take Harris with me? I'm going to need someone to watch my back, and he's good at picking up intel."

The old man glanced over at Harris, then shook his head as he turned to Rio. "No, take Rio with you. He keeps talking about how valuable he is to us, so let's see what he can do."

I don't think anyone in the room was more surprised than Rio—except maybe Harris, who looked like he'd just lost his best friend.

My father asked, "So, Rio, think you can handle this?"

"Uh, yeah, I can handle it," Rio replied, rather shaky.

"LC, this is kind of important. Don't you think this deserves a more experienced hand?" Harris asked. He sounded a little desperate, and I was sure it was obvious to everyone in the room that he felt slighted. "I'd be glad to—"

The old man turned to Harris, cutting him off mid-sentence. "No, I think he can handle it. Besides, after Trevor's funeral, I'm gonna need you and Junior to go talk to some of our Korean friends. They've wanted to do business with us in the past. I'm not too keen on their product, but right now beggars can't be choosers. You okay with that?"

"I'm fine with it, LC. Perfectly fine." Harris glanced over at me with that stupid smirk of his. It looked like he was making a competition out of this. Stupid thing was that if he was able to make a deal with the Koreans and I came back from Detroit with my dick in my hand, I was going to look mighty stupid.

"What about me, Daddy?" Paris squealed with excitement. "Where you gonna send me?"

"I'm not sending you anywhere," my father stated frankly. "You're gonna stay here with me, so I can keep an eye on you until this whole Trevor mess blows over."

I wanted to laugh when Paris pouted like a little kid.

"But, Daddy—"

"Don't 'but, Daddy' me. I've got a lot on my mind right now, girl. If your brothers and Harris aren't successful, I'm going to have to eat a lot of humble pie. And I can't stand pie."

Harris

16

A cold, biting rain was my uncompromising companion as I joined the large crowd lined up outside First Jamaica Ministries for Trevor Sims's wake. Councilman Sims and his wife had wanted it this way, a public wake, then a private funeral and a discreet burial sometime tomorrow. I hated going to funerals, but it was a duty I'd become used to as LC's right-hand man and legal counsel for the family.

It had been three days since Trevor's death, and so far, I'd been able to keep Paris and the Duncan name out of the press. A few more days of damage control and this whole thing would be water under the bridge. Not that things would be any less stressful for us with all the problems we were having with our distributors. Junior and I had met with our Korean contact, but that didn't pan out at all. Once again, LC was right. Their product was just too inferior for a high-end operation like ours. What's more, even if we wanted to go with them, they couldn't put us in their distribution pipeline for a good six months to a year. By then our competitors would have eaten our lunch and taken over our markets.

Getting back to the task at hand, I followed the line of mourners into the church, to the open casket. Like everyone else, I stopped briefly to look at Trevor's body before offering my condolences to the family. I had to admit that J. Foster Phillips Funeral Home had done a great job with him, because the kid looked good—almost as if he were sleeping.

I offered my hand to the grieving father. "Councilman Sims, I'd like offer my condolences. I'm—"

"I know who you are, Mr. Grant," he replied curtly. "And what you do for the Duncans." He maintained a gentle hand on his wife's shoulder to console her. Their grief had to be terrible. I don't know what I'd do if someone took Mariah from me in such a horrific fashion. I cringed at the very thought and shook my head to erase such an idea.

"I was expecting to see LC Duncan and the rest of his family, not his lawyer, but . . . but thank you for coming."

"A lot of people don't know it, sir, but I am part of the family. I'm his son-in-law."

"Well, then I hope you and your family will be a part of the Stop the Violence campaign we're organizing, along with the Cash for Guns rally we're having this weekend at Baisley Park."

"I'm not sure if it will be me, but I'm sure someone from the family will be in attendance. I hope you will also accept our family's condolences and our deepest sympathies on Trevor's death. Paris was planning on attending, but she didn't want anything overshadowing such a private time. We know how troubling this must be for you."

"Wait a minute. She's not coming?" Diana Sims questioned, her voice slow and wavering, either from medication or just plain old grief. "She was there when . . . when my baby was murdered, and she can't come to his funeral? Show some sort of respect for Trevor? My son would never have been in that area if not for her. He doesn't go to places like that! He's a good boy!" She shifted her eyes toward her husband, and he lowered his head as if she were using telepathy and had just told him off.

"Mrs. Sims," I replied, maintaining a low voice in my most sincere manner, "Paris would be here, but to be quite honest, she's currently under a doctor's supervision and heavily medicated. This whole ordeal has traumatized her. I'm not sure if you're aware of it, but she actually watched Trevor die in her arms."

"I don't give a damn about any doctor's supervision!" she yelled at me. The disturbance caught the attention of half the church, freezing them in place as they stared in our direction. Not what I was trying for. "She should have died too. She should be dead just like my baby is!"

"I know whatever I say won't be sufficient at this moment, ma'am, but if there is anything we can do, please don't hesitate to ask." I handed her husband my card, but she ripped it out of his hand and tore it to pieces.

"You wanna know what you can do? You can give me my son back! Can you do that? Can you give me my son back?"

I paused before answering gently, "No, ma'am, I can't. Only the Almighty can do—"

"Then what you can do, Mr. Grant, is kiss my ass!"

The councilman raised his hand in a gesture to calm his wife. "What you can do is tell us what your employer's daughter knows about the night Trevor was murdered," Councilman Sims uttered.

"She already told the NYPD all that she knows, Councilman, I assure you. We've even gone over it repeatedly with her to see if there was something she missed. Believe me, we want these murdering dogs brought to justice as much as you. Given time, I'm sure the police will turn up some leads."

"Mr. and Mrs. Sims," a low feminine voice called out, interrupting our exchange.

I whipped my head around in shock, and I couldn't believe my eyes. It was Paris! What the . . .

"I'm sorry. I'm so sorry." Paris, adorned all in black, with a matching fur and a pillbox hat, wept openly. The way she was dressed, you would swear she was the boy's widow. What the hell was she doing? This was not what we agreed to.

She stared at Trevor's parents before shifting her gaze to the casket. She slowly moved in its direction, seemingly oblivious to the other people trying to pay their respects.

"I thought you said she wasn't coming," Trevor's father snapped accusingly.

"I . . . I . . ." I've just been made a fool of is what it looks like.

Although the mother said that she wanted Paris there, now I could see just how socially inappropriate it was. Paris must be out of her friggin' mind.

"They tried to keep me at home, but . . . I had . . . to," Paris answered for me, still staring in the direction of the casket. "Trevor was so sweet to me. He didn't deserve this. I'm sorry that I didn't see the thugs who did it, but . . . but I was so scared . . . and Trevor was so brave, stepping in front of me." She wiped her eyes, although I didn't see any tears.

"I can still hear the gunshots over and over in my head. I didn't know what to do. Thank God Trevor squeezed himself through that window and followed me, otherwise I would have been face-to-face with that gunman by myself. Mr. and Mrs. Sims, Trevor saved my life." Paris looked like she was about to faint.

Mrs. Sims was becoming more visibly upset by the moment. I could tell her husband was becoming concerned about the effect that Paris's ramblings were having on her. Then Paris walked over to casket and grabbed Trevor's face, kissing him passionately.

"I'm sorry, baby. I'm so sorry," Paris said between kisses.

"What the hell is she doing?" Mrs. Sims had screamed. She clutched her heaving bosom and shook her head.

I was so shocked by Paris's actions that I couldn't even speak. Paris had done some crazy shit over the years, but this by far was the craziest.

"Stop that! Stop that right now!" Councilman Sims shouted. When he grabbed his chest, I thought he was going to have a heart attack. "Mr. Grant, I think it's about time the two of you left."

"I completely understand," I said as I snapped out of my trance. I grasped Paris by her shoulders and led her away from Trevor's casket. I gave the boy's parents a final nod as I maneuvered my dazed and emotional sister-in-law past the other visitors, who were still gawking. From the snippets of conversation I heard as we passed by, I realized that, much to my chagrin, a few recognized her as the ubiquitous socialite that she was.

Leaving the confines of hallowed ground, we stepped back outside into the chilly, damp air. "What the hell were you doing in there?" I snapped, turning Paris around to face me. I wanted to push her down the stairs in frustration for pulling a stunt like that

"Paying my respects and giving these people what they wanted—answers to their son's death. What did it look like?" she replied, her numbed state giving way to her typical demeanor. Obviously, her incoherent babbling had been a show for Trevor's parents. "I don't think they wanna ask me any more questions now, do they?"

"It looked like you were creating a scene and adding to those poor people's misery. Your father told you—"

"Hey! Hey!" Paris exclaimed as we walked down the stairs toward the parking lot. "He's my daddy, not my master. Maybe you should learn that, brother-in-law. Then again, if you had, Orlando wouldn't be the one running things, would he?"

Now, that was hitting below the belt, and I wanted to punch her for it.

I stopped and turned to her at the bottom of the stairs. "You're not going to taunt or shame me into thinking or behaving like you, Paris. Have some damn decency. Maybe your sister is right about you."

"Whatever. Maybe my sister is just as bad as me—or worse." Paris smirked, rolling her eyes.

She was purposely trying to bait me. Everyone in the family knew London and I had been arguing the past few days over this Jesse guy she'd dated and never told me about. I still couldn't believe she'd had me thinking I was the only man she'd ever slept with for all these years.

"Anyway, all this death and sadness has me feeling all chilly. I need something to warm me up. Wanna get some coffee—or better yet, a drink?"

Before I could answer, a man's loud voice interrupted us. "Harris Grant, why does someone always have to die for me to run into you?"

I turned to the voice, recognizing the impeccably dressed Vinnie Dash right away. Vinnie was my law school rival at Georgetown. We graduated first and second in our class. Unfortunately, I was number two, something he would never let me live down. Funny thing was that regardless of my second-place status, he'd been trying to get me to come to work for his family's business for years.

I gave him a polite wave, hoping he wouldn't make the trek down the stairs. Of course you know he did, and a lump formed in my stomach as he approached. I discreetly turned to Paris. "You better get out of here. This is business, and he's very close to the press."

"Yeah, that's cool. Like I said, I need a drink," Paris replied. She walked out of earshot just as Vinnie loped up to me, grinning from ear to ear as he offered me his hand.

"What? Now you're following me?" I asked, taking his hand.

"No. Coincidence. Or maybe just karma," he said, taking a sip of the coffee he was carrying in his free hand. Two of his employees walked behind him, pretending to be disinterested. "I'm paying my respects to the Sims family, just like you. Well, maybe not just like you." He laughed. "Duncan's kid can't stay out of trouble, huh?"

"Nothing I can't handle."

"Is that the best use of your talents? Playing babysitter to spoiled brats? Jesus, Harris, you were number two in our class. You need to leave the amateurs. Come work for me, and this whole stinking borough can be yours."

I cut my eyes at him. "Careful. That's my family. And the only reason I was number two was because you cheated. Why don't we compare our bar exam scores, see where that gets you?"

"You're still a competitive fuck, aren't you? I like that." He eyed me from head to toe as if he were evaluating me. "I can see Duncan's treating you good, but I can treat you better."

I shook my head. "Vinnie, what are you doing here?"

"My family's contributed a lot of money to the councilman's campaign. My father thought I should pay my respects. This thing with his son may be just what he needs to cruise to the finish line. Big-time sympathy play. Unfortunate, but great if you're trying to win an election. We like to be on a winning team." He leaned against a car that was parked on the sidewalk. "So, did you think about my offer?" he asked. "It's a sweet deal, and you'd be running the show without interference from us."

"I did, but the answer is still no. I'm a Duncan, Vinnie. They're not my employers. They're my family. And I've already got a pretty sweet deal now."

He chuckled. "Harris, Harris, Harris. You're only a Duncan by marriage. We both know about your real family." Vinnie smirked. "And you know how clannish the Duncans are. You'll always be second, third, or even fourth place in their eyes when it comes down to it. Need I remind you of the old saying, 'Blood is thicker than water'?"

"Maybe, but I'm obviously the wrong color for your organization," I said, holding my hand up and placing it near his face. "I mean, you may have a nice tan, but my melanin's a little stronger than that."

"Didn't you hear? It's a new day. Black president. Yes We Can and all that candy-ass, Oompa-Loompa bullshit." He laughed, then said, "Black is beautiful."

"In other words, you want this nigger to open doors in the black community for you and your people. And maybe help you move in on LC's business."

"First of all, I resent the fact that you used the N word in association with anything I do, especially since you know how fond I am of black people."

This time I had to laugh. "Black pussy maybe."

"That, too, but on the serious side, we don't give a damn about LC Duncan's business. He's a small fish in a big pond. But there is a lot of money to be made in the black community, and history has shown us that it's best to have a black face deal with black people," Vinnie said with actual sincerity.

"I hear you, but I'm not turning my back on my family, Vinnie. They need me."

"Yeah, LC sure proved that when he passed you over for the big chair. I mean, I could see if it was Vegas, but Orlando? That kid's gonna run that business into the ground."

"LC's not going anywhere," I said, chuckling for his benefit. I was rattled that maybe somebody within our organization had told him about LC's pending retirement.

"Maybe, but if he doesn't leave or croak, where does that leave you? Stagnant. Come work with me, and you'll make more money in the first five years than you can in a lifetime with Duncan. There's more to life than those stupid car dealerships."

I cut my eyes at him, the head of competitive business interests in the New York area. At the same time, knowing I despised him, I was always willing to listen. Opportunities in life often came from unexpected quarters. I was a living, breathing testament to that.

Vinnie looked at his Rolex, lifting himself off the car. "Harris, I've got to go pay my respects, but I just want to remind you that you got a beautiful wife and lovely daughter to think about in this competitive market. Are you going to be the man of your household or forever beholden to your in-laws?"

"Speaking of that, tell your people to quit calling me. My wife thinks I'm having an affair."

Vinnie didn't respond at first but waited till he was almost halfway up the steps before acknowledging my last remark. "But aren't you? Having an affair, that is," he teased with a smirk. "We have eyes everywhere, Harris, my man. Ears too."

LC

17

Orlando walked into my office, looking tired and run down. He and Rio had come straight from the plane to the dealership after their final meeting with the cooperative up in Detroit. From the look on his face as he sat down in the chair to my right, I could tell he'd been unsuccessful in securing a distribution deal. Truth be told, I didn't think they had a snowball's chance in hell of negotiating a deal when I sent them, but as desperate as we were, it was worth a shot. Hell, I don't think if I'd sent them up there with a suitcase full of money, they could have gotten those old boys to help us.

"How did it go?" I asked, more to break our silence than anything else.

"They said no, Pop." Orlando leaned back in his chair, sighing as he loosened his tie. Like me, he hated failure.

"It's okay, son. I figured they would." I nodded my head in understanding as I ran my hand through my hair. "There's a lot of bad blood between us and the cooperative since we went foreign and high-end. I guess they feel like I got too big for my britches. Who knows? Maybe they're right."

Orlando said, "Yeah, I got the impression they didn't like you too much, Pop. Quite a few of them, especially Richard Coleman, seemed to be enjoying the fact that you were having problems."

"Yeah, well, Coleman's got an axe to grind. I'm sure that when I left the cooperative, it took a lot of money out of his pockets just in margins alone." I sat back in my chair, second-guessing my decision to leave the cooperative. I was now seeing the wisdom behind the old adage that there's safety in numbers. It was not good news to hear that the chairman of the cooperative was still holding a grudge.

"Enough about Richard Coleman," I said. "How'd Rio do?"

Orlando sat back in his chair. "Surprisingly well. He kept his mouth shut when he was supposed to and did what he had to do when the time came. We may not have gotten what we wanted, but we left there with quite a bit of information about how they do business. I take it you knew Simons was gay?"

"Let's just say I was pretty sure Rio was right up his alley." I'd sent Rio with Orlando, instead of sending Harris or Junior, because I knew Mark Simons, the number two man behind Richard Coleman, had a thing for young men in their twenties. "So what did Rio find out?"

"Well, for starters, they're hurting far worse than we are from the slowdown in production and government intervention. Coleman's looking to make a deal with Alejandro from out west. For some reason, Alejandro doesn't seem to be affected the same way as we are on the East Coast and the cooperative in the Midwest."

"I haven't figured it out quite yet, but there is something up with Alejandro. I wouldn't be surprised if he turns out to be the reason for all our problems."

"I hope not."

I raised an eyebrow. "Why's that?"

"Well, I know you don't particularly like him, but on the way home I was thinking maybe we should give him a call. I mean, it can't be any worse than talking to Coleman. Besides, he always seemed cool to me. He's never seemed disrespectful when I've seen him, and he always asks how you and Momma are. You always told me business was business, never personal, so I never understood why you didn't wanna do business with him in the first place."

"It's a long story, son, but I'm glad to see you're thinking. And you're right. Business is business." I was about to explain myself when Paris poked her head in my office.

"Daddy, your three o'clock is here."

"Thanks, princess. Why don't you send him in and ask Harris to join us."

"Okay. You want me to sit in on this as well? I can take notes," she replied.

"No, I don't think it will be necessary."

Paris looked like she wanted to say something, but then she must have thought twice about it, because she pulled her head back through the door. She was still on relatively good behavior after her incident with Trevor.

"Listen, Pop, if you've got a meeting, we can talk about this later." Orlando stretched, getting up from his chair.

"No, no, son. I want you in on this. I think you're going to see that I can think outside the box as well."

"All right, but can I ask you a quick question?" I nodded as he sat back down.

"Why'd you send Rio up there to seduce that man? You would have never let Paris or London do anything like that."

"I sent him there because this family is in trouble and I had to use everything at my disposal to save it. Make no mistake. Every member of this family has talents that are very valuable to our operation. If you're going to lead this family, you better understand it and be ready to use those talents whenever it's necessary." I took a cigar out of the box on my desk and clipped the tip. "Son, we'll have to finish this conversation another time. It looks like our guest has arrived."

Orlando turned to the door, and we both stood up to greet the handsome and well-dressed Latino gentleman in his early thirties that Paris had ushered into my office.

"Daddy, this is Miguel Sota. Miguel, this is my father, LC Duncan."

"Buenos días, Miguel," I said as he shook my hand. Paris's eyes lustfully lingered on Miguel before I shooed her away. Orlando saw it as well, but he didn't bother to react. He was learning.

"Miguel, this is my son Orlando."

"Señor Duncan . . . er . . . both of you, it is a pleasure to make your acquaintance." He spoke with a heavy accent. I liked his manners, as well as his composure, especially after whatever his employer had told him about me before he came from California. To some in the business, I could be the devil; to others, something worse.

"No, no, Miguel, the pleasure is ours. Come, have a seat." I motioned toward the open leather chair next to Orlando.

"Would you like something to drink?" Orlando asked, stepping up so as to not be a spectator in what he now perceived to be an important meeting.

"No. I'm fine," Miguel replied. "Paris already asked me. And after a long flight, I'm just ready to get down to business. That is, if you don't mind, sir?"

"No, not at all. Orlando, Miguel works for Alejandro."

Orlando nodded his head with a smile. "I see. How is he?" Orlando asked as Harris entered the room, carrying a folder. He sat to the right of Miguel.

"Doing good, in spite of the economy. When some of our competitors struggled and failed in Las Vegas, he managed to move right in and expand into that market."

I glanced over at Orlando. "Yes, I hear he's doing a lot of that lately. Is he being backed by anyone?"

"No, sir. Not that I know of."

I studied him, hoping to see some type of chink in his facade. He gave away nothing.

He continued, "He just sees opportunity and takes it."

"That sounds like him. Did you know I used to do business with Alejandro a lot back in the day, when I was getting established and branching out? We were just two up-and-coming minority dealers from two opposite sides of the country, looking to make moves in their respective markets. I learned a lot from him about distribution and networks. I hope he learned a lot from me about sales."

"Yes, he has mentioned this many times," Miguel stated, making me feel a lot better about the possibilities of working with Alejandro. "He says that you are a great businessman and we can all learn much from you."

"I hope so, Miguel, because this deal he proposes could change the way we all do business. He must really trust you to have you broker it."

"I believe he does," Miguel said, pride evident on his face.

"Good! Then I must trust you too. Y'know, even though me and your boss butt heads from time to time, there is always respect."

"With that in mind, he wanted me to discuss the final terms of our proposal to become your new distributor. I know you and Señor Alejandro have discussed the basics, but I thought you might want to see the numbers in black and white."

He handed me a folder, which I in turn handed to Harris. He opened it and scanned the paperwork it contained. When he finished, he smiled and handed it to Orlando, who did the same when he was done reading.

"Alejandro did tell you that this deal hinges on one thing, didn't he?" I asked.

He nodded. "Yes, you want Señor Alejandro's 1957 Corvette Roadster."

"He did tell you I used to own that '57 Corvette Roadster? It's been a sore spot between us for years."

I pointed to a picture of me standing next to a fully restored red and white classic 1957 Corvette Roadster with barely one thousand miles on its engine. I'd lost the car to Alejandro in a poker game almost twenty years ago, during a business trip to Las Vegas. That was the last business transaction we'd done, because I believed he'd cheated in that game, miraculously pulling a straight flush to my full house. In any other situation I would have protested, but considering I was in his part of the country, he had several of his men there, and I was alone, I figured it was best to give up the keys. I'd regretted that mistake to this day, but my baby was finally coming home. Of course, now I had to pay 2011 prices for its return, but I was glad Alejandro had taken good care of it.

"I hated parting with that car."

"And he equally hates parting with it now, sir, but in the interest of business and good relations, he has agreed to your terms."

"Glad to hear that." I glanced over at the boys. "Orlando, Harris, what do think of the deal we've made? Should we do it?"

"I can't see any reason not to. It gives us a steady supply of inventory for the next five years and covers all my concerns," Harris explained.

"It's a no-brainer, Pop. These terms are almost as good as Lee's when you take out the shipping."

"Very good," I said, reaching across my desk to shake his hand. "Miguel, it looks like we have a deal—as long as I get my Roadster back in one piece."

"I can assure you we will take the utmost care in delivering the Corvette to you, Señor Duncan, as I will be here personally to ensure delivery once payment is made. That is why Alejandro wanted to make sure we met."

"My brother Junior will be your contact for transport on our end," Orlando said. He was all into the details, back from whatever mental vacation that trip to Long Island had him on. "How do you plan on making delivery of the Roadster, considering its value?"

"A special tractor-trailer transport fitted with special bracing and retrofitted to fit classic cars. It keeps them from picking up any damage during the trip. We use them a lot for this type of transport," Miguel replied calmly.

"Yeah, so do we. What about security? I mean, we're not talking about a few Camrys here. If that car is what you say it is, it's worth more than both our paychecks."

"It's worth more than both your lives," I interjected.

"Of course. All will be secure, as per your father's arrangement with Alejandro. We, of course, will guarantee delivery."

"Sounds good. You can see me about payment," Orlando confirmed, looking at me with a smile as he checked off on everything. He handed Miguel his card. "Junior will get with you and nail down the route and delivery date in the next few days, but don't hesitate to call me if something comes up."

"Bien."

"How long are you in town?" I asked as we walked out of my office.

"I head back to L.A. in the morning, but I will be back a few days before the first shipment."

I patted him on the back. "Well, let me see you out, then. I have an apartment nearby that you're free to use, if you'd like. Anything else you need while in town, just let me or Orlando know. My son Rio owns a club that I think you might like also. You have our numbers, and we'll be sure to answer," I said, cutting a look at Orlando.

Outside my office, I led Miguel to the showroom floor, while we waited for Orlando to double-check all the facts and figures of our agreement. Miguel was drawn to the black Continental GT instantly, peering in its windows and admiring its powerful lines as he circled it.

"You like?"

"I love it. It's beautiful," he gushed, his eyes ablaze. "Señor Alejandro does not deal in such expensive European cars as you. He is more comfortable with domestic brands and Japanese cars, as you know."

"When you're ready for one, come see me. I'll let you have one at my cost," I said with a smile. Even though I wasn't actively involved in sales these days, the allure of a potential deal still gave me a rush.

"You are most generous, Señor Duncan."

"Daddy, here are those purchase orders you asked for," Paris said as she approached us. This could've waited, but at least she was following my instructions and being productive in the office until she was needed.

"Thank you," I said curtly, letting her know I was still busy.

She hadn't noticed Miguel, who was now seated inside the Bentley, and broke into a wide grin when she did. His smile for the car was now devoted to my daughter, as he tried to discreetly check out her body.

"That'll be all, Paris. Go check on Orlando to see if he's done back in my office," I directed. She moved on, but not before eyeing Miguel a final time and flicking her hair. I could've sworn she had a little extra bounce in her step.

Wait. Don't fucking answer that," I said as my mind was filled with the image of some bitch giving him head.

I knew I probably should have stuck to the flat tire issue, but the minute I heard his voice, I couldn't help myself. I wanted to jump through the phone and strangle him.

"London, I'm busy and don't have time for your shit, okay?" he snapped.

Damn. He didn't even deny it. "My shit! I'm the one out dropping off your laundry while you out getting your dick sucked by God knows who."

"You know what . . .?" He hung up, which pissed me off even more.

I called him right back. "Don't be hanging up on me."

"You keep talking to me about nonsense, and I'm gonna do a lot worse than hang up. Now, I told you I have a meeting."

I'm not going to lie; his threat scared me, but I tried not to let it show. "Well, I got a flat tire by the dry cleaners, and your daughter's in the car."

"The one over by Farmers Boulevard?"

"Yep, and the only reason I'm here is because you said you don't want anyone else doing your shirts but them."

"You said Mariah's with you?" The way he said it made me feel like he didn't give a shit about me, just Mariah.

"Medium starch? We'll clean it good," was all she said as she handed me my ticket.

I sucked in some air, lifting my head as I walked out of the dry cleaners, wishing Harris's clothes were in a burning heap.

As we walked through the parking lot, Mariah asked questions about every little thing she saw, as she was apt to do, but I didn't respond. My fucking philandering husband was consuming my thoughts, along with ideas about just how I was going to pay his ass back.

I buckled Mariah into her car seat, then walked around to the driver's side.

"No, no, no," I said with a groan when I spotted the flat front tire. This could not be happening to me. Not today.

"Mommy, what's wrong?" Mariah shouted from her seat. It was the first time I actually heard what she said since we'd left the dry cleaners.

"Hang on, baby. Mommy needs to make a call." As much as I hated doing it, I needed to call my husband.

"Where are you?" I barked when Harris answered.

"In Manhattan. I have an important meeting."

"You sure you're not in some hotel with that bitch whose lipstick was left on your shirt? How the hell do you get lipstick down there, anyway?

Once she disappeared around the corner, I leaned over and placed my arm across the roof of the Continental GT, peering inside.

"Miguel, that's my daughter," I offered, not sure if he was aware.

"Yes, sir," Miguel responded, trying to be nonchalant about the obvious rise she'd gotten out of him a minute ago.

"This car, you can have one day. Matter of fact, once this deal goes through, maybe I'll give it to you. We'll call it a finder's fee. But my daughter, you can't have. Comprende?"

"Yes, sir."

"Good," I said, looking him dead in the eye as I gave him a fatherly pat across his chest. "Because if you touch her, I'll kill you."

London

18

I walked out of Queens Village Montessori School, holding Mariah's hand, styling and profiling like I owned the place. With the tuition I was paying them for Mariah to go to school there each week, I probably should have had Daddy buy the joint, because it would have been cheaper.

I'd picked her up a little early in hopes of using her as an excuse for stopping by the office and running into Harris. We'd been arguing nonstop since he found out that he wasn't my first lover. I'd hurt his ego pretty bad. He hadn't come home from the office before midnight for the past few nights, and he was out the door before seven every morning. I was hoping that bringing Mariah by the office to see him would be enough of an olive branch for us to at least talk. We had a fundraising dinner with my parents in a few days, and I did not want my mother or father picking up on just how bad things were between us.

I knew that once we started talking civilly again, I'd ease my way back into his good graces. He was a sucker for a good blow job, so it might just take giving him some head from under his desk for him to forgive me. I was going to have to do something, because that man had a high sex drive, and I wasn't about to let any other woman step into my shoes. I'd given up my professional life and had a baby years before I was ready, all in the name of making him happy, so you best believe I wasn't about to let anyone step in my way.

"So how was school today?" I asked my daughter as she leaped into her seat in the back of my Mercedes SUV, her curls bouncing wildly.

"Good. Jermaine was bad again today. He couldn't play at recess," she rattled off without taking a breath. Kids. As I buckled her seat belt, she gave me a kiss on the cheek. "We goin' to see Grandpa now?" she asked, almost pleading.

"Yeah, baby. Mommy's gonna take you to see Grandpa. But I want you to find Daddy first and give him a big hug. He really misses you."

"Okay, Mommy, but then I'm gonna find Grandpa and help him, because I run Duncan Motors."

As much as Mariah enjoyed pretending she was an employee, barking out orders and charming the car shoppers, my father loved having her around the dealership even more. I kind of think his spoiling Mariah was an attempt to make up for how hard he was on us growing up—well, all of us except Paris. Perhaps he should've been harder on her. It might have saved us all some trouble.

On the way to bring Mariah for her visit, I stopped at the dry cleaners on Rockaway Boulevard to drop off Harris's clothes. Mariah stood at my side, counting the articles of clothing as the woman behind the counter separated them. Everything was as usual, until I sifted through the crisp whites. As I grasped the third one from the pile, a red streak near the last button on the bottom of the shirt caught my eye. I studied it harder, realizing it was a woman's lipstick smudge—and it wasn't mine. It was far too bright.

"Son of a bitch," I muttered.

"Oooh, Mommy, you said a bad word," Mariah chastised.

"I know, baby. I'm sorry," I apologized as tears welled up in my eyes.

"Mommy, you look like you're crying. Is it because you said a bad word?"

"No, I'm not crying, baby. I just have something in my eyes. Mommy's fine." I wiped away the tears. The Asian woman behind the counter met my dazed stare, offering either solidarity or pity as she took the shirt away from me and squirreled it out of my view with the rest of the dry cleaning.

"Medium starch? We'll clean it good," was all she said as she handed me my ticket.

I sucked in some air, lifting my head as I walked out of the dry cleaners, wishing Harris's clothes were in a burning heap.

As we walked through the parking lot, Mariah asked questions about every little thing she saw, as she was apt to do, but I didn't respond. My fucking philandering husband was consuming my thoughts, along with ideas about just how I was going to pay his ass back.

I buckled Mariah into her car seat, then walked around to the driver's side.

"No, no, no," I said with a groan when I spotted the flat front tire. This could not be happening to me. Not today.

"Mommy, what's wrong?" Mariah shouted from her seat. It was the first time I actually heard what she said since we'd left the dry cleaners.

"Hang on, baby. Mommy needs to make a call." As much as I hated doing it, I needed to call my husband.

"Where are you?" I barked when Harris answered.

"In Manhattan. I have an important meeting."

"You sure you're not in some hotel with that bitch whose lipstick was left on your shirt? How the hell do you get lipstick down there, anyway?

Wait. Don't fucking answer that," I said as my mind was filled with the image of some bitch giving him head.

I knew I probably should have stuck to the flat tire issue, but the minute I heard his voice, I couldn't help myself. I wanted to jump through the phone and strangle him.

"London, I'm busy and don't have time for your shit, okay?" he snapped.

Damn. He didn't even deny it. "My shit! I'm the one out dropping off your laundry while you out getting your dick sucked by God knows who."

"You know what . . .?" He hung up, which pissed me off even more.

I called him right back. "Don't be hanging up on me."

"You keep talking to me about nonsense, and I'm gonna do a lot worse than hang up. Now, I told you I have a meeting."

I'm not going to lie; his threat scared me, but I tried not to let it show. "Well, I got a flat tire by the dry cleaners, and your daughter's in the car."

"The one over by Farmers Boulevard?"

"Yep, and the only reason I'm here is because you said you don't want anyone else doing your shirts but them."

"You said Mariah's with you?" The way he said it made me feel like he didn't give a shit about me, just Mariah.

"Mm-hmm. You coming to get us or what?"

"I can't right now, London. I'm just about to start this meeting. Just call Junior's people. They'll send somebody over to change it."

I exhaled loudly into the phone. "I guess."

"Listen, I love you, London. Now, get back inside with Mariah and lock the doors. That's not the best of neighborhoods. I don't want anything happening to you before we have a chance to talk."

Don't ask me why, but I hung up with a smile— before someone frightened the hell out of me.

"Miss—"

I screamed, turning around to find a man standing between me and the back of my car, where my daughter was sitting, watching this whole thing. He looked dirty and disheveled, but I told myself that didn't automatically make him a bad person.

"Miss, everything okay?"

"No," I said, embarrassed by being rattled. "My tire. I had a blowout."

"That's too bad," he chirped.

At that point, I was about to show him where the spare tire was, because I assumed he was about to offer assistance. Well, you know what they say about assuming things.

"Guess I can't drive it off, then," he continued as he pulled a gun on me from under his hoodie. I gazed down its barrel.

"Please. My daughter—"

"Will be okay if you hurry up and hand over all yer shit!" he snarled, cutting me off.

"Mommy?" Mariah called out from inside. Thank God the man's back was turned to her, so she couldn't see the gun.

"Wait a minute, baby. The nice man is going to help us." I looked at him and pleaded, "Please . . . just leave us alone. You don't want to do this."

"Who the fuck are you to know what I want and don't want? Lady, I'm losin' my patience. Now, give up your shit!"

"Okay. Okay, here." I was willing to give him everything, as long as Mariah and I could walk away from this alive. I let my purse slide off my shoulder into my hand, then tossed it to him.

"What else you got? What about that jewelry and that watch? Don't even think about holdin' out on me."

I took off my wedding ring and watch and handed them to him. "That's it."

"What you got in the car? I said I want it all," he shouted.

"Nothing. Just my daughter."

"Check again, or I'll make her check." He glanced in Mariah's direction. Just the thought of him going near her was enough to make me take action. I opened the car door. Behind me, I could hear him riffling through my purse with his free hand. I knew he was distracted, so I began fishing beneath the driver's seat for something he hadn't bargained for.

"Mmm . . . you got a nice ass."

I dreaded that his eyes were on me again rather than on my purse. I reached around a little more frantically for what should have been easy to find. Then it hit me—my gun wasn't there. It was in the glove compartment, locked away so Mariah wouldn't find it. Damn, motherhood had made me sloppy, but I had to think of something. This guy was starting to act creepier than before. "Um, my glove compartment is locked. I'm gonna need the keys out of my purse."

"Nah, now that I think about it, that wheel and tire ain't that bad. Why don't you get in? We can drive around the corner . . . talk. Maybe I'll change it fer ya. Afterwards." I jerked up when his hand touched my ass.

"Look," I said, turning to face him. "You really don't want to do this. Check my wallet. There's—"

"I'm already gonna get the money, lady. What I want is between your legs. Now, get your ass in the car."

He glanced over at Mariah, and I made a decision right then and there. I was not going to let that man rape me, especially not in front of my child, so we were about to see who was stronger.

I was about to try to wrestle that gun away from him.

I took a deep breath, but before I could move, someone rushed up behind me and bowled the fiend over. He fell against the fender of my Mercedes, busting his mouth wide open and sending the snub-nosed revolver spilling onto the pavement, along with several rotted teeth.

My sudden rescuer, a very handsome, dark-haired white man, delivered a knee to my attacker's ribs as he tried to scamper to his feet. Leaving his gun, my personal effects, and the teeth that no longer mattered, he fled up the avenue with his busted mouth.

"Get the fuck outta here!" my rescuer hollered, kicking at the open air in disgust.

"Mommy!" Mariah screamed as she tried to undo her seat belt. I rushed to the backseat, opening the door to check on her.

"Shhh, shhh. Hey, baby, it's okay," I said, delivering my best smile to calm her as I brushed her curls aside. "The man fell, and this gentleman tried to help him up."

"I thought he was tryin' to hurt you."

"No, no, baby girl. Everything's fine. This nice man is going to help us instead. That's all."

Mariah looked at the new arrival, waving at him with a warm smile. He returned her smile and waved back. I was still trying to remove my heart from my throat as the adrenaline wore off.

"Thank you," I offered as he handed me back my purse.

"Glad to help. I was across the street. I didn't think anything was wrong until I saw him going through your purse. Didn't know about the gun until I hit him. Whoa," he said, looking down at the ground as he suddenly realized his mortality in this situation.

"I didn't know this city still had Good Samaritans. That was very brave of you."

"My mom would be glad to hear that, but it wasn't nothin'. I don't like to see women in trouble," he said with a smile. He had this rough charm about him, and he was easy on the eyes too. "You still need your tire changed, right?"

"I guess I do. London," I offered, suddenly self-conscious about how this mom looked after a near-fatal encounter.

"Anthony. But my friends call me Tony," he replied. "You think we should call the police?"

"For what? So we can be knee-deep in paperwork and waste the next five hours? I think he already got what he deserved."

"Suit yourself. Where's your jack?" he said, bending over to get a better look at the tire. I went to the trunk. "Beautiful daughter you have there."

"Thank you."

"She obviously gets it from her mom," he added with a slight change in his voice. Was this white boy flirting with me?

As I smiled, I wondered whether I should even tell Harris or the rest of my family about this. For now, I would clear my head of such things and enjoy the view as Tony rendered assistance—while my husband was across town, once again too busy for me.

Orlando

19

I hadn't been back to my apartment since that night with Ruby. Not that I hadn't wanted to, but I'd been busting my ass day and night trying to get a handle on things and prove myself to the old man and my siblings. I'd completely forgotten about doing anything for myself. That in itself wasn't necessarily a problem, except that I'd been thinking about Ruby almost every day. I couldn't seem to get her out of my head, so with the distribution deal with Alejandro well in hand, I had called Remy and set something up to relieve my sexual tension.

"We've been expecting your call," Remy had told me through the phone receiver. "We haven't heard from you in quite a while. You're breaking routine. That's not like you," he noted. "I was afraid you might have gone to another service."

"No, no, I'm very happy with your service. I've just been very busy."

"Ah, yes, the new promotion at work. How is it going?"

"It hasn't completely begun yet. I'm still in training, but even that's not easy."

"I see. Well, maybe we can make you feel better...." he'd said and then we proceeded to make arrangements.

When I strolled into the condo, the aroma coming from the kitchen was teasing my nose, much like how, in the next hour or so, the cook would be teasing my dick. I know it might seem selfish of me to be out whoring around in my condo when my family's business was in trouble, but nobody had put in more work than me this week. I was doing the best I could, and consequently, I hadn't had a good night's rest, eaten a decent meal, or screwed in more than two weeks, and I was bound and determined to kill three birds with one stone that night.

I quickly tried to erase the self-serving thoughts from my mind. Pussy should never interfere with blood—although I'd be a lying bastard if I said a little pussy wouldn't give me just the boost I needed right about now. After all, what's more rejuvenating and energizing than a little pussy? Hell, a big pussy. And thanks to Maria and Remy, whose services I could always count on, that was just what was about to go down.

"Dinner is served."

Just the words I needed to hear as I turned my attention to the antidote to cure my day's woes.

Seeing her standing there in nothing but stilettos and a black-and-white lacy apron would have made any man forget his troubles and get lost in the sheer anticipation of what was to come. But I knew what was to come. I'd been there before, to that place that washes all a man's troubles away just long enough for him to recoup and prepare for the next day's concerns.

"I hope you like." Her accent was so sexy. She licked her lips, batted her eyes, and beckoned with her index finger, luring me into the kitchen. Even though I'd been there before and almost knew what to expect, I followed.

"Allow me to get your chair, Mr. Orlando," she said, then proceeded to pull out my chair.

I sat and gave the spread on the table the once-over. I'd eaten an identical meal before. I hated repeating meals almost as much as seeing the same girl twice. Had I done the right thing, letting Remy send me this girl, or should I have listened to my gut? The hell with your rule, my conscience had tried to tell me.

Ten minutes into our dinner, it got to the point where it all seemed like déjà vu. I wasn't even taking part in the conversation anymore. Just nodding.

"Is everything okay?" The poor girl almost looked offended that I had only picked at my meal. "The rice not good? You like sweet and sour chicken, no?"

"You wouldn't happen to know how to make jerk chicken, would you?" I looked up at the Asian beauty and then at the native cuisine that sat on the table. I meant to keep my laughter inside, but it seeped out. Now she wasn't almost offended; she was offended. I knew this because even though I had absolutely no fucking idea what she was saying in her native tongue, I could tell she was cussing me out.

Once I was able to contain my laughter, I knew I had to make nice with her. The last thing I wanted to do was to hurt her feelings. Still, I couldn't help it. It wasn't really her fault, I suppose, but all of a sudden everything seemed so redundant. I'd never been with this particular Asian girl before, but I'd been with plenty just like her. Plenty who looked like her, talked like her, even cooked that same damn meal like her. The meal was a dead giveaway that none of them really knew how to prepare their native cuisine. Sweet and sour chicken? Come on. Even I could pull off that entrée.

"Look, I'm sorry . . ." I searched my mind for her name.

"Candy," she replied when she saw me grasping at straws.

I spared her feelings by suppressing my laugh this time. Candy—so typical. Remy had even sent me another "Candy" before. I was beginning to realize just how I'd been fooling myself, thinking that my second-date rule made any difference. It didn't matter that I never saw the same girl twice. No matter how I looked at it, it was the same broad, different name. Or in Candy's case, same name.

Ruby was the exception. I'd never met any woman like her before. I had never even given one of Remy's girls a second thought after our night together, but I'd given Ruby more than just a second thought. I'd given her a fraction of my mind, and in order to reclaim my full sanity, I knew exactly what I had to do.

"Candy, you are a wonderful, beautiful young lady. And a hell of a cook, I'm sure." I had to soften the blow, didn't I? I had to place a soft pillow over her head before I pulled the trigger to blow her brains out, so to speak. "But this isn't gonna work."

"Save it, asshole." Her accent was gone. She stood up from the table in a huff. "I don't need to hear the speech about how it's not me, it's you, and you don't know if you can do this, blah, blah, blah." She slammed her chair into the table. "And Maria said you were one of the good ones. Huh. You waste time is what you do." Her accent was back—a little. "You still pay. Just know that," was the last thing she said before she exited the kitchen to go change.

"I'll call Maria and let her know to send the car service for you," I shot over my shoulder as she proceeded to curse me out.

The escort service was one of the first numbers, after my family members', that I'd programmed into speed dial when I got my new phone. I pulled it out now to make the call.

"Orlando. How's our favorite client?"

"Remy, my man," I replied. "It's all good, but look, check this out. I'm going to need you to send the car for Candy a little earlier than scheduled."

"Oh?" He sounded disappointed, nervous even. "Is everything okay? Was something wrong with your girl?" I could hear him flipping pages in the background. "She wasn't a repeat, was she? Damn it, I told Maria to always make sure you never get the same girl twice. Look, I'll send you someone else. Just let me—"

"No, listen, Remy. Everything is fine. Candy is fine. She wasn't a repeat. You guys are on the J-O-B," I explained. "But, Remy, if you don't mind, you can send me someone else."

His voice was now a mixture of excitement and relief. "No problem. We have this half-African princess that does this thing with her—"

"Look, Remy, I'm sure she's the finest the motherland has to offer, but I kind of have a special request."

"Anything, anybody for you. Just name it."

I couldn't believe I was about to say the words that eased out of my mouth. "Ruby. Send me Ruby."

There was crazy silence on the line, and it made me uncomfortable. Finally Remy said, "But you never see the—"

I had to cut him off. I didn't have an appetite for my own words. "Remy, man, when the driver comes for Candy, just make sure he drops off Ruby."

I thought everything was settled, until Remy informed me, "Ruby is no longer with us."

It took a few seconds for his words to register before I could ask, "What? Excuse me?"

"I'm sorry, Orlando, but you were Ruby's first and last. She said this line of work didn't suit her, after all."

I felt . . . hell, I didn't know how I felt, but it wasn't good. "Remy, I have a craving for the Caribbean beauty by the name of Ruby. You get paid to cure my cravings. Need I search for a new chef?"

"No, no, no! That won't be necessary. I'm sure we have another island girl who will suit your needs just—"

I was cutting Remy off for what was hopefully the last time. "Maybe you didn't hear me, Remy. I want Ruby. Get me Ruby. Money is and never has been an issue."

There was a sigh from Remy. "I'll do my best, Orlando." He didn't sound too convincing.

"Do better than your best, Remy. Get Ruby here by tomorrow." I ended the call, knowing that if Remy didn't make this happen, I'd be cutting him off, all right—and hopefully finding Ruby on my own.

LC

20

My wife walked into my office and sat down on the small sofa, smiling for what seemed like the first time in weeks. You could always tell just how the Duncan family was doing by her mood, and this day, well, this day was good all the way around. We'd gotten our first shipment of cars from Alejandro earlier that day, and my '57 Roadster was due at our Long Island City warehouse sometime the next day.

To top that off, Chippy and I were going to be receiving a lifetime appreciation award from First Jamaica Ministries for all the charity work she'd done for underprivileged children. I really didn't want to take any of the credit, since all I did was write a check. She and London had done the work, but she insisted that I accept with her because we were a team.

"Daddy, you have a phone call on your private line," Paris said from my office door.

"Thanks, baby girl." I reached for the phone.

"Paris," Chippy called, giving our daughter a disapproving look. This prompted me to hesitate before hitting the talk button to connect the call. "Don't you know how to use the intercom?"

"Yeah, Ma, I do," Paris confessed, "but the view's so nice at this end of the hall today, I decided to walk down and tell Daddy about his call."

Both Chippy and I were shaking our heads as Paris walked slowly back down the hall. We heard her stop at the next office, where Orlando was having a meeting with Miguel. He'd flown in from California the night before to supervise the first shipment of cars and to make sure the Roadster was delivered unharmed. It was pretty obvious that he was the view Paris was talking about. I just didn't understand why my daughter kept putting herself out there like some common slut. She was by far the most beautiful of all my children and could have any man of her choosing if she decided to settle down.

Frustrated, I hit the button, connecting the call.

"LC Duncan," I spoke into the phone.

"Greetings, LC, my friend." It was Alejandro. I would know his raspy voice and thick accent anywhere. "I call with great thanks for the payment, and with well wishes for our continued business. I also would thank you for the hospitality you have shown Miguel. He's mentioned quite often what a wonderful time he has had in your city. In fact, it was his diligence that insured that the Roadster will be delivered tomorrow."

I had to smile. Miguel must have really wanted that Bentley I hinted at during his first trip to New York. That was a good thing, though. The more he was in tune to my needs and wants, the better. Now, if I could only keep him away from my daughter.

"Glad to hear that, Alejandro. Even though things have been strained between us, I'm glad we're able to do business again," I stated in the spirit of the moment.

"As am I, my friend. Let this be a new beginning. No longer competitors, but partners of a sort. I look forward to making much money with you, my friend."

"I'll toast to that."

"Good. Maybe we can share a bottle or two of some of my best tequila. If I can get you back out here to L.A., mi amigo, maybe I'll arrange for some sexy ladies, like we used to do. I remember that time with me and you and those four señoritas from Cozumel. Those were the days, huh?" He laughed loudly.

I glanced at Chippy, happy that I didn't have this on speakerphone. "I've gotten a little too old for that, Alejandro, but thank you for the offer.

These days, I'm just a 'community' sort of guy who enjoys time with his family. I don't really travel much anymore outside of New York. Like how you don't leave the West Coast, eh?"

"You got me there. I guess at the end of the day, we're both just kings captive in our own little castles."

"Good way of putting it," I commented, thinking of the world beyond my castle walls that awaited me and Chippy down in Florida. "We'll talk further once we take delivery from your men."

"We most certainly will. Best wishes to your family, my friend," Alejandro stated, presumably with other thoughts kept to himself for another time.

"Yours also," I replied, then disconnected the call.

"Do you trust Alejandro?" Chippy asked.

"Have I ever, sweetheart?" I answered. "You know how it is. Same as it's always been. Every man for himself, or in this case, every family."

"Except the competition has never been this fierce. There's no loyalty in business, and you're not the sexy young man I fell in love with."

I chuckled at her latter comment. "There was somebody before me, and there will be somebody after me. Alejandro can say whatever he wants. He has plans to take over our territory.

He's just using this as a way to get his foot in the door. That's why I've been readying Orlando."

"But Orlando's not you. He's his own man. He's going to want to do things his own way."

"And he'll have that freedom. But if he plans on making wholesale changes . . . too much, too soon, he'll have to answer to me. A lot of people, beyond our immediate family, depend on what we've established here, sweetheart. This isn't just a business."

"I know, baby," Chippy stated as I stood up to give her a hug. "But to say I would mind having you all to myself would be a lie."

Our embrace was cut short by Paris, coming to inform me of a call from Harris.

"Sorry to bother you, LC," Harris said when I answered. "But did you take care of London's problem?"

"No. I never heard from her," I replied. "But I've been on the phone with Alejandro in L.A. Maybe she spoke with Junior."

"No, I called him first. He never heard from her either. Shit."

"Is something wrong? What was she supposed to talk to me about?"

"Oh . . . nothing major. She had a flat tire and I had a meeting, so I couldn't get to her in time. I told her to call for someone over there to come out."

Just as I became concerned, I heard the familiar laughter of my granddaughter coming from the showroom floor.

"Was Mariah with her, Harris?"

"Yes. Why?"

"They're here. No need to worry anymore," I assured him.

"Good," he said with a deep sigh over the phone. "Just have her call me later."

London came down the hall, walking past the window to my office. She looked unfazed to my eye, which made me feel better. As the door cracked open, Mariah stormed in ahead of her.

"I see you, Grandpa!" Mariah shrieked, full of youthful innocence and glee. She ran behind my desk and jumped into my outstretched arms. As I hugged her, I reflected on how grateful I was that London had provided me with such a lovely and caring grandchild, my only one. In stepping down from her responsibilities around here and marrying Harris, London had given me an even greater gift than her mere talents.

"Is everything okay? I just got off the phone with Harris," I said to London.

"Oh. Yeah. Everything's fine. I had a flat—my front tire. I have the spare on now. One of your men is going to put on a new tire," my daughter answered as she embraced her mother.

"Mommy had two guys help her. But the stinky, dirty one left," Mariah said, smiling at me with a fresh missing baby tooth evident.

"Is that so?" I looked to London to elaborate.

"Uh-huh," my granddaughter continued, volunteering what she knew in her own unique way. "He hurt his mouth and went home. And the nice one that Mommy likes stayed and put on the good wheel for us."

"Oh, really?" Chippy asked this time, with a sly grin on her lips.

"Just somebody who helped, that's all," London replied with an equally sly look adorning her face. This wasn't like London. Paris, maybe, but definitely not London.

Orlando

21

I left the dealership and dropped Miguel off at his hotel. He was going to catch a flight back to California right after Junior got confirmation that the truck with the Roadster was securely in our people's hands. I was looking forward to a little peace and quiet now that things were starting to look up. With his beloved car on the way back to him, my father was content, and I was feeling like I finally deserved a little time to myself. I loved my family, but with all the stress lately, living and working with them 24/7 was really starting to grate on my nerves. I'd never been more convinced than right now that buying a private condo was a good move on my part. Even more than the privacy it afforded me, my place allowed me to indulge in something else that I needed—something that was waiting for me on the other side of the door to my condo.

I entered the condo and before I could stop myself, I shouted, "You're here!" I tried to play it off once those words escaped my mouth, but there was no hiding my excitement. I was breaking my own rule about never seeing the same girl twice, so no doubt Ruby was already feeling pretty full of herself. I didn't really want to add fuel to that fire, but just seeing her again, I couldn't help myself. For a while I'd worried that Remy wouldn't be able to find her and I might never see her again.

"Were you not expecting me?" Ruby rose up off the couch. Her voice was like music to my ears.

"Oh, uh, yeah, I guess I was." I looked everywhere but at her eyes, as though I had a million things on my mind—and that she wasn't one of them. She was, though. She had been on my mind plenty since our first encounter. Damn, it was proving to be hard work to maintain my cool around this woman.

"You don't sound so sure about that." She began to undo her blouse. With any other escort I would have appreciated that she was ready to get right down to business, but there was something about Ruby's eyes. They looked empty, like she wasn't even really in there, and it was almost painful for me to see. Clearly, she had left Remy's service for a reason. This was not the type of work she wanted to be doing.

"What are you doing?" I asked.

"Remy and Maria said that you're paying twice the usual amount and you don't want me to cook. So, I am preparing myself for what I know you want. Why you asked to see me again. My body." The melody was gone from her voice, and it kind of scared me how much I missed it.

"I don't want that, either. At least not that way or right now. Can you put your clothes back on, please?" Anything to bring back the Ruby I'd been thinking about ever since our first meeting.

She shook her head and clutched her unbuttoned blouse to cover her breasts. "I don't understand." She sounded agitated, maybe even embarrassed. This was not turning out at all the way I'd hoped.

"You don't understand what?"

"Why I'm here. Remy and Maria, as well as yourself, made it very clear that you never see the same girl twice." She quickly buttoned up her blouse. "So why am I here?"

"Well—" The chirping of my cell phone interrupted me. It was probably a good thing, because it gave me a minute to collect my thoughts, so I didn't slip up and admit to this woman how much I'd been thinking about her.

"Hold on. Let me check this." She waited patiently while I read the text from Junior: On my way to the rendezvous spot.

This made me happy. Soon LC would have his Roadster, and all would be right with the Duncans' world—and I could celebrate with Ruby all night. I texted back: Cool. We exchanged a few more quick texts before we were done, and I turned my attention back to Ruby.

"Where were we?"

"I was asking you why I'm here."

Because I've been thinking about you, every inch of you. Because there's no one else Remy could have sent who holds a candle to you.

Those were the things I wanted to tell her but never would. Instead, I said nonchalantly, "Guess I made an exception," as if breaking my own rule wasn't the monumental thing that it really was.

Her confusion seemed to be giving way to a little bit of an attitude, complete with hands on her hips and the hint of a sour frown, which she was trying hard to conceal. Either she just didn't like being confused, or she could see right through me and knew I was full of shit. Maybe she knew just what her beauty was doing to me. The growing excitement in my boxers sure wasn't helping to disprove that theory.

"Here. This is for you," I said, holding out the garment bag I'd been carrying, in the hope that I could distract her before she noticed she was making me hard.

"What's this?" she asked, though her bright eyes and quick smile made me think she already had some idea.

"Open it."

Her smile grew even wider when she opened the bag and took out the silk halter dress I'd bought for her. When I spotted it in Bloomingdale's, I'd instantly envisioned her gorgeous mahogany skin against the white silk.

Her eyes met mine, and for the first time that night, I heard that sweet island music again. Now, that was more like it.

"Put it on," I said.

She turned to head to the bedroom to change.

"No, here. I want to watch you put it on."

She stopped in her tracks and turned to face me. This time when she began unbuttoning her blouse, she kept her eyes on me, and that vacant look from before was replaced with . . . Was that admiration? Desire? Either way, I liked the way she was gazing into my eyes as she undressed for me. I guess a three-thousand-dollar dress can turn a bad situation good, just that fast.

By the time she was down to her bra and panties, she had me rethinking the plans I'd made. Maybe we'd have to order takeout, because I didn't know if I'd be able to wait until after dinner to bury myself deep inside her warmth.

Just as I was about to tell her to take off the rest, my phone rang. I looked down and saw my father's number on the screen. As much as I hated to tear my eyes off Ruby's body, I'd already learned my lesson about ignoring calls from my family, so I turned away and answered the call. Behind me, I heard Ruby sigh. Guess she didn't like being interrupted while she was seducing a man.

"Junior's on his way to the rendezvous spot," my father said when I answered.

"I know. He texted me already." I hoped the annoyance wasn't evident in my voice. It wasn't so much my father that was annoying me, just the fact that I had much better things to attend to at the moment. Work could wait.

My father must have sensed something, because he kept the call mercifully brief. It wasn't long before he said, "All right, son. I'll talk to you tomorrow at the office."

I hung up and turned around. I didn't know what was more gorgeous, Ruby in her bra and panties, or in the dress she was now wearing. The rhinestones sparkling along the neckline drew my eyes to her succulent cleavage.

"You look . . . beautiful," I said, at a loss for words to truly describe her.

"Thank you. This is very generous of you."

I didn't answer. She was so stunning, I felt like I could barely form a thought in my head.

"So," she asked coyly, "do you do things like this for the other girls too?"

That was enough to snap me out of my stupor. Ruby was fishing for some kind of confirmation that she meant more to me than all the other girls, and it was way too soon for that. While she might very well be more special, I still didn't know where this was going. Shit, it had been a big step for me to break my rule, so I was not about to take it a step further and profess feelings for this woman.

"Nah, never have, but it's no big deal," I said coolly, then changed the subject quick. "You hungry?"

She looked disappointed by my less than enthusiastic response, but knew enough not to complain like she was my woman or something. "Sure. Did you change your mind? Should I cook for you?"

"No. You're wearing the hell out of that dress. I thought I'd take you out to a restaurant. No doubt you'll be the most beautiful woman there."

I was right. There was not a woman in the place whose looks came anywhere close to Ruby's. One woman actually had to smack her husband to make him stop staring. I knew how dude felt, though. Halfway through the appetizers I thought

I was going to lose my mind watching the way she ate her shrimp cocktail. She dipped a fat, juicy shrimp into the cocktail sauce, brought it up to her mouth ever so slowly, rested the tip on her tongue, then wrapped her full, sexy lips around it, sucking off the sauce before she bit into it. I don't have to tell you what she had me thinking about. I was so into this sexy show that a moan almost escaped my lips right there at the table.

"So, you broke your rule for me, Mr. Orlando," she said with a flirtatious smile. "And not only have I been invited back for a second time, but you're taking me out in public—and to such a fancy place."

Again, she was fishing for compliments or commitment or something, but I wasn't going there. "You know, I was a little worried that Remy wouldn't be able to find you. He tells me you're no longer working for him."

She lowered her eyes. I'd hit a sore spot. "Yes," she said with a sad little sigh. "After my night with you I told him I didn't think I was cut out for this line of work. I was not raised this way. My parents would die if they knew what I was doing here in the States."

"They're still in Jamaica?" I asked.

"Yes. My family is the only reason I agreed to come back when Remy called. I had no other way to earn money to send back to them."

Now, I understood family loyalty, but damn, this was taking it to another level. "You're saying you can't find any other line of work? Something that will make you happier?"

The way she appeared to withdraw into herself, I realized maybe my question hadn't been very sensitive. After a long moment of silence, she practically whispered, "I don't have a work visa."

I nodded. "Say no more. Forgive me for prying."

She seemed to relax a little, I guess since she saw that I wasn't going to report her to the INS or something. "I only plan on doing this for a while. Once I've earned enough, I will go home to my parents and my daughter."

"You have a child?"

She nodded, then looked away quickly. "You must think less of me now, no? What type of woman leaves her child behind and goes to another country to sell herself to strangers?"

Rules be damned, this woman was arousing feelings of tenderness in me I thought I might never allow myself to feel again. I reached across and put my hand under her chin to make her turn and look at me. Her eyes were glistening with tears. "Hey, you're doing what you have to do to take care of your child. I don't judge you for that, and you shouldn't be so hard on yourself."

"Thank you," she said and wiped her eyes.

To lighten the mood a bit, I asked, "So, since your papers are a little funny, does that mean that anytime you won't do what I say, I can just threaten to call immigration on you?"

Luckily, she understood I was joking, and she joined right in. "Mr. Orlando, I'm not afraid of you. Besides, you never have to worry about me refusing to do whatever you want me to do for— or with—you." With that, she picked up another shrimp and did that thing with her tongue again.

For the rest of the meal, we kept the conversation pretty light. Any time a subject seemed to make her uncomfortable, I changed it in a hurry. Ruby gave off this air of vulnerability that just made me want to protect her. At the same time, she exuded a sexuality and a confidence about herself that just made me want to peel off her dress and make love to her right on the table in the restaurant. This woman had me going in so many different directions at once that I didn't even notice my brother walk into the restaurant until he was standing directly in front of me, looking ready to punch somebody.

"Yo, uh, Junior . . ." I glanced at Ruby, who was looking nervously up at Junior's hulking presence. "What are you doing here, man?" This was not exactly the kind of restaurant my brother frequented, especially since it was way the hell out on Long Island, where my family rarely went.

He shot a disdainful glance at Ruby and shook his head. "I shoulda known you was with a b—"

"Junior!" I stopped him before he could call Ruby a bitch. "I said, what are you doing here? And what is your problem, man?"

"What I'm doing here is trying to find you, fool. Good thing I put that damn GPS tracker on your car last time it was in the shop. Why the hell aren't you answering your phone?"

"What are you talking about?" I asked. I addressed the phone first; the idea that he was tracking me would be dealt with later. "My damn phone ain't rung once since I've been here." I looked to Ruby. "Isn't that right, Ruby?"

She didn't answer, and the strange look on her face told me I was about to find out something I wouldn't like.

"Ruby?" I said again.

"I'm sorry," she admitted. "When you went to the men's room, your phone kept ringing and then a few texts came in. We were . . ." She glanced quickly at Junior, maybe to be sure he wasn't ready to hit her. "We were having such a nice conversation. I didn't want it to be disturbed by phone calls. I didn't think you'd mind if I turned off your phone."

I shook my head and counted to ten as I gripped the sides of the table to keep myself from going off. I could not believe I was about to get cursed out again by my old man for not answering my phone, and it wasn't even my fault.

I was almost afraid to ask Junior, "What were you calling for?"

He tilted his head in the direction of the door, so I got up and followed him outside, where we could have some more privacy. I didn't even look in Ruby's direction as I left.

Outside, Junior blurted out, "The shipment's been hijacked. Somebody stole the truck with the Roadster on it."

I suddenly wished I hadn't eaten so much at dinner, because I felt like I was about to throw up. "Not the shipment. Tell me you're fucking kidding around."

Junior shook his head solemnly. "Dude, I would not joke about this. Pop is damn near ready to have a heart attack."

As the recently appointed head of Duncan Motors, I had to keep my bearings. I wanted to flip out, but I tried to remain calm as I asked, "Okay, look, any idea who could've done it?"

"Nope, but Pop wants us all back at the dealership ASAP. I'm sure he's got some thoughts."

"I've got a few of my own. I'll meet you back at the shop."

"Cool. Don't take too long," Junior said.

"Don't worry. I won't," I said over my shoulder as I headed back into the restaurant.

At the table, Ruby was sitting there with a contrite look on her face, but if she thought she was getting off that easy, she was mistaken. What the hell was she thinking, turning off my phone? This was what I got for breaking my own damn rule, I guess.

I snatched my phone off the table, and sure enough, the screen was black. I hit the button to power it back on.

"Orlando, I—"

I cut her off quick. "Look, it's too late to apologize. Something's come up, and if I had gotten the call when I was supposed to . . ."

"I'm really so—"

"Look, you don't get paid to touch my fuckin' phone, got that?" I snapped. She looked ready to cry. "I'll have Remy send a car to pick you up here." I threw some money down on the table to pay for dinner, then left without another word.

London

22

The water running down my body had turned icy cold, but I barely felt it as I leaned against the wall, still trembling from the powerful orgasm I'd just given myself. I'd been doing a lot of that lately, pleasuring myself like a horny teenager. Instead of fantasizing about my husband, though, I found myself thinking about Tony, the guy who saved me from that mugger outside the dry cleaners.

Maybe it was kind of cliché, you know, the damsel in distress falling for her knight in shining armor and all that; but once I got past the fact that he'd saved me from an attempted rape, it didn't take me long to notice that Tony was pretty damn hot. Coincidentally, his look reminded me a lot of my ex-boyfriend Jesse—the same guy I'd been fighting about with Harris. Maybe that was why I took Tony's number when he started flirting and offered it to me.

Speaking of Harris, he was still barely talking to me. Oh, he showed a fair amount of concern when I told him about the mugging, but that only garnered me sympathy but for so long. We made love that night, but he'd hardly looked in my direction since. I assumed he was still mad about the whole Jesse thing, but he wasn't the only man in the house who was out of his mind lately. My father and my brothers were all on edge too. I didn't know all the details, but I knew some serious shit had gone down, and it had every one of them stressed out. When I approached Harris one night and asked why he hadn't made love to me in a while, he actually told me he had too much on his mind to think about sex. He suggested I take care of myself, and so I'd done just that. I figured, hell, if Harris was too busy and stressed out, fantasies about Tony would do the trick just fine.

When the tremors between my legs subsided, I turned off the now frigid water and stepped out of the shower. I wrapped myself in a huge, fluffy Egyptian cotton towel and headed into the bedroom, where I thought I'd lie down and watch Regis and Kelly for a while. I was so glad my father had taken Mariah to preschool so I could have some time to myself.

The peaceful moment was soon interrupted, though, when I heard a ringing sound coming from my walk-in closet. At first I thought it was my phone, but as I got closer to the door, I heard Harris in there answering his phone.

"Hey, what's up?" he said warmly. He lowered his voice almost down to a whisper. I was sure he didn't realize I was on the other side of the door and could still hear everything he said. Whoever he was talking to sure had him upbeat and happy.

"Yeah, I miss you too, but things are a little hectic right now at the office. . . . I'll be free this evening. I'm not gonna have much time, so it will have to be quick. But I'll make it count. You got my word on that."

I'd heard enough. The least the messy bastard could have done was told the heifer he'd call her back when he left the house he and his wife shared. "Make what count? And who the hell is she that you miss her so much?" I blurted out as I pulled back the partially closed door and stepped into the closet with him.

"Damn it, London!" Harris snapped, like he was pissed that I was interrupting his call with his mistress. Like he was mad at me for talking so that she could hear me. He quickly hung up the phone, and when I went to reach for it, he pulled away.

"Give me the phone, Harris," I demanded. "Who is the bitch? Have some balls about your shit. Man up and let me have the fucking phone!"

He wasn't giving it up without a fight, that was for sure. I could feel my towel loosening as we tussled, but I didn't care. I was determined to find out who the hell was coming between me and my man.

"London, you're acting like a fool. Stop it!" Harris shouted, still holding the phone out of my reach.

I continued to press forward, trying to grab the phone out of his hand.

"Did you hear me? Stop it!" Harris followed up with a slap that I swear made me lose my hearing for a few seconds.

I stood there, still a little damp, with the towel now at my ankles. I was holding the side of my face and head where he had laid one on me. The pain was excruciating, enough to make me cry.

Harris had put his hands on me before, but this time there was so much rage behind it. So much power. Even he could tell he'd landed a mighty blow. It showed in the look of instant regret that shot across his face.

"London . . . oh my God. Baby, I'm sorry." He took a step toward me, but I jerked back.

"Don't. Don't touch me." I held the side of my face gingerly. "Harris, I swear, if you ever put your hands on me again, I'll kill you," I said in a low growl.

"What?" His regretful tone suddenly vanished. "Look, I said I was sorry, but don't make this worse by making idle threats. You ain't got the guts to kill me."

He was right. I didn't have the guts, but I knew who did. "Maybe, but let's see if I have the guts to tell my father you've been hitting me. I didn't have a problem telling Vegas that time, did I?"

The first time he'd ever hit me, I told my brother Vegas, and it wasn't pretty. I actually had to tell Vegas I was lying to stop him from killing Harris—and I made sure Harris understood that I'd saved his life. Now anytime things got too out of hand, all I had to do was threaten to tell my father or my brothers, and Harris would snap right back in place.

"You'd do that? You'd tell your father something like that and ruin our family?" Harris shot back. He was forever trying to play the family card. What he failed to understand was that husband or not, I was a Duncan long before I was a Grant, and I wouldn't hesitate to play my own family card if he ever got too heavy-handed with me.

"I will do whatever I have to do to stop you from hitting me," I threatened, although I had already decided that at least this time he was off the hook with the family. There was too much drama with the business right now for me to distract everyone with this bullshit. Besides, this whole fight had started because of a stupid phone call. Last thing I wanted to do was start some shit between my husband and the family.

Then my marriage would be over, and the home-wrecking bitch would have won.

"I am not your punching bag," I reminded him.

He sighed, taking a second to reflect. "Look, I know that. I'm sorry, but you just know how to push my buttons," he replied, walking over and gently touching my shoulders. "If you want, I'll go to counseling. I'll do whatever it takes, but I want you to keep this between us."

"I don't know who she is, Harris, but get rid of her before I get rid of you. That punch I just took woke up a lioness that's about ready to go on the prowl. You don't want to see that side of me."

"You wouldn't," he challenged.

I countered with, "Let that disrespectful bitch call you one more time and I guess we'll both find out, won't we?"

He stared at me for about three full seconds. He was breathing heavily and was clearly still agitated. For a second I thought he might wind up and smack me again, but then he turned and stormed out of the bedroom.

I walked over to the mirror and observed the area where he'd just hit me. It wasn't too bad considering how hard he'd hit me. Thank God my mother and father had both already left the house. Rio was the only one home, and he was asleep, no doubt.

What hurt almost as much as the slap was my bruised ego. I couldn't believe the disrespect Harris had just shown me by answering that call—and in our bedroom, no less! Well, I thought, let's see how he likes being disrespected.

I found my own cell phone on the dresser and picked it up to dial. After the first ring, Tony's voice penetrated my ear. It was like an instantaneous healing.

Paris

23

I checked my watch as I stepped onto the elevator at the LaGuardia Airport Marriott. It was a little after eight, so I had about one hour to accomplish what I'd set out to do. On the seventh floor, I stepped out and headed for room 726. I knocked, and when I saw the light disappear from the peephole, I knew he was on the other side of the door, looking out at me. I smiled seductively and held up two fingers.

"I come in peace," I said.

Miguel opened the door and stuck his head out, checking left and right down the hallway.

"I'm alone," I reassured him. I couldn't blame him for looking. My brothers and my father had a knack for scaring off men I was interested in.

"Señorita Paris, how did you find me?" He sounded a little nervous, but still sexy as hell with his accent. He had that Tony Montana–Scarface swagger, and it turned me on—hence, the reason for my visit.

"Shhh." I placed a finger over his lips and pressed my body against his. He took a step back, but I didn't mind, because it just gave me space to enter the suite. "We don't have time for twenty questions. Your flight leaves in two hours, so you'll be heading to the airport in an hour, right?"

"Sí." He nodded.

"Then you need to stop wasting time."

"I don't understand. Wasting time?"

I guess the language barrier was greater than I thought, because he really wasn't getting it. Oh well, time to be blunt about it. "You're standing here talking when we could be fucking."

I closed the distance between us. Every time I stepped closer, he moved back, until his legs were against the couch. All it took was one slight push against his chest and he was sitting down. I wasted no time, straddling his lap and wrapping my arms across his shoulders.

His mouth said, "Holy mother of God, your father's going to kill me," but the rise in his pants told me he liked the position we were in.

"Don't worry about my father. He's not going to kill you, because he's not going to find out about this. But what I'm about to put on you . . . yeah, it just might kill you." I pressed my body against his and started grinding. I wanted him to feel the warmth that was radiating between my thighs.

"No, señorita, please." He placed his hands on my hips to stop them from swaying. "That is what he told me. He said if I touch you, he will kill me."

Damn, damn, damn! My father must have really scared the crap out of him, because very few men could resist me once I gave them the green light. I was beginning to think I was wasting my time here. I climbed off his lap.

"So you want me to leave?" I looked down and saw that his dick definitely didn't want me to leave. His face, on the other hand, still wore a mask of concern. Fortunately, after a moment of hesitation, his dick won the battle. He reached out and pulled me back down onto his lap.

I leaned back a little so I could gain access to the bulge in his pants. I caressed the raised outline, tracing along its considerable length, until I came to his plump, swollen head. It jerked and throbbed noticeably to my touch, like a dog standing on its hind legs for attention.

I approve this massage, his dick said. I liked that.

A moan escaped from Miguel's mouth, and finally I could see the lines in his face relax. That was all the encouragement I needed as I went to work, grinding my pelvis against him again.

"You a bad girl, huh?" Miguel uttered, his smile indicating he'd completely forgotten about my father.

"Sí," I replied softly. "Wanna spank me with your stick?"

His hands were on my ass in no time. He pulled me in even closer and pressed his delicious hardness up against me. When he started whispering in my ear in Spanish, I thought I might come right then and there.

Miguel kissed me deeply, and I was brought back in time, to someone I met in boarding school in Europe. He was a Spaniard who maintained the school's security; much older than I was, but I learned a lot from him. He was dangerous, like this one, and perhaps where I first developed a taste for the thrill of danger.

I tugged on Miguel's shirt, pulling the black cotton tee over his head and exposing his smooth, sculpted chest and abs. I could tell he had a nice body under those suits he always wore to the office, but now that I was seeing him in the flesh, I realized my imagination hadn't done him justice. Papi's body was definitely a ten out of ten. He looked like he could be on an infomercial for one of those exercise programs, like P90X or something. I wondered if he spent hours in the gym, or if his lifestyle just made it a necessity to be that hard. Either way, he looked damn good.

Miguel yanked my blouse loose from my skirt, then began unfastening it, each button yielding with only the slightest effort. He bit at my neck, almost to the point of leaving a mark, as his hand grasped at my back, pulling me closer. As I ran my fingers through his hair, he went for my bra. The straps went slack and fell off my shoulders, and Miguel cupped my bare breasts, placing his warm, wet mouth on each. He teased and nipped at my sensitive nipples and sucked on them with a passion that made my juices start flowing.

"Let me see it," I gasped as I unbuckled his belt. He finished for me, unzipping his jeans and pulling them down, along with his boxers. His manhood jutted out at me in invitation, and I was glad to accept. I unzipped my skirt and discarded my last bits of clothing, except for my Louboutins. Placing my hands on Miguel to steady myself, I got down on my knees to serve him.

As I took him deep inside my mouth, he let out a loud, satisfied moan. Finally, he was relaxed, and I was determined to make sure his attention stayed focused on me, not on who my family was. I worked my lips, keeping a tight seal around his dick as I bobbed my head, making it nasty and wet for him. The more I gagged and slurped on the pole, the deeper he tried to go down my throat. He got so into it that he stood up from the couch and put his hands on the back of my head, thrusting against me. I sucked him long and hard, until I felt his body tightening. I looked up into his eyes, letting him know how much I was enjoying giving him pleasure and coaxing him to let it go like he wanted.

"Ay, caramba. Señorita, you are very good at this," he said, smiling wickedly as his eyes rolled back.

It didn't take long before his body began to shake. I sped up my motion, and Miguel released himself with sounds of passion that could probably be heard by half the hotel.

"Shit. Where you been all my life?" he gasped approvingly in heavily accented English. I rose to my feet, not surprised by his compliments. Not to brag or anything, but my blow jobs always made men lose their minds.

"Just waiting on you, Daddy," I replied, grasping his waning stiffness in my hand. Despite my mouth showing signs of my labor of lust, he kissed me with an abundance of passion. I liked that. It showed he appreciated me and what I had just done.

"Señorita, a man could fall in love with you very easily. The way you talk and act . . . You are a very dangerous woman."

"Much more dangerous than you can ever imagine. So don't use the L word with me. I have a tendency to take what men say to me to heart."

He looked right in my eyes and insisted, "I say what I mean and mean what I say."

Damn, he sure knew how to talk that romantic shit, didn't he?

"Now it is my turn to show you the stars and the moon." He lifted me up with ease and carried me into the bedroom, where he placed me on the bed. I opened my legs so that my shaved, plump pussy was on display and ready to be sampled. He dropped to his knees before me and nuzzled his face into my lips, where his nose and then his mouth sought out my clit. He licked and probed first with a firm tongue, then pushed deeper into me, making my clit throb and my pussy cream. I convulsed, popping my hips toward him with each uncontrolled eruption on his face.

My body had barely stopped trembling from the first orgasm when he dove in for another. "Don't stop till you get enough," I teased, grateful for this man's skills. I could fall in love with a man like this.

As he went to work with his tongue, I turned my head to the side and noticed a black handgun on the nightstand beside me. Miguel hadn't even bothered to try to hide it. It was so close, I could have reached out and touched it if I wanted—which I definitely didn't. Something similar had snuffed out Trevor's life. A solitary tear escaped down my cheek as I closed my eyes.

"What?" Miguel asked. "Am I doing something wrong?"

I opened my eyes, hating that he'd noticed my momentary emotional lapse. "No, you're perfect," I replied with a smile at the inquisitive face between my legs. I quickly wiped away the rogue tear. "Don't stop. Talking gets me in trouble."

I gently pushed his head back down, coaxing my pussy onto his face again. As he resumed a gentle tongue massage on my clit and slid two fingers inside, I closed my eyes and started grinding against his face.

Just as Miguel brought me to the edge of orgasm once again, we heard a crash coming from the living room. Miguel jumped up and went for his gun. He was no Trevor, that was for sure. Miguel was 100 percent man.

Before Miguel could even take the safety lock off his gun, though, three masked men burst into the bedroom. Shit, this was even worse than that night with Trevor. These dudes were huge, and they had shotguns pointed right at us. Miguel lowered his gun.

"Don't move, or we'll blow your fucking heads off," one of the masked men yelled.

"Oh shit," was all I could say when I recognized the voice.

One of them switched on the light.

"What the fuck? Paris, put some fucking clothes on!" Junior pulled off his mask. The look on his face scared the hell out of me, but of course, I wasn't going to let him know that.

I pulled the sheet up to cover my naked body. This was so fucking embarrassing. Not only had my brothers just seen me naked, but they'd probably heard me screaming in ecstasy right before they barged in. "What the hell is going on here? Is this some kind of joke?"

"Does it look like a joke?" Orlando spat angrily as he grabbed Miguel by the arm. "We're taking this motherfucker for a ride. Pop wants to see him—and I'm sure he's gonna wanna see you too. Get some damn clothes on."

All three of them pulled Miguel out of the room. Rio came back in a second later, but instead of coming to smooth things over with me, he just shook his head and then threw my clothes at me. I didn't know yet what was going on, but maybe Miguel was right, after all. My father was going to kill him.

LC

24

"What time is it, Harris?" I growled.

Harris glanced at his watch. The way he was frowning, I know he wanted to tell me, "About three minutes after the time I told you three minutes ago." But he wasn't stupid enough to say that shit to my face, especially considering the mood I was in, so he just said, "Ten forty-nine."

"I thought you said they were on their way. They should have been here by now."

"That's what Orlando told me, LC," he replied.

We were sitting in my SUV in a warehouse I owned in Long Island City, Queens, waiting for Orlando, Rio, and Junior to return with Miguel. This was part of the reason why Harris had an attitude. He didn't like the fact that I'd sent my sons to get Miguel in the first place. To be frank, he damn near pleaded with me not to, spewing legal jargon, but I didn't want to hear that mumbo-jumbo shit. That suave Latin punk Miguel had a hell of a lot of explaining to do. I mean, damn, it wasn't like I didn't warn him.

"LC, as your attorney, I must ask you to reconsider this. The boys may have already crossed the line, but there is no reason you should be involved. There is such a thing as plausible deniability. And if we—ah, I mean you—are here when they arrive, we may all be implicated in a crime."

"Harris, do me a favor. For the next hour or so, can you be my son-in-law and not my goddamn lawyer? If you don't have the balls for this, you can take your ass home, because you sound like a little punk. You're either part of this family or you're not. Which one is it?"

Harris sat back in his seat, a little thrown off by my question. He might have been formulating some lawyer-bullshit response, but before he could speak, one of my men covering the door yelled, "They're here."

I heard the sound of a car door being slammed, and then the side door of the warehouse opened. Orlando stormed in, with Rio on his heels.

"Yo, Uncle Lou. Open the garage doors," Orlando barked.

Lou, my brother, did what he was told, and then a white cargo van entered the warehouse and parked beside my SUV. I rolled down my window so I could watch everything. Junior jumped out of the van, walked to the side, and opened the sliding door.

"Jesus Christ, LC! This is even worse than I thought. This is kidnapping, straight up," Harris shouted when he saw Miguel lying on the floor of the van, bound, blindfolded, and gagged.

Without even looking in his direction, I raised a hand to get him to shut the hell up. I loved Harris's legal mind, but sometimes that law rhetoric he spouted just got on my damn nerves. This was one of those times.

Junior and Lou removed Miguel from the van and dragged him to a chair at the center of the warehouse. Miguel kind of slumped over in the chair, and Junior used that as an excuse to strike him in the side of the head with his gun. "Sit the fuck up!" he shouted.

Blood trickled down the side of Miguel's face as he did what he was told. I didn't even have to look in Harris's direction to know that he was ready to lose it. I told him, "Don't say a damn word, Harris. If you can't handle this, you know where the door is."

"You move, I do it again! Comprende?" Junior yelled as he yanked the blindfold off Miguel's face.

"Fuck you," Miguel spat, looking directly at me as I sat in the SUV. This motherfucker had some balls; I'd give him that. His eyes almost looked like he was challenging me. "Wait until Alejandro finds out about this. He will kill you all for your insolence."

Junior raised up to strike him again, but I shouted, "Hold on, Junior." I got out of the SUV. What Miguel had just said didn't sit right with me.

I walked close to the chair and stood over him. "Alejandro will kill us for our insolence? Do you even know why you're here?"

He nodded. That son of a bitch had the nerve to hold his head up like he was proud of what he'd done. I had to admire him in some ways, though, because even in the predicament he found himself, he still tried to maintain his dignity. You don't find many men who can do that. Most men would have been begging for their lives as they were dragged from the van.

"Tell me, Miguel. Why are you here?" I asked.

"Because I fucked your daughter."

I felt his words like a punch in the gut, and I did the only thing a father could do upon hearing those words: I hauled off and swung as hard as I could, hitting him square in the jaw. His head snapped back, and as he righted himself, blood began pouring from his nose.

I pulled a handkerchief from my pocket and wiped the blood from my hand as I turned to Orlando. "What the hell did he just say to me?" I asked.

"We caught them right in the act, Pop."

"Son of a bitch. Where is she?" I looked back at Miguel. His bloody face and swollen lip had gotten rid of any bravado he might have had left. I had a momentary urge to wrap my hands around his fucking neck and choke the life out of him, but I could already hear the lecture I would get from Harris, so I restrained myself.

"I sent her to the office," Orlando told me. "Figured you'd want to speak to her away from this situation."

"Damn right I wanna talk to her. Rio, call Paris and tell her I said to keep her ass at the office until I get there!" I turned my attention back to Miguel. "What did I tell you I would do if you touched my daughter?"

He wobbled in the chair but remained silent, until Lou popped him in the head with his open hand. "Answer the man."

"You said you would kill me," he slurred.

"But you did it anyway . . . because you don't fear me, do you? You think Alejandro will save your ass from my wrath. Maybe make you marry her or something like that?"

"Señor, I swear, she came to me. I did not mean for this to happen," he pleaded. "But if you want me to marry her . . . she is a very beautiful woman and would make a good wife."

"You arrogant little bastard!" I landed another punch, which started a fresh wave of blood streaming down his face. I was ready to keep swinging until this son of a bitch was nothing but a bloody pulp, but Harris knew me well enough to step in before my temper reached the point of no return.

"LC!" he yelled to get my attention. "Remember the reason we're here. Deal with Paris later."

I turned to Harris and took a few deep breaths to bring my blood back down from the boiling point. "You're right."

"You are one lucky man," Lou said to Miguel, who just nodded.

"You know, Miguel," I said, "I'm not quite sure you understand how serious this situation is. Maybe you're even more stupid than I thought. Now, why don't we talk about the real reason you're here."

"I don't know, señor." His voice cracked, and even covered in blood, his face clearly reflected the fear he was feeling.

"Oh, you don't know, huh? Well, let me explain it to you." I started circling around the chair as I spoke. "Right after your people handed over the truck carrying the Roadster, someone hijacked my people, and now my Roadster is gone. Funny thing is, you were the only one other than my people to know the route."

His eyes got huge. He actually looked like he might shit on himself.

"You know anything about this, Miguel?"

"Sir . . . Señor Duncan," Miguel started breathlessly. "I know you're upset about your car. I know how much it means to you. I just want you to know—"

"I don't give a fuck about that Corvette!" I tipped over the chair, and Miguel fell to the ground. "I want what was in it! Fuck the damn Corvette!"

With both hands around his throat, I lifted Miguel to a sitting position on the ground.

"Where . . . is . . . my . . . shit?" With each word I squeezed his neck a little tighter. "Where the fuck is my heroin?"

Even if he wanted to answer me, Miguel could not talk with the way I was cutting off his air. His face was starting to turn blue at this point.

"Pop! Pop! He's no good to us dead." I could feel Orlando trying to pry my fingers from around Miguel's neck as he pleaded with me. I released Miguel, and he fell to the ground in a fetal position.

"There was supposed to be a shipment of two hundred ki's of Alejandro's best product stowed in that car. Ki's that are bought and paid for and belong to me. I want my shit, Miguel." I kicked him hard in the gut, and when he tried to crawl away from me, I kicked him again.

"Señor Duncan, I swear, I had nothing to do with this. Por favor," Miguel pleaded. At this point, I didn't give a shit what he had to say. I just needed a place to take out my aggression, so I kept kicking him repeatedly until I was too tired to kick him anymore.

I grabbed him by the hair and, with Lou's help, lifted him back into the chair. I patted Miguel on his shoulder as a father would his son. "You say you have nothing to do with it? Well, I guess we'll see about that, won't we? And God help you if you did, 'cause I still haven't forgotten that you slept with my daughter."

Harris

25

I will never forget the day that I learned the truth about my wife's family business. When I first met her, I saw the Duncans just like the rest of the gullible, admiring public did—as legitimate businessmen who'd made it big by selling cars. Their wealth was something to be admired among black families in Queens—but that was only because they did an exceptional job of hiding their dirty little secret.

Their family business was based on a union of three things: cars, drugs, and violence. LC had taken a legitimate car dealership and a lucrative exotic auto transportation business and turned them into a front to supply New York City and most of the Northeast with all the illicit drugs they could handle. The operation was backed up and enforced by a criminal enterprise of loyal men and women willing to do whatever it took to make the almighty dollar. There are still times when I look in the mirror and wonder how I let myself get so deeply involved in all of it.

It was a week before my wedding, and LC had asked London to have me stop by his office for a little chat. I didn't think much of it, assuming he wanted to have one of those father-of-the-bride conversations. You know, "Take good care of my little girl" and all of that. I was a little nervous to meet with LC, because I hadn't spent much time with him up to that point. Except for a couple of family gatherings during the holidays, London never seemed to want to bring me around her family. At the time I just figured they were a little more dysfunctional than she wanted me to know about, but I would soon find out the truth. She didn't want me to know she was the offspring of one the biggest drug dealers on the East Coast. That kind of thing might have put a slight damper on our marriage plans, you know?

When I arrived at LC's office, he asked me to take a ride with him to South Jamaica. During the drive, just as I expected, he went into this speech about how much family meant to him and his wife, then went on and on about how much he loved his daughter.

"You know, Harris, I like you, and I'm really happy London found you. You seem like a nice kid with a good head on your shoulders," he said as we parked in front of a Crown Fried Chicken.

"Thank you, sir." I worked to rid my voice of any evidence of nervousness. I wanted to make sure I spoke clearly and articulately. After all, I was speaking to the head of my fiancée's family—not just any old family, but one of the most prominent and wealthy black families in the city. LC Duncan and Duncan Motors stood for strength, power, and respect. They were so well known that my boss at the law firm was begging me to set up a meeting. He wanted Duncan Motors as a client. So, I had multiple reasons to want to impress LC, although I had a sense already that he was not an easy man to impress. If I was ever going to fit in—to be like one of the family—I knew I'd have to work overtime in order to do it. Now was the time to start proving that no matter what my last name was, I could be a Duncan.

"But when you get to be my age, you understand that women are funny about certain things—especially money. My daughter is no exception to this rule, probably because I spoil her and give her anything she wants. So, I have to ask you." He took his hands off the steering wheel and turned to me. "Harris, are you going to be able to keep my child in the lifestyle she's accustomed to?"

Now, I hadn't been expecting the conversation to go in this direction, but I'd done enough job interviews in my life to know how to give an answer on the fly. "Well, sir, as you know, I'm an associate at Brask and Williams. The managing partner says I'm on track to be a partner one day, but to be honest, that's some years down the road. With that being said, I still make a nice salary for my age, and, well, London seems to be okay with that." I thought my answer was fine, one that would satisfy any future father-in-law, but like I said, LC Duncan wasn't easy to impress.

He laughed as he reached for his car door and opened it. "So, as her husband, you're not going to mind if she comes to me for money?"

I got out, and we stared at each other across the roof of the car. "Sir, with all due respect, that's not going to happen. London and I—"

He cut me off. "Harris, how much do you make over at Brask and Williams? Sixty, maybe seventy grand?"

I nodded. "Something in that neighborhood."

"You're right. That's not bad for a man your age. But did you know that Mercedes coupe London drives cost almost double what you make in a year?"

LC Duncan was no joke. I could feel my ego shrinking by the moment, and he managed to do it all with a smile on his face. "No, sir, I didn't know the price of her car."

"Did you know that London's credit card bill was a little over five grand last month?"

All I could do was shake my head.

"I didn't think so." Apparently tired of humiliating me, he turned his attention to the Crown Fried Chicken in front of us.

I wasn't done with the conversation, though. Whatever kind of a test this was, I couldn't let him insult me like that without defending myself. Shit, I was pretty damn successful for a guy my age. Any father should be glad to have me marry his daughter. LC needed to understand that while he might have spoiled London, he had to accept the fact that I was going to be the man in her life soon.

"Mr. Duncan, you don't have to worry. We'll make do. London may have to cut back on some things, but we're happy, and that's all that matters for us. We're gonna make it."

"I see. Well, I guess you've got everything all figured out, don't you?"

"Yeah, we're happy, we're in love, and we're going to have everything our hearts desire in just a few years, when I make partner." I was trying to stand my ground, but I was starting to realize how hollow my words must have sounded to this powerful man. I was losing all self-esteem, and LC's continued smirk told me he thought the whole thing was pretty funny.

"You hungry?" he asked, still staring at the chicken joint. "You look hungry."

"I guess I am a little hungry." I shrugged, feeling defeated.

He leaned in and said seriously, "Be a lot hungry, and stay hungry. That's the only way you're going to be able to provide for my daughter. That's how you're going to be able to get the house, the cars, the clothes, and all the things that are going to keep her happy. Being happy right now doesn't mean shit. It's staying happy that's a muthafuck." On that note, he started walking toward the chicken spot. He shouted over his shoulder at me, "Let's go."

What the fuck was that? was all I could ask myself as I headed toward the entrance.

"No, this way," LC ordered, opening the door next to the one I was standing at.

I stepped back, a little puzzled, but followed my future father-in-law's orders. He led me up a flight of steps, stopping in front of one of several apartments above the restaurant. He knocked on the door, then turned to me.

"You're gonna need more money than you make to support my daughter. And I need a good lawyer, someone who's smart, hungry, and most of all, loyal. So, Harris, my man, I'm offering you a job. Do you want to be my exclusive lawyer?"

Even if I had known what to think or what to say, he didn't give me time. He pounded on the door again, until it finally opened a crack. I saw half a man's face eyeballing us. Before I knew it, LC raised his foot and kicked open the door, busting the man upside the head.

"LC, please, man, I just need a little more time!" The man held out his hand as if it might keep LC at bay. With his other hand, he covered the side of his face, now bloody from the door strike.

I hadn't a clue what the hell was going on. It was all going down so fast.

I heard three loud pops. One, two, and then a third hole appeared in the man's chest and stomach. As blood began to seep out of the wounds, I looked over at LC, who was tucking a silenced pistol into his coat pocket.

"He wasn't hungry like you, Harris. He was a slacker—didn't take care of his business—and he talked too much. Namely, about me and my business. But you . . ."

I felt LC's hand on my shoulder, only I couldn't tear my eyes away from the man who was taking his last breath on the floor.

"You are still hungry, aren't you? And as my lawyer, you're honor bound to keep your mouth shut, right, Harris?"

I nodded, feeling numb.

"Good. Then here's the first order of business, counselor." LC reached into his jacket, and my heart started pounding. Was he reaching for that gun again? I had no idea if I would be joining the man down on the floor. "Here, take this."

I looked down to see LC handing me a piece of paper. Once it was in my shaking hand, I realized it was a check. I read the figure, and my knees were so weak, I almost fell to the floor next to the dead man. "This is a check for a million dollars."

"That's your retainer. You're now my lawyer, and you work exclusively for me and Duncan Motors. I want you to give Brask and Williams your walking papers in the morning. . . . Unless you have a problem working for me?"

"Mr. Duncan . . . I . . . I can't—"

"Sure you can," he stated without a hint of doubt. "Let me help you out here, son." He put his arm around my shoulder and led me away from the pool of blood that was forming near our feet. "You have three choices. You can work for me, you can pretend this never happened and go about your business, or you can go to the cops and talk to them. Your first choice is going to make you rich beyond your wildest dreams. The second choice will probably mean you'll be alive, but would also make you an accessory to murder—something to think about just in case you ever consider changing your mind. And the third, well, if you decide to go to the cops, you might as well lie down with the guy down there, because you're as dead as he is. If I don't kill you, then I promise you that my sons will."

I stood there silently, taking in LC's words and trying to breathe. A sudden wave of nausea hit me, and I didn't know if I was going to throw up or pass out. One thing I did know was that of the three choices LC had given me, only one guaranteed that I would live.

"So, Harris, future son-in-law, are you my lawyer or not?"

I couldn't speak. My words were somewhere frozen between my throat and the tip of my tongue, so I relayed my answer the best way I could. I folded the check and tucked it into my pocket.

LC patted me on the back. "Welcome to the family. Now, let's go get something to eat, because I'm famished. Killing a man really helps you build up an appetite, you know?"

So, for the past ten years, I'd been learning and mastering both the public and private side of the family business. Unlike him or his children, though, I was not willing to get my hands dirty, especially when it came to the violent side of the business. Don't get me wrong. I was far from innocent, and I understood the need for the heavy-handed approach, but I preferred to stay in the shadows, walking that thin line between attorney and crook.

Still, what I'd just witnessed LC doing to Miguel was just plain stupid and a little scary.

Aside from that first murder I saw him commit, LC usually had other people handle that type of thing. He claimed to be proud that he stayed above the fray, but as we drove back to the dealership and I looked in his face, I was starting to think that he enjoyed it—which was probably why I was scared to death by my wife's threat to tell him about our physical confrontation that morning.

"Orlando, I wanna know who's got that damn truck and my dope, and I wanna know now. We don't have much time before Alejandro realizes that Miguel wasn't on his plane and starts asking questions about him," LC barked at his son, who was sitting in the front passenger seat while Lou drove. "I want you to put it out on the street that I got a hundred grand cash to anyone who tells me where to find that truck. No questions asked. We only have a short window before that shit hits the streets—if it was even in the car."

"Already on it, Pop," Orlando replied, pulling the phone from his ear. "With that kinda money, we should have every crackhead in the five boroughs turning over every rock to find it."

"What about Alejandro? When he finds out we have Miguel, he's gonna go through the roof. You want me to—"

LC cut me off. "Don't worry about Alejandro. I'll take care of him when the time comes. What

I want you to do is call our friend at One Police Plaza and see if he can offer any assistance. Have him check the stoplight cameras and all the toll cameras. If that truck left the five boroughs, I wanna know it."

I reached for my phone to make the call, but my finger froze over the send button when Orlando turned around and said, "Pop, Pablo's dead."

"What did you say?" LC asked, even though he sat only a foot or two away.

Pablo was one of LC's best friends and a trusted lieutenant. He ran most of the drug trade in Spanish Harlem and the Bronx. By taking him out, someone was sending us a message. From the expression on LC's face, it was a message delivered loud and clear.

Orlando elaborated. "His brother Carlos said some people busted into his brownstone and shot him in the head in front of his wife and kids."

"Shit! Does Carlos know who they were? Did anyone recognize them?" LC asked, surprisingly calm in the face of this gruesome news about his friend.

"No, but he said they spoke Spanish fluently."

"Some of his Bronx beef coming back to bite him. I told him to let the Puerto Ricans have that block," Lou complained. "He was just too stubborn."

"No, Uncle Lou, I don't think so. Carlos said they weren't Puerto Rican or Dominican," Orlando retorted. "Pablo's wife thought they sounded Mexican from their dialect."

Everybody quieted, probably thinking the same thing as me: Alejandro. This wasn't common knowledge, but Alejandro was the middleman for most of the Mexican drug cartels.

"Son of a bitch!" LC shouted out, breaking our silence.

"You want me to turn the car around so we can go back and talk to that motherfucker Miguel again?" Lou asked, looking at LC in the rearview mirror.

"No. Let him sit on ice while we figure this all out. I don't know what it is, but I think we're missing something."

"Well, I hope you figure it out fast, or we're going to be in the biggest damn fight of our lives," I warned.

London

26

I took a deep, nervous breath before I stepped out of the cab when it finally pulled up in front of the Long Island Marriott. I'd had the cabdriver circle the block five times before I built up the courage to ask him to stop. I still couldn't believe I was sneaking around behind Harris's back to have drinks with Tony. Less than a month ago, you couldn't have paid me to talk to another man, let alone meet him for a drink, but Harris and his bitch had really pushed my buttons this morning. Granted, I had no intentions of doing anything other than having a drink. I mean, yes, I was meeting him at hotel, but the hotel was nothing more than a convenient meeting place, because it wasn't likely I'd run into anybody I knew on this side of town at a hotel. After all, who would be hanging out at a bar at the Marriott in the middle of the week other than someone from out of town . . . or someone having an affair? We weren't having an affair, but if I was being honest with myself, it sure as hell would look like it, wouldn't it?

What the hell am I doing? I asked myself as I paid the driver and headed toward the lobby. I wanted to believe I was only getting a little payback for the smack I got this morning. So why the hell was I feeling so guilty? I didn't know which emotion was more overwhelming at the moment as I made my way through the hotel entrance: guilt or fear. I was feeling guilty about sharing my time with another man, but also fearful about what could happen if someone saw me.

"Can you point me to the bar, please?" I asked the bellman, wondering if I looked like someone who might be getting ready to cheat.

"Right that way, ma'am." He pointed over his shoulder, barely even acknowledging my presence.

It's just a drink. It's just a drink, I kept telling myself as I headed toward the bar. There was nothing to feel guilty about. The man saved me and my daughter, for Christ's sake. Couldn't this friendly little meeting be considered just a form of thanks? That was all it was—a drink and conversation. Lord knows I could use a little adult conversation these days. Harris always acted like he was too damn busy to give me the time of day, so I was left to converse with no one but my four-year-old daughter. Hell, if no one else could be bothered with me, I was going to talk to Tony.

It sure wasn't hard to spot Tony in the small bar. All I had to do was follow the stares of the women in the bar, every one of whom seemed to be ogling him. Maybe it was the light in the bar, or maybe it was just all the attention he was getting, but I suddenly realized just how attractive he was.

"And the lady has arrived," Tony stated, looking down at his watch and then back at me.

"Fashionably late." I slid into the seat next to him.

"No worries. I was expecting as much," he replied with a wink.

"And just what is that supposed to mean?"

"Well, if you're like most women, you're always running late. That way, when you make your grand entrance, all eyes are on you."

"Humph!" I grunted, not sure if I should be offended. After all, there was some truth to what he was saying. "Anyway, I'd say all eyes in this place are on someone else tonight, wouldn't you?" I teased, looking around the bar at the women who were still staring in our direction.

He ignored my comment and also ignored all those other women as he looked me up and down. "Well, Ms. London," he said as he raised his glass in a toast, "I must say, you were definitely worth the wait."

As much as I didn't want to be, I was flattered by his obvious flirting. He stared at me with those golden brown eyes, which I hadn't really noticed the first time we met. Here in this bar, surrounded by other women who wished they were sitting in my place, I was starting to think they were the most beautiful shade of brown I'd ever seen. The uneasiness I'd felt evaporated from my body. He was making me feel very at ease, maybe even too much at ease. As a matter of fact, every emotion I might have been feeling before walking into that bar was no more. Now the only thing I felt was—and I'm ashamed to say this—wet.

He gestured to the empty space in front of me on the bar. "So, what can I get you?"

"How about an apple martini?" I'd never had one of those in my life, but I'd just seen a rerun of Sex and the City on cable and one of the ladies had ordered one. What woman didn't live vicariously through Carrie, Miranda, Charlotte, and Samantha?

Tony ordered my drink, and while we waited, I started in on the small talk. "What about you? What are you drinking?"

He picked up his glass and took a sip. "Hennessy." Another sip. "But I usually drink rum." He shrugged, looked at the drink in his hand, and then looked at me. "For some reason I felt like trying something different today." He swal-lowed the last of his Hennessy.

"So, how was it?" I wasn't intentionally trying to flirt with him, but I think it came across that way. I'd have to work on that. Be more careful. I didn't want to give him the wrong idea. I was just here to talk; that was it. And to get back at Har-ris for the smack and that bitch he was seeing behind my back.

"It was good, but then I expected it to be. Dark liquor never lets me down. It's the only thing I drink. I have this thing for dark . . . stuff." While I was worrying about sending the wrong mes-sage, Tony was sending his message loud and clear. And it scared the hell out of me that I was becoming aroused by it.

The bartender set my drink in front of me and took away Tony's empty glass to get him another. I picked up the martini and took a sip, then another, and then a gulp.

"Thirsty?" Tony asked with a chuckle.

I looked down at my glass. On Sex and the City, the woman had sipped it, not drunk it down like Gatorade after a soccer game. "Oh, uh, yeah, I guess I really needed that drink."

"Nervous?" Tony inquired.

"A little. But more stressed than anything," I replied, taking another gulp.

"Listen, I don't mean to be stressing you out."

"It's not you. I wouldn't be here if it was you," I assured him. "It's my life that's stressing me out."

"Maybe we need to change that?"

"Maybe you could start with my husband. . . ." I allowed my words to trail off. Did I really just almost make the mistake of telling another man about my issues with my husband? I wasn't a cheat, never had been, but even I knew that the rules of Adultery 101 included not feeding the other person information about your spouse.

"You're married. I figured as much," Tony said as the bartender placed another Hennessy in front of him. "I mean, you have a daughter. I can't imagine her father ever letting someone like you get away. He'd be a fool." He picked up his drink. "Besides, that rock is a dead give-away." He winked and took a sip.

"So, it doesn't bother you to have a drink in a hotel bar with a married woman?"

"Should it bother me? I mean, you did call me. If it doesn't bother you, why should it bother me? We're just two adults sitting at a bar, having a drink, talking." He shrugged, then pierced me with those beautiful eyes. "Why? Does it bother you, London?"

He said my name like he knew me, like he knew things about me I'd yet to tell him. "Yes . . .

no . . . Hell, who am I fooling? Sure it bothers me. I'm a married woman. Tony, I love my husband, and we have a good marriage. It's just that every once in a while I need someone to talk to and he isn't there."

"I believe you, London, and I understand. Everyone should have someone to talk to. So, I guess the only real question is, why me?"

All I could do on that one was call out to the bartender for another drink, because I didn't have a clue how to answer him. In one of those saved-by-the-bell moments, my cell phone rang, only this was a call I didn't want to have to take. Adultery 101 again: put that shit on vibrate. I contemplated letting it go to voice mail, but why? I was there only to have a drink and talk. Ignoring my husband's call would make it look like I was doing something wrong. I hit the talk button.

Harris's voice shot through the phone. "Where are you?"

"I'm out having a drink with a friend. Why?" Unlike his angry tone, I kept mine calm and even.

"Get home right now, London!"

I felt my stomach tighten up with fear. My heart was pounding as I searched the bar area for a familiar face. Was someone reporting back to him?

"Did you hear me? Get your ass home now."

I flashed back to that morning, when he dared to raise his hand to me, and I felt some fire return to my attitude. He was not going to bully me, dammit. Besides, I didn't see anyone in the bar that I recognized, so there was still a possibility he didn't know anything. Maybe I wasn't busted; maybe he was just in one of his macho moods, the ones that seemed to be becoming more frequent the deeper he got into the family business.

Well, I could give as good as I got. I answered him with, "You're not my daddy. I'll come home when I damn well please."

"I don't have time to argue with you. Now, get home right now."

If he knew I was in a bar with another man, he would have said so by now. It was safe to say that this particular ego trip was for some other reason. Just Harris trying to force me to do what he wanted. Except this time, I decided, I was done playing by his rules.

"I'm not going anywhere until I finish my drink. Not after the way you put your hands on me this morning. If my father—" I was about to scare him with another threat to tell my father but realized it was best not to get into all of that with Tony next to me, listening to every word. "You know what? Never mind. Just go to hell,

Harris. I'm not coming home until I damn well please!" I hung up the phone, pissed that he had fucked up my buzz.

"Wow, sounds like trouble in paradise," Tony said.

"Who said anything about my marriage being paradise?" Shit! I did it again. I gave him information about the home front.

The bartender had brought me another drink during my phone call. I finished it off quickly and ordered another. "Look, let's talk about something else. Something nice," I said to Tony and then proceeded to sit there and say nothing. I was too busy fuming about Harris's macho ass.

Tony reached out and put a hand on my shoulder. "Hey, it's fine. We don't have to talk at all if you need a minute."

I gave him a nod to let him know that was exactly what I needed. From guilty and nervous to turned on and then angry, my emotions had been all over the place in the last hour or so, and I needed a moment to sort myself out.

Tony picked up his drink with his free hand, but the other one stayed on my shoulder, patting it gently. Then, ever so subtly, it traveled up from my shoulder to my neck. I felt myself relaxing as he massaged my neck and the base of my head. Before I knew it, his fingers were all up in my hair, and he was stroking it. It felt so good that for a second I thought I moaned with pleasure—until I realized it was Tony who was moaning.

"Uh . . . hello?" I said, pulling my head out of his reach and breaking the moment.

"Oh, I'm sorry," he apologized and dropped his hand into his lap. "It's just that your hair is so beautiful."

"Thank you." Okay, so the hair-stroking moment was a little weird for a public place, but what woman doesn't like to hear compliments about her hair? And then Tony ruined it by opening his mouth and saying the stupidest possible thing.

"Is it real?"

I snapped my neck around and glared at him, all attitude now. "Excuse me?"

"Is it real?" His tone was innocent, but I didn't care. First, the comment about me being late, and now this. Until now, Tony's whiteness hadn't really been an issue for me, but hair is a sensitive subject for a black woman, and if he didn't know that, then maybe there was such a thing as being "too white."

"I heard you the first time," I said, my voice laced with contempt. "I just can't believe you asked me that. I mean, why wouldn't it be real?"

"I don't know," he answered. "But I do know that sometimes women get weaves, extensions, or whatever."

"Women, or black women?" I was feeling defensive, but incredibly, he still looked bewildered, like he truly didn't understand how his question had offended me.

"All women," he answered. "It seems like half the women in Hollywood are doing it now, aren't they? I mean, how else did Britney Spears get her hair back so fast after she shaved her head? But to answer your question, it is popular among black women, isn't it?"

"Humph!" was all I said.

He was right, of course, but he still needed to know that just like you don't ask a woman how old she is, you don't ask if her hair is real. But since the question was already out there, now I had to defend myself.

"As a matter of fact, it is real," I finally added. "I don't do weaves, wigs, or chemicals. My family comes from good stock." I took his hand and placed it on my head. "You can pull it if you like."

"No, I believe you." His smile traveled all the way up to his beautiful eyes and made me forget that a moment before I'd been offended. I considered the thought that maybe I was just on edge and being too sensitive. It was possible, after all, that he was making innocent conversation that had nothing to do with race. I just needed to chill and let the buzz from my drink kick back in.

"So, Tony, now that you know that I'm married and that my hair is not fake, tell me a little bit about yourself. What type of business are you in?"

"Garbage," was his one-word answer. I sensed he was being a little evasive.

"Garbage? What is that? Code for the Mafia?" I was joking, but as soon as the words came out, I realized how offensive they were.

"When an Italian guy says he's in the garbage business, why does everyone assume it's the Mafia or something?" It was his turn to sound defensive, and I couldn't blame him one bit.

"I know, I know, and I'm sorry. I shouldn't have said that. That's just as bad as when a black man says he's a deliveryman, and people automatically think that's code for drug dealing."

"Exactly. Now, how would you have felt if I automatically assumed you were somehow involved in the drug business just because you're black—correction, African American?"

Oh, if you only knew . . .

"Point taken," I replied. We both retreated into our drinks for a minute to avoid any more uncomfortable conversation.

After a while, Tony looked at me with a mischievous smirk on his face.

"What's so funny?" I reached for a napkin, thinking maybe I had something on my face.

"No, no, I'm sorry. I just had a thought . . . ," he said, still with that smirk on his face.

"A thought about what?"

He shook his head. "Nothing. It's totally inappropriate." Of course, this just made me even more curious.

"You can't just look at me like that and then not tell me what's going on," I protested.

"London, it's inappropriate," he said, looking at me again with this half-lidded seductive gaze. I swear to God I thought he was going to lick his lips like LL Cool J or something. If it had been some other random dude in a bar, I might have found that look corny, but I was actually kind of turned on.

"Why don't you let me decide if it's inappropriate? I'm an adult."

He hesitated, but only for a few seconds. "You have to promise me you won't get offended if I say something fresh."

"I promise, I promise. Now, tell me."

"Okay. I was just thinking that you look like you're the kind of woman who loves oral sex. Receiving, not giving."

He said it so nonchalantly that it took a moment for it to register in my brain. When it did, I lowered my head, because I was sure all the blood in my body had rushed to my blushing face.

"See, I told you it was inappropriate. Look, I'm sorry—"

I squeezed his wrist to stop him. "It's true."

"Excuse me?" he said, suddenly sounding a little breathless.

"Yes, it was inappropriate, but it's also true. I do love to receive oral sex. I don't mind giving it, either." For the record, I was now even wetter than before. "I just don't get it like I used to. You know, husband's too busy and all. . . ."

"My God, what is wrong with him?"

"I wish I knew," I said, not wanting to get into the fact that I believed he was too busy giving it to someone else these days.

"London, what would . . . Never mind."

"No, go ahead and say it." I was starting to find this conversation very intriguing.

He sighed. "Ah, what the hell. You only live once." He turned his whole body to face me. "London, what would you say if I told you I wanted to perform oral sex on you? No strings, no reciprocating, just me doing you until you come."

Okay, at first I was wet, but now I was fucking soaked. Just the thought of this dreamy olive-colored man wanting to kiss me between my legs had me ready to go home and make love to my shower massager. I didn't need the real thing; just the imagery was enough for me. After all, I was a married woman.

I opened my mouth to respond, but the phone rang again. I snatched it up furiously. "Harris, didn't I tell you I wasn't coming home?" I yelled.

"This isn't Harris." The baritone male voice was like a bucket of cold water over my head, extinguishing any flame that Tony might have ignited. It was my father. "But you stand corrected," he said. "You are coming home. So whatever you're doing, drop it and get home now." And that was that. He ended the call.

Grown woman or not, Daddy was Daddy, and if he said I needed to come home, then something was going on. I picked up my purse. "I'm sorry, Tony, but I have to go."

"Oh, the hubby not taking no for an answer?" he joked.

"No, that was my father. I have to go." I stood up to leave, but Tony grabbed my hand.

"Before you go, I just need to know one thing."

"No," I answered before he could even ask the question. "No, even if the phone hadn't rung, I would not have let you go down on me. Does that answer your question?"

He let go of my hand and turned back toward his drink.

I leaned in close to his ear and whispered, "But I do appreciate the offer. If I wasn't married . . ."

I'd like to think it was the alcohol that made me do it, but I can't say I was all that drunk.

No, I was fully aware of my actions as I grabbed Tony by the back of the head and pressed my lips against his. I got a taste of Hennessy from his tongue as he explored my mouth. God, if he was half as good at oral sex as he was at kissing, he'd have me wide open. It was a good thing I was going home.

"Thank you," I said to him, staring into his soulful eyes. "You don't know how bad I needed someone to talk to."

LC

27

"Alejandro, we have a problem," I said plainly, though it took all of my resolve not to fly off the handle. The morning had come without sleep and without news of the Roadster or the truck it was being hauled in. It would be an understatement to say that I was unhappy, but I would keep my rage in check for the time being. At least for now, we would pretend to be gentlemen.

There was a slight hesitation on the line before he said, "What kind of problem?"

"Right after your men made delivery, the truck was hijacked with the car inside it. As you can imagine, I'm not a very happy camper."

"I am sorry to hear this. Perhaps your misfortune has something to do with my dilemma. I was just going to call you myself," Alejandro explained. "You see, I haven't heard from Miguel or my drivers who delivered you the fine automobile last night. Do you know anything of their whereabouts?"

"Your drivers, I have no idea where they are. But I'm sure you can understand that we've been a little preoccupied. Especially since I paid for the delivery in full in advance . . . as a sign of good faith. Now I find that faith in question, and I have nothing to show for it."

"And you suspect me or my people of hijacking the truck?"

"As you know, I am not a trusting man, Alejandro. I suspect everyone, and your man Miguel was the only one other than my people to know the route we planned on taking."

Again he hesitated. I was sure that like me, he was weighing his words carefully for two good reasons. One, we were feeling each other out, getting a sense of the situation before making rash moves. And two, in this post-9/11 world, a man can never be sure whether his lines are being tapped. "I see. Well, have you heard from my man Miguel?"

"As a matter of fact, we have. He's talking to my son right now."

"And?"

"We're still listening to him," I answered, letting him know Miguel was alive—for now. "We'd like to listen to you, too, if you have something to say."

"I'm in the dark about this as much as you, Lavernius. But with the loss occurring on your turf, after you took possession, you're probably best equipped to find the answers you seek."

"We're looking into it—and also into the murder of one of my employees last night. A man who worked in my Harlem operation. We called him Pablo. He was killed in front of his family. It's a very troubling time."

"My condolences on the loss of your worker, and his family's loss as well. Speaking of that, has Miguel mentioned mine? The ones that accompanied him? Should I be contacting their families as well?"

"Can't say, Alejandro. Your guess is as good as mine. Also, can't say what happened to my cherished Corvette . . . yet. Just an unfortunate set of circumstances all around. How about you replace what I lost, or at least refund my money?"

"Ahhh, I cannot do that, my friend. You know how it is. Caveat emptor. Let the buyer beware. That money has already been spent. You must remember, I am just a middleman."

"Oh, yes. Your expansion into Vegas. Miguel told me about that. I'm just glad you're not trying to expand into New York. Competition can sometimes be a killer—as I'm sure you know."

"Yes, it sure can," he said grimly. "Lavernius, may I speak with Miguel? Maybe we can get this misunderstanding worked out."

"No can do, my friend. He's a little tied up at the moment," I taunted. "If you haven't heard from him, I would assume he is too busy. Like I said, it's a very troubling time for us. Luckily, Miguel's volunteered to help us figure out what happened . . . and where my car went. Really generous of him. Of course, I knew that when we met."

"That's Miguel. Always willing to go the extra mile."

"Which he is doing right now. We'll talk more soon," I stated. "Maybe you'll have some answers on your end by then."

"I hope one of us gets some answers for us, my friend, because I do not like the direction this is going." His voice was low, but I could feel his anger.

"Neither do I, Alejandro," I said, matching his intensity. "Neither do I."

Orlando

28

The Van Wyck Expressway was crowded, and as I sat in traffic on the way back to the warehouse where Miguel was being held, I finally had some time to think about the events of last night. Before now, things had just been moving way too fast, and everything felt so fucking out of control. My father was on edge, and when he was stressed, everyone felt it. So, of course, we were all in panic mode, trying to figure out where the Roadster was and the quickest way to get it back.

The most logical answer was that Miguel had something to do with the hijacking, but something about that didn't feel quite right. If Miguel was involved, why would he waste his time fucking around with Paris instead of getting the hell out of New York? Hell, he could have jumped a plane ten minutes after I dropped him off. I didn't care how good looking or persuasive Paris could be; she wasn't worth his life, which was now clearly on the line. I guess it was possible he was just that cocky and thought he could play us dumb-ass niggers, maybe even use Paris as an alibi. Or perhaps he was just plain stupid. But I'd spent a lot of time with the man while putting the finishing touches on this deal, and I never saw that. Then there was the possibility he was innocent and was being played by Alejandro. I didn't know what the truth was, but I was damn sure going to get to the bottom of this mystery. By the time I finished pumping a couple hundred cc of sodium amytal into his system, he was going to tell me anything I wanted to hear.

Most people didn't believe in truth serums, and that included my father, until he'd seen it work for himself. Now he had me keep enough of the stuff around to interrogate an army. I wondered what Ruby would think if she knew how I was really using my pharmaceutical degree.

Ruby. Believe it or not, even with all this crazy shit on my mind, I was still constantly thinking about Ruby. I didn't like the way I'd left things with her. I just kept seeing that expression on her face when I snapped at her about turning off my phone. But what did she expect? His cell phone and his radio: every woman should know those are two things you don't fuck with when it comes to a man's stuff. Of course, the real reason I was so pissed off that night was that someone had dared to steal from the Duncans, but Ruby's stunt with my phone made her the target for my anger. Still, I felt bad about hurting her feelings, and something inside of me just needed to make things right with her.

I took out my phone and hit one of the speed dial buttons.

"Remy. It's Orlando."

"Orlando. It's always a pleasure. What can I do you for?" Remy said.

"I need something from you."

"Well, you know I've got you covered. And your call is perfect timing. We have this new girl that—"

"No. I don't want to meet a new girl. I want you to set up something with Ruby again."

"Oh?" Remy sounded confused. "But after the way you left her at the restaurant, I thought—"

I interrupted him. "Can you do that for me?"

"I'm afraid not, my friend. Ruby has once again decided that she's through working for us. Perhaps it is for the best, anyway. She was very emotional after your last date, and you and I both know that emotion is a no-no in this business."

"Get her back. I'll pay triple if I have to."

"I don't think you understand. She's moved on. But there are others. I've got plenty of girls."

"Not like her, you don't."

There was silence on the line. Remy probably didn't know what to think. Me, the originator of the one-date-only rule, suddenly demanding to see the same girl again, no matter what the cost. I was still a little shocked myself by how into this girl I was, so I was sure Remy was beyond confused.

"Look, Remy," I started. "I've been one of your best customers for a long time. If you won't get Ruby back, then I need you to give me her phone number."

This time he wasn't silent. This time Remy laughed at my request. "Come on, now. You know I'd do anything for you, but I can't give you the personal number of one of my girls, current or former. If I did that, I'd be putting myself out of business here. You're a businessman. You know that's not how things work."

"I understand, but it's not like that. I'm not trying to score behind your back," I reasoned. "It's just that something went down with Ruby and me. It was less business and more personal. I just need to clear some things up with her. That's all. You can understand that, can't you?"

"Something like what?" I could hear the suspicion in his voice, but I didn't blame him. I was acting way out of character, and he was just trying to protect his interests. Knowing it would only make him more leery if I tried to bullshit him, I went for the direct approach and told him the truth.

"I flipped on her for turning off my phone. I think I hurt her feelings."

Remy laughed. "That's what she gets paid for, Orlando, to take whatever you dish out. It doesn't matter if you had a bad day. She's supposed to grin and bear it. If she let her feelings get hurt, then that's her own fucking fault. Don't worry about her."

"I hear you, but I'd still like to get that number. Please, man." Yes, I was that damn close to begging. Something about this girl had me wide open.

I could almost see Remy shaking his head through the phone. "Come on, Orlando. Don't put me in this type of position. You're one of our best customers, but this goes against all the rules, and there are no exceptions to the rules in my line of work."

"I get where you're coming from, and I assure you that I'm not trying to fuck up your business. As a matter of fact, as a show of good faith, I'm going to throw you two grand. That's Ruby's fee for a night, right? That's two grand you never would have gotten, since she stopped working for you."

"Two grand . . . just for a phone number?"

I knew that would get his attention—being the businessman he was, of course. He could say what he wanted about there being no exceptions to the rule, but I knew that just like most people, Remy had a price.

"I know favors and exceptions don't come free, Remy. I'm willing to pay. So, what do you say?"

Again, Remy paused. He was doing either one of two things: trying to recall Ruby's number, or deciding whether breaking one of his sacred rules was worth two thousand dollars.

I decided to call his bluff. "You know what? You're right. Forget I even put you in this position."

"Oh, no, wait. I have her number right here."

"Cool." I scribbled the number on the back of an envelope as he rattled it off. "Thank you, Remy, and as always, it's a pleasure doing business with you." I ended the call with a smile on my face. Remy might have been a good businessman, but I was better.

I wasted no time calling Ruby.

"Hello," her voice greeted through the phone.

"Ruby?" There was a silence after I spoke, which told me she recognized my voice.

"Orlando." Her tone wasn't welcoming. It was more like a what-the-hell-you-doin'-ringing-my-phone kind of tone.

"Yeah, it's me," I said.

"What do you want? How did you get this number?"

"I got it from Remy. I needed to talk to you about how things ended the other day. I'd like to see you." Without trying to sound too desperate, I hoped she could hear how sincere I was.

"I know you think of me as just some piece-of-trash prostitute, but I have feelings, Orlando. Crazy as it sounds, I had feelings for you. I didn't deserve the way you treated me. All I did was turn off your lousy phone."

"You're right. I shouldn't have done that. But because of what you did, I missed a very important business call. A call about something that might have bankrupted my family business." I took a deep breath to calm myself down. I was starting to get worked up just thinking about it, and I didn't want to take it out on Ruby this time. I tried again, in a calmer tone. "Look, I apologize for the way things went down, but there is just so much going on."

"Let me guess. With work, right?"

I overlooked the obvious sarcasm in her voice. "Yes, work. But look, I can't really get into things over the phone." By now I had arrived at the warehouse and was parking my car. "If you'll just agree to see me, then we can talk, and I promise I'll tell you everything."

"Not interested."

"Excuse me?" Now, that was a surprise. I knew she was hurt, but I definitely didn't expect her to be such a hard-ass about this. "I know you feel the connection between us."

"Anything that was there is gone, Orlando. I just want to be left alone—by you, by Remy, and all the rest."

"Please don't be like this. Just give me ten minutes of your time." I definitely hadn't begun this call planning to beg, but she was being so stubborn, I felt like I had no other choice. In the midst of all this chaos surrounding the Roadster, I had this inexplicable desire to be with Ruby, like a calm port in the middle of a storm. "Please, Ruby," I begged as I shut off my car and headed toward the warehouse. "I really need to see you. I can't leave things like this."

I could hear her sigh. It was so cold, I could imagine a frost coming out of her mouth. For a moment I really thought she was going to say no, and I didn't have it in me to beg anymore. Instead, she gave in. "Sure."

A slight victory smile spread across my lips, until she said, "Set it up through Remy. And, Orlando, don't call this number again."

"I won't, but we don't need Remy."

"Yes, we do."

Needless to say, the smile disappeared from my face. I choked out a laugh as I walked inside the warehouse, where I was greeted by Junior's men. I lifted a finger so they wouldn't interrupt my call. "Oh, so it's like that?"

"It's business. Just like your reason for yelling at me in the restaurant. You chose to make it about business then, and I choose to keep it about business."

Again, she was so cold that I could imagine icicles hanging off her words. "All right, fine," I agreed. "I'll call—"

Boom!

A loud blast echoed throughout the warehouse.

"Look, Ruby, I have to go. I'll see you soon."

"Orlando! My God, what was that?"

"That was business. I'll see you soon." I ended the call, stuffed the phone in my pocket, and pulled out a gun.

LC

29

"Alejandro, are you able to talk?" I was seated in the conference room at our offices. It had been almost two days since Alejandro and I first spoke about the hijacking. I was not any happier now than I was then. I motioned for Harris to come closer as I placed the phone on speaker.

"Yes, the line's secure. Speak freely," he replied.

"There have been new developments on our end. I just wanted to know if you have anything for me. I'm starting to lose my patience about the loss of my product."

"I can only imagine, my friend. You have remained remarkably calm during a difficult situation. Unfortunately, I have no answers for you. I'm afraid my resources on the East Coast aren't as reliable or thorough as they should be."

Does he really expect me to believe that? I wondered as I glanced over at Harris, who just shook his head. We both knew Alejandro had been supplying the Mexican gangs on the East

Coast for years; I had just never cared, because they weren't anything significant or challenging to my network. Besides, I had some very reliable people I worked with on the West Coast too.

"Has Miguel helped you any?" he asked.

"No. He hasn't done shit but proclaim his innocence." I was starting to get tired of this.

"And what do you think?"

"That he's a liar," I replied, my voice rising in the specially equipped soundproof room. "And that you took my money, then sold my shit to someone else."

"Lavernius, my friend, I give you my word. I have nothing to do with the travesty that has happened to you. I only want good relations between us."

I sighed long and hard. "You want good relations between us, you fucking Latin viper, then give me my shit back!"

"I give you my word, and then you raise your voice and accuse me of being a snake?" I heard a loud thump, which I assumed was him pounding his desk.

"That's because you are a fuckin' snake. You were when I met you, and you are now. But I'm used to dealing with snakes in this business. It's the thieves and crooks I have a problem with, and you've become a first-class crook."

"I am no crook!" he yelled, his anger matching my own. "I could sell my 'shit,' as you call it, to the Italians or the Jamaicans and not have to deal with your arrogance or accusations. I do this only because we were once good friends."

"That's right, once good friends. Past fucking tense. Now, who did you sell my shit to?" I asked.

"I don't believe this. It's like talking to a petulant child with you."

"Ha! I'm not the one who killed his own men to cover up my crime."

This news seemed to take him off guard, as he grew silent for a while. "What are you saying? My men are dead?" His voice cracked. If he was putting on an act to seem innocent, he was doing a damn good job. I still wasn't convinced, though.

"I told you there have been new developments," I said coldly.

Harris had gotten a tip less than an hour ago that the truck was in a warehouse up in Orange County, New York. I'd sent Pablo's brother Carlos and his crew up to check it out, since they were the closest. They reported back that the truck was there, but the car was gone. They also found two dead bodies, two men who appeared to be Mexican. In truth, I wasn't so sure that the Mexicans were really dead before he got there. There was no one Carlos loved more than Pablo, and if he had the chance to avenge his brother's murder, well, let's just say God Almighty couldn't have stopped him.

"What are these developments?" he asked cautiously.

"We found the truck that your men delivered. My car's gone, of course, but there are two dead Mexicans there. If we ID them as your men, then we have a serious problem, Alejandro, because there's no fucking reason that your men should have been anywhere near that truck after it was delivered to my men."

He remained silent.

"Nothing to say, huh?" I asked. "That's okay, because remember I still have Miguel, and he'll eventually spill the truth. If I have to, I'll rip out his fucking liver to make him talk, and then I'll mail it back to you."

"Don't touch him, Lavernius. I am warning you," Alejandro threatened.

"My, my, my. You're awfully touchy about your employee, señor, which is surprising. I mean, if you think about it, Miguel may be the one who planned the hijacking and then set them up to be murdered. After all, who else knew the truck's route?"

"He would not do such a thing. He would not betray me."

As I considered the theory I'd just put forth, I realized it could be true. Miguel might very well be the mastermind of the hijacking. "You seem so sure of Miguel's innocence, Alejandro. Perhaps you put more faith in your men than is warranted."

"Lavernius," he said, his voice barely above a whisper, "Miguel would not betray me. Miguel is my son."

This time, I was the one stunned into silence, during which Alejandro's confidence returned.

He warned, "If you harm my only boy, Lavernius, I promise you I will not rest until one of yours is hanging from a stake."

I looked over at Harris, who was undoubtedly thinking the same thing I was. Thank God I had not given a final order regarding Miguel's fate. Family members were generally off-limits, unless you wanted a war. I had no idea that Miguel was family, but that wouldn't matter to Alejandro. He would not hesitate to even the score if we harmed Miguel.

"Why didn't you tell us he was your son?" I asked, trying to keep my tone more neutral than it had been.

Thankfully, Alejandro seemed willing to dial his anger back a notch too. "Miguel's all about proving himself in my organization," he explained. "He doesn't want anything handed to him. I'm sure your sons feel the same way."

"Yes."

"So, can I speak to him? You have not killed him, have you?"

Hearing the fear in Alejandro's voice, I realized that holding his son was a dangerous thing, but it was also a good bargaining chip. "No, no, Miguel's alive. But I'm still not in the mood to share him with you. Not until I check out this trailer personally."

"You do understand I cannot let you hold my son any longer without a sign of good faith?" he said.

"How about you return the money I gave you and I return your son?"

"You know I cannot do that. It would be an admission of guilt, and I am not guilty of anything. I was thinking more like a sign of good faith on your part. You have my son. For all I know, your people murdered my men and are processing the delivery as we speak."

"Ridiculous! You already had my money. Why would I jack my own shipment?"

"I don't know. To discredit me?" he speculated. "Maybe you're just looking for an excuse to end our arrangement and go with someone else. Still, I'm going to need something to keep this from turning into some very bad shit for both of us."

"Okay, you're right. How about I send one of my people to L.A. to keep the lines of communication open until we get this sorted out?"

"Agreed. But I don't want it to be some flunky. I want it to be someone high up in your organization who you value. One of your family members."

"Fine," I answered. As long as we held Miguel, I had to assume that Alejandro would never be stupid enough to harm my family. "I'll send one of my sons."

"Fair enough. There is a flight that leaves Kennedy in two hours. I will expect your son to be on it. We will speak again soon."

I ended the call and sat back in my chair, rubbing my eyes to relieve the throbbing pain behind them. My blood pressure must have been at an all-time high.

"Can this get any worse?" Harris blurted out.

"I sure hope not," I replied.

"You're not really going to send one of the boys out west, are you?"

I turned my head to look him directly in the eye. That was enough to let him know his question was a stupid one. What choice did I have but to send someone?

Harris continued. "I mean, now that we know Miguel's his son, why not give him back to Alejandro? Or at least let him speak to him. We don't war with these people, LC."

"Harris, we're blind right now. Someone's gunning for us, and we don't know if it's Alejandro or someone else. Miguel is our only hope to get to the bottom of all of this. Let's just hope Orlando can get what we need out of Miguel without hurting him worse than he already is."

"I hate to say this, but maybe this is a sign that it's time to get out of all this. Look at it as an opportunity. We've got some pretty successful legitimate businesses."

This wasn't the first time Harris had suggested this, and once again, it was the wrong time. "I appreciate your idealism, but our legit businesses don't bring in a tenth of what the dope money does. With our overhead and expenses, things would not be as pretty as they might seem. Besides, there would be blood on the streets if we suddenly left the game. Nature abhors a vacuum. All our lieutenants and their crews would be fair game for every fool wanting to make a name for himself. I go back too far with some of those men to abandon them like that."

"Look around, LC. There's blood on the streets already. Alejandro's people are dead, and Miguel's damn lucky we didn't pop him. And just how loyal are your lieutenants, anyway? We still don't know if Pablo was working with someone against our interests when he got popped."

"Your arguments aside, we're staying in the business, and I'm still sending somebody to L.A."

"Okay. I tried," Harris said with a shrug. "But you're not really gonna send one of the boys to L.A., are you?"

"Yes, I am. We have to show a sign of good faith," I said, shaking my head. "It'll be okay. We'll send Rio."

"Rio?" Harris snapped back. "Rio doesn't have anything to do with this. He runs a club and distributes designer drugs. You don't even think of him as an executive."

"Exactly," I responded. "He's not essential to our operations."

"Damn, LC. That's cruel."

"It's a cold, hard fact. We can still function while Rio gets a little vacation out west."

"But it could be dangerous. He could get killed."

"That's life. Everything we do is dangerous and comes with risk. Do you think peddling club drugs all over Manhattan is safe? Sometimes celebrities and entertainers are more irrational and unpredictable than the criminals we deal with day in and day out. And besides, Rio's never shied away from wanting to prove himself. Now's his opportunity."

"But he's your son," Harris said. "How are you going to tell him you're sending him to his possible death?"

"I'm not. You are," I stated flatly. "I want you to make arrangements right away for him to be on that flight."

Harris stared at me for a moment, his face twisting and contorting as he mulled over a response. I could've sworn real concern flickered in his eyes for a nanosecond.

"That is, unless you plan on taking Rio's place. Otherwise, I suggest you get moving so he doesn't miss his flight." I sat back and folded my arms.

"Nah, I'm good." He stepped toward the door. Now that he knew his own ass could be on the line, he was all business, no more protecting his brothers-in-law. "You don't have to worry about it. He'll be on that plane if I have to carry him on myself. Should I send a security detail to keep an eye on him out there?"

I shook my head. "No, Alejandro and his people are too smart for that. Our people will stick out like a sore thumb out there among those Mexicans. Rio's going to have to be on his own on this one."

Harris

30

I pulled up to the family residence and got out of the car. It was about a thirty-minute ride to the house, but it felt like forever with all the anxiety building up inside me. I loved being LC's right-hand man and lawyer, but telling my brother-in-law he was being exchanged for that scumbag Miguel was not something I was looking forward to. I just hoped Rio was awake so I could tell him what he needed to know, get him on a plane, and put this whole ordeal behind me.

As I entered the house, I ran into London, with purse and keys in hand, getting ready to exit.

"Oh, honey, you're home," she said with such a lack of emotion that I couldn't tell if she was happy or disappointed to see me. For some reason, my wife was very hard to read as of late. Perhaps it was because my mind was so preoccupied with the task at hand.

"And you're leaving," I replied. "Where are you headed?"

"Oh, well, uh, just out to grab some lunch. Maybe go over to Roosevelt Field and do some shopping." She kept her eyes focused on some point behind me, and the lack of eye contact made me suspicious. I was about to accuse her of something when she offered, "Would you like to join me? I could use the company, and we do need to talk."

"I wish I could, but I have to do something for your father. Is your mother home?"

"No, she went to a doctor's appointment."

I nodded, thankful. I had been dreading the possibility that Chippy would be in the house to ask a million questions about where Rio was going.

"Okay, what about Rio? Is he up? I need to speak to him."

"Believe it or not, he's in the kitchen. What do you have to talk to him about?"

"Nothing. Just business." Now I was the one avoiding eye contact.

"Do you want me to wait for you? I'd love to do lunch. And we really do need to talk."

Did she want me to say yes? Did she want me to say no? This was the first time she'd spoken more than five words to me since her threat. What did she mean by "we do need to talk"? I was not going to talk with her about that phone call again. I still couldn't read her, but I thought she was happy—or at least pretending to be. In any case, I had more important things to take care of at the moment.

"Uh, no. You go ahead and enjoy yourself. Buy yourself something nice. "

She smiled. "Don't worry. I will."

"Where's your bodyguard, anyway? I don't want you going anywhere without protection. These are bad times, London."

"I know. He's in the car, waiting for me." She kissed me on the lips and then galloped off.

She was happy, all right, but I had no idea what she was so happy about. Then again, why shouldn't she be happy? She had a nice house, a luxury car, the family she had always wanted, and she didn't have to deal with half the shit I did. I'd be happy, too, if I had nothing better to do than do lunch and have Mommy-daughter time.

I walked toward the kitchen, dreading my assignment. It wasn't that I was nervous about the assignment LC had given me. I was nervous for Rio, because we were about to serve Rio up to Alejandro. I might as well have been sent to the house to cut his head off and then deliver it to Alejandro on a silver platter. Today's lunch special: Rio Duncan. Man, I could have used a stiff drink at that moment.

"Harris, what's up, man?" Rio said upon my entering the kitchen. He sat at the island bar, nibbling on a sandwich and sipping a cup of tea.

"Hey, what's going on?"

He looked down at his plate. "Just having something to eat before I head down to the office. Figured with everything going on, I should try and get down there before the sun goes down. Show Pop and Orlando a little support."

"You wanna show the family some support, I've got just the thing." Like an actor who hadn't expected to win the Oscar, I didn't have a speech ready. So, without further delay, I just got right to it. I reached into my breast pocket, pulled out an envelope, and threw it down on the bar. It landed right next to Rio's glass of orange juice.

"What's this?" He dropped the sandwich, brushed the crumbs from his hand, and then picked up the envelope.

"Tickets," I said as he pulled the contents out of the envelope.

"Tickets for what?" He began reading the details on the tickets.

"To L.A. We have a job for you."

"L.A.? What kinda job?" He looked a little upset as he tossed the tickets onto the bar. "Don't tell me you have some gay man out there you want me to sleep with for information, like you did in Detroit. You can tell my father I'm not a hooker and I won't be pimped out."

"It's not like that, Rio."

"Then how is it?"

I lowered my head and cleared my throat, wishing I had spent my time in the car preparing a speech instead of worrying. Did I really think he was going to accept his assignment, no questions asked? Now, I had no idea how to sugarcoat this. I went for the straightforward approach. "Well, you know how we're holding Miguel as a marker . . . ? Well, I guess you could say you'll be a marker for Alejandro."

"What the fuck are you talking about?" He pushed his plate away and stood up. I couldn't blame him for losing his appetite. "Y'all want me to be Alejandro's collateral?"

"Trust me, Rio, if I was in charge, this wouldn't be my call."

He shook his head. "I can't believe this. Orlando actually wants me to go to L.A. and play hostage? If anything goes wrong, I'm a dead man."

"Nothing's going to go wrong. We're not going to let anything happen to you."

"You can't guarantee that! I can't believe Orlando."

"Orlando has nothing to do with this," I corrected him. "He doesn't even know I'm here. This is what LC wants. He's the one who sent me here."

I might not have been able to read my wife, but I could read Rio's expression loud and clear. He was hurt. I would say this about Rio, though: he was loyal to a fault. Once he learned that the order came from his father, he gave up all protesting.

He examined the tickets again and said, "At least it's a round-trip ticket," with a nervous laugh.

I didn't have the heart to tell him that my orders were to get him a one-way ticket. I'd opted for a round-trip. It made it feel a little less like I was handing Rio a death warrant—though there was still a good possibility that was exactly what it was.

"Guess I better go get packed, huh?" In an attempt to ease the tension in the room, he added, "Wonder how the weather is. I have this killer purple outfit that has L.A. written all over it."

I hated to rain on his gay pride parade, but I had to. "Actually, you don't have time to pack. You have to leave now. A car is waiting outside to take you to the airport. You can shop for the things you need in L.A."

"Oh, it's like that, huh? Well, do I at least have time to grab my new pair of sunglasses? Although for some reason I have a feeling the sun is not going to be shining bright."

I nodded. "The car is waiting."

"Yeah, I get that," Rio said. He took one last bite of his sandwich and then looked at me as if to say, "Hey, you never know. This could be my last meal."

"Fuck!" I cursed under my breath after he left the kitchen. It was tasks like this that made me hate my job sometimes. When my mother-in-law found out it was me who sent Rio to L.A., she was going to hit the roof.

My cell phone rang, and I looked down at the caller ID. "Shit! Not now," I said and ignored the call. It rang again almost immediately. I knew he would just keep calling until I answered. I hit the talk button.

"Yeah."

"Hey, Harris. It's Vinnie Dash, baby." Had he been in front of me and not on the phone, he probably would have tried to give me some corny hand-slap secret handshake type of shit.

"Look, Vinnie, now is not a good time. I'm in the middle of taking care of some serious business."

"I'm sure you are, but that's because of me, isn't it? I'm just calling to find out when I'm going to get my money."

Okay, so now he'd piqued my interest. "And exactly what money are we talking about?"

"The hundred grand you owe me."

"Hundred grand? Vinnie, I owe a lot of people a lot of things, but I think I'd remember if I owed you a hundred grand."

"Don't act like you don't know what I'm talking about," he said.

"I'm not acting at all. I don't know what you're talking about." If he didn't stop bullshitting soon, he was going to be the recipient of all my pent-up tension.

"You and your people put it out on the street that you were paying a hundred grand for any information about that truck."

Shit. Now I knew exactly what he was talking about. Earlier today Vinnie had called me with a tip on the truck. This information was just what I needed to prove my value to LC, to prove once and for all that I was more than just the convenience of a son-in-law with a law degree. No, I wasn't a blood Duncan, but surely this would help me move up in rank. His tip had turned out to be right on the money, except for the car being missing from the truck.

"Vinnie, you never mentioned that you were looking for the finder's fee when you told me about the truck."

"Didn't know I had to, but I did give you a tip that helped you find the truck, didn't I?"

"Yeah, I guess you did, but the car's not in it."

"Don't know anything about a car. I was looking for the truck." He laughed, probably reveling in the fact that he knew something we didn't know. Smug bastard.

"How'd you know where the truck was, anyway, Vinnie?"

"Someone offered us the truck. We declined, of course, but still, we acted just interested enough to get a location."

"Who offered it to you?"

"Now, that's something you're going to have to ask my old man about. I can set up a meeting."

"Let me get back to you on that."

"That's up to you, counselor. I just wanna know when I'm gonna get my money."

"I'll make arrangements. Don't worry, Vinnie. You're gonna get exactly what's coming to you."

After I hung up, I walked over to the window and pulled back the curtain. Rio was just getting into the car. He looked over his shoulder and spotted me staring out the window. Slipping on his diamond-studded sunglasses, he waved and then slid into his seat. I watched until the car headed down the driveway and was out of sight.

I called LC and let him know. "He's on his way. He should be at the airport in fifteen minutes. My men will let me know the minute his flight takes off, and I'll call you."

"Good. Junior and I are on our way to the truck. I just texted Paris to meet us up here. Why don't you check on Orlando and make sure Miguel's okay."

Paris

31

I walked up to the large steel doors and gave the secret knock. I knew I shouldn't be there, especially since my father and my brothers had chewed half my ass off for sleeping with Miguel in the first place, but I needed some answers. Sure, Orlando had promised to get to the bottom of things with all that chemistry mumbo jumbo, but I didn't want to wait for that. Besides, I had my own agenda, my own set of questions. I needed to know that I wasn't wrong about Miguel, that his swagger wasn't anything more than confidence, not conspiracy, and our lovemaking was filled with affection, not betrayal.

I had always said that talking got me in trouble, but handsome men who showed me affection were my true Achilles' heel. My therapist had tried to tell me I had Daddy issues, but I stopped going to that bitch right after I whipped her ass for bringing up that crazy shit. I hated it when people talked bad about my father.

The steel doors opened, and a large, bald-headed black man holding a sawed-off shotgun gestured for me to come in. The man's name was Kennedy, and he, along with two other knuckleheads, worked directly for my brother Junior. They were assigned the duty of keeping secure the fifty-plus classic cars my father had collected over the years. Kennedy and his men also doubled as muscle for our family during times of trouble. They were all highly trained and would give up their lives to protect Junior and our family without a second thought.

"Hey, Miss Paris," one of the men said, lifting his head from the desk where he'd been sleeping.

"What are you doing, Freddy? Sleeping on the job again? Wait till I see Junior," I scolded halfheartedly. I wasn't about to snitch on him, because I liked Freddy. He wasn't much to look at, but he was a nice guy and knew how to handle a gun under pressure—something I admired in any man.

"No, no, I was just resting my eyes. Whatchu here for, anyway?" He walked over and gave me a hug.

"Business," I replied, turning toward the bolted door to the room where they were holding Miguel. "Our guest doin' all right in there?"

"Yeah, he's a'ight. I gave him something to eat about an hour ago. Junior just said to keep him tied up until someone from the family called or came by," Kennedy replied.

"Well, here I am."

I took a step toward the door but was cut off by the third man's rolling office chair. His name was Kareem, and he was a good-looking brown-skinned man about my age. I'd given him some ass a couple of years ago, but that nigger didn't know how to keep his mouth shut. He was lucky that shit didn't get back to my brother, or I would have killed his ass.

"Where you think you're going?" Kareem asked, blocking my way.

"To see the prisoner. You gonna let me by, or are you gonna stand here and jack off for shits and giggles? Lord knows your dick's small enough to make a bitch laugh."

Both Kennedy and Freddy started cracking up.

"What you trying to say? That shit ain't funny," Kareem barked.

"If that shit wasn't funny, then you better talk to your boys, 'cause they sure as hell laughing. Now, open the damn door and get your ass out my way before I move it for you. I told you I have business with that man."

He stood his ground, until Freddy said, "Yo, man, you better let her pass before she fucks you up. You know she's not someone to play with." Freddy shook his head at Kareem's stupidity.

Kareem moved aside, mumbling under his breath, and Kennedy walked over and unlocked the door. I entered with both Kennedy and his shotgun on my heels.

"I need to speak with him. Alone."

"You sure?" He looked surprised by my request. "Junior said that man is dangerous."

Yeah, maybe with his tongue and dick, I thought. I glanced at Miguel, who was lying motionless in his underwear across the bed. He was blindfolded, and his hands were tied behind his back.

"Is that what you think?"

"Well . . . yeah," he said with a shrug. "Dude's down with them Mexicans. Can't take no chances with that."

"He's tied up, for crying out loud. What's he going to do? Shoot me with his big toe? Don't worry. I can handle him. Just wait outside," I ordered.

Kennedy hesitated for a moment, probably wondering whether he should challenge me, but deciding against it. "A'ight, if you say so. But if he gets outta hand, just holler and we'll come runnin'," he offered.

I might holler, but you better not come running in until I'm finished.

He exited the room, and I closed the door behind him. I stepped out of my heels and headed to the bed, treading softly across the cement floor. I stopped alongside the bed, taking a moment to quietly observe him as he slept. I took in all his sexy-ass tattoos that covered his back. He was bruised and beaten, there was no question about that, but not broken. I was actually surprised they had let him sleep. My daddy was getting soft, though I'd never say it to his face. Five years ago Miguel would have told him everything he wanted to know by now, or they would have dumped his lifeless body somewhere in a landfill on Long Island.

Placing my purse on the table next to the bed, I reached out and shook Miguel gently. "Hey, wake up. It's me, Paris."

Miguel flinched at first, spinning around quickly to confront me. I wasn't really sure what he planned on doing with his hands tied. I eased off his blindfold and saw that his eyes were blackened and his lip was busted, but his face was still pretty.

"Señorita Paris." His shoulders relaxed, and he gave me a weak smile. That was a good sign. It meant he trusted me. We could get a lot accomplished as long as he trusted me.

"Daddy's not happy with you," I said, arms folded.

"Yes, I noticed. He thinks I stole his dope." His mouth twisted into something I couldn't quite interpret. Was he smirking, or did it just look that way because his face was so damn busted up? I sure hoped it wasn't a smirk. As far as I was concerned, that would be almost like an admission of guilt. The uncertainty made me angry.

"Did you? Did you take our fucking shipment, Miguel?"

His entire demeanor changed, all trust replaced by fear. He pleaded, "No, I did not. I tried to tell your people that . . . the night they beat me." He sat up in the bed with a grimace. He probably had a few broken ribs, and in spite of myself, I felt sympathy.

I placed my hand on his chest, touching him softly. "I hate seeing you like this. But you need to try harder. Give us what we want. Just tell me where it is, and I can get you out of here."

"I can't, Paris, because I do not know. I swear on my mother. You know I would tell you."

I backed away from him with a sigh. "You takin' me for a fool, Miguel? Because I'm not a fool. I know you know something."

"No, no, I do not. You know how I feel about you. I swear I would tell you."

His statement stopped me in my tracks. What did he mean, how he felt about me? And why did I care so much? I mean, the sex was hot, but what did I really know about this guy? I definitely wasn't used to feelings getting involved when it came to the family business, but there was something about Miguel that was tugging at my heart.

"You told my father you would marry me. Is that true?"

"Yes, Paris. I would marry you."

"You don't have to lie to me."

"I'm not lying. I told you I could fall in love with you when we made love, did I not?"

He did say that, but did he mean it? Was it just a moment of passion, or was he falling for me? Maybe this was just the attempt of a trapped man who would say anything to get released, but I wanted to believe him. I sat on the bed next to him and leaned down to kiss him, as if the truth might be found on his lips. The heat between us was instantaneous.

I stood up and unzipped my dress, letting it fall to the floor. "Enough talk," I said. "I've got something that will ease your pain." I took off my bra and slid my panties off my hips. "They're outside the door, so we're gonna have to be quiet," I told him, though I didn't think I had to worry about him making any noise. He was staring at me, dumbfounded, looking like he couldn't form a thought in his head. Who could blame him? I'd had sex in plenty of strange places, but never with a man in captivity. As crazy as it was, I was totally turned on, and from the way his dick was straining against his boxers, I could tell he was too.

I removed a switchblade from my purse and cut the cord that was binding his hands together. Instead of trying to escape, he fell back onto the bed and reached his arms out to me. I climbed on top of him and then moved up until my pussy was right over his face. He wasted no time going to work. I could feel his warm tongue on my thigh, and then across my clit, again and again. I wanted to cry because it felt so good. I rode his face like a jockey, and it wasn't long before I came.

I slid down to his hips, guiding his already hardened dick out of his underwear and deep inside of me. Certainly this had to be a treat after what he'd endured. I placed my hands on his chest, bracing myself as I brought my hips up before dropping them down with a corkscrew of my waist. I worked myself up, riding that dick good as I came all over him.

"Oh, oh. Damn, girl," Miguel gasped, ignoring the pain, courtesy of my father's beating.

"That's it. Just close your eyes and enjoy it, baby. Take this here pussy," I coaxed. My ass cheeks clapped together, grasping his long shaft as I bottomed out on it. His breathing became shallow as he reached up to take both my breasts in his hands. I let a moan escape as another shudder ripped through my body. From his intensity, I could tell Miguel was close to blowing his load.

A beep from my cell phone brought me back to reality. Miguel had me so hot that for a second I'd almost forgotten where I was. I wasn't about to stop riding him, but I knew I couldn't ignore the text, either. I reached for my purse and pulled out my cell phone so smoothly that he didn't even notice.

I'd gotten a text from Daddy: We found the truck and Alejandro's men. You may need to go to California and take care of it. You need to meet me in Orange County ASAP.

I tossed the phone on the table and began slamming my hips even harder against Miguel, watching his face contort in ecstasy as I reached for my purse again. This time I pulled out a Glock 17, similar to the one he favored, but the latest model. Without breaking my stride, I suspended it scant centimeters above his face, placing my finger on the trigger.

"I love you," I purred in his ear, smoothly bringing my motion to a halt.

"I love you too," he said with that accent I absolutely adored. When he opened his eyes to find out why I had stopped, he gasped, simultaneously erupting inside of me against his will. I don't think I've ever seen a man make a weirder face.

"Señorita Paris, why are you pointing that gun at me if you claim to love me?"

"Because you're a lying son of a bitch. You don't love me. And you really shoulda told us what you did with our shipment before we found it, Miguel."

His face, that beautiful face, froze in terror. "I did not know where it was to tell, Paris. I swear to you!"

"Well, your two men were found with it," I said angrily. "What the fuck have you done? I was defending you, and now you've made me look like a fool, Miguel."

"No!" he protested, but I kept going.

"I was falling for you, but you're just like the rest—which makes what I have to do here that much easier."

"And what is it you must do?" he asked tearfully.

"My job. You do know my job description, don't you?"

He shook his head. "Receptionist? Secretary?"

"No, I'm the company troubleshooter. I shoot anyone who gives us trouble. And you and Alejandro have just made it to the top of my list," I stated, sliding a bullet into the chamber.

"Paris, you have to believe me. I do love you, and I don't know anything about the truck."

"Sad thing is, I actually believed you until about a minute ago," I replied, with a feeling of genuine sadness, right before I squeezed a single round into his already swollen eye. As the bullet slammed back into his brain, Miguel's body spasmed, legs protesting with a violent twitch before falling limp.

I climbed off of him and grabbed a corner of the sheet to wipe away his essence as it oozed out of me. Unlike most hits, I felt a twinge of regret. I realized that maybe I had actually been falling in love with Miguel. But it didn't matter now. When duty called, my family would always come first. I wasn't just Daddy's baby girl; I was his avenging angel. Miguel and his lies would disrespect our family no more. I only hoped my father would let me go to California and finish off that scumbag Alejandro.

"Damn it, Paris!"

I turned instinctively, gun in hand, and aimed directly at the voice, only to realize I was face-to-face with Orlando, Freddy, Kennedy, and Kareem, whose guns were also drawn.

"What the hell did you just do?" Orlando shouted.

"My job. After all, I am the family's assassin, aren't I?" I lowered my gun as I spoke. "Now, can you get the hell out of here so I can get my clothes back on?"

London

32

Twenty minutes into my shopping trip at Roosevelt Field Mall, I ditched my security. I just needed some time alone to think, without some hulking guy following my every step. I was still a little disappointed that Harris hadn't taken me up on my offer to go to lunch. He didn't have a clue he was doing it, but he was pushing me away, and Tony was standing right there with open arms to catch me when I fell. It wasn't that I didn't love Harris, but damn, can a girl get a little attention sometimes? Yes, I'd made a conscious decision to retire from my role in the business, but that didn't mean I wanted to feel left out and alone. And that was how I felt when it came to Harris. Who could blame me for wanting to escape that type of life? And escape was just what I planned to do as I picked up my phone to call Tony.

"Hey, can I still take you up on your offer?"

"What offer?" he asked.

"You know, your no-strings-attached offer?"

"Oh, yeah!" The excitement in his voice was just what I needed for my self-esteem. "My offer still stands. Anytime you'd like."

"Right now. I'll meet you at the Marriott. I'm going to leave a key at the front desk for you."

"I'm on my way," he said.

I left the mall and hopped in a cab with my heart pounding. I'd been standing at the edge of infidelity for a while now, and I felt like I'd just jumped off.

Instead of meeting Tony at the bar, I'd decided to cut to the chase and meet him in a private suite. We were both grown. I knew a booty call when I made one; he knew a booty call when he received one. This was something I never dreamed I'd be doing once I walked down that aisle with Harris, but the deeper he got into the family business, the further apart we were drifting. I had to save myself before my bad marriage devoured any self-esteem I had left.

When Tony opened the door, I was already naked on the bed. You should have seen the expression on his face as he climbed next to me, looking like a kid in a candy shop. He barely spoke a word before he proceeded to rock my world.

He slid down the bed and took my foot in his hands, giving me a gentle massage. When he went to put my toes in his mouth, I almost stopped him. I'd never had anyone suck my toes before, nor did I think I'd ever want to, but once he started, not once did I think about telling him to stop. He kissed and sucked every inch of my skin from my toes to my kitty, and by the time he reached it, I'm sure the bed was soaked with my fluids. I'd had men go down on me before, but Tony took it to the next level. He licked and sucked until I came—multiple times. Finally, I was so sensitive down there that I pleaded with him to stop.

That wasn't the end of it. He made his way up to my lips, and we kissed like we were teenagers. Before I knew it, I was pulling down his pants and admiring the biggest dick I'd ever seen. I guess the rumors were true about Italian men—they did have a little "brotha" in them.

"Your skin . . . ," Tony purred as he rubbed my arm. "It's so soft."

I put my hand on his dick, which was growing harder by the second. "Ummm, I can't say the same about you," I purred.

I was about to dive right into an ocean of lust as I stood over the hotel bed, looking down at Tony. He was waiting—waiting on me to dive right in and ride the wave—and I had every intention of doing just that. Before doubt or guilt could prevent me from engaging in the screw of a lifetime, I lowered myself on top of Tony. As I rocked back and forth, my wetness against him was like the water splashing up against the rocks on the shore.

As I popped my hips back and forth, I could feel Tony staring at me. At first it made me self-conscious, but then I was flattered. He couldn't take his eyes off of me. What woman wouldn't be turned on by a man who couldn't dare turn away from her? So, the more he watched, the more I performed, rolling my hips like a tidal wave.

"Damn, baby. Slow down. I don't wanna cum," he pleaded.

I fell over on him, my hair surrounding his head, my hips still working his manhood out. "Isn't that the whole point?"

"I mean I don't want to cum yet," he said, trying to muffle a moan.

"I wouldn't be doing my job if I didn't make you cum, baby," I teased, slowing down and then speeding up again.

"Oh, you like to play, do you?" He grinned. "Then let's play."

Before I knew it, Tony had lifted me off of him and flipped me onto the bed, flat on my stomach. He spread my legs with his, then entered me.

"Ohhhh, Tony." I couldn't help but moan his name as he pumped into me.

He leaned down and whispered in my ear, "Say it again. Say my name. What's my name?"

"Tony," I whispered, totally turned on by his aggressive dominance. He thrust in and out of me, and I appreciated every inch of his well-endowed manhood.

"Again," he ordered as he pumped faster and faster, each of us on the verge of a climax.

"Tony. Tony . . ." By the third "Tony," we'd both been wiped out as our wetness collided.

"Oh, baby girl." Tony exhaled as he fell next to me on the bed. "You . . ." He searched for words. "You're incredible."

"Hmmm, you think so?" I asked as I rested my head on his hairy chest.

"Yes. Trust me. I'm not lying when I say that was the best sex ever."

"I beg to differ," I teased. Before his ego could deflate, I said, "Because this right here"—I got up and mounted him yet again—"is the best sex ever."

I placed him inside me, and we went at it once again. And again, until two hours later, we were both laid out, exhausted.

"I think you better go. It's getting late," Tony said, looking over at the clock on the nightstand.

"Oh, I see. You're kicking me out. Got what you wanted and now you're kicking me to the curb," I joked.

"No, never that," he said, kissing me on the forehead. "I just wouldn't want the missus getting into any trouble with the mister. I heard what you said the other day on your phone call with him. Does he hit you?"

I immediately got up out of the bed. If I had a dick, it would have just gone limp.

"Hey, come here." Tony gently pulled me against him. "I'm sorry. I didn't mean to spoil the mood. But you deserve better, and for as long as you'll let me, I'll give you better."

And just like that, he won me over, and I was leaning over to give him a deep, soulful kiss.

"Now, get on out of here. It's getting late." He smacked me on the ass and nudged me to go.

He was right. I needed to get going before Harris started blowing up my phone—or worse, before Daddy called. I took a quick shower and got dressed.

"Do you want me to walk you down?" Tony asked.

"Nahh. I'm good," I said. I was already taking a big chance. The last thing I needed was to get spotted being escorted down from a hotel suite by some sexy-ass Italian guy.

"Oh, I know you're good." Tony smiled, still lying across the bed, looking like he belonged on the cover of a romance novel. "Now get. How many times do I have to tell you that?" He swished his hand as if scooting me out of the room.

"I'm going. I'm going." I opened the door. "But I'll be back."

LC

33

"Rio's plane is in the air."

"Very good. Junior and I are at the warehouse now. I'll call you later," I told Harris and then ended the call.

So, Rio was on his way to California, and Junior and I were with six of our men, preparing to examine the hijacked truck and the dead bodies in the warehouse. Best-case scenario would be that the dead bodies were not Alejandro's men, so that somehow we could avoid an all-out war. I'd been around long enough to know that war wouldn't be good for any of us, especially Miguel and Rio, but I wasn't holding out much hope.

"Carlos," I said with open arms as I greeted the brother of my deceased friend Pablo. He was standing at the entrance to the building, flanked by two very large Dominicans, each holding a TEC-9 semiautomatic machine gun. "My deepest sympathy for your loss. Pablo was a good man and a good friend."

"Thank you, LC," Carlos said as he gave me a firm handshake. "You were a good friend to my brother. He talked about your many adventures in Asia."

"Yeah, me and Pablo went way back," I said. "He saved my life on more than one occasion, so I can promise you I will not rest until the people responsible for his death are wiped off the face of the earth."

"I know this, LC, and my boys and I will help in any way we can."

I glanced at the men carrying the TEC-9 handguns. They looked like they meant business, which was something I liked.

"So, with that being said, where are the men and the truck you found? It's time we found out who we're up against."

"Right this way." Carlos gestured with his arm and led the way down a corridor. Stopping in front of a large sliding steel door, he stepped aside and covered his nose with his hand. One of his men opened the door, and the odor hit us immediately.

"Holy shit," I mumbled, taking one step in and another one back. The indescribable stench of death filled my nostrils.

"Yeah, the smell takes a little getting used to," Carlos explained. "Try not to breathe through your nose."

It took me a few moments, but I finally walked inside and was met with something that looked like a scene out of the St. Valentine's Day Massacre. Blood and guts were splattered all over the cinder-block walls. Both men lay dead on the floor with their hands tied behind their backs, their bodies riddled with gunshot wounds. This wasn't a shooting; it was an execution.

"Johnny, are these the men?" I waved over my guy who'd taken possession of the truck from Alejandro's men.

He studied the bodies only briefly before declaring, "Yep, that's them, all right. You can't see his face too well anymore, but this one has that tattoo of a spider on his neck I was telling you about."

"Son of a bitch," I spat.

"You know what this means, don't you, Pop?" Junior asked.

I ignored Junior's stupidity, still focused on the two men before me. Of course I knew what it meant. It meant that son of a bitch Alejandro and his piece of shit son had been playing me all along. And to top that off, now they had Rio.

"Junior, I want you to get a hold of all the men loyal to us and have them meet us at the usual spot in three hours."

Junior came closer and said under his breath, "So, what do we do now, Pop? We going to war?"

"I don't think we have any choice, Junior. But we're going to wait till Orlando and Paris get here. I need to know what Orlando got out of Miguel, and I have a job for your sister." I checked my watch. "I texted them both before we left. They shoulda been here by now."

The warehouse door creaked open. Every gun in the room was drawn and focused on Orlando as he walked into the room.

"Hold your fire! Hold your fire! That's my son!" I shouted, my heart in my mouth at the thought that one trigger-happy finger could have lost me my son. "Orlando, where the hell have you been? I texted you almost two hours ago."

"Sorry, Pop, but some stuff came up that I had to deal with," he answered, seeming a little distracted. As he took in the bloody scene around him, he turned to me and said, "Jesus Christ. So, what's the verdict? Are these Alejandro's men?"

"They sure as hell are," Junior answered.

Orlando acknowledged his brother's words but turned to me for verification.

"It's his men." I nodded. "Johnny confirmed it."

Orlando looked at the bodies again, and then at the truck. "You know, Pop, I've been thinking about something the entire ride up here. If these men hijacked the truck, then who shot them and stole the car?"

All heads turned to the first people on the scene: Carlos and his men. A few of Junior's people even drew their guns.

"Put your damn guns away!" I shouted. "They didn't have anything to do with this. They're on our side. Can't you see these men have been dead for at least a day?"

After a few seconds of silence, during which everyone got their tempers under control, Carlos spoke. "LC, I think my part here is done. We will leave you and your men to take care of your business."

"Will you be there tonight?"

Carlos looked over at Junior and my men, then shook his head. "No, but when this war starts, I want you to know that as many of my men as you need are at your disposal. Just say the word."

"I appreciate that and all you've done, Carlos." I shook his hand before he and his men exited.

Junior turned to me and said, "I'll put a team together, and we'll be on the red-eye tonight, Pop. We're gonna need all the intel we can get on Alejandro and his people. I'd like to take Paris, if you don't mind. With her skills, she might be able to take out Alejandro with one shot."

I still didn't know how the hell I was going to tell their mother about Rio. Last thing I needed was more of my family on Alejandro's turf.

"No, you're staying here. I've already got a man on the ground out there."

Orlando and Junior exchanged glances before they said in unison, "You do?"

"Yes, I do." I didn't elaborate, and they knew enough not to ask for more explanation. "Orlando," I said, "I'm not totally convinced, but there might be some merit to what you said. These men didn't shoot themselves, so what the hell happened here? Now, it could have been Alejandro trying to cover up his tracks. Or it could be there's a third player in this little game that we don't know about. What you two need to do is find out who killed these men, and that should lead us to the Roadster and my heroin."

I turned to my men and instructed them to start removing the bodies.

"Ahh, Pop," Orlando said, sounding nervous. "I know it's not a good time to discuss it, but we have another problem."

"What kind of problem?"

Orlando washed his hands down his face. He clearly did not want to speak up, and I knew that whatever it was, it was big.

"I asked you a question. What kind of problem?"

"Miguel." He said it in a whisper, but to my ears it sounded like he was screaming at the top of his lungs. "He's dead."

His words almost brought me to my knees. "What?"

"I said Miguel is dead."

My mind immediately went to Rio. I had sent him out to California, into the hands of a man who would undoubtedly kill him now. As if I had no control over them, my hands went right around Orlando's throat. "What the hell did you do to him? Why did you kill that boy?" I was screaming like a madman.

Orlando grabbed my wrists, pulling them down until I had to relinquish my grip around his neck. He gasped for air. "I didn't kill him! Your daughter did!"

For the second time I felt like the earth had dropped out from under me. I could only manage to mumble, "Paris?"

"Yes, Paris," Orlando said angrily as he rubbed his throat. "I told you about her. We've all told you about her. She's out of control, and now she's killed Miguel, the only chip we had over Alejandro."

"No, Orlando," I said as I walked away in anger. "She didn't just kill our only chip. She killed Alejandro's only son. And she may as well have killed your brother Rio too."

Paris

34

"Hey, watch it!" I yelled. I had just stepped over a puddle, careful not to mess up my shoes, but the two burly men shadowing me didn't have such concerns. The heavy-footed one stomped down, splashing the back of my legs, as well as the Alexander McQueens I was trying to protect.

I glared at both of them, lifting my hand in a fist. One of them flinched, prepared to defend himself with the revolver he probably kept holstered inside his suit jacket, and I almost laughed out loud. If I wanted to take him out, he would have already been on the ground. I stopped to wipe the drops of muddy water off my calves, scowling at the stains on my shoes. Now my palm was wet and dirty, so I dried it on the front of the guy's black jacket. Neither of them reacted—no complaining and no apology. Instead, they just motioned for me to continue walking straight ahead. Sucking my teeth, I turned and resumed trudging on the uneven ground.

As we entered the building, Orlando passed us on his way out, looking evil and not saying a word. He was not a happy camper when he busted in on me taking out Miguel, but now he looked straight up heated. What the fuck was up his ass? I was the one in trouble. Or was I? Perhaps Daddy saw things my way and Mr. High and Mighty was sent home with his tail between his legs.

At the end of my escorted walk, we entered a room where Junior's men were huddled around him, talking, and my father was standing off to the side, talking on his cell phone. I walked over to Daddy, who immediately ended his phone call.

"Daddy, you wanted to see me?" I asked warily.

"She clean?" he shouted over my shoulder to the men who'd brought me there. It wasn't like him not to look me in the eyes when he spoke. Under normal circumstances, it would've made me feel guilty and insignificant. Instead, it made me a little bit fearful this time. He looked almost too calm. Calm wasn't good when it came to my father, because it usually meant he was about to explode.

"Yeah," one of the men replied.

"No. They missed one," I quickly corrected, kicking myself for being so honest. "I've got a thirty-two in my garter holster."

"You fucked up!" He smacked me with a gloved backhand that knocked me off my feet. I went tumbling to the worn wooden planks and almost unholstered my stashed .32 on instinct. I bounced back up, shaking off any signs of weakness I'd just displayed. I was a soldier. I was his soldier.

"Daddy, I—"

"Shut up!" he yelled, punching me directly in the face as he would a man.

As I fought back the quivering of my bloody lips, his men remained still, not coming to my aid. It was better that way. I didn't want their pity.

"Don't you dare interrupt me!" he continued. "Do you understand? I sure as hell hope you do, because I am dead fucking serious."

"Yes, sir, I understand," I answered, holding back tears. He ignored the fact that I was still strapped, or else he just didn't care. I could have blown him away right then and there—but he knew I wouldn't. That was why he let me keep it. He knew I loved him as any girl should love her father. I wouldn't raise a hand to him.

"Why did you kill that boy?"

To me, the answer was simple. "Because he was a liar and had double-crossed us, Daddy. He stole our shipment, and he had to pay the price. I didn't do it for myself. I did it for you." I still couldn't understand what the hell everybody was so worked up about. It wasn't like this was the first time I'd taken care of business for the family. Apparently, Daddy felt like I'd overstepped my position.

"I don't remember naming you my successor," he said. "And I sure as hell didn't tell you to shoot Miguel. Since when did you start calling the shots around here?"

"I don't."

"You damn right you don't. That's my job. I give the orders."

My body tensed in anticipation. I knew I was about to get hit again. It was the only way, short of killing me, that he could save face in front of his men. I understood his reason, but I wasn't a glutton for punishment. I had to state my case.

"Daddy, I was just sending a message to Alejandro and anyone else who wants to mess with the Duncans. We are not to be fucked with!"

He looked like he wanted to smile, but instead he mocked me with his laughter. "Sent a message? Sent a fuckin' message? You don't send messages around here unless I say so. Do you even know who that boy was?"

"Yeah, he was Alejandro's messenger boy and a thief," I replied, although doubt was starting to creep in. Usually, I could talk my way out of any situation with Daddy, but this time he was mad as hell. Had I killed a Fed? Had I slept with a Fed? Fuck.

Then Daddy told me who he was, and it was much, much worse than a Fed.

"Paris, he was Alejandro's son. Do have any idea how badly you screwed up?"

"Oh. No." I suddenly felt sick to my stomach. "I . . . I'm sorry, Daddy. I didn't know."

"Of course you didn't know! It's not your job to know! You're trained to kill, Paris, but only when I say so. What do you think Alejandro is going to want now in exchange for his son's death?"

I didn't reply, but I knew the answer.

"You've started a fucking war . . . and the only way out is to give them the life of someone in our family."

I spoke in a terrified whisper. "What are you saying, Daddy?"

He reached in his jacket and pulled out a .38, pointing it directly at my head.

This couldn't be happening. A few hours ago I was getting fucked by a hot Latin man, and now here I was, with my father holding a gun to my head. I refused to accept that this was real. Daddy wouldn't kill me. I was his baby girl, the apple of his eye, the child that could do no wrong. Still, Daddy had taught me a rule a long time ago, and now his words were ringing in my head: Never pull out your gun unless you plan on using it.

"Paris, you're turning into more of a problem than a problem solver. And we can't have that."

He looked like he was about to cry. "I sent you to the best schools in Europe. Paid hundreds of thousands of dollars to have the very best teachers mold you into a woman of substance. You were supposed to be better than all the rest, and look how you turned out."

I gathered my nerve and tried to talk some sense into him. It was my only hope of survival. "Let's be real, Daddy. I turned out just the way you wanted me to. You didn't send me to boarding school over there in Europe. You sent me to mercenary school, and I'm just a product of my environment. You didn't want me to be a linguist like London, or a chemist like Orlando, and you wanted something different than Junior. And that's what you got—a killer nobody would see coming. Your own personal hit woman."

In his eyes, I thought I saw his resolve wavering, so I went for his sentimental side. "I'm your baby girl. All I ever wanted to do was please you. So, if it's going to make you happy by pulling that trigger, then do what you gotta do, because I love you, Daddy." I closed my eyes and waited for the end to come.

Orlando

35

The cold gray walls and the sound of metal clanking only intensified my anxiety as I walked down the long corridor. I wondered what the old man would think of me if he found out I was here. Stupid. That was what I'd be labeled. I'd be dethroned as the new leader of the family before my reign even started, but I guess that was just a chance I'd have to take, considering the circumstances. Besides, he could blame this on me all he wanted, but this wasn't my fault. If anyone should take the blame for me coming to this god-awful place, it was him.

I'd made arrangements to come here right after I left the warehouse in Orange County in a huff. I can't begin to tell you how pissed off I was when I found out that the old man had sent Rio to Alejandro. I didn't know why the hell he was using my brother in his little game of chess, but it sure as shit had blown up in his face. Now that Miguel was dead, he could pretend he had everything under control, but I knew better. We needed help, or at least I needed help figuring this whole thing out, and there was only one person I could really trust in this situation.

"You here to see Mr. Johnson?" the sandy-haired white man sitting behind the desk asked.

He'd caught me off guard with the "Mr. Johnson" crap. For a minute there, I almost said no.

"Yes, I'm here to see Michael Johnson," I confirmed.

He glanced down at the notepad in front of him, then back up at me, smiling. "You got something for me?"

I reached in my pocket and slipped out five bills, discreetly handing them to the man. His smile became a smirk now that he was five hundred dollars richer. This was the third payoff I'd made since entering the prison, but it was the only way to bypass the BS and get an undisturbed one-on-one sit-down with the infamous Mr. Johnson.

"Have a seat. Mr. Johnson will be right with you."

I walked into a small room and sat down at a table with two chairs on one side and one chair on the other. It wasn't long before I heard the door open, and in walked Michael Johnson, wearing a pair of jeans and a wife beater. It had been more than three years, but he was bigger than I remembered, better looking too. He still had that same charismatic aura about him, that little something that made women love him, men admire him, and enemies fear him. My respect for him forced me to stand, as if royalty had entered the room.

He didn't say anything at first. He just stood in the doorway, staring at me, as if he wasn't quite sure who I was or why I was there.

Finally, he spoke in an agitated tone. "Orlando, what the hell are you doing here?"

"What do you mean, what am I doing here? What do you think?" I stepped closer, although my stature couldn't hold a candle to his. "I'm here visiting my brother in prison. How you doing, Vegas?"

He eyeballed me for another few seconds before he reached out and hugged me tightly. I returned the embrace, holding back tears. He patted me on the back, then pulled away. Once again, his eyes locked in on me.

"You know you're not supposed to be here," he said with a tone of warning. "Pop's not going to like it."

"The last time I checked, I was a grown-ass man," I spat.

"A grown-ass man still living under his daddy's roof," he threw back with a chuckle.

"Yeah, well, if I remember correctly, you used to live under that same roof when you were my age. Besides, I do that just to appease Momma."

"Momma," he repeated, a slight smile touching his lips. "How is she?"

"Momma's good. She's been under the weather a little as of late, but nothing serious. She talks about you every day. She misses you."

"I miss her too. Man, I miss all of you. How's Pop?"

I was surprised to hear him ask about the old man, especially since it was LC's fault that he was locked up in this hellhole in the first place.

"He's good," I said, hoping he didn't plan on going down the list of family members one by one. I didn't have time for all that. That was not why I was there. "But how are you, Vegas? How you been holding up?"

"I'm fine, but don't call me Vegas in here." He pointed a finger at me. "Vegas is dead until the day I walk outta this place. In here I'm Michael Johnson, and Michael Johnson doesn't know nothing about the Duncans." He sat down in the single chair across from me. "Now, tell me about all this shit that's going down with the Mexicans and our stolen shipment."

My eyes bucked and he smirked. That damn Vegas was always two steps ahead of us. "How'd you—"

He cut me off with a chuckle. "What? You think just because I'm locked up, I don't hear things? You wanna know what's going on in the streets, pick a cell. We've got the best gossip network in the world right here behind these walls. And I run this place, so I hear it first, before them all. Now, tell me what's going on. Is it as bad as I hear?"

"Bruh, shit is crazy," I said.

"Yeah, from what I'm hearing, it sounds like we're going to war. I'm trying to keep it from spilling over in here. Mexicans trying to recruit everyone who speaks Spanish. Only ones on our side are the Dominicans. I got a sit-down with the Jamaicans tonight. Other than that, I've got all the brothers lined up. We need every black face we can get on our side."

Just hearing the word Jamaicans made my mind travel to Ruby. In between making arrangements to come up here to see Vegas, I'd called Remy and asked him to set things up so that Ruby and I could meet. He didn't seem to have a problem with it, but five minutes later he called me back, telling me Ruby's number had been disconnected and he had no other way of contacting her. I tried to call her myself and found out that Remy wasn't lying. Ruby had turned off her phone that quick.

"O!" Vegas shouted, snapping me out of my thoughts. "What's Pop talking about? We going to war or what?"

"Oh, we're going to war, all right." I shot him a serious look. "And your baby brother is right in the middle of it, about to get his ass killed."

Vegas sat erect in his chair. "What are you talking about? Are you in some kind of trouble?"

"Not me, but Rio's in a hell of a lot of trouble."

He leaned in close and asked, "What kind of trouble? What, he get his boyfriend pregnant or something?" He began to laugh.

It didn't take long for Vegas to realize that I wasn't laughing with him.

"You're serious. He really is in trouble, isn't he?"

I nodded. "Guess there are some things you don't hear in this place."

"What's going on with Rio? What's he gotten himself into?"

"He hasn't gotten himself into anything. It's what LC has gotten him into."

Vegas sat back in his chair, listening intently as I continued.

"Alejandro's son, Miguel, is dead—under our family's watch, if you know what I mean."

Vegas nodded to confirm that he knew exactly what I meant.

"To make a long story short, LC sent Rio to California as a good faith trade for Miguel. Two hours later, Miguel was dead."

"That stupid son of a bitch!" Vegas banged his fist on the table, then shot out of his chair and began pacing the room. "He promised me he'd never do that again."

Vegas's outburst had drawn the attention of the guard outside the room. He rapped on the window a few times and glared at us until Vegas took his seat again.

"Rio ain't cut out for that shit, man. I mean, yeah, he's a Duncan, but fuck!" He caught his fist in midair before it landed on the table once again.

"Calm down, man. That's why I'm here. LC has told us not to do anything, that Rio's on his own," I said. "But that don't sit well with me at all."

"Me either, O. Me either." Vegas shook his head. "So, what's Junior got to say about all this?"

"I haven't talked to him in private, but you know Junior. He's never gonna go against Pop, even if he's wrong."

"Yeah, kinda figured that. Junior's not exactly a free thinker when it comes to Pop."

"So, what should I do, Vegas?"

"What the hell do you mean, what should you do? You get our little brother back here . . . alive. That's what the fuck you do. You put our people on the next thing smoking and go get Rio."

"But what about Pop?"

"Fuck Pop. He's the one who got us into this. Now, you came here to get my advice. Well, I just gave it to you. And here's a little more. You want the old man to respect you, then sometimes you gotta stand your ground. Now, go do what you gotta do to get my little brother."

All it took was that assurance from the one person I knew would see things the way I did. Some people ask themselves what Jesus would do, but I ask myself what would Vegas do—then I do it.

I stood to leave. The clock was ticking; time was wasting. Although I hadn't seen my big brother in a long time, I had another brother who, despite LC's orders, I had to save.

"Thank you, Mr. Johnson." I extended my hand.

Vegas stood and shook it, then pulled me in for a quick chest bump and a pound on the back.

There was a knock on the door.

"What the hell do they want?" Vegas asked. "We ain't even been in here half an hour. They told me I had an hour visit. When I get out there, heads are gonna roll."

"That might be my fault," I said, pulling away. "I got a little present for you."

"A cell phone?" He could hardly contain his excitement. He went from being this big bear to acting like a little kid over the possibility of a cell phone.

I laughed. "No, bruh, it ain't a cell phone. But I can make that happen. What I got is better than a cell phone."

I walked over to the door and knocked a couple of times. The guard looked in at me. I nodded, he nodded back, and a few moments later the door opened.

"Well, I'll be damned. I guess that is better than a cell phone," Vegas said as he gave Maria, who stood in the doorway, the once-over.

"Mr. Johnson," I said with a wink, "I leave you with Mrs. Johnson."

"You did good, O. You did real good," Vegas told me as I left.

As I sat in the back of the Town Car, waiting for Maria to finish her business inside the jail, I tried to get in touch with Rio. His phone went straight to voice mail, so I left a message for him to call me ASAP. That was not a good feeling, being unable to reach my brother, knowing he was alone and vulnerable. I prayed he was going to be okay until I could get someone out there to bring him home.

I heard a tap on the tinted window, and I looked up to see Maria standing outside. I unlocked the doors, and she climbed in.

"Mrs. Johnson, how was your conjugal visit?" I joked.

Always discreet about her business arrangements, Maria didn't kiss and tell. She sat there quietly, looking down with an expectant look on her face. And I knew exactly what she was expecting.

I reached into my jacket pocket and pulled out an envelope, which I handed to her. "That had to be the fastest twenty Gs you'll ever make. I hope you left him with a smile on his face."

Maria didn't respond with words, but the look on her face said it all. She'd had a pretty good time, probably better than she'd expected—or at least faster. Sure, she did have to ride four hours upstate with me, but at least she didn't have to do it on her back.

She was still looking down at the envelope, but her expression had changed.

"What's wrong?" I asked. "It's all there. You can count it if you like."

She opened the envelope and flipped through the money halfheartedly. "This is wrong."

"No, it's not. I counted it myself."

"No, I don't mean that." She handed the envelope back to me. "I mean I can't take this, Orlando." She turned her body toward the door—as if turning away from the money—and stared out the window. "Remy's gonna kill me."

"I don't understand," I said.

"I don't either." She turned back to me. "Have you ever just felt this strong connection with somebody? You don't know what it is or why. You just feel it."

Instantly, Ruby entered my mind. "This might surprise you, Maria, but yeah, I have."

"Well, that's what I felt with your brother. So, you understand why I can't take the money." She gazed out the window as she spoke. "There's just something about him. He's not like any other man I've ever been with . . . anyone I've ever known."

"Yeah, that's my brother," I said with a proud smile on my face. "Mr. Charming."

She looked at me. "Then can I ask you something? A favor."

I nodded.

"Would you mind if I saw your brother again? No charge. I'll come see him every week. Bring him money, whatever it takes."

"Are you serious?" For a minute I couldn't imagine anybody being sprung like that, but once again, Ruby entered my mind.

"Dead serious," Maria replied.

"Okay then, no, Maria, I don't mind at all," I said without hesitation. "But now I need your help."

"Whatever you need," she said.

"Can you set me up with Ruby? I tried going through Remy, but your brother is trippin', talking about he can't, all the while trying to pitch another girl at me. I don't want another girl. I need . . . I want Ruby."

A look of disappointment crossed her face. "I'm sorry, but I can't. Remy can't either. Ruby wasn't cut out for the business. She was simply paying off her brother's debt. With your help, she paid it off a lot quicker than any of us thought possible." Maria shook her head. "What some people will do for family. But I don't blame her. I'd do anything to keep my brother alive too."

Rio came to my mind. "Yeah, me too."

"Just do it, Daddy," Paris said as I held my .38 snub-nosed revolver to her head. "If I'm that much of a burden, just pull the damn trigger and get it over with."

I took a deep breath to calm my nerves. My usually steady hand began to tremble as I stared in my little girl's face. Taking a life, although necessary sometimes, was never as easy as it seemed; and this was my baby girl, not some thug I was trying to keep in line, which made it so much more difficult. Nonetheless, just as I helped bring her into this world, I was prepared to take her out—or so I'd thought before now. Why couldn't she have just done as she was told?

"Pop!" I heard Junior shout from the other side of the room. "Pop, no!"

"You've really fucked things up, Paris," I said.

I heard the sound of Junior's footsteps as he rushed toward us. They stopped, though, when I commanded, "Junior, you fucking stay out of this!"

"Give me one good reason why I shouldn't handle you the same way I would anyone who crossed me." I pressed the barrel of the gun deeper into the flesh of my baby girl's forehead. If she had just followed directions, I wouldn't be standing here, struggling with the decision I had to make: kill my own flesh and blood, my favorite daughter, or let her live, which meant Rio would surely die. I was losing control not only of my business, but of my family as well.

"Because . . . you love me. And I'm still useful to you. Please." Although she was pleading, it wasn't out of fear. Not fear of death, at least. I remembered seeing this in her even as a small child. Paris had always been afraid of displeasing me. That child lived to win my approval, and it led her to be one of the best at what she did. "Give me another chance, Daddy. I won't prove you wrong."

Paris looked in my eyes, and I was transported back in time to the day she was born. She was the most beautiful thing I'd ever seen, and as the years passed, she just became more beautiful. How in the world could I take such beauty away? I paused, with my finger resting on the trigger and my hand trembling even more.

"Daddy?" she called out. "I'm sorry."

"Why?" I asked with a voice somewhat weaker in tone. I eased up on the barrel just a little bit. I let her take a breath.

"Why what?" she asked with sincere puzzlement.

"Why did you have to make this so hard, Paris? You think I want to do this? Huh?"

She shook her head, blinking her eyes to dissipate a tear before it slipped free. Its presence seemed to anger her. I knew my baby girl. She didn't like to cry unless it was planned. Crying equaled weakness, and she detested weakness, especially in herself.

"Pop, dammit, someone's coming!" Junior called out.

I finally looked in his direction just as a dark sedan rolled into the warehouse and two men jumped out.

An ambush. Shit.

"FBI! Drop your weapons and put your hands up! Now!"

FBI. Double shit.

"How can I help you fine gentlemen?" I called out, quickly placing my revolver back under my jacket and trying to will my hands to stop shaking. If I'd given in to my anger and shot Paris, this scene would have been very different.

"You can help yourself to a jail cell, LC Duncan," the one I would peg as the lead agent replied. His gun was pointed directly at me, and his partner's was pointed at Junior. Clearly, they knew who was in charge. Of course, our men had their guns drawn on each of the Feds. "Now, tell your fuckin' thugs to drop their weapons and nobody has to get hurt. We've got a whole team on the way."

"Fine, but let me see some badges first," I yelled back. They were wearing FBI windbreakers, but that didn't mean shit. They looked at one another, then moved their jackets aside to expose gold badges and IDs attached to clips. Thank God our weapons were legal and we'd already removed Alejandro's men's bodies. The blood on the walls, however, was going to take some explaining. For now, I preferred to think of it as a mere technicality for Harris to handle, nothing more.

"Good enough for you, old man?" the other one called out. "We really don't want to do this the hard way, do we?"

Paris slowly rose to her feet, while I nodded for my men to obey the agents. They begrudgingly dropped their weapons. Squinting into the sunlight that was peeking through the warehouse skylights, Paris began ambling toward the agents in an unsteady manner.

"Paris, stay put, dammit," I ordered under my breath. "I have this under control."

That damn girl was ignoring me again. Now a part of me was wishing I'd shot her ass when I had the chance. She was going to make dealing with her that much easier when this was all said and done.

The agents yelled for her to stop but kept their guns trained on Junior and me.

"He . . . he was trying to kill me! You have to help!" she cried out, rushing toward the agents.

"Paris!" I yelled. Betraying me. My own flesh and blood. Shame on me for showing weakness and not doing what I should have. I couldn't believe that of all my children, she was the one turning on me. As angry as I was, my heart was breaking.

"Miss! Move aside!" the two agents shouted in unison as Paris put herself between them and me, directly in the line of fire.

She was jumping around hysterically, screaming, "Please don't let them kill me!"

"Ma'am, shut the hell up and move out of the way!" the lead agent growled, coming from behind the boxes that partially shielded him. His gun was no longer trained on me.

When he approached Paris to shove her aside, she tumbled forward, pulling a hidden Taurus .32 from under her skirt. She placed a single shot through the back of his skull, sending a fine red mist spraying out of the chasm that was once the front of his forehead. His partner hesitated, deciding now that Paris was more of an immediate threat than my men. By the time he'd trained his gun in Paris's direction, his partner was falling over, deconstructed, face-first. When he squeezed off at her, she was no longer there.

Dropping to one knee, Paris leveled two quick shots, one missing, but the second catching the agent directly through the bottom of his jaw and exiting his skull at an odd angle. He collapsed, slumped over his car door, blood flowing down its dark painted surface before collecting in a dark puddle amid the dirt on the ground.

Paris walked over to both bodies, calmly examining them as we ran over.

"What the hell is wrong with you? It's not bad enough that you've killed your last couple of boyfriends? Now you've resorted to killing Feds?" I yelled with more anger than I thought possible.

"Nope. I'd never be that stupid," she responded with a wicked smirk so typical of her.

"What the hell are you talking about? First, you kill Miguel; then you kill not one, but two Feds, and now you stand here and say that you didn't? Have you lost your motherfucking mind?"

"Daddy," she said, still as calm as if we were discussing the weather. "Those aren't Feds. Those are hit men. Look at their shoes and their guns."

Junior and I both looked down at the bodies to see what she was talking about.

"Those are hard-bottom shoes, Daddy. What Fed do you know wears hard bottoms? And I don't know any Feds issued TEC-nines as their service revolvers."

I bent over and studied the guns. I'd be damned. That girl was right. They weren't Feds. She had saved our lives and her own . . . for now.

Orlando

37

"You okay, man?"

After about eight hours of calling, I finally reached Rio. I'd never been so happy to hear his voice, to know that he was alive and well. I'm not going to lie; I'd pretty much written him off when he didn't answer the phone last night. I had a sick feeling in my gut every time his voice mail picked up—probably the same way Alejandro was feeling every time he asked to speak to Miguel and was denied. So, hearing my brother's voice gave me some relief, though I wouldn't truly be satisfied until he was back on the East Coast, safe and sound, eating my mom's home cooking.

"I'm doin' all right," Rio replied in his typical laid-back, "everything's good" tone. I wasn't sure if everything was really okay or if it was for show, just so those sons of bitches couldn't sense fear in him. He had to be scared. I knew I'd be scared if I was in his position, but at least I'd had some training. This type of shit was far from his usual job description.

"Have you seen Alejandro? Is he treating you all right?" I asked.

"Yeah, I seen the man, and his people ain't treating me bad. At least not yet," Rio answered. "I've had men treat me much better, though, if that's what you're asking."

I chuckled, only because he was trying to make light of the situation—and I damn sure needed a light at the end of the tunnel.

"I hear you, man. So, what's the weather like out there in Cali?" It might seem strange that I was making small talk at a time like this, but I was still trying to get a sense of what his situation was without asking him outright. I had no idea who was surrounding him as he spoke.

"Sunny skies, palm trees. Just like a postcard, bruh," he replied. "Only the postcard's written in blood—my blood."

Okay, so now I knew he was alone and we could talk openly.

"Look, man, don't talk like that. We're gonna have you home in a flash."

"I hope so," Rio said. "To tell you the truth, Alejandro is getting a little antsy. He keeps making slick-ass comments out the side of his neck about my well-being."

I tensed up. "Comments like what?"

"Never mind all that," Rio replied. "Just tell Pop to let him speak to Miguel, for crying out loud. I'm sure that will calm his happy ass down some. I know he's stubborn, but what's a five-minute phone call just to make the playing field even?"

Fuck! I lowered my head. A phone call wasn't asking too much—if only Miguel was alive to do any talking.

I didn't have the heart to tell my baby bro that Miguel was dead, so I said, "I'll see what I can do." And I wasn't lying, either. Not only was I going to see what I could do, but damn it, I was going to do it.

"Thanks, Orlando, man. I know you'll come through for me. Pop didn't choose you to be in charge for nothing."

That one last vote of confidence nearly crushed me as the phone went dead. Now, if I was any kind of brother or leader of the family business, then I had to see to it that the phone line was the only thing that went dead.

"So, how is Rio?"

I turned to look up at Paris, who was standing next to me impatiently, waiting on word about her twin. Harris was sitting on the sofa across from us, and Junior stood behind him. I'd asked them to come in right after the old man left for the office. I thought it might be a good time to hear everyone's honest opinions of our situation without Pop's presence looming over them.

"Rio made it and he's alive is all I can really say," I replied.

"What do you mean, he made it? Where is Rio?" London asked as she strolled into the room. We all turned to Harris, because from her reaction, it was obvious he hadn't told her a thing.

"Rio's in California with Alejandro," Harris said calmly, as if this were no big deal. "He was supposed to be a gesture of good faith while we held Miguel."

London stopped in her tracks, and I watched the expression on her face quickly go from shock to anger. "How's that working out for you now that Miguel's dead?" She turned toward me. "Y'all gonna get that boy killed. Does Momma know about this?"

"No, and no one is going to tell her anything until we get him home," I warned.

The tension in the room was terrible. Everybody was on edge, and Paris was the first to let it get the best of her. She got up in Harris's face and screamed, "You coulda talked Daddy out of this!"

Thankfully, Harris kept his emotions in check. "We're not all as persuasive with him as you are, Paris."

"This is not his fault, Paris. This could all have been avoided if someone we know hadn't killed Miguel," I said.

"What! You shot Miguel?" London glared at Paris, who looked like she was about to break down in tears. Then London turned to Harris and let him have it. "Another secret, huh, Harris? I'm getting sick of all this mystery lately. What the fuck is up with you not telling me things?"

Harris started to get up off the sofa, until London said, "Oh, really? You gonna show out in front of my family? I dare you." He sat right back down.

"I wasn't trying to worry you," Harris offered weakly as an explanation. There was definitely some unspoken shit going on between these two, but now was not the time to address it.

"And what would you recommend?" I yelled, turning my attention back to Paris. "Just go bat-shit crazy and start blazing on them?"

"Maybe. I dunno," she said, still smoldering. "But I'm not going to let him die."

Junior pounded his fist on the table, silent until now. "Shit! Y'all some fuckin' kids! I got my boys out there on these streets, feelin' heat, and we got no answers! Is this how it starts? The end? Everything we worked so hard for? Damn."

"We might not be alone in this situation," Harris noted, using his most lawyerly tone. As usual, he'd calculated things and waited for the right time to offer his input.

"We're listening," I said, moving around Paris to better address my brother-in-law. "Spit it out."

"Others have expressed to me that they're feeling pressure too."

"From?" I pressed.

"Mexicans."

"Shit," Paris cursed a half second before Junior.

"And that they're actively trying to cut out the middleman here," Harris continued.

"Using our shipment," Junior muttered as he shook his head.

"The people that expressed this to me want to speak with LC."

"Who?" I asked.

"The Italians. Sal Dash and them."

"And why did they pick you to speak with?" I was suddenly curious as to what else my brother-in-law hadn't shared. Maybe I would have to keep a closer eye on him.

"Being a lawyer in this city, I guess they felt approaching me might result in a less violent reaction than from one of you," he replied.

Part of me wanted to punch him in the face for his arrogance, but he did have a point. Even Junior shrugged his acknowledgment of the facts. "You believe them?" I asked Harris.

"I don't know."

"You're a lawyer. You deal in lies twenty-four/
seven. You can't tell if they speak with forked
tongue?"

"No. I haven't spoken with Dash," he said,
ignoring my insult. "Mainly a go-between, one
of his errand boys. Sal wants to speak with LC—
family head to family head."

I took a moment to assess the body language
of the three of them—Harris, Paris, and Junior.
If we still had anything left, I would have to learn
to depend on these three. "Okay," I decided. "I'll
tell LC. Make the meeting happen, counselor.
Right away, but on our terms. We don't need
any more fake Feds showing up, trying to take us
out. If this is a setup, it's on your head, brother-
in-law. And family or not, I mean that literally.
It's on your head." I tried to give Harris my best
LC glare.

"If what the Italians say is true, then Rio is as
good as dead," Paris pointed out, and a notice-
able pall fell over the room.

I needed to keep everyone focused on the
business at hand, before our worst fears paralyzed us.

"Junior, find our shit. Or at least find out who
has it. Do whatever you need to do. We've played
nice for too long. Duncans don't do nice. It's time
to remind the streets of that."

I turned to my sister and continued handing out orders. "Paris, get a small team together. Discreetly. We need most of our people here, but you're going to L.A. If I'm wrong and things get royally screwed with Alejandro, I'll deal with it. But this . . . ," I said, thumping my finger on the table for emphasis, "this ain't happening to my brother. Our brother."

"Did LC approve of this?" she asked.

"No. And maybe you can get some shopping in on Rodeo Drive when this is all over. Isn't that why you're going? Just another shopping trip and a chance to see your girls on the West Coast?" I asked coyly.

"What has gotten into you?" she asked, smiling wildly.

"Taking a stand. We have to do something," I said. "Rio said everything is all right, but I know better."

"Why? What exactly did he say?" Paris was practically bouncing around the room at this point. She was hyped for a fight. She lived for this kind of high drama.

"Alejandro wants to talk to Miguel. Rio says he's getting antsy."

"That's not good," Harris stated.

"Tell us something we don't know," Paris snapped back.

"We have to do something," Junior added.

My pulse was racing from the tension and anger that were building up inside of me. I was about to give the order to go over Dad's head. If only there was a way to get my brother back without risking the wrath of LC. But if I was going to step up and be the head of the family business, then I couldn't waver in my decision.

Pushing any doubt to the back of my mind, I said, "You damn right we have to do something, and we are."

"Yeah, right," Harris said as he stood up. "It goes without saying that I'll have no parts of going against LC." On that note, he straightened out his suit jacket and exited the room.

As he passed by, Paris mumbled under her breath, "Bitch ass. To this day I have no idea how London got pregnant by a pussy."

Junior let out a chuckle. Even London, who would normally set Paris straight, just shook her head.

"What do you think, Junior? We need to get Rio out of Cali alive."

Junior's answer surprised me a little. "Orlando, we all know what being a Duncan is about. Risk is just part of the package. I don't mean to sound heartless, but Rio is no exception. Believe it or not, I'm with Harris on this one."

I looked to Paris. "What do you think?"

"Well, isn't anyone going to ask me what I think?"

I turned to see my mother entering the living room.

"Momma? I thought you were lying down," I said, regretting the fact that we'd held the meeting in the house.

"Well, do you or do you not want to know what I think?" she repeated.

"Of course we do," Paris said, jumping in. As usual, she was trying to kiss up, but my mother wasted no time putting the freeze on her antics.

"Quiet, Paris," she shot. "In all honesty, we wouldn't even be having this conversation if it weren't for you and your whorish actions."

"I know, I know," Paris said, clearly tired of being reminded. "And I feel like shit."

"As you should," Momma snapped. "Your brother may not live through the night because of you. This is all your fault." Her tone was acid, but she looked like she might cry.

Junior walked over and rested a hand on each of her shoulders. "Relax, Momma," he said, comforting her. "And of course we want to hear what you think."

She walked out of Junior's caress and over to me. "What I think, Orlando, is that you need to see to it that I get my baby home safe." Her bottom lip was trembling.

"I will," I assured her. "I'll go get him and bring him back personally."

"No. You need to be here to run things," she said sternly, then turned to face Paris. "You go."

I didn't know if she thought it was some type of punishment for Paris, but that was like a Scooby Snack for her. Her eyes lit up, and her bags were as good as packed. "I'm on it," she said, then immediately turned to go start taking care of her business.

"Hey, wait a minute here. What about Pop?" Junior was trying to be the voice of reason.

"Don't you worry about your father," my mother was quick to say. "I'll take care of him."

LC

38

"Been too long, LC. We should see each other more often." The silver-haired man with the shark-like smile and trademark pocket square extended his arms as if expecting a hug. Behind him were four goombahs I didn't know.

"I don't know about that. Last time I saw you, I didn't plan on seeing you again . . . at least alive," I said, denying him the disingenuous hug he sought for appearance's sake.

At my side were Orlando, Harris, and Sihad, a trusted soldier. In all honesty, I didn't want Harris there. His attitude about what we had to do lately had me on guard, but Orlando insisted, because Harris was the one who had brokered the meeting. Orlando had also taken it upon himself to send Paris out of town, due to her unpredictable nature. I'd kept Junior away as a precaution, but he wasn't far. I had him waiting nearby with his boys, in case the man I was meeting had plans to suddenly increase his numbers beyond the five who accompanied him per the ground rules. It wouldn't be the first time he had broken the rules, and I wasn't going to get caught out there.

Our relationship was fragile, to say the least. We'd had some minor business dealings together over the years, and we shared some mutual enemies. There was an understanding that we would leave each other alone, allowing us to conduct our businesses without interference.

Our groups stood face-to-face inside the service bay of my flagship dealership, nothing but tension, disdain, and opportunity sharing the space between us.

"And yet here we are, old friend," said the nattily clad Italian, whose very voice left a bad taste in my mouth. Sal Dash, the owner of Dash Realty, and his entourage, mostly armed goombahs, had dared to step foot in Jamaica, Queens, rather than scurrying around the other boroughs like cockroaches on the perimeter. I'd closed the dealership down early and sent my employees home with pay, using inventory as an excuse, so we'd be undisturbed and unobserved.

"Harris tells me you wanted to talk. So. Talk," I urged. Both of us had lost good people in our last flare-up, so it took a lot of self-control not to order a hail of bullets to be pumped into him and his crew on the spot. Still, his daring to meet with me on my terms spoke louder than any gunshot. Sal was either scared, crazy, or desperate.

"We might have a mutual problem," he said.

"No problems other than a need for more customers on these streets," I joked. While almost all of us laughed, Harris seemed fidgety, never comfortable with discussing our major source of cash flow. Staying a step or so removed from the nitty-gritty had always worked in both our interests. Still, I made a mental note to keep an eye on my son-in-law in Dash's presence, to see if anything else should give me reason to be concerned. Something about his demeanor this time didn't seem quite right.

"I think our mutual problems might lie not with customers, but with product—and its delivery. Capisce?"

"Yeah. I think so. Know anything about an item I'm missing, Sal?" I asked, tired of avoiding the obvious with this Sicilian fuck.

"Only what my people report back to me. Hearsay."

"And what have they heard?"

"Heard the men who killed your little Dominican Pablo were Spanish-speaking too, but not from around here. Maybe a similar accent is associated with whatever it is you're missing. Hear that maybe this Pablo had some kind of deal with these folks, but suddenly he wasn't useful."

"That's a big stretch with no proof," I said, while admittedly intrigued. I needed to end this rumor immediately. If word got out that my men had started making deals behind my back, that would be a sign of weakness, and everyone would start gunning for my operation. This whole situation could turn into an even bigger problem if what Dash was saying was true.

"Unless you have a little more involvement than just hearing things from the sidelines," Orlando said, entering the discussion to Dash's annoyance. "Someone tried to kill my father the other day. They were white boys pretending to be Feds. No Spanish accents at all. Know anything about that? I mean . . . since you're in such a helpful mood."

One of Sal's men, who commanded respect by virtue of his proximity to Sal, tried to stifle a laugh after Orlando spoke. I could not tolerate rudeness and disrespect aimed toward my son on my turf.

"What's so fucking funny?" I asked him.

The arrogant one exchanged looks with Sal rather than acknowledge me. Another strike against him. One more and bullets would start to fly.

"Control your pup before I put him down," I said to Sal.

"No. I agree with you, LC. This is serious business, and my son can be an idiot sometimes. Apologize to Mr. Duncan. Now," he said with a snap of his fingers.

"Sorry, sir." The young punk apologized directly to me in compliance with his boss's orders. The words were there, but they didn't match the feelings behind them. I fixed my eyes on him, imagining giving the order to end his life one day, perhaps one day soon, if I ever saw him again. While he was not a killer, by any means, Harris's expression told me he shared similar feelings toward Sal's arrogant son. I made a mental note to add that to the list of out-of-the-ordinary reactions from Harris.

"Harris, is this all Mr. Dash had when his people reached out to you for this meeting? Gossip and rumors? If so, you just wasted my day with this bullshit."

"No. They insinuated there was more, LC," my son-in-law offered frantically.

"Sal?" I asked, turning back to my counterpart.

"The Mexicans," he said. "I'm hearing they're trying to gain a foothold here, beyond supplying the region. Maybe to cut out the middleman and supply directly. I don't know about you, but I'm not ready to become irrelevant."

"When you say Mexicans, who? Mexican Mafia? Los Zetas? Cali Cartel?" I asked, intentionally omitting someone.

"No. Somebody based stateside, out west. Alejandro Zuniga is his name, I believe. At least that's what my men tell me. Ever heard of him?"

Sal waited for an answer, but I hesitated. This all seemed a little too coincidental. A little too contrived. I glanced over at Orlando. His eyes told me he was thinking the same thing.

"Tell me you didn't hit my shipment," I said.

"No, but this Alejandro's people offered it to me. I was about to take it when my son Vinnie over here informed me that you'd put out a bounty on that truck," he said, shark teeth in full view again.

"So you just turned down two hundred ki's of dope at fire sale prices. Do I look like a fool, Sal?" My blood started to boil, but I needed to keep it under control if I was to get to the bottom of who was fucking with my product. My mind was flying in all different directions. I couldn't narrow it down; there were too many people who would love to have control of my territory. Too many people who would be willing to do whatever it took. One of those people was standing directly in front of me.

"No, of course not," Sal insisted. "Why would I want to go to war with you? Look, we may piss each other off from time to time, once in a while, but we're both successful men with way too much to lose."

"And a lot would be lost," Orlando said not so nicely to Sal. He was definitely more assertive than I'd seen him of late. Maybe he'd finally caught on about just how serious running the family business was, and why I did the things I did.

Sal had a point. I didn't trust him, but why would he risk everything to go to war with us? It would turn out badly for all involved. "Thank you for passing on this information to me. I'll be in touch, Sal." We shook hands. I still didn't trust him 100 percent, but I was feeling a little more cordial than when Dash and his men first arrived.

"Grandpa!" I heard a tiny voice emanating from the dealership floor. Startled, Dash's men went for their guns, which in turn made us do the same. It looked like we were about to get that standoff after all. As fingers rested on multiple triggers and everyone took aim, Harris, who was unarmed, looked to me to stop things.

"Stop. It's my granddaughter," I said, extending my hand toward the men aiming at us, as well as in the direction of Mariah's voice. "That's all."

"Graaaaandpa!" she called out again. It sounded like she was coming closer to the service bay.

Sal's arrogant son made an odd facial expression, then whispered something to Sal as he lowered his weapon. Sal nodded at whatever was said.

"I don't want anyone knowing we're here," Sal said as he motioned for the rest of his men to put away their guns. "Whoever that is, stop them."

"No worries," I said, gesturing to Harris. "Go." As my men stowed their weapons, he ran to intercept his daughter. He caught Mariah just as she was pulling on the door.

"Grandpa, you in here?" she asked into the dark as Harris embraced her.

"Yeah, Mariah," I replied, my eyes fixed on Sal. "I'm busy right now. Go with your daddy, and I'll see you in a minute."

"Kids. They'll be the death of us all," Sal said with probably the first genuine smile of this meeting.

London

39

When Harris escorted Mariah from the back of the dealership, I was startled to see him. Our daughter had run ahead of me when we arrived, but we couldn't find anybody at work other than the one employee who let us in as he closed up.

"What are you doing here?" Harris asked, almost whispering. I was wondering the same about him.

"Mariah likes to visit. You know that."

"Not today," he said firmly.

"Excuse you? You don't tell me when to visit my father's place."

"Okay, okay. That's not what I meant," he said, waving to diffuse the tension. "We have guests. No one's supposed to be here. No one."

"We? You mean LC has guests. When did you get so deep in the business?"

Harris cleared his throat, reminding me that Mariah was listening. I hated to admit that he was right. I knew better than to talk about any of this in front of my child. I was restless as of late, caught up in betrayal, both Harris's and my own, and it was causing me to be careless.

"What's gotten into you?" he asked, a lawyer's suspicion keenly alerted. "Damn, London. I'm trying to keep you out of trouble."

"I was doing just fine before I met you, and I'm doing just fine now," I snapped as images of Harris's lipstick-stained shirt came to mind. If I ever came across the bitch who left her lipstick mark, I would beat her ass good. For all I knew there was more than one.

"Something you want to talk about?" he asked in an irritated tone.

"No. I just wanted Mariah to see Daddy."

"He's in the bay with Orlando and the rest, but you can't go in there. Look . . . why don't you take our daughter home? This isn't the place or the time. I'm sure your father will be there soon."

"Yeah, you're right," I replied, feeling a little stupid for being so ornery when Harris was only considering our daughter's safety. "Who's in there?" I asked as I placed a hand on Mariah's head to guide her out of this place. I used to know something about how this stuff ran. Now it seemed like I was always the last to know. I wasn't exactly sure when it happened, but I was becoming an outsider in my own family.

"Italians," he replied.

It took me a second to react. I heard Italians and thought about Tony. I hadn't let a man make me feel like a silly schoolgirl since, well, school. He was making me feel alive again. I hated that he'd had to cancel our rendezvous earlier today.

"Dash?" I asked, stunned at the possibility.

Harris nodded.

"I'll see you at home. C'mon, baby. We'll see Grandpa later." Knowing the implications, I hurried Mariah away from the potential war zone.

I drove back to our home in Far Rockaway more uneasy than I'd ever felt. Paris had been sent off somewhere after a whispered meeting with Harris and my brothers. Rio was missing, as far as I knew, and no one wanted to give me a straight answer. Now, after a major drug shipment had turned up missing, my father was meeting with a man he'd rather see dead than breathe the same air with him. Strange times calling for strange alliances—and me being left on the sidelines. I didn't know what to do. Not only was my husband pushing me away, but now my family might be doing the same. Again, I thought of Tony. He made me feel wanted.

I smiled at Mariah, turning up the volume on her Dora the Explorer DVD. The sounds of childhood innocence came from the backseat, while in my mind I worried, with the knowledge that life seemed to be changing for all of us.

Rio

40

"It has been three days since you arrived here, and we have treated you well. So, I must ask, when you last saw him, how was my son?" Alejandro asked from behind his desk at the auto dealership. Same M.O. as LC, except this place sold Chevys. He was a volume dealer in more ways than one, with lollipop-colored Camaros and big trucks stretching as far as the eye could see on his lot. Alejandro snagged a few cashews from the glass bowl in front of him and plopped them in his mouth as he waited for my response.

"He was good. Said for you to hurry up and get this straightened out. He wants to come home. Misses his mom's home cooking," I replied, making up shit off the top of my dome. What kid didn't like his mom's cooking?

"Hmm. That's interesting—especially since she is a terrible cook. Sometimes I question that boy's sense."

"Maybe it's some kind of code he was trying to relay to you. All I know is that's what he said before I left," I offered, not missing a beat after fumbling on my ad-lib.

"Perhaps," he said as he tried to read my bullshit.

"You wanna share what it means, then?" I raised my eyebrows, continuing to perpetuate my game.

"Maybe later," he said as he attempted to be coy. The pudgy, balding motherfucker was acting like I'd given him some valuable intel, when I'd just pulled it out of the air. Dumb ass. Then that dumb ass got right to the real point of our meeting. "Your father thinks I stole his dope. That I double-crossed him."

"I'm not an expert on these things, but look at it from his side and you might agree. Why don't you just give him his stuff back and call it a day? I mean, here I am on the West Coast, and I'm stuck down here in L.A., when I could be in San Fran, partying like it's 1999."

"You are young. You're strange," he said, making a whistling sound and motioning with his hand in a way I didn't like. Another homophobe. Just like LC. I was getting sick and tired of being surrounded by people threatened by my sexuality. I was probably more of a man than half these motherfuckers. "I gave your father my word. A true man would understand that should be enough."

"I know men lie. Gay or straight . . . if that's what you're getting at," I said, giving back the same wagging hand gesture. "LC doesn't like this any more than you, and the sooner the two of you can reach a resolution, the sooner I can head back to my fabulous life in New York. And your son can be back chowing down on his mom's awful cooking."

Alejandro let out a hearty laugh, not really appropriate for what I'd just said, and suddenly my two escorts appeared in his office. I figured it was a sign of some sort. They'd already frisked me for weapons and removed my phone, so I assumed this might be when my torture or beat down commenced. Give them a chance to get back in the wife beaters they preferred, instead of the suits they were wearing at the moment.

As I contemplated what was to come, all I could think was, Lawd, not the face. Don't mess with the moneymaker, gurrl. Okay, maybe not the most appropriate thought for a time like this, but what can I say? I'm vain.

Alejandro said, "To show you that I don't run things the same as LC, I want you to enjoy your stay in L.A. Go. Have fun. Wherever you like Except, my men will accompany you, never leaving your side. This is still, after all, a sticky business situation we find ourselves in."

"Oh. Okay," I said, breathing a sigh of relief. My pretty face—and my life—were safe for now. So then why were these two goons staring me down? If their expressions were any indication, this trip was not going to be all fun and games.

"Despite that, I have to go with my gut," Alejandro added, downing another cashew, right before his jovial eyes went cold with a menacing glare. "And my gut's telling me all's not well with dear Miguel. So, I'm giving LC forty-eight hours to let me speak with my son. I no hear from mi hijo, then these two gentlemen will start cutting body parts, and we will send them to LC until I have my son back. Comprende?"

"Sí," I replied casually, hoping to mask my nervousness. In truth, I was scared shitless. LC had better work this situation out in a hurry.

"Good, good," he said heartily. "Until then, enjoy yourself as my guest. Eat. Drink. Be merry."

In other words, enjoy yourself as best you can, because tomorrow there's a good damn chance you shall die.

As scared as I was, I still couldn't resist playing with my two new best friends a little. "Okay," I said, "but I hope your boys don't mind gay bars, because I plan on visiting The Pink Lion, picking up a pretty young thing, and getting laid."

Both men glanced at each other, then turned to their boss. It was quite obvious they wanted no part of a club like The Pink Lion.

"Take him where he wants to go, but don't let him out of your sight."

As Alejandro had promised, they treated me as well as could be expected; but the clock was ticking, and I could feel the pressure mounting as Alejandro demanded answers from LC back in New York. The dirty looks and less than hospitable attitudes of my escorts were evident, and it made me nervous as hell. I didn't want to die. I tried to console myself with the thought that at least the weather was nicer out here. And the shopping was off the hook! Oh, and all the fine wannabe actors swarming around meant I had plenty to look at to keep my mind off my current predicament.

"Got anything to say?" my de facto chauffeur asked as he pulled the black Suburban with darkly tinted windows to a stop. His eyes were like daggers in the rearview mirror.

I felt as though he was asking me for any last words before I was sentenced to death. "I don't know what else to say," I said with a shrug. "I just want to enjoy my stay out here while our bosses have their Doctor Phil moment."

"Just have your boss turn over Miguel, puta, or I'll be the one to kill you myself," the more angry one, seated next to me, snarled. It was obvious he'd hacked a body or two in his time.

"If I had that kind of power, I wouldn't be here with you two handsome gentlemen. Oh, and I'm being sarcastic when I call you handsome. Just so you know. Now . . . can we go inside, please?"

Before exiting the vehicle, both men were sure to remind me that they were packing.

"Roger that," I said as I sarcastically saluted. We had parked a block away and made the trek up Santa Monica Boulevard so as not to run the risk of a nosy valet discovering the rest of their arsenal.

"How do you know about this place?" one of them asked as they trailed behind me, hands on triggers, no doubt.

"I heard about it online and always wanted to see it. Somewhere I can have some fun," I replied, leaving off the unspoken before I die. I continued to step lively down the sidewalk. I would play my role and go along with LC's plan as long as possible, but I had to start thinking about a last-minute escape. The problem was that I was more MacGruber than MacGyver. I guess that was the real reason Pop chose me. If I didn't make it out alive, the organization wouldn't lose a beat. That old softy. In my case, it was business before family.

"Fuckin' maricón," one of them muttered when he realized just how out there and flamboyant The Pink Lion was.

"Yo' mama," I commented back. "Ain't been out to West Hollywood much, huh?"

If they weren't so dangerous, I would've laughed at the impotent expressions on their otherwise hardened faces. Rather than enter The Pink Lion, one of the hottest gay clubs in Cali from what my friends had told me, one of my chaperones went for his cell. He probably wanted to call for further instructions.

"They got me," I said to the doorman, quickly entering. I figured they wouldn't dare create too much of a scene in front of everybody.

"Uh . . . they're at the right place?" the door-man asked as the two Mexicans in suits broke out into a shoving match and started cursing in Spanish.

"Yeah, they're just having a lovers' spat," I lied as he watched the two of them argue. I didn't speak more than a few words of Spanish, but I assumed they were fretting about catching coo-ties or something if they followed me inside.

I took in the European-themed interior, bathed in red lights, and observed the couples on the dance floor and the onlookers on the second-floor balcony. If I weren't so stressed, a pretty brotha like me could do some damage in here. It took all my might not to try to blend into the crowd and escape out another exit; but I was unarmed and alone, so I knew my chances of a successful escape were slim to none. When his men came rushing in, I was standing there waiting on them, acting nonchalant and playing my part in this fucked-up shit.

"This shit ain't cool, homeboy," our driver said, looking like he wanted to swing on me just for making him come inside.

"Relax. This ain't prison, like you're used to, muchacho. Nobody's going up in your ass without your permission. And looking like you, you'd have a hard time anyway," I taunted, so glad I could make them uncomfortable for a change.

"Alejandro said to let you do your thing, but I say we ain't staying for long."

"Soon as I find a little playmate for the night, we out. Meanwhile, you guys need to relax while I go get me a drink."

They motioned for me to go ahead, taking strategic positions, with their backs to the walls, so as to keep me in their direct lines of sight at all times.

"Cîroc and cran. Two of 'em," I requested of the bartender over Usher's "DJ Got Us Fallin' in Love" mixed in with some Swedish House Mafia dance track.

As my drinks were brought to me, I saw a face that didn't belong. Not because he wasn't attractive, but because I knew him from New York. Italian boys always caught my eye. It took me a moment to recognize him, but when I did, I took my two drinks, which were originally both for me, and made my way to where he sat.

"Here," I said as I bumped his arm. "I bought this one for you."

When he noticed it was me, his eyes lit up. We'd chatted from time to time but never hooked up. Now that I was a dead man walking, I thoroughly regretted it.

"Oh my God! Rio!" he yelled over the music. "What are you doing here?"

"Just visiting. You know how I do. If there's a party . . . ," I joked, maintaining pretense. "And you?"

"Business," he said with a sigh as he gladly took my drink, giving up on his attempts to get the bartender's attention. "But I had to slip away. Mix in a little pleasure." I knew what he meant by "slip away." From our talks back in New York, I recalled that he was leading a double life, even though we never got too deep into what he did or from whom he hid his true sexual orientation.

"Well, cheers," I said, clinking glasses with him. For the life of me, I still couldn't remember my friend's name, but I continued to smile. It was welcome company, no doubt.

My two shadows grimaced at my flirting, choosing to look away in disdain as long as they knew I wasn't going anywhere.

"How long you in L.A.?" he asked just as I remembered his name—Martino. At least that was what he'd told me.

"Till tomorrow. And you?"

"Not sure. Waiting on instructions from my boss," he said, his Long Island accent broadcasting loud and clear from his vocal cords despite the pounding bass in the club.

"Your boss. You sound like a gangster," I teased, deepening my voice.

"I don't like those terms," he responded, looking down momentarily into his glass. "I prefer 'businessman.' I ain't into breakin' kneecaps 'n stuff. Unless absolutely necessary."

"Okay, okay. I didn't know you were dangerous like that, Martino."

"Does that bother you? That I might be a little dangerous?" he asked sincerely.

"Ooooh, no. I like danger. Like it a lot," I said with a big grin. "Makes things more interesting. Why didn't you tell me before?" I reached out and caressed his shoulder and bicep in a reassuring way. Also, I just wanted to touch him and feel his sculpted arms. So sue me.

"Back home I gotta be more discreet. Y'know, my people wouldn't appreciate my . . ."

"Lifestyle?" I said, completing his thought for him. I'd heard the term enough times from my pops.

"Yeah. Not so understanding. And I like livin', y'know?" he admitted, with a little bit of nervous laughter escaping. It felt like I was his priest or something.

"Well, relax, 'cause I ain't tellin' no one. Lips sealed 'n all," I commented, being a bit suggestive at the end.

"Good," he said with a grin of his own. "Where are you staying?"

"Wherever I choose to lay my head," I answered, knowing it couldn't be further from the truth.

"Oh, because I was—" Martino stopped mid-sentence.

"What's wrong?"

"Those two men over there . . ."

"Where?" I followed his gaze and nearly panicked when I realized that he was referring to Alejandro's men.

"The two Mexicans. In the suits."

"Oh . . . what about them?" Shit. I'd thought I was heading at least toward a blow job in the bathroom with Martino, but now their presence was cramping my style.

"They must be following me."

"You?" I asked, stunned. "Why?"

"Things. Stuff with their boss. They must be onto me . . . somehow," he said, panic showing for the first time. "Look, I gotta get outta here before they find me. Now."

His sense of urgency swept over me. It made my hands tremble ever so slightly, and I almost dropped my glass.

"Let me help you," I said, my mind racing. What the hell had I stumbled into? I needed to know more. I had a feeling that my life depended on it.

Orlando

41

It had been seventy-two hours since Miguel's death, and there was no doubt in my mind that it was just a matter of time before all hell broke loose. From what I could see when my newly assigned driver and bodyguard turned into the garage at Uncle Lou's auto repair shop, that time was now. To make matters worse, I'd just received a blocked call from Ruby, during which she proceeded to drop a bomb on my head.

"Orlando, did you hear me?" Ruby asked, her accent heavier than ever.

"Yeah, I heard you," I said, though her words went in one ear and out the other. I was too pre-occupied with the scene of carnage before me as I got out of the car.

"What happened?" I yelled.

"Motherfuckers sprayed us, O!" Junior yelled, his T-shirt smeared in crimson as he and Sihad carried the still body from his bullet-riddled and smoking Trans Am.

"Orlando . . . I'm pregnant," Ruby repeated again. This time I heard her. The noise and commotion continued around me, but I tuned it out. Ruby's words hit me like a left hook.

I turned away from my brother. "Are you sure?"

"Orlando! What are you doing?" Junior yelled, bringing my attention back to the situation at hand.

"Of course I'm sure," Ruby answered at almost the same time as Junior's grunt. "I know my body. I'm two weeks late, and I'm never late. This isn't my first time being pregnant, Orlando."

"I have to call you back. We've got sort of an emergency here, but we'll deal with it, baby. Trust me." I was supremely shocked but unable to process the news at the moment. There was far too much chaos for even me to handle.

"Orlando!" Junior yelled.

"Deal with it?" Ruby snapped, her disgust far from concealed. "Fuck you. I knew I shouldn't have called you. You're just like the rest. Don't worry. I'll deal with the baby on my own."

I wanted to apologize, tell her that it had just come out wrong, but Uncle Lou, LC's brother, lay dead on the ground at my feet. His eyes were still open and they were accusing me. Junior knelt down and closed them with his blood-stained fingers.

Without a good-bye, I hit the button to end my call. I was undoubtedly doing damage to my budding relationship, but I couldn't concern myself with that now.

"What happened?" I asked Junior.

"We were hittin' the streets. Like you said to do," Junior replied, still out of breath. "We were out there searching for our stolen shit. One of Lou's boys had a tip, so he went with me to check it out. Lou felt he needed to be out there again, you know, trying to help as best he could. He knew how bad things were. The tip turned out to be a dead end, so we came back to the shop—and this happened. They were laying for us, O. No doubt this was a setup."

"Who did it?" I asked.

"Dunno, bro. Old car pulled alongside us when we were parked. They just unloaded on us. We had no time to react. Couldn't even see their faces or nothin'. I was too busy tending to Lou, otherwise I woulda chased 'em."

"What the fuck are we doin'?" Sihad yelled, taking shit hard. Boy probably thought he was immune from such violence since coming up from the ranks. "My boys talkin' about defectin', and now our own people settin' us up and sellin' us out. Who the fuck is in charge around here, anyway?"

"Certainly not you. Now, shut your fuckin' mouth!" I yelled, still trying to process the fact that I was going to be a father while everything else was in jeopardy. The last thing I needed was Sihad's played-out act.

Sihad came at me, all common sense gone. Junior went to make a move, but the look I gave him held him in place. Two more steps closer and I coldcocked Sihad with the nine millimeter I had begun carrying everywhere for protection. Sometimes a direct statement was needed with insubordinate employees. Sihad added to the blood on the floor of the warehouse with his own, the fresh gash on his forehead spewing a fine mist.

"You's a weak-ass bitch, yo!" Sihad cried out from the floor, where he held his bleeding face. As I raised the gun to strike him again, Junior kicked him, eliciting a yelp from Sihad, like a wounded dog being punished by his owner.

"You lucky my pop likes you, or I'd put a bullet in your head!" I yelled.

"We lost Pablo, now Lou. Control yourself before you join them," my brother warned, towering over our mouthy lieutenant.

Then things got even worse as three new visitors entered the garage. It was unsafe for him to be here, but LC walked in anyway, with two bodyguards shielding him. The bodyguards refused to put their guns away until absolutely certain there were no threats around.

"What the hell is going on here?" LC asked, noticing that Junior was pulling Sihad up off the floor.

The shop fell silent. We were all too embarrassed that things had devolved to this point, that we had let down our leader. We solemnly moved aside as Pop took slow, deliberate steps toward his brother's body.

He knelt down and placed his hand on Lou's heart. The little brother who had come up in the game beside Pop was now lying motionless in front of him. In a low voice, Pop spoke somber words of parting. It was a sentimental side of our father rarely witnessed by any of us.

"Who did this?" Pop finally asked, still on a knee. He kept his head down, depriving anyone of the opportunity to see the pain that had to be etched on his face.

"We don't know," I said, embarrassed to have been saying that way too often these days.

"Oh, I think I do. Dash was right," Pop said, his voice cracking under the strain. The sound of it had me fearful of what was to come. "No more. No more Mr. Nice Guy," he chanted, his words sounding like drumbeats to a war slowly building.

As Junior tried to console Pop and convince him to go back home, I stepped away to place a call.

"Yo."

"Where are you?" I asked Paris.

"On the ground. Palm trees, sunshine, and movie stars. Oh, Crips and Bloods too. La-di-da."

"You got him yet?" I followed up, cutting through the fluff.

"No, but I'm on his trail as we speak," she answered. I heard car noise in the background.

"Hurry. Uncle Lou's dead and Pop's about to go scorched earth. If you don't get him soon, Rio's gonna be collateral damage."

Harris

42

"I want you to reach out to the Italians again," LC said after summoning me to his office at the dealership.

"Me?" I asked, incredulous. "I'm just—"

"Part of this family," LC said swiftly. It took a moment for his words to sink in and for me to understand that he was saying I was part of this family, not theirs. With everything that had been happening, it was normal for a little paranoia to be creeping in, wasn't it?

LC continued, "And they think they have some kind of connection with you, so let's use it. Thank them for reaching out."

"Okay," I said, trying not to sound hesitant. The last thing I wanted to do was spend more time in the company of Sal Dash and his Mob associates.

"There's more," my father-in-law said, motioning for me to make sure his office door was closed firmly and that no one was eavesdropping. I should have known that wasn't all he wanted of me. There was always more when it came to LC and his orders. "We're about to move on Alejandro's organization through our California affiliates."

"Really? I mean . . . at a time like this? A war on both coasts? If this spills out onto the streets and the general public gets wind of this, it will be disastrous. We're talking about everything you've worked so hard to build going up in flames," I argued, doing my best to make him see the downside of this course of action without pissing the man off.

"You think it's still about my shipment, Harris? It's not. Lou's dead. They killed my brother. Took him out in a drive-by. And they almost got Junior. Now they're going to kill Rio—if they haven't already. We're already beyond disaster, boy."

"Are you sure it's the Mexicans? Alejandro and them?" I asked, needing to hear it.

"Yes. What Dash was saying makes sense, as much as I hate to admit it. If I'd had that info earlier, I would've never sent Rio to L.A."

I had never seen LC second-guess a decision before, but I had a sense that was what was going on as he dropped his head and went silent for a second.

When he looked up again, he said, "The Mexicans have been playing us for fools all along, while slowly working the edges of our organization. Pablo probably had some deal with them that ended when he got cold feet or outlived his usefulness."

If they were killing lieutenants, and if Pablo's killing was tied in, then LC's dream of getting away to Florida with my mother-in-law was now a pipe dream. This was going to take his life in years, if not through bullets.

"Do you trust Dash?" he asked me.

I hesitated, unsure what he was implying. How much could you trust a Mafia boss, especially considering the history of competition between his camp and ours? Especially when you had the history of him and me.

LC must have read my puzzled expression. He said, "You're a lawyer. You saw the man up close. Do you think he's a liar?"

"Yes," I replied without hesitation this time. "But that doesn't mean he was lying about what he said."

"Hmm. I agree," LC said, then went briefly silent again, deep thoughts consuming him. "I want you to assure Dash that any aggression that might spill over near their interests or within their boundaries is purely unintentional. Tell him we are looking to do business with the Italians and welcome him and his people as allies."

"Got it," I said as I prepared to leave. More contact was not something I wanted when it came to Dash, especially after I'd been promised absolution from my father's debt back in Maryland. Out of sight, out of mind was how I wanted to be with Dash, but this whole mess wasn't going to allow me that comfort.

"And another thing," LC added as he tapped a pencil like a drumstick on his desk calendar.

"Yes?" I asked, waiting for the other shoe to drop.

"Whatever's wrong with you and my daughter, I want you to fix it. It's not good for my granddaughter. Nor my trust factor."

I considered some methodical response. Maybe some laid-out, scholarly argument. Instead, after a long pause, I surrendered a simple, "Yes, sir."

London

43

"I'm sorry about canceling the other day," Tony said, holding me tightly. "And glad I got to make it up to you."

"I'm risking a lot by coming here," I remarked as I placed several kisses across his muscular chest.

He lifted my face so he could look in my eyes. "Why? Your husband suspects?"

"No. He's too busy with his head up my father's ass to notice. That and the bitch he's fucking keep his mind totally off me." I felt pitiful admitting that to him, but as usual, Tony did what he could to lift my spirits.

He joked, "Lucky for me, I guess."

Unfortunately, I was too preoccupied to relax. When I didn't respond to his gentle kiss, he asked, "What's wrong, baby?"

"Family. Things are a little crazy at home—besides my marriage. Security concerns. I'm pissing a lot of folks off by ditching my detail to meet with you."

"Whoa. Security detail?" He leaned on one elbow and looked down at me. "A rich girl, eh? I figured that with that expensive Mercedes of yours and the nice clothes you wear, but rich, like security-detail rich, I had no idea."

"Don't judge me." I sighed and turned my head away from his inquiring eyes. "I would trade it all in for a nice, quiet life away from it all. Once upon a time, I thought I'd get that."

"Maybe you still can. With me," he said, and I felt him beginning to harden again under the sheets as he rubbed his legs against mine.

"Look," I said, "that's sweet of you to say, but I have no illusions about what this is between us."

"I understand. Me neither." He began to stroke my hair. "The last thing I want to do is cause more problems for you and your family. So, if this ever becomes too much for you to handle, just let me know. I'll back off. I promise."

I turned to give him a kiss. "Don't worry. I don't plan on asking you to go anywhere. You're the only real break I get these days."

Mercifully, he changed the subject. "Speaking of family, how's that sweet girl of yours?"

"Mariah's doing fine. She's at school right now. She still talks about you since that day, you know."

"I was just glad I was able to render assistance, m'lady," Tony commented in jest.

"What time is it, anyway?" I asked. "I don't want to be late picking her up."

"It's early still," he said, putting a hand on my shoulder to send a subtle signal that he wanted me to stay put in the bed with him. "I'll make sure you get there on time. What school is she at?"

"Ralston Academy."

"Yeah," he said, "I've heard of it. I think my sister was looking into that place for her kids."

I raised an eyebrow. "Really?" Ralston was a historically black institution.

"Yeah. What's so funny about that?" Tony asked, looking genuinely confused.

Shit. I had no intention of getting into another discussion of race, like the one we'd had about hair on our first date. And I had the perfect way to change the subject.

"Oh, nothing," I said as I took Tony's penis in my hand and stroked him.

"Mmmm," he moaned with a grin, sinking into the mattress as he relaxed.

I slid beneath the sheets and took him in my mouth. Cradling his sac in my hands, I was slurping mightily, and from the sounds of appreciation above, I knew I was doing my job right.

I heard Tony's phone vibrate and felt his body twist and shift on the mattress as he reached out to retrieve it. I kept sliding my wet mouth up and down his shaft, daring him to try to hold a conversation while I sucked him.

"Hello?" He tried to move to exit the bed, but I purposely let him feel the slight grazing of my teeth on the tip of his dick—my way of telling him to stay put. I gripped the sides of his hips and went at it with no hands. I bobbed my head as I sucked his dick even harder, playfully trying to fuck with his concentration.

"Thanks. We appreciate that. Um . . . when? Uh-huh. Uh-huh. No . . . I'm fine. I'll check with my boss and let you know about his availability."

"What's her name?" I asked, poking my head out of the sheets as he ended the conversation.

"No, it's not another woman. Just business. One of the prospective stores we've been courting for expansion wants to meet with my boss again. I think we've come to an understanding."

"So it's good news?"

"Yeah. No . . . fuck yeah," he said, correcting himself with a big grin similar to some of the joy I'd brought to his face before. "Our plans are really coming together."

"Then why did you sound like you wanted to get off the phone?"

"Uh, because you were sucking my dick. Some things are a little more pressing—and a lot more satisfying," Tony said just prior to flipping me over and penetrating me again with that wonderful dick of his.

And for an hour longer, I was free of the violent specter of death hovering over our family.

A part of me wanted to check Tony's phone later, to view the number and see if he was lying to me, as Harris had done repeatedly. But then I realized it didn't matter. Like I said, I had no illusions about this particular relationship. Worrying about the fidelity of one man was enough for me. I would keep this fling simple: no questions asked and no worries. Just what I needed.

Rio

44

"Oh my, they do look pretty scary, don't they?" As hot as he was, I'd just determined that Martino was a damn punk. He looked terrified by my two Mexican friends. "You sure they're after you?"

"Do those motherfuckers look like they belong in a gay bar?" Martino replied. "Of course they're after me. They work for the guy I'm spying on. That son of a bitch I got on the inside must have ratted me out."

As scared as he was, I wasn't about to alleviate his terror and tell him that Alejandro's men were really after me. He was a gift from heaven that had suddenly fallen into my lap, and he could quite possibly get me home and back into LC's good graces without even breaking a fingernail.

"Christ Almighty," he said in a voice made breathless with fear. "They're gonna kill me."

"Not if I can help it. I haven't even had any of that tasty dick yet." I stood up from my bar stool. "C'mon, I'll get you outta here." I pulled Martino along. Usually, I relished being the center of attention, but at a time like this, I wished my hair weren't dyed quite so blond. It made me too easy to spot in here.

I faked a sudden move to my right, somewhat shielding Martino in an effort to play along with his notion. Both of Alejandro's men bit on my action, waking from their dazed stupor and flinching to attention. They were trained too well, neither one overcommitting as they maintained their spacing to keep me pinned in their sights.

Rather than waiting for me to make another move, Martino panicked and darted out from behind me, heading toward the back of the club. With his distraction, they pivoted toward the potential new threat to them. When this happened, the one to my left suddenly fell over, clutching his chest. His surprised partner reacted to the unseen threat the only way he knew how, by whipping out his gun. This sent the whole club into a panic and stampeding for the front door. I now had a wave of bodies momentarily between me and Alejandro's remaining man.

I ran out the back door a few seconds behind Martino. I found him scrambling down the alley, and I screamed for him to wait the fuck up. When he saw it was me, he gladly halted for a moment to catch his breath.

"What happened back there? I thought you were right behind me." He stood panting, hunched over with his hands on his knees.

"I . . . I held them off. Got the drop on one of 'em," I said, sucking wind and lying my ass off. I didn't know what happened to the one that keeled over, but I wasn't complaining. "But the other one is still coming."

"Thank you." He stood erect and loosened his collar. "If they found me, then that means everything's blown up. I gotta get back to my hotel, grab my shit, and get back to New York."

"Well, they've seen me helping you, so I'm leaving if you're leaving!" I said, doing my best damsel in distress for his benefit. All that was missing was for me to bat some false eyelashes.

"C'mon," he said.

When we turned to resume our escape, two shots landed near us. I yelped, feeling flakes of brick separate from the wall and ricochet across my cheek, leaving bloody scratches on my pretty face. It was the other one of Alejandro's men, storming down the alley in pursuit. He was still aiming at us, and I was sure he did not intend to miss again.

"Run!" I yelled.

There was another shot, and then Martino grunted in pain. I looked behind me to see that he'd been shot in the lower back. He reached out his arm toward me.

"Go . . . let's go. I'll be all right," he urged, grimacing in pain.

With me yanking on his arm, Martino got up to a pretty good pace.

We ran as fast as we could toward the end of the alley, quickly cutting across a parking lot and then into a neighborhood bustling with pedestrian traffic. I hoped we could get lost, at least temporarily, in the crowd. We dipped into another alleyway so Martino could catch his breath.

"Do you have a gun?" I asked, figuring it was somewhere on him based on his job description.

"No. Stupid on my part," Martino replied as he reached toward his back to check how bad it was. "It's back at the room. No one knew I was going to be here. I didn't think I'd need it. Just trying to enjoy a little downtime, like I said."

His trembling hand came out with a good bit of blood from his wound.

"We need to get off the streets. Is your hotel nearby?" I had to get this guy to a safe place and get him talking before he passed out from blood loss.

He told me where his hotel was, and we scurried across the intersection, hustling past a hamburger joint and a dry cleaner. I kept looking over my shoulder, and so far, it looked like Alejandro's man hadn't spotted us. All the couples out strolling on this warm night had provided cover.

As we passed the high-end boutiques, I did my best to act as if we were drunk lovers window-shopping. I pretended I was hugging him, when I was really just trying to bear the big lug's weight. By the time we'd reached Melrose Avenue, fear of dying in a hail of bullets had gripped me in near paralysis, yet I pressed on. I had no choice. If our reduced speed didn't allow Alejandro's man to catch up, the trail of blood drops running down Martino's leg might.

My brothers and sisters were better at this sort of thing. Me? I just went haphazardly along tonight, trying to outthink a professional killer while not giving in to the panic ripping my gut apart. As we crossed Melrose, I decided to take a wild right on Rangely Avenue. We used the tree-lined residential street to give us some cover, hoping every car, tree, bush, and shrub would afford us some protection if he was still following.

When I saw the hotel, I could still hear the police sirens back around The Pink Lion as they fanned out over the area. I considered getting us arrested, as it would get Martino the medical attention he needed and would get me out of Alejandro's reach for a minute. But I quickly dismissed that idea, because I was sure Alejandro would have someone on payroll on the police force, and then I'd be without whatever information Martino possessed. And I did believe he possessed some.

I led Martino into the hotel and up to his room; then I quickly got us behind closed doors. Inside the room, I removed his shirt and had him lie on the bed while I wet a towel to wipe the bloody wound. I didn't really know what the fuck to do, but I talked a good game to keep him from panicking.

After double-checking the locks on the door and peeking out the curtain, I struck up a conversation with a semi-delirious Martino as I went about trying to tend to his wound.

"Why you out here, baby? Least you can do is tell Rio why that man's trying to kill us."

"He . . . he works for Alejandro Zuniga," he said through teeth gritted in pain. "I—I gotta call in. Let 'em know I'm safe . . . thanks to you. Give . . . give me my phone."

"I'll get your phone in a minute, but you need to lay still, okay? I used to be a nurse. Let me take care of this," I urged. Of course, I'd never been a nurse a day in my life, but it sounded good. "Your boss let you come out here with these crazy mofos?" I asked as I tended to the blood steadily trickling from the hole in his back. We had only so many clean towels, and the comforter was already ruined.

"Yeah, I got somebody inside their organization. Paying him for info. Found out the beaner's shippin' crazy shit to these niggers back in New York," he said.

Humph. Guess his delirious ass didn't know that just because I was gay didn't mean I suddenly wasn't black. My previous crush on this fool was now officially over. Not only was he on the down low, but he was also a racist who liked to fuck black men. What kind of self-hating faggot was he? I made a mental note that if this racist faggot survived, I would make sure to literally bite his dick off.

"Hold still. I think I can get it out." I dug a finger into Martino's wound, acting like I was searching for the bullet. Really I was just punishing his racist ass. He let out a loud grunt, which brought a smile to my face. "Sorry," I said, containing a giggle. "Shippin' shit? Like stolen car parts?"

"Nooooo. Drugs. Coke. Heroin. Heavy shit, Rio. But get this. Niggers didn't get their shit," he said, laughing even through his pain. "My boss used the info I got out of the beaner over here, and he jacked the shipment once it got back east."

"Niggers and beaners ain't comin' after you and your paisans over it?" I asked. Incredibly, he totally missed the irony in my tone.

"Nah," he answered. He was so proud of the work he'd done for his boss that he suddenly seemed to regain some strength as he explained, "No one knows we knew about the shipment, so each side thinks the other's lying. We're turnin' them against each other, and then we just wait to pick up the pieces. Some beautiful, wicked shit my boss thought of. When it's over with the niggers, our guy out here will be in charge of Zuniga's old operations on the West Coast. And I get more trips out here to keep an eye on things." He turned his head to try to look at me. "You wanna move out here with me? We could go out and party every night. Fuck 'n shit, and nobody would know."

I wanted to slap this silly-ass fool. "Doesn't seem like it's gonna happen now, Martino, since Zuniga's men came after you in the club. Remember? They shot at us."

"Y-yeah, you're right. Damn," he said, his voice trailing off as either the blood loss or shock began to take over. "Our guy musta gave us up and told his boss everything. That's how those Mexicans knew to follow me out tonight. Aw. Everything's fucked now."

"That bastard."

"Yeah. As much money and pussy as we supplied him with. We should cut off his dick and feed it to the dogs. I . . . I really gotta call my boss, I think. He's gonna be pissed."

"What's the guy's name?"

"My boss? We call him Mr. Dash. Respect, y'know," Martino rambled, his eyes barely open now. I couldn't believe how much information he was giving up so easily. I figured he must be in shock.

"Noooo. The guy inside Zuniga's organization. That double-crossin' bastard who sent them to kill you. What's his name? If I get out of this alive, I'm gonna kill him myself."

"Oh. We call him Road Map."

I mean, this was just too damn easy. I felt like a detective on some television drama the way I was getting this dumb ass to spill his guts—figuratively and literally.

"Road Map? What the fuck kinda name is that?"

"He got jacked-up skin," Martino said with a groan as he tried to laugh. "Face look like a . . ."

"Road map?" I said, completing his sentence for him.

"Yeeeeah, you got it. Now . . . hand me my phone. I'ma send somebody to help get us outta here. Just won't tell 'em about us or where I was at. I'll say you were a Good Samaritan 'n shit."

Yeah. A blond, gay brother in the hotel with the supposedly straight Martino. Like they wouldn't kill my ass on sight if I let him send his boys over. Now it made sense to me why he was so loose with his tongue. He probably figured telling me wouldn't hurt, because I wouldn't be around to share it with anybody.

I took his phone, looking through numbers in the directory first. Then I placed a call of my own.

"Hey, O. It's me."

"Rio? Thank God. You need to get as far away from Alejandro and them as you can. Pop just had both his brothers killed. In retaliation for Uncle Lou's death."

"Uncle Lou's dead?"

He hesitated, then said quietly, "Yeah, man. Lou's dead."

"Oh, shit. So I guess I'm next."

"Not if I can help it. Now, I need to know exactly where the fuck you are, man. I got Paris on the ground, looking for you."

"Hotel Beverly Terrace on North Doheny, room three forty-eight," I said. "And tell her to hurry. The block is hot, O, and they're out to get me."

I hung up. Once I got out of immediate danger, I'd call Orlando again and tell him everything I'd just learned about the Italians setting us up.

"Who was that?" Martino asked, a surge of consciousness allowing him to raise his head.

"I just called your people for you and told them where we're at. They said for you to lay still and they're on their way."

"Damn. I owe you my life. Still wish we coulda fucked tonight."

"Yeah. That woulda been some incredible shit," I said with an eye roll.

With a crash, the door flew open. Shit. Martino's blood drops must have led him right to the hotel. I tried to use Martino's phone again, but our pursuer pointed his barrel dead at me.

"No . . . w-wait," I stuttered as I slowly lowered the phone. Martino groaned as he tried to turn over in our direction. "He . . . he needs medical attention."

With rolled-up sleeves exposing the extensive ink down his forearms, he brought his aim in Martino's direction. He fired two shots into Martino, killing him on the spot. Before I could yell or scream, he turned his gun back toward me.

This was it. I closed my eyes, not wanting to know when the fatal shot was coming.

"If it was up to me, I'd kill you right now," he hissed. "But Alejandro wants to see you. You're one lucky fuckin' maricón."

I kept my hands up in the air as I opened my eyes and glanced at Martino, who hadn't been nearly as lucky. It looked like Alejandro's man didn't realize who Martino was or his significance. Our meeting up and his saving me was really a crazy coincidence, but I was alive because of it—something that didn't make Alejandro's man too happy.

"Of course, he didn't say nothing about your condition when I deliver you," he scoffed just before he cracked me upside my skull with his gun.

As everything faded to black, the only thing I could think of was that I hoped LC was proud of me. I was unconscious before I hit the floor.

Paris

45

"Awww, fuck me!" I'd arrived at the hotel on the edge of Beverly Hills too late. The kicked-in door and the dead white man on the bed were clues that I was in the right room, just at the wrong time. I must have just missed them, though, because no one had discovered this mess yet. A cell phone lay on the carpet. I picked it up and checked the call history.

The last call was to Orlando's number. I hit the button to redial.

"Rio!" Orlando yelled.

"Guess again," I replied. "I got here too late. There's one dead dude on the bed. All ventilated. Whoever he was, I guess he wasn't important. No Rio in sight. That's a good sign, I think. I mean, who's to say the dead son of a bitch isn't the result of Rio's handiwork? Perhaps he's learned a thing or two from his li'l sis."

There was silence on the line for a second. Guess Orlando wasn't in the mood for jokes. Me, I preferred not to get too wound up, too serious, because it made me lose my focus.

"No," Orlando explained. "The only reason Rio isn't laying right there next to him is because he's the only chip they have left. They still think Miguel is alive. But with what Pop just did with the two brothers, I don't think they're gonna think that for long. You better find him, Paris. Find him and get the two of you home in one piece."

"A'ight, a'ight. I'll call you later," I remarked, taking one final look at the dead body before quickly exiting the room with the dude's phone.

At least I kinda knew what to look for—the black-tinted Suburban I'd tailed from Alejandro's dealership to West Hollywood. I just had to find it again. It was what led me to Rio inside The Pink Lion after I found it parked near a bunch of clubs and restaurants. Leave it to my brother to convince Alejandro's men to take him out to a gay bar before killing him.

Out of all the clubs and venues in the area, I went with the newest, shiniest one in sight, figuring that was where someone with Rio's tastes would be. And, of course, my instincts were right. Inside the club, I spotted the two goons pretty quickly as they tried unsuccessfully to blend in with the gay crowd. With no time to canvass the whole place, I had no idea how many more might be around, so I prepared to do some reconnaissance work.

Figuring I'd play the role of a lipstick lesbian, I found a nearby butch chick and approached her. From my vantage point at the bar, I could watch the goons while they watched my brother. I made some small talk with the lesbian and got her worked up over my boobies, which were peering over the top of my dress. Then I convinced her to show me around, taking a route past one of the thugs.

Dude was so out of place in a gay bar, and unlike me, he couldn't play gay, even for a minute. As I walked by with my fake date, he took notice. Bold motherfucker actually reached out to caress my free hand as I moved past him. It was just what I was hoping he'd do. The touch was just long enough for me to stick the prick with a prick of my own—a tiny needle to his wrist that I'd concealed in my hand. Probably felt like a static shock to him, or the electricity that existed between us in his deluded mind.

It was going to take a minute or two for the poison to make its way to his heart. So, after only a few more steps with my impromptu companion, I suddenly declined my "tour," leaving her to curse me out as a fickle bitch.

I was moving into position to take out the other goon when his partner keeled over, grasping his chest. Rio suddenly bolting threw a monkey wrench into my plans. When I got caught in the stampede of bodies fleeing the building, I was unable to move, swept up in the sea of people rushing for the front door. I watched my remaining target take off in the direction of Rio and the soon-to-be dead dude from the hotel. I waited outside the club with the rest of the confused and curious, but neither Rio nor the Mexican exited my way.

By the time I made it around to the alley, no one was in sight, so I hopped in my rental and went driving in circles, trying to find that Suburban again. I got the lucky break I needed in the form of Orlando's call telling me to go to the hotel. As I left there now, I hoped I'd catch another lucky break, because I had no idea where Rio had gone.

On Santa Monica Boulevard, I decided to head back toward Alejandro's place as fast as I could. That was when I spotted the Suburban, just as it was about to enter the 405. Too many cars separated us to do anything, so I had to follow it onto the freeway. The closer I let the SUV get to Alejandro's turf south of here, the stickier the situation would be. I had to think fast. I had to think of something that would get my brother out of there without getting both of us killed.

As I shifted the Mustang GT and picked up speed, my mind went to a bad place. What if Rio was already dead? If anything happened to my brother, I would damn sure release my anger on more than just the guy driving the SUV. Shit, I'd take down the whole population of Mexicans in L.A. if I had to.

C'mon, girl. Stay focused, I reminded myself. Negativity wasn't helpful at the moment. I had to remember my training and keep my eyes on the prize.

Thinking on the fly, I switched lanes to the right and accelerated to overtake them. I stayed within the flow of traffic, gradually easing along-side so as to get a look, but the damn tint didn't yield much info for me. The only person I could see was the driver. I was pretty sure it was the one from the club that I didn't get to. I was re-solved to rectify that like a mutha now.

I let him get a look at me as I pretended to be texting while driving; then I reduced my speed to fall back ever so slightly. A loud pop rang out, followed by swerving as the right rear tire on his SUV blew out, courtesy of the shot from my Wal-ther .380. I moved the Mustang in his direction, guaranteeing the collision I was trying to accom-plish. With a wrenching crash, our vehicles made contact.

I clenched the wheel as I rode my car to a stop. Both cars were scraped up, and only one was drivable—mine. It was decision time. If he want-ed to escape, he'd need my car. If he wanted to stay, he would be calling for backup to come pick him up. When I saw him on his phone, I knew his decision. I needed to hurry. I didn't have enough firepower for a shoot-out on the 405.

"What's wrong with you?" I screamed, exiting the Mustang on the passenger's side. "I need your license, registration, and insurance!"

"You don't know how to drive, bitch?" he yelled back as he exited the Suburban in a huff and came around to inspect the damage. "Fuckin' textin'. I saw you!"

"And you fuckin' came over into my lane. Comprende, estúpido?"

"You got a fuckin' mouth on you. You know that?"

"Whatever. This mouth wants to see your insurance 'n shit. Same thing happened to my last car. Motherfucker drove off. Ain't happenin' this time," I said.

He shook his head, obviously wanting to strike me. With so many witnesses driving by, he restrained himself . . . for now. Then his eyes turned lustful. That caught me off guard a bit. I wasn't expecting that with the high pressure conditions he was under, but I guess transporting bodies, pulling guns out in clubs, and shooting up hotels was just another day for him. Wow. A potential soul mate? If that bitch didn't have my brother in there, maybe we . . . Oh, who was I kidding? We'd kill each other on our honeymoon. Literally.

"Tell you what. Give me your number, and I'll get your car fixed at our shop. Good as new, no charge. Plus a little cash for your inconvenience," he offered.

"For real? How am I supposed to believe you? You might be lyin' to a sista 'n shit," I said flirtatiously, playing in my hair and flashing my "you might get you some eventually" smile.

"Look, just give me your number. I'll have a tow truck come over now and take care of you."

"Okay. You sound like a man who knows what he's doin'. You got a pen on you? 'Cause I don't have one."

"Just give me the number and I'll put it in my phone."

"Nah, I don't trust that. You could put in the wrong number or just delete it. I wanna see you write it down on paper. Make it official. Old school. Like we in high school and you gonna ask me on a date." I was making this thug think we were truly vibing.

He smiled, then sighed as he looked back at the Suburban. It took him a minute to decide, but just like all men, he couldn't resist my charms in the end. As he walked toward his car, I followed on his heels.

"What's your name, anyway?" I asked. "Somethin' sexy soundin' I bet. I was just breakin' up with my man before you hit me."

"By text, huh?" he said with a laugh as he reached over into the center console. He still didn't give me a name.

Bet he'd tell me more if I let him hit it, I thought. I'd already let Miguel get some of this, though, and my rule was only one dick per organization. Too bad for this dude. Besides, I had much more important things to do at the moment, like getting my brother back.

Before he had a chance for more conversation, I wedged my gun up under his jaw.

"Is he alive?" I asked coolly as I removed his concealed handgun from his shoulder holster.

"Y-yeah," he said, straining to swallow with my barrel pressing into his trachea.

I tossed his gun over the freeway railing, then hit the button to unlock the passengers' doors. "Show me," I ordered.

When I let him stand, he was smiling again. Trying to dazzle me with charm still. "You can't be his girlfriend," he joked.

"What I am to him and what I am to you are irrelevant. Move," I said, shifting my gun to the base of his skull.

We walked to the rear, and I nudged him to make him move faster. I had to be gone from here soon. He opened the door just enough for me to see Rio lying in the back. He was bound with zip ties, with a knot as big as an egg in the middle of his forehead.

"See. Alive. We good?" he said.

"Totally," I replied as I pulled the trigger, sending my love through his brain.

Rio, semi-awake, must've heard my voice. He let out a shrill scream as Alejandro's man fell over beside him. I hated when he did that. Shit hurt my ears.

"Boy, shut the fuck up," I scolded as I yanked on him to sit up. "Once I get those zip ties off, we gotta move."

My warning to my brother couldn't have been more timely. As soon as I removed the ties from his wrists and ankles, I spotted a matching black Suburban coming up the 405 toward us. I doubted this one had only one occupant.

"Oh, shit! Rio, get to the Mustang." I had my brother, but we were still far from safe.

Orlando

46

After my conversation with Paris, I was even more worried. It was a risk sending her into an unknown situation, and now both of them were in danger. I didn't know who the dead guy in the hotel was, but the body count was racking up on both sides. It was already a foregone conclusion that LC was going to ream me out for keeping him in the dark, but he just might kill me if anything happened to Paris.

As I stood outside the bar, I stared at my phone, half expecting another call, another disaster, another fire to put out. But no call came, so I entered the bar to take care of another responsibility.

"You haven't been answering your phone," I said, interrupting Ruby's conversation with some young punk who was getting too friendly. I didn't bother acknowledging him.

"I've been busy too," she answered, gesturing to all the customers around the bar. She'd been working there as a bartender ever since she left

Remy and Maria. "You buying a drink?" she asked, her demeanor strictly business. She knew it would piss me off, and it did.

"Look. I didn't come here for bullshit chitchat. We're way beyond that. I need to talk to you."

"You need to talk, or we need to talk?" She wasn't about to give up the attitude she was giving me.

"We need to talk."

Ruby rolled her eyes before fixing them on me in a deadpan stare. "Now you have time," she said, overtly disgusted. "Maybe my life's not as important and urgent as you and your 'empire,' but it's something."

"I'm sorry. It's hard to explain, Ruby, but things are out of control. I'm just trying to keep my head on straight." I wanted to tell her everything, but it was safer for her if she didn't know.

"Then what you doin' at a bar, bro? Go home," busybody joked as he came way too far into my space. His breath didn't reek, so it was more simple asshole than alcoholic.

"Look. Can you take a break?" I asked Ruby as I continued to ignore her patron.

"No," she replied as she grabbed two chilled longnecks and popped their tops, plunging lime wedges into each. "Leave me alone." She strutted to the other end of the bar to serve another customer.

"See, I think the lady asked nicely," the man chimed in as he stood up from his seat.

"You don't know what you're getting into, so I suggest you butt out and sit your ass back down. Besides, she's pregnant with my child. Being the big hero won't benefit you," I warned.

"You really slept with this asshole, Ruby?" he said loudly across the bar.

Ruby turned in embarrassment at the sound of his voice.

I shoved the man, and of course, he shoved me back. Fed up with the silliness, I swung on him and connected. Unfortunately, the boy was one of those wrestling types that liked to grapple and wear you down. He tried to bear-hug me before I did damage.

Ruby came from around the bar, hurriedly separating us just as I was about to bust him in the head with a nearby bottle.

"Stop! Stop!" she shouted as some of the other staff gathered.

I wasn't about to stop, though. With the problems in my life, my stress level was maxed out. If that meant that I was going to have to bust this dude's ass at Ruby's place of business, then so be it.

"You don't know who you're fuckin' with!" I yelled, jabbing my finger in the air toward his face.

"Whatever, man," he conceded, throwing his hands up and walking away in search of his lost buzz. "They got better drinks and better-lookin' women across the street."

"You're fuckin' crazy, you know that?" Ruby scolded as she slapped the open palms of her hands into my chest. "A madman."

"You make me crazy," I said, sulking. "Please. Just talk to me." I grasped her hand. "Okay?" I needed to fix this part of my life so I could focus on the business.

Ruby looked mad enough to slap me, but I didn't care, because I deserved it. "Lisa, can you cover for me for a sec?" she asked the redhead who was still manning the bar. Her coworker nodded, and Ruby motioned for me to follow her as she went on break.

Outside, I offered her my jacket, but she refused. She just stood there with her arms tightly folded, bouncing up and down to stay warm. She couldn't even look me in the eyes.

"All this fuckin' stress. Gawd, I need a smoke," she said.

"Wouldn't be good for the baby," I noted.

She stopped her bouncing, suddenly immune to the effects of the weather. She stared at me with a blank expression, said nothing for a moment, then, "I'm getting an abortion."

My stomach did a flip. "What? Why?"

"Notice you didn't tell me not to," she noted with a sad smile. "I'm too old for this. I'm already doing the single mom thing after one failed relationship. And you've already shown me that you don't have time for me . . . or this baby."

"And that needs to change," I said quickly. "I'll admit that I'm not ready for this. But who really is? I wanna try to make this work. For real. But, Ruby, my life is dangerous, and you need to understand what that means."

Just as I thought I saw a hint of reconciliation in Ruby's eyes, my phone rang. Talk about fucked-up timing. I motioned to Ruby that I had to take it. She shrugged, that angry scowl returning to her face. At least she didn't storm off.

I was hoping it was Paris reporting back, but it was Junior.

"Yeah," I said, keeping my eye on Ruby so she wouldn't leave.

"Pops wants to know where Paris is and why she won't answer her phone. He also wants to reach out to the El Salvadorans. Apply some pressure out west in retaliation. Where are you?" my older brother asked.

"I'll have to call you back. I'm with my woman," I replied, to which Ruby frowned.

I abruptly hung up. They'd have to get along without me for a moment. My relationship with Ruby needed immediate attention. The family could wait; my ambition would have to wait even longer.

"You acknowledging me to your family now, Orlando?" she asked, her features softening a bit, giving me a glimmer of hope.

"Yeah. I need to if I'm really as serious as I feel. I want you to have the baby. Our baby."

I was going to be a father. No matter how hard it was, I would make it work, and I'd be a good one.

London

47

"Just wait here."

"You keep leaving us behind," my bodyguard said. "Ma'am, our orders are—"

"I don't care what your orders are," I said, cutting off the man who was supposed to protect me. "I'm not walking into my daughter's school with armed men. That's where I draw the line. I still want Mariah to at least think she's having a normal childhood. Do I make myself clear?"

"Yes, ma'am," they both agreed, no attitude apparent. One exited the vehicle and went around to open my door for me.

"But we'll pull up to the entrance when you come out," he informed me as I exited.

I smiled and nodded, allowing them at least the appearance that they were in control. It was a two-way street, after all. They hadn't told on me yet, so I let them feel like they were doing their job, even though I'd been ditching them pretty often to be with Tony lately.

I entered the school and signed in to pick up Mariah. Even though they knew me, they always asked for identification, which I didn't mind at all. A lot of wealthy parents sent their children here, so nothing was taken for granted.

"Any problems with my baby today?" I asked Miss Abernathy, the head administrator. I could swear the woman had a computer inside her head the way she remembered everyone.

"None at all, Mrs. Grant," she replied. "Just the usual sweet bundle of energy. Want to kiss her to death."

I grinned, thinking how glad I was that Mariah had such a joyful spirit. Looking at how Paris and I turned out, I sometimes wondered if perhaps my baby had been switched at birth.

After a few minutes, Mariah was delivered to me, her uniform still clean despite her love of cookies.

"Hi, Mommy!" She jumped into my outstretched arms for a kiss.

"How was your day?" I asked as I led her outside and down the stairs to where our escort waited.

"Good," she said, making that adorable face of hers. It meant she was about to ask for something. Maybe she was related to Paris, after all. "Dora's coming to town. Ayanna told me. Her mommy's taking her and her sister. Can we go see Dora too?"

I pretended to consider her request, even though I already knew my answer. "As long as you promise to behave, we might be able to do that," I said, squatting down to face her and adjust her shirt collar in a motherly fashion. Of course I would take my daughter, but I had to teach her that you couldn't just get anything you wanted. My daughter would not be growing up to be like my spoiled sister.

"Thank you, thank you, thank you," she gushed, hugging me tightly.

I buckled her into her car seat, and we headed away from the school. As soon as the car was moving, Mariah had another request. "Can we go see Grandpa today?"

"No, baby. Grandpa is kinda busy today."

Saying he was busy was an understatement. As bad as things were sounding, I wondered if maybe I should head out to the Hamptons, or perhaps Florida, to get my daughter clear of what was becoming a militarized zone at the mansion. It bothered me that I should have to be thinking of those plans on my own. Harris was supposed to be the man of the family. Pity he hadn't considered moving us out of there long ago.

At the red light, a scraggly-looking panhandler was coming up to cars with a bucket in hand. I wasn't paying him any mind, until he became aggressive at our window. The driver motioned for him to go on, but the man in the old army jacket and cheap sunglasses kept knocking.

"C'mon, help a vet out," he chided our driver as he shook his bucket again.

"If you blast his ass, he'll stop," the other escort joked, until he remembered Mariah was present. "Oh. Sorry, Mrs. Grant," he offered as he looked back, regaining his professional demeanor.

The man continued knocking even after the light ahead turned green. Traffic had snarled in front of us, so we had no escape from his persistence.

"I'ma just give him some change so he can be on his way," our driver said.

"Ain't he in the wrong part of town?" our other escort joked, leaning over to better see the panhandler.

"Probably makes more money on this side," our driver joked.

"Bless you, sir," the man said before the window was fully down. He tilted his bucket inward, giving us a glimpse of his success—several crumpled dollars. As our driver reached to drop some loose change, his head suddenly exploded, sending a gruesome spray of blood onto the dashboard. The shotgun blast that killed our driver had rung out from the bottom of the panhandler's bucket, peppering the front cab with pellets and torn remnants of the dollar bills.

I screamed and covered Mariah's eyes, trying to shield her from the horrible sight of the twitching body slumped over the steering wheel.

"Oh, shit!" The bodyguard in the passenger's seat reached for his gun. That was when I noticed the three ski-masked men coming up along both sides of our van. I screamed for him to look out, but he didn't have a chance as they sent a hail of bullets in his direction. The poor man howled in pain from the pellets that ripped into his body.

Mariah was my sole concern now, and I unhooked her seat belt as fast as I could. One of the masked men turned his gaze inside the van, toward us, and motioned to cease fire. In addition to my daughter's sobbing, I could hear people outside as they screamed and ran for cover.

When the man reached to open the door, I kicked against it with all my might. It came open, bowling him over. I yanked Mariah up with me and darted out of the van.

I bounded over the downed man, holding Mariah like a sack of potatoes. He reached up and grabbed my ankle. Robbed of my momentum, I suddenly tumbled forward. My poor daughter fell from my grasp, yelping in pain as she bounced off the concrete. I went down face-first near her feet.

As the other masked men and the panhandler came around, I tried to get up and grasp a hysterical Mariah. Instead, I was viciously stomped and tumbled back down to the ground again.

"Mommy!" Mariah shrieked. My poor baby. The panhandler chambered another round with his shotgun and took aim at me, smiling with pride over being the most effective of them all.

"No," said the one who'd just stomped me, commanding my would-be executioner to stop. "Get the girl."

"No . . . no! No!" I pleaded as I crawled toward Mariah, her arms outstretched and begging for me. I was shoved aside as I watched my daughter get scooped up by one of them.

"Mommyyy!" My panic-stricken daughter screamed just before they covered her mouth and threw her into an old van that had driven alongside us. The masked one in charge quickly followed them.

Adrenaline took over, and I rose to my feet, quickly closing the distance behind him. He swiftly turned around, as if sensing my approach. He had to know a mother wouldn't just give up, despite the odds.

"Don't be stupid," he said as he pointed a nine millimeter at me. "She won't be hurt as long as you do what we want," he said in a voice that was both chilling and calming, for reasons unbeknownst to me.

"What do you want? Whatever it is, I'll give it to you." I could still hear her muffled screams, yet I was powerless to advance.

"We'll be in touch." When he turned and jumped into the van to leave, I swiftly lunged at him, stabbing him in the back with the pen I'd snagged off the floor while shielding Mariah.

"Ow! You black bitch!" he yelled as he swiveled and kicked me dead in my stomach. I fell over, barely able to breathe as the van's doors shut.

"Mariah . . . ," I called out before succumbing to the pain. Curled up in the fetal position, I helplessly watched them pull off as tears streamed down my face.

Rio

48

"Rio! You okay?" Paris reached over from the driver's seat to feel if I had any bullet holes in me. The Suburban that had just shot at us had been joined by another, following in close pursuit, probably trying to herd us into a trap.

"No, dammit! Will you keep your eyes on the road?" I pleaded, trying to open my eyes sparingly. Even if it was keeping me alive, her intense driving was making me sick to my stomach. Just let it end already, I prayed.

"Bro, I'm almost out of gas. And these putas know L.A. too well for me."

"What are you saying?" I almost yelped as we took another freeway exit at speeds way in excess of the limit.

"Three options," she said, calmly checking the rearview mirror.

"Other than dying right here? Okay, I'm listening."

"One, I get the po-pos involved and we go to jail. Their helicopters are gonna be out soon anyway. News choppers, too. But that doesn't mean we don't get shot up before the arrest."

"On the plus side, we'd be famous," I offered. "And maybe die on camera. Next option."

"Two, I go somewhere crowded like a mall, and we probably get away. Probably. But it would be wet for civilians. Very wet," she said. "Don't matter to me, 'cause I'm down for whatever."

"Going out as baby-killers. Tasty. And the final one?"

"We find somewhere secluded, like under the freeway, and play hide-and-seek. Give me a chance to do what I do. Pop, pop, pop. Can't guarantee that one, though, 'cause I didn't do any advance recon. All I can say is I'll do my best, bro. Maybe we get lucky and my team gets here before it's over."

I opened my eyes just in time to see that we were drifting sideways into oncoming traffic on Venice Boulevard. I clenched the door handle in a death grip and stifled a scream, squirming at the sight of passing cars swerving to avoid us.

Once we straightened out and got back into the correct lane, I reached over and touched my sister's arm, acknowledging my choice to her.

"Suit yourself," she said, although I knew my sister well enough to know she would have picked the same one with or without my input.

The SUVs drew closer, and one of the drivers shot off the door mirror near Paris's hand. She cursed out loud over the near miss. Our choice made, she began looking for the right conditions to end this.

As the low-fuel indicator light came on, our search became a little more desperate. Paris made a hard right turn onto a side street off Sepulveda, then crashed through the chained gate of a warehouse complex near the airport.

"Paris, they're speeding up!" I yelled as the two black Suburbans in hot pursuit moved quickly to close the distance between us.

"Thanks. You're such a fountain of information, bro," my sister spat as she made a beeline for a warehouse and office building that reminded me of LC's back home. She was gunning the Mustang's motor, which seemed to be suddenly failing us. "Overheating," she stated grimly.

"Give me a gun! Give me a gun!" I screeched.

"Here," she said, tossing me something other than a gun.

"A phone? What the hell do you want me to do with this?"

"It's off your buddy back at the hotel. Figured he had no use for it."

"Oh! Wait! He told me stuff before Alejandro's man busted in and killed him. I need to tell you—"

"Tell me later," she blurted out in a tone that worried me.

I looked in the rearview mirror. The lead van looked like it was going to ram us.

"We gotta run as soon as I stop," she said.

With the last surge of the Mustang, Paris brought it into a sideways slide, leaving the driver's side exposed to Alejandro's people, who'd declared open season on us. When it came to a halt ten feet away from the front door of the warehouse, I felt adrenaline surge within me.

"Get out! Go! Go!" Paris yelled, almost jumping over the center armrest as she shoved me ahead of her. Our remaining windows exploded just as I got the car door open. I rolled onto the ground, afraid to stand up as bullets sprayed the car, popping some of the tires.

Paris closed her eyes, talking to herself at a volume I couldn't hear as she gripped her gun firmly in both hands. Was that a prayer? When the tiniest of breaks took place, she popped up and fired a shot toward the closest Suburban. The single bullet went through the windshield about where the driver should be. The van rolled to a stop just as she began dragging me along.

I could hear bullets whizzing by our heads as we came upon the locked door. Again, my sister fired a single shot, this time directly into the door's key cylinder. With a huge tug, the door came open and we darted inside.

On the first floor, Paris had me wait while she ran down the first-floor hall, knocking things off the wall. Then she ran back toward me, yanking me up the stairs two at a time. Even I was smart enough to realize she was trying to slow Alejandro's men and throw them off our trail.

Ignoring the sounds that might be either behind us or below us, we darted down one entire hall and around a corner before finding an open break room on the right. Paris told me to remain still. After getting our breathing under control, she looked at the remaining weapons she had, checking the clips of two guns and some knife she had stowed God knows where.

"I'm running real low on ammo, Rio. I'm going to have to get the jump on one of them and draw them away," she said in between gulps of air. "When I leave out, move that table in front of the door. Take this gun and hide, but don't let anyone come in. Stay low, and I'll try to be back as soon as I can."

"But I gotta tell you," I blurted out as I grabbed her arm to prevent her from running off. "That guy back at the hotel, he's with the Italians back home. We're all being manipulated. This whole thing has been a setup."

"Damn, that's good shit to know, but I can't deal with that right now. Use the phone. Call Daddy and tell him what's up. Love you, bro," she said, kissing me as she removed her expensive Manolos, then disappeared into the darkness outside.

"Ditto, sis," I whispered, scared as hell for both of us. But she'd already gone. I just hoped she was as good as LC thought she was.

I tried to quietly slide a break table against the door, then hurriedly stacked several water cooler jugs atop it. In the far corner there was a snack machine and a Coke machine. I ran over there, wedging myself in the space between the two as if willing myself to disappear. At least from this location, I could shoot at them first.

For several moments, the silence was deafening. It was like every swallow I took was the loudest noise ever and my heartbeat was a thundering drum. After what felt like an eternity, I heard footsteps. I closed my eyes so tight, it hurt. I had no idea what kind of nine millimeter she'd handed me, but my fingers were going numb from gripping it so hard. Before long, a barrage of shots rang out from somewhere in the building.

There was a loud bump against the wall outside, and then a bloodcurdling scream erupted that almost made me piss in my pants. I could hear more yelling coming from different places, then someone calling out in Spanish for someone else.

This wasn't going to get any better anytime soon. Using the phone she'd given me, I called Orlando back in New York.

"Paris?"

"No, it's me," I said in a near whisper as I locked in on the barricaded door for any sign of movement.

"She found you. Thank God," Orlando said.

"Look. Listen to me. You have to stop them, Orlando. They're trying to kill us, but I know what happened."

"What are you talking about, Rio?"

"Gawd, I don't want to die," I moaned, succumbing to the stress.

"Rio, you gotta get it together and tell me what's going on," Orlando said.

He was right. My sister was out there risking her life. I had to man up and keep my head on. "Orlando, you gotta make them stop, or Paris and me are dead. She's good, but she ain't got but so much ammo. It's not the Mexicans we're up against."

"You mean the same ones trying to kill you right now?"

"Yeah. Right. But wait," I said, confusing even myself. "Listen. It wasn't Alejandro that jacked the shipment. It was the Italians."

"Italians. You mean Sal Dash and them? Are you serious?" Orlando asked, his attention heightened.

"Yes, that's exactly who I mean."

LC

49

I took a long, slow breath to steady my emotions before I dialed the phone. I'd really screwed up, letting my emotions over my brother Lou's death get in the way of making a sound decision for my family and my business. By ordering my West Coast affiliates to take out Alejandro's brothers, I'd as much as signed Rio's death certificate. It was a move that would not go over well with any of my children or my wife. Right now I didn't have time to worry about what they thought, though, because the task at hand was way more important. Its outcome could determine the survival or demise of us all.

"Alejandro, are you ready to talk?"

"You murder my brothers for no reason. Now you're attacking and killing my men all over L.A., and you want to talk?" Alejandro bellowed, his voice coming through the speakerphone and filling my office with his venom. "I will talk once your son and that tramp bitch are chopped up and delivered to your doorstep! Now, I ask you this one last time. Let me speak to Miguel—if he is not already dead as well. Por favor."

Tramp? Rio was gay, and the local talent I rented to take out the brothers were all men. Who was Alejandro referring to?

"What tramp?" I asked.

"The one my men said you sent to rescue your son. Do not deny it. She is at this very minute fighting to protect him, but believe me, neither she nor that little woman you call a son will leave L.A. alive."

Orlando was standing near me, waving his hands wildly to get my attention. I hit the mute button on my phone and asked him, "What is it, dammit?"

He answered me breathlessly. "Paris is out there. With Rio."

My chest tightened, and it took me a moment to catch my breath. Now two of my children were in danger. I could only assume that if Orlando knew about it, he was the one who sent Paris out there. He was giving orders without me. Once my kids were home safely, I would kick his ass for insubordination.

Thankfully, Alejandro did not seem to know that the tramp was actually my daughter. I wanted to keep it that way.

Still glaring at Orlando, I picked up the receiver and continued my call off the speakerphone.

"Alejandro, I'm only calling to get you to stop," I said.

"Then you don't know me after all," Alejandro said. "This stops when the streets flow with blood. Revenge for my brothers—and for your arrogance."

"And what about your arrogance, Alejandro? You stole my shipment. You killed my only brother first, and now you tell me your men are going to kill my son."

"We did not steal your shipment or kill your brother. But I will kill your son," Alejandro answered with absolute determination.

Orlando's phone rang. I continued to trade accusations and threats with Alejandro, until something Orlando said caught my attention. "What are you talking about, Rio?"

He was talking to Rio. My son was still alive. With my attention now divided between two phone calls, I was waiting to hear Paris's name come out of Orlando's mouth. I needed to know that she was still alive too. Instead, his face went pale, and he rushed over to me and whispered in my ear.

It was information that nearly knocked me out of my chair.

"Alejandro, wait." I interrupted his tirade. "My other son has just given me some very disturbing news."

"I am not interested," he answered.

"No, I think you should hear this. He's telling me that we've both been played."

"I do not have time for this!" he raged. "Next time we talk, it will be in the afterlife. And I am pretty certain we're both going to hell."

"Wait!" I had to get him to listen before any more blood was shed. "Someone in your organization has been working with the Italians out here."

"Your attempt to stall and save their lives is futile."

"Goddammit, Alejandro!" I slammed my fist on the table. "I swear on my granddaughter's life that I am not lying to you. They've played us both."

I held my breath during the silence that followed, feeling each thud of my racing heart. Finally, he spoke, slowly and cautiously, his voice still full of suspicion. "And you know this how?"

"Just . . . don't kill my son. Or the tramp. Call your men off. We need to talk about this, Alejandro." It was the best I could do. I still didn't have all the information I needed, but Orlando was claiming Rio had proof.

"You're not giving me anything, Lavernius. Make me a believer. Make me believe that you are an old, senile fool and not simply a ruthless man who deserves what's about to happen all around him."

Orlando slipped me a piece of paper.

"Who is Road Map?" I asked Alejandro.

"Who?" he asked in return.

"Road Map," I repeated, worried that I'd misread the paper Orlando slid in front of me.

"We don't know any fuckin' Road Map."

I looked at Orlando and shook my head. He understood my message and spoke quickly into his phone to try to press Rio for more information. I imagined Rio on the other end, God knows where, terrified for his life. Of all my sons, he was the least equipped for a situation like this. And it was my fault he was there. A sense of regret threatened to overwhelm me now.

Orlando glanced at me. My face must have betrayed my emotions, because he quickly took control of the situation. He pressed the button to put my phone back on speaker.

"Mr. Zuniga," he said, "someone there with you is nicknamed Road Map. I don't know his description, but he's apparently working for the Italians. He is responsible for our shipment being stolen and, indirectly, for our mistrust of you, sir. He is responsible for my uncle's death, your brothers, and your son. For that, we apologize, but we were misled."

"You, whoever you are, are sounding as desperate as Lavernius. And you are a worse liar." Alejandro's voice turned ominous. "But at least now I know my son is dead. And so is Lavernius's son."

"No!" Orlando pleaded. "It's not a lie. My brother has proof. Call your men off."

Alejandro laughed wickedly. "Based on what? My son is dead. There is nothing more we have to say to each other."

Orlando did not give up. "Please. My brother has a phone. It belonged to Dash's man on the West Coast. He was working with this Road Map."

"And why should I care?" Alejandro asked.

"He's going to call Road Map now."

"You are stalling for time," Alejandro said. "But it is of no consequence to me. If you'd like your brother to spend his last few minutes on earth playing this silly game, then so be it."

Orlando barked into his cell phone, "Rio, call the number now! Do it!"

He ended his cell phone call with Rio, and it was like a knife in my heart. Would that be the last contact any of us ever had with him?

Alejandro's voice came through the speaker. "Lavernius, this—"

Suddenly we heard the sounds of a scuffle, and then silence. The call was disconnected.

Orlando and I sat staring at each other in paralyzed silence. The future of my family hung in the balance, and we were cut off from all contact with Rio and Alejandro. There was no way of knowing what was taking place on the West Coast. All we could do now was sit and wait.

Harris

50

Frangio's, a little Italian bistro in Long Beach, Long Island, was a place where someone with my complexion was not really welcome, no matter how nicely dressed. I would never have come here, except for the fact that this was where Vinnie Dash said he wanted to meet. I was there to speak to him on behalf of LC. With any luck, Vinnie would agree to talk to his father about joining forces in our fight with Alejandro. Unfortunately, it was starting to look like Vinnie was a no-show.

I was beginning to feel a little antsy. The guidos milling about weren't making me feel all that welcome, and with all the drama happening, there was no use in tempting fate. If Vinnie wasn't here in the next few minutes, I was leaving. I was picking up my phone to send him a text when suddenly I noticed someone at a table across the room. It was Sal Dash, the head of the family.

I hadn't noticed him earlier, probably because he was without his signature suit. He was dressed simply in a golf shirt and a pair of slacks, looking nothing like the violent crime boss he was. He was sitting alone, eating a bowl of soup. I guess this was him in his environment, free from threats.

I knew this to be an illusion, though. Someone like Sal never traveled alone. From the look of the hulking goons seated at tables around him, he'd obviously come with protection. I was beginning to second-guess my own decision to arrive at the restaurant without security, especially with the news of Uncle Lou's death still so fresh in my mind. Nevertheless, I was here now, and Sal had turned and looked me dead in the eye. There was no turning back.

As I approached his table, he dabbed his mouth with a napkin and gestured for me to take a seat. I remained standing.

"Where's Vinnie?" I asked.

"Indisposed. Come. Sit down," Sal said with a grin. Actually, it was more like a smirk—the same arrogant look I remembered from our first meeting, all those years ago at Georgetown. "You don't like meeting with me, do you?" Sal said when I declined to sit for a second time. "Not many get to break bread with a man like me on a regular basis. You're lucky, son. Soon the Dashes are going to have a seat on the commission, and then there will no longer be five families running New York, but six."

"I'm not your son." I felt my blood pressure rising as I realized that I'd been set up. Vinnie had never intended to meet me here. It was Sal all along.

My phone began to vibrate on my hip. I checked it quickly, then hit ignore. It was London, but she'd have to wait until my impromptu meeting with Sal was over. As much as I hated being in this man's presence, I was there to do a job for LC. It was not going to be easy to convince Sal to join forces against Alejandro, and I didn't need any distractions making it even harder.

Sal rose up out of his chair. If I wouldn't sit, then he would stand up to meet me face-to-face. "No, you're not my son," he hissed. He was close enough that I could smell the minestrone on his breath. "But you are my brother's bastard son, which makes you a part of my family. In my world, we treat even our nephews like sons." His words spoke of family bonds, but his expression revealed the truth: it pained him to think that his family's blood was running through my veins beneath my black skin. The feeling was mutual.

"That man fucked my mother and left her with a child. He is a coward, not a father, and I am not part of your family."

He laughed. "Oh, you have it so wrong, Harris. He loved your mother. He was going to leave his life—this life—for her." He shook his head. "We can fuck niggers, but we can never really be with them. I tried to explain it to him, but he wouldn't listen. He would have shamed my family. He had to be taken care of."

"You killed your own brother," I stated, summing up the root of my disgust for this man.

"I did not kill my brother. I had someone else do that." His explanation was flippant, as if these things happened to normal people every day. "It's the price you pay for stealing from the family."

"I don't have time to stroll down memory lane with you," I said, anxious to end this meeting and get the hell out of Long Island.

My phone vibrated, and I reached down to silence it again.

"You might wanna answer that. I'm pretty sure it's your wife." Sal's voice sounded sinister, and I felt a chill run down my spine.

"How the hell did you know that?"

"There are a lot of things I know. One of them is that you should answer that call from your wife. I'm sure she has something important to tell you." With that, he sat back down and resumed his meal calmly.

I hit speed dial for London's number, my anxiety skyrocketing as she picked up before the first ring was complete.

"Harris!" she howled. "Mariah! She's gone!"

I almost dropped the phone when Sal flashed me a knowing smile. "What?"

"Someone kidnapped Mariah," she blubbered through her sobbing.

"What do you mean, someone kidnapped her? How did you let this happen? You're supposed to be her fucking mother!"

"You son of a bitch! Do you think I wanted her to be kidnapped?"

The line went silent for a few seconds; then I heard Junior's voice. "Harris, man, you need to get home. This shit is serious."

"I'm on my way." I ended the call. That was when I noticed that all the goons from the surrounding tables had moved in, ready to pounce if I made a move on Sal.

"What do you know about my daughter's kidnapping?" I said, barely able to control my breathing to speak.

"Have a seat, counselor," he requested again, and this time I had no choice but to comply. "Our plans have changed. Called for some improvisation."

"I don't give a shit about your plans. I want my daughter back. What do you know?"

He made me wait for his answer while he took another spoonful of soup. Each second that passed was torture.

"You know, it's kind of a shame it had to get to this point. Things were really heating up between you niggers and the Mexicans. For a while we thought you'd all just take each other out. No more competition for us."

As he slurped the last bit of soup, I had to grip the table to keep myself from strangling him. If his goons killed me, there was no hope for Mariah.

"But we've had no word from California," Sal continued. "Our guy inside the Zuniga organization hasn't checked in, which means he's probably been found out."

"What the fuck does this have to do with my daughter?"

"Don't you get it?" Sal said, sounding exasperated. "We have your daughter. That's why I agreed to meet with you over here."

I lunged for his throat, overcome with anger and grief, but two of his men pushed me back down in my chair and held me there. Their massive hands felt like vice grips on my shoulders, but I refused to give them the satisfaction of seeing me wince in pain. One politely jammed a gun into my ribs, while normal families quietly enjoyed their meals all around us.

Sal looked me straight in the eyes and said, "Relax. She's okay—for now. I'll show you."

He snapped his fingers, at which point one of his men produced an iPhone to show me a video of Mariah. I saw my daughter sitting on the floor in a tiny room. Poor thing was spooked. She refused to play with the toys in front of her as she sat crying for her mommy. I wanted to reach through the phone and rescue my child, but the gun in my side reminded me how defenseless I really was.

When the video was over, I asked, "What do you want, you piece of shit?"

Sal smiled, glad to have arrived at the crux of his lesson for tonight. "Take care of LC," he replied as he broke off a piece of focaccia bread and dabbed it in the bottom of the soup bowl. "That's it. And your dear, sweet Mariah's returned to you unharmed. It's really quite simple."

"I want my daughter, and I want her now," I growled.

"And I just told you what you need to do. Capisce?"

I tried to appeal to reason. "I don't know shit about killing someone. They'll just wind up killing me instead, and then we all lose."

"No. You're too brilliant, boy. You're close to them. You'll figure out something, and they'll look to you to steady things in the aftermath."

"I won't. They're my family."

"Bullshit. You're nothing like those common street thugs and drug runners. LC has always been nothing more than a petty crook with delusions of grandeur. A wannabe king who won't admit he's still a stable boy. Besides, it's easy for you to cut ties. You did it with your father all those years ago. Come back to your real family."

I was reduced to begging. "Please. Just give her back to us. Anything but this. I'm not a killer."

"Oh, I know that," Sal said, causing the men on both sides of me to laugh. "That's why they won't expect anything from you when it happens. Now, do the right thing. Don't make me have to show you how a killer acts—at your daughter's expense."

Orlando

51

Pop and I stared across the conference room table at one another with horrified expressions. Between us were two phones, neither one providing answers, only a tortured silence. We'd been blindsided from the beginning by Sal Dash and the Italians, and it had most likely cost us the lives of Rio and Paris. I'd wanted to sit in Pop's chair all my life, but how the hell could I have ever thought I was ready for this? No one was ready for this, not even Pop. It was a dark day for us that I'd surely never forget.

"What do you think happened?"

"I don't know, Pop," I replied. "I don't know, but I think we fucked up."

"How am I ever gonna tell your mother this?" Pop asked in frustration, as close to tears as I can ever remember seeing him. "And who told you to send Paris out there?"

I knew that was coming. He needed a recipient for his rage, and I didn't blame him. His eyes were flashing red, like they did when he dealt with Alejandro.

"No one," I replied, trying not to blink with LC dead in my face. I understood his anger, but I was not the only one to blame for the predicament we were in. "I took it upon myself to undo what you set in motion. That was my brother you sent out there to die! He was your son. Rio was your son, Pop."

"And Paris is my daughter! Damn you to hell!" he yelled so loud that they probably heard him outside his office, in spite of the soundproofing.

I could tell he wanted to hit me, but he put some distance between us before things got physical. He was a tough old man, but without a piece of steel, he couldn't take me—unless I let him, and I was no longer willing to let him. I think he knew that.

"What is it with my children no longer listening to me? Why do they think they can do whatever the fuck they want?"

"I can only speak for myself," I started, "but your children are no longer children. We've grown up. You have to see that. Would you even be having this conversation with V—"

"Shut up!" he bellowed. "Just shut your mouth, boy."

The conference phone rang, interrupting our heated battle. There was a moment of hesitation between us. I didn't know if I should pick up the phone or defer to him. He looked down at the phone and then to me, sending a silent message that it was up to me now.

"Alejandro?" I said into the phone.

"Yes. . . ." He paused long enough that I started to worry that it was all he was going to say. I listened for any noise in the background that might give me an indication of where we stood now. Finally, he broke his silence with, "My apologies for ending our call so abruptly."

I held back the sigh of relief that wanted to escape. "What happened? Were we correct?" I looked across at Pop. He looked like he was holding his breath in anticipation.

"Sí," Alejandro said, the bravado in his tone replaced with pure sadness. "You were right. I know now why this Italian used the term 'Road Map.' The man has some face issues. Pockmarks, I think you call them. His phone rang just as he was about to plant a bullet in my head. He proclaimed his guilt easily enough, but he won't trouble anyone anymore."

"This is good," I said, feeling the tension rush out of my body. My brother and sister had a fighting chance now—or at least that was what I thought until Alejandro reminded me of the blood that had already been spilled.

"The man was one of my trusted people. Under normal circumstances, I would thank you for exposing scum like this. But I have a dead son and two brothers I must bury."

The situation between us was still tricky, to say the least. I needed Alejandro to stay focused on the fact that we had a common enemy, rather than on the fact that he'd lost family members at our hands. "I'm sorry for your loss. I have an uncle I must bury too," I reminded him. "We've both lost loved ones—just as Sal Dash wanted, I'm sure. But now is the time for us to put an end to the fighting, not to finish each other off. I want you to let my brother go." I purposely left Paris out of it, since Alejandro didn't seem to know she was family. No need for him to feel like he had an extra bargaining chip, in case he wasn't ready to call a truce just yet.

To my relief, he said, "Enough blood has been shed between our families today."

I nodded to my father and gave him a thumbs-up to share the good news, but Alejandro wasn't done yet.

"Hostilities have ended between us—for now," he said gravely. "But this does not mean we have settled the score. You must pay a price for the death of my son."

Oh my God, he was still going to kill Rio. I had to convince him to stop. "No! Your son's death was an ac—," I started frantically, but he cut me off.

"I do not want to hear the details surrounding my son's death. You have taken my only son, and for this you must pay. I expect no less than the head of Sal Dash. This is nonnegotiable."

That was it? He only wanted us to kill Dash? As far as I was concerned, that was on my agenda anyway. "Done," I told him.

"One more thing. Tell your father that I will no longer be doing business with him. Tell him to keep out of the West Coast, especially Los Angeles."

Before I could respond, Alejandro hung up. If it was still in LC's plans for me to succeed him, I would be dealing with the new frienemy we'd made. For now, I just wanted my brother and sister back . . . alive.

I needed to get to L.A., to see what I could do about getting them out of there myself. I was picking up the conference phone to make flight arrangements when my personal cell phone rang. It was a number I didn't recognize, and the connection was spotty. I had to call out a few times before I heard a recognizable voice.

"Rio!" I yelled out in a fit of relief. "Thank God."

Paris

52

The old Israeli from boarding school never put me through anything as brutal as this, but he'd be so friggin' proud of me right now.

Eight of Alejandro's men were dead, another two wounded, and I still stood, using everything in this warehouse to my advantage as I ran around wreaking havoc, pretending to be Uma Thurman in Kill Bill. I'd done everything but telepathically tell Rio to make a run for it, having drawn all their attention. I didn't know whether I'd saved my brother's life or merely bought him time, but I couldn't focus on that right now.

Even with all my masterful technique, I'd finally been run into a corner with no means of escape. Options were few. My left arm burned from gunpowder, sweat, and dirt entering my cuts and scrapes. Adrenaline, which I'd tried to regulate with breathing control, was failing me now. My legs were wobbly, and the last sidearm I'd pried from dead hands was out of ammo. Still, I crouched low, gripping my last usable weapon—a karambit knife—in my shaky hand. I waited for the

assault, ready to use the tiger-claw blade on the
throats of however many were gathering around
the corner. Last I counted, thirteen still stood.

For about half an hour, I tried to remain alert,
but I was worn out. It was when I found myself
resting against a wall, my eyes shut and the knife
hanging at my side, that I realized something
wasn't right. I sprang to attention, grimacing in
pain from the soreness that had gripped my right
arm. I swiftly moved to defend myself from certain attack, but the attack never came. I slowed
my breathing in order to hear my surrounding
environment—and heard nothing.

"What the fuck?" I gasped.

I cautiously crept to the end of my hallway,
not believing what my ears were telling me. I
was alone. No ambushes or traps were waiting
for me as I carefully combed the warehouse.
They'd even dragged off the dead ones. The
only reminders of this orgy of violence were the
pieces of broken office equipment, bullet holes,
smeared blood, and shell casings. And I had to
walk through it barefoot. Ewww.

But what had led Alejandro's men to cut out?
Rio. Had to be. He must have gotten hold of
Daddy and our men. I wasted not a moment longer, heading back to the barricaded break room
where I'd left him.

The door was partially ajar. Not knowing what
to expect, I pushed the door open a little bit more

and squeezed through. The table he'd wedged against the door had been pushed aside. There was space enough for someone to have gotten inside before me.

Oh, dear God, please let this boy be alive.

"Rio, it's me. Don't shoot," I called out, seeing at least three bullet holes in the wall to my right. I assumed he'd missed whomever he had shot at. Now, if only they had missed too. "Rio?" I called out again. I took another step, almost slicing my foot open on a busted cell phone. A few more curse words escaped my lips. I checked my foot: cut, but not a mortal wound.

"Sis?" a worn voice finally responded, followed by a head peering out from between the snack and Coke machines. "Oh . . . my God," he said as he took in the sight of me, the blood splattered all over my clothes, along with the complimentary bruises and cuts I'd suffered.

I limped over quickly, relieved that we'd both survived. "What the fuck did you do to the phone?" I asked.

"I ran out of bullets, so I threw the phone," Rio said with a shrug, then gave me a long hug, despite my being a bloody mess. "He left after that. I must've run him off."

"A phone. Yeah. I'm sure that did it," I said with a smirk. "I'm just glad you're alive, bro."

"Me too, sis. Thank you for not giving up on me," he said, kissing me on the cheek.

"Never," I said, fighting off a tear. "You kept my shoes safe, right?"

"Yeah," he replied, pointing to my discarded Manolo Blahniks in front of the Coke machine. "Nobody touched them, but I was about to throw them next if the phone didn't work. You know I'll beat a bitch with some heels if I have to." He snapped his fingers, back to the sassy Rio I knew and loved.

"If you had messed them up, I'd have killed you myself." The jokes were a welcome release of tension for both of us. I got back to business. "Speaking of phones, I take it you reached Daddy 'n 'em before you used it as a lethal weapon."

"Yeah. And it worked, I guess. Sure didn't seem like it at first. Orlando had me dial the number to this guy called Road Map. They had Alejandro on the other phone or somethin', everyone screamin' 'n shit—including me. Everything stopped not long after I dialed the number, though. Right around when I had to throw the phone at the door. Then it all just stopped. No noise. Nothing. I thought they'd killed you. Thought I was about to die too . . . but no one ever came back."

"No need to try and make sense of it now. We just need to count our blessings and get the hell out of here. Need to find a phone ASAP too," I said as I bent down to put my shoes back on my sore dogs.

"Oh shit, Paris! You been shot."

"I have?" I saw blood right before I met the floor with a harsh thud.

London

53

"Harris thinks this is my fault, doesn't he?"

Junior shrugged his shoulders as he handed me my phone. "I don't know, sis."

Oh, he knew, but he was trying to stay impartial, which pissed me the hell off. He was my brother; he should have had my back no matter what, even if it was my fault my baby was taken.

I walked toward the back door of the mansion, unable to control the tears that escaped from my eyes. I raised my hand at Junior, who was right on my heels, so that he wouldn't follow me outside. He hadn't let me out of his sight since we'd walked through the door.

"I'm not going anywhere. I'm just going to get some fresh air. Can you give me some space so I can fucking breathe?"

I was out the door before he could answer me. I wasn't trying to be rude to Junior, especially not after the way he'd broken every speed record known to man to get to me when I called for help after the kidnapping. I just needed to be alone—

to hate Harris and this life that had taken my daughter.

As I dialed Tony's number, I felt like I was on the verge of a mental breakdown. "Tony, honey, I . . . I need to see you," I whispered into the phone.

"Can't. I'm in the middle of something."

Why now, of all times, was he saying no? He'd never refused to hook up with me in the past. As a matter of fact, he was always the eager one, but not this time. This time he sounded distracted, uninterested.

"Tony, I need to see you," I repeated. "Something terrible has happened."

"Look, I'm busy, all right? I don't have time to be holding your hand because your nail broke." His patronizing attitude was something new. I was taken aback, but I persisted, sharing with him the horror of my daughter's kidnapping.

I finished with, "And all my husband did was yell at me and say it was my fault. When this is all over and I have Mariah back . . . I want to run away with you, Tony."

His reaction nearly knocked me off my feet. "Look, I'm sorry about your daughter, but I've got problems of my own." Who the hell was this man? What happened to the sweet, kind man who'd swept me off my feet? I was seeing a whole new side to him.

"Tony, I need you. You're the only one who can make me whole," I pleaded as the tears flowed freely.

He sighed loudly. "You sure you don't want to do this some other time? I mean, with your daughter missing and all, shouldn't you be with your family?"

That stung a little bit. Family loyalty. Maybe Mariah's kidnapping was punishment for me and Harris, for not staying loyal to each other and our marriage.

"Please, Tony," I persisted. "Just for a little while."

He finally relented, saying, "Meet me at the Howard Beach Motor Lodge in twenty minutes. I'll text you the room number."

"I'll find it," I said with relief. "And, Tony, I love you."

He didn't say it back before he hung up. In fact, I could have sworn I heard a laugh as he disconnected the call. But I had bigger things to think about now. I headed back into the house.

Twenty minutes later, I arrived at the Howard Beach Motor Lodge, a serious step down from our usual five-star rendezvous spots. I always swore I'd never go into one of those short-stay motels, but then again, I never thought that

I'd cheat on my husband, or that my daughter would get kidnapped. My life had taken a drastic turn from the path I always thought I'd be on.

I knocked twice before Tony opened the door. I felt my chest tighten at the sight of him. He took me into his arms, but it was far from comforting to me. I could almost feel his eyes surveying the parking lot as he hesitantly welcomed me inside.

"Oh, Tony, they've got my baby." In spite of his strange behavior, I collapsed against his chest and sobbed.

He led me over to the bed and helped me sit down. "This world is so crazy. Nowhere is safe anymore." He was saying the right things, but it sounded so mechanical, so cold.

"They took her and shot my security in cold blood." I looked deep into his eyes as I asked, "What kind of people do this?"

He looked away quickly and answered, "Animals, only animals. . . . Maybe they're after a ransom or something."

"That's what the police said, but no one has called about a ransom yet."

The color drained from his olive skin. "Police? You called the police?"

I felt it in the pit of my stomach; my instincts had been right. There was only one reason Tony would be concerned about the police being involved.

"Oh, Tony. Just hold me, please," I said, though the last thing I wanted was to feel this man's arms around me now. I just needed to check one thing to confirm what my intuition was already telling me.

As he leaned in close, I placed my hands on his back and felt it: a bandage on his back, in the same spot where I'd stabbed my attacker with a pen. Ever since the shock of the attack had subsided a bit, I'd had this nagging feeling that I knew the voice of my attacker. At first my brain— or maybe it was my heart—wouldn't allow me to acknowledge the painful truth that it was Tony's voice. I hadn't wanted to believe it, but feeling this bandage now, I had the proof I needed.

Tony pulled back a little when he felt my hand on the bandage. As our eyes met, a sinister grin passed over his face.

"Something wrong?" he asked.

"You . . ."

His hands were on me in an instant, throwing me around like a rag doll. I tried to fight back, but he effortlessly pinned me on my stomach, yanked up my skirt, and tore off my panties.

"No," I gasped as he plunged into me violently.

"Shhh. Relax. I just want to take away your pain," he hissed into my ear as he rammed himself into me over and over again. The weight of his body made it hard to breathe. I lay there, crying silently, as he tore me apart. It wasn't long before he finished his business and got up off me. He pulled up his pants without even cleaning himself.

"I hate you, you son of a bitch!" I yelled as I jumped off the bed and yanked my skirt back down.

He laughed. "You have no idea how much you're gonna hate me. Now, get your black ass outta here."

I wiped the tears from my eyes and left without another word to Tony. I would get payback later. Right now I had only one thing on my mind—getting Mariah back.

"Was it him?" Junior sat up in the backseat when I got into the car.

After my call with Tony, I'd gone back in the house and admitted everything to Junior. It was humiliating to have to admit my affair to him, but I would do whatever it took to get Mariah back home safely. Shoot, I'd publish my shame in the newspaper if I thought it would help. Junior didn't pass judgment. He didn't curse me out; he didn't ask me how I could have been so stupid. Maybe that would all come later, but for the time being, he was focused only on his niece.

"It was him," I answered. "That motherfucker has my baby."

We watched as Tony rushed out of the motel room and into a black Cadillac. He was on his cell phone. It looked like he was having a heated discussion with someone.

"I remember him from our meeting at the dealership," my big brother said. "He's definitely Sal Dash's big-mouth son."

"Well, I plan on shutting it. When I get my baby back, Junior, I want him to die, and I want him to know it was me who ordered his death."

Junior leaned back and watched as the black Cadillac exited the parking lot, recording every detail about his new target.

LC

54

"Why didn't somebody tell me about Mariah?" I asked my wife when Orlando and I returned to my near-empty house. When we should have been a tight, cohesive unit, everybody was out pursuing their own agendas. That was why we were so easily manipulated by Dash. Our self-ishness was our weakness. It was time for us to stop acting on emotion and start strategizing as a family. Order had to be restored.

"We didn't want to upset you, dear. You know, the same way you didn't want to upset me by telling me you sent Rio out to L.A. to get his head blown off." Chippy's hands were trembling as she cast an accusing eye at me. I had no defense for my bad decision, so I just let her comment hang in the air between us.

She was looking worn down. The stress of everything that had gone on lately was obviously taking a toll on her. Then again, I hadn't looked in the mirror lately. She could probably say the same thing about me.

"She's my granddaughter, Chippy! I had a right to know. I could have done something."

"Not while you were negotiating with Alejandro, you couldn't. You're her grandfather, LC, not her parent. Her mother made the right decision not to tell you right away, and I stand behind her."

"You've gotta be kidding me. Has everyone lost their mind around here?"

"Pop, please. You and I both know we need to stay focused to get Mariah back. We can't be losing our cool," Orlando said. So noble of him to finally be getting his head in the game. I was beginning to rethink my decision of handing the family business to him.

"That's just it, Orlando. Nobody's been focused. Paris killed that boy Miguel when I expressly told her to leave him alone. Then you send her out to L.A. without my knowledge, putting both her and Rio at risk. Harris and London are God knows where, when they need to be right here, together, waiting on either the police or the kidnappers to call. Together," I stressed as I motioned at our empty abode. "And you," I said, pointing at him. "You've been disappearing at times when we needed you most. Seems the only dependable one is Junior, and he isn't even . . ."

"What? Junior isn't what?" Orlando asked.

"Junior isn't even the one I chose to lead this family," I replied quickly, turning the conversation back to him. "But you haven't been yourself lately. Not answering calls when people try to reach you, disappearing to who knows where. What exactly have you been doing all this time?"

"Well, for starters, I've been starting my own family. I'm going to be a father," he said, dropping another overwhelming revelation at my feet.

"Oh my goodness!" Chippy looked stunned, but equally elated. "Who is she? Do I know her?"

"I didn't even know you were seeing someone." I offered my hand, but I was skeptical. "Why didn't you bring her around?"

"Because it was my business alone," Orlando replied with a bit more attitude than I was used to from him. "But with someone taking my niece, that changes everything. I've sent some of our people to watch over her."

"Orlando, if this woman is having my grandchild, I need to meet her," Chippy started, but I put an end to it before she launched into an interrogation.

"We'll have time for this later," I told her, then turned to Orlando. "But when things calm down, your mother and I would like to meet this woman."

"Hey." We all turned at the sound of Harris's voice. He entered the room, looking like death warmed over. He'd obviously been crying. "Any news? Have they called?" he asked.

I hated to have to tell him no. "Nothing yet, but we're pretty sure the Italians are behind it."

He flinched, as if he'd been punched in the gut.

"Don't worry, son. We're going to get her back," I said.

"How do you know it's not the Mexicans that took my daughter and almost killed my wife?" Harris asked, his voice sounding hollow and weak.

Orlando explained, "It's all been a setup. We got verification that the Mexicans had nothing to do with any of it. It was Sal Dash and those scumbag sons of his—all of it."

Again, a look passed over Harris's face that I couldn't quite read. His daughter was missing, but there was something else on his mind too.

I asked him, "Have you talked to Dash like I asked you?"

He didn't even look up from the floor when he answered. "No, they haven't returned my calls."

"Goddamn cowards!" I exploded. "They're using my granddaughter as a shield. They must know that we're onto them, that Alejandro and I have called a truce."

"Thank God for that," Orlando uttered. "Rio and Paris are alive. They're both coming home, and so is Mariah. You got my word on that."

"I just want my baby girl back," Harris said as he collapsed into a chair. "I can't lose her. I won't. Not for anything." Behind the sad look in his eyes, there was something else going on. His teeth were clenched, and the muscles in his neck were tense. Was I sensing anger?

Something about the way he wouldn't look me in the eye had my radar up.

As I was trying to figure out why Harris's energy was off, London arrived home with Junior. Harris rushed toward her.

"Where the hell have you been? You do know our daughter has been kidnapped, don't you?"

"We were following Dash's boy," Junior growled in response for his sister.

We were all surprised, but Harris's reaction was over the top. He seemed downright panicked. "Who?" He wasn't looking to Junior for answers. He was looking directly at London. "And how did you find him to follow?"

"That prick motherfucker, Dash's son. The one who was disrespectful when we met at the dealership," Junior stated, answering Harris's first question only. Those of us who had been there knew exactly who Junior meant. He and London exchanged a glance.

"You know . . . ," Orlando said, turning to Harris, "you arranged the meeting with Sal and Pop. The one where he convinced us the Mexicans were gunning for us. The Italians came to you to set it up."

"You accusing me of something, you insecure little fuck?" Harris got in Orlando's face, looking ready to fight. "My daughter is out there somewhere, all alone, and you want to take this time to score points? I've about had it with you."

My family was self-destructing before my eyes. Dash would be laughing his ass off if he could see it.

Junior slid away from his sister, heading toward Orlando and Harris as their words got louder and hands were clenched into fists. Chippy broke down in tears and began flailing her arms for them to stop making fools of themselves. A security guard stuck his head inside the door to check on things. When he saw it was a family matter, he quickly retreated.

I was just about to raise my voice, but London beat me to it.

"Stop it! Stop it!" she shouted over the din. "It's not Harris's fault. It's mine."

Fists were lowered. Mouths at full bore suddenly fell silent. A pall fell over the room as all eyes fixed on my eldest daughter.

. "This isn't your fault, baby. You couldn't have known they were going to kidnap Mariah," I assured her.

"No, but I know the person who did it," she said with her head lowered. "I'm the reason they have Mariah. It's my fault. I know Dash's son Tony."

"How . . . do . . . you . . . know him?" Harris asked with deadly calm.

London didn't answer. She just looked down at the floor in shame, giving us all the answer she didn't want to speak. My daughter had been sleeping with the enemy.

Harris

55

My in-laws usually saw me as a rational man who sought answers through logic rather than violence. Unfortunately, when it registered in my mind that London was sleeping with Tony, I was incapable of rational thought. All I could see was Tony Dash taking what belonged to me. First, he'd taken my wife, and now he had my daughter. No wonder Vinnie was always smiling and laughing in my face when we met. He had a secret. Vinnie, his brother Tony, and their father, Sal, had their own private joke at my expense—and it was all London's fucking fault.

I have no memory of how I got across the room, but before I knew it, I'd grabbed London by the shoulders and was shaking her violently.

My mother-in-law screamed first.

London didn't fight back. She just stared at me with a blank look as I yelled in her face, supremely hurt and betrayed. Orlando and LC were yelling something, but I didn't hear them. I didn't really hear myself, either. I was in a rage.

It was like I was out of my body, staring down a dark tunnel. Events unfolded over which I had no control. Everything seemed to be happening all at once.

Orlando was trying to pull me off. Junior brought his large arm between London and me, forming a wedge that he used to pry me away. I fell backward as my feet became entangled with Orlando's legs. The two of us hit the floor, and something came tumbling out of my coat pocket with a dull thud.

Someone yelled, "Gun!" and the entire house went silent, except for the security guards running in, weapons drawn.

Junior came over and casually picked up the gun, holding it up to the light for inspection.

"Hmm. This yours, Harris?" he asked me. Of course he knew it was.

"Um, yeah," I said, coming up to one knee. I wasn't sure if my brother-in-law was going to allow me to take another step, so I stayed put.

"What are you doin' with a gun, Harris?" Junior probed further, trying to hold back an amused grin. I was never one to carry a firearm, and they all knew it. I fought my battles with words and the law, not with bullets. When I needed that type of help, I went to them.

"Serial number's been filed off," Junior announced, no longer sounding so amused.

"You planning on shooting someone?" Orlando asked.

I had to think fast. "Someone took my daughter. When I catch up with them, I plan on putting a bullet in their head personally."

"Where'd you get it?" LC asked.

"On the street," I answered honestly, hoping that would be the last of the questions.

LC nodded to Junior, giving him permission to hand it back to me. Junior removed the bullets, then handed it over.

"This is a piece of shit," he said. "No accuracy from over a few feet. When you're ready for a real gun, ask us for one."

He handed it back to me pistol grip first—the same way Sal Dash's man had handed it to me a mere hour ago. I hated having it in my hands. I had always avoided guns like the plague. They reminded me too much of my father's life, a life I'd spent my whole youth vowing never to emulate. And now here I was, married into a crime family, with the Mob holding my daughter hostage. If Junior had left the bullets in, I might have used the damn thing on myself right about now.

Instead, I stowed it once again in my coat pocket and stood up. I came at London more calmly this time. Her brothers stood by her side, in case I erupted again.

"You said you've been . . . following Tony?" I asked, avoiding the question I really wanted answered, which was, how long had she been fucking this mobster? That discussion would have to wait until we had Mariah back. After that, I had no idea if we'd be able to salvage our marriage, or if I'd even want to.

London didn't speak. She looked to Junior, who answered for her.

"I got my boys on him now. Been following him since—" He stopped, and a glance passed between him and my cheating wife. London's eyes welled with tears, but I felt not an ounce of sympathy for her.

"Now that we know who we're lookin' for, we'll probably find our shipment too," Orlando commented.

"Fuck the drugs. I know they're important to you guys and whatnot, but I want my daughter. That's all," I said, reminding them where my priorities lay and where theirs should be as well.

"Oh yeah, we're gonna get her back," Junior assured me. "You don't have to worry about that."

"Then we need to get moving," Orlando said. "'Cause if none of us have heard from them, that's not a good thing."

"True," LC said. "I'll contact Dash. Try to see what his game is. In the meantime, Junior, you stay on Tony. We're going to get Mariah back. Alive. Then we take them motherfuckers down, but we have to do it together, as a unit."

Junior nodded. "Don't worry. We got this, Pop."

"I'm going to help Junior," London said, finally joining in the discussion.

"No. You're not doing this. I forbid it," I said.

"You don't get that choice anymore," she shot back. "Not when it comes to my daughter. I need to be there when we find her. I failed her once. Not again." She looked so worn down, so damaged, and for a minute I realized that she had been there to witness Mariah's terror during the kidnapping. She would live with that guilt forever. It almost made me pity London. I almost wanted to reach out and comfort her, but then I remembered that none of this would have happened if she hadn't been a cheating whore.

Lucky for London, her mother still cared about her feelings. "Baby," Chippy said, reaching out for London's hand, "maybe you should stay out of this. You've already been through too much."

"No, Momma," my wife said. "Paris is not here. They . . . they need me. Mariah needs me. My family needs me."

"Very well," LC said, putting an end to the discussion and granting London the opportunity to atone.

He turned to Orlando. "I want you to make arrangements to get Rio and Paris back here to the house, safe. After that, I'll need you somewhere coordinating things. Reach out to some of our friends. See if they can give us a hand with this. Although I didn't like you going behind my back, in the end, you did good sending Paris to L.A. Now I guess we'll get to see what you can do in this situation."

Orlando stared at his father for a moment, processing the respect LC had just paid him. Then he nodded.

I was the only one left without an assignment—other than the one I'd received from Sal Dash. "What about me?" I asked LC.

"You're my right-hand man, aren't you?"

I nodded.

"Then stay by my side. I'll have you there with me when I meet with Dash. It'll show him I didn't come to wage war."

"'Cause we'll be busy doing that," Junior said.

I followed LC outside, with my mind on the decision I had to make: obey the family of ruthless criminals who held my daughter, or remain loyal to the family of killers I was a part of.

God help me if I made the wrong decision.

London

56

The motorcycle came around the corner, one helmeted man in black and bright blue leather revving it as it traveled down the tree-lined street toward us. He came to a halt beside us just as Junior lowered the driver's window of the van.

"Any movement?" my brother asked.

The man in the helmet shook his head. "No."

"A'ight. Thanks, bro," Junior said, extending a fist bump out the window to the man.

I checked the gun clip one more time, removing it and counting each bullet it stored before slapping it back into the SIG Sauer. It was an old ritual of mine that I'd thought was long in the grave.

"Soon?" I asked.

"Like you anxious for this," he joked dryly.

"Just to get Mariah back."

In the back of the van, the other three of our party were suiting up.

"Bro, how many black faces you seen around here?" Sihad asked from the back as he zipped up his National Grid jumpsuit. The other two men selected by Junior were doing the same. These three were the best of the best, along with Junior and Paris, when it came to taking down enemies. Daddy called them our own personal black ops team.

An NYPD cruiser made its rounds. Junior nodded at the two officers from under his hard hat—just a big grin from another utility worker. There were a lot of police roaming around the residential neighborhood just off Richmond Terrace in Staten Island today.

A gas line had "conveniently" ruptured this morning, resulting in a suspension of service while National Grid worked on the repairs. Workers were going around notifying residents on the next block over, which was also affected, while we were concentrating on this block.

LC's man Sihad was right about us sticking out in this predominantly white Italian neighborhood. Even dressed as gas company employees, we were sure to get cross looks. That was one of the reasons we needed to hurry—the other being that my daughter was probably being held here.

We split into two groups and walked down the street, clipboards and tool bags in hand. We went door to door, meeting with elderly women who spoke English as a second language, inspecting around their homes for any residual damage from the gas-line explosion—excellent work, which Orlando had arranged on short notice. All the while we were methodically working our way toward one particular home from two ends of the block.

"Think these are the ones who offed Pablo?" Sihad asked my brother, refusing to keep quiet. I think he was pretty close with Daddy's old friend.

"Yeah. And Lou," Junior answered.

"I just wanna get some get-back on that ass."

All five of us convened in front of the house. The van parked outside was the same one used to take Mariah away from me. Chills overcame me as I recalled its sliding doors cutting me off from Mariah. Further proof that we were at the right place was the presence of Tony's black Cadillac parked directly behind the van. Since Tony knew our faces, we had one of Junior's boys go up the stairs to the front door, while Junior and I pretended to inspect the gas line on the side of the house. Gossip traveled quickly in this tight-knit community, so news of the gas-line rupture had surely made its way around the neighborhood, adding legitimacy to our presence there. Tony and his crew would have no reason to doubt utility company workers.

"She's in the basement," I gasped, staring at the unassuming slender window by my ankles, remembering the words Harris had whispered to me before we left to go our separate ways. He said he suspected our daughter was being held in a basement and that she was alive. He wouldn't tell me how he knew this, but he swore me to secrecy. I would uphold my promise to keep it secret—for now.

"How do you know, sis?" Junior asked, eyeing me suspiciously.

"I just know. Mother's intuition," I answered.

"Then we can't risk it. If we bust in there and blaze on 'em, there's no guarantee someone don't harm Mariah first," he hissed, his confidence wavering.

But there was no time for second-guessing our plan. We needed to get in there fast. It came to me to "call an audible," as they say in football.

"Leak! We got a leak!" I yelled from the side of the house to our men in the front.

"What?" one of them hollered back, no doubt unsure what I was pulling.

"We got a major leak," I said, poorly disguising my voice. "People in there need to get out till we get it repaired."

I tugged on Junior to follow me to the front of the house before something went wrong. I kept my head low, fearful of Tony walking outside and recognizing me. My brother quickly communicated to Sihad and the rest with eye signals not to do anything yet. After delivering the message to the man who answered the door that it wasn't safe for them to remain inside the home, we retreated to the van with the fake National Grid magnetic signs on the exterior. One of our group remained on the side of the house, pretending to call in an emergency repair order.

"What the fuck is going on? We got them to open the door," Sihad said, out of breath and obviously nervous over the sudden change in plans as we regrouped following the retreat.

"My daughter. If she's in the basement and someone's down there with her—"

"Shit! We coulda had her!" he yelled, cutting me off. "Our chances don't get any better than that."

"Watch your tone, bro. I ain't gettin' my niece killed. We wait," Junior urged Sihad as he motioned toward the home.

As we went about acting like a normal work crew gathered around the van, a flurry of activity erupted from inside. Two men exited first onto the porch, checking outside for any signs of trouble. Like rats creeping out of their rat holes at dusk.

"See, they're relocatin'. Afraid o' gettin' blown the fuck up. Now they comin' outside to us," my brother said, glad I was right with my gamble.

"This is it," I said, reaching into my tool bag for the SIG Sauer pistol. "Silencers, since we're outside."

"Damn. You is used to gettin' wet," Sihad joked with a smile. "Let's do this."

Keeping my hard hat low over my face, I saw him. Tony. He came out of the house and beat a path straight to his Cadillac. He was by himself. If we were wrong about Mariah being here, we'd need him to help us find her. We couldn't let him drive off.

"Your call, sis," Junior said, his hand resting inside his tool bag as he prepared to set up road cones around the van in the continuance of our ruse.

"Green light," I said just as three more men exited the home and walked across the lawn to the van. Still no sign of Mariah. Once Tony was clear, they'd be free to drive away too.

Tony pulled away from the front of the house and drove straight toward us. When we were just about to unload on his car, he slowed anyway.

"Hey, man. How long is this gonna take?" Tony chirped in our direction out his lowered passenger-side window. Despite the disguise I wore, I almost couldn't bear to look in his direction. I felt my hand trembling as I placed my finger on the trigger. Eventually, Junior took it upon himself to respond.

"Waitin' for the big boss to send another inspector," my brother replied, trying to keep a sufficient distance so as not to be recognized, but still close enough to shoot.

I couldn't take it any longer. I slowly turned to steal a glance at the man who'd snatched my child from my arms. In that instant, his eyes locked on me and our path was set. No cheap disguise could obscure the eyes of someone from their former lover. A second later and he'd taken an accounting of the other gas company workers.

"Shit," Tony muttered as he turned toward the road, preparing to gun the car.

"Junior!" I yelled.

He knew what it meant, bringing his pistol up from his tool bag and squeezing off a quick zip of silenced rounds into the cab, at Tony. The Cadillac still lurched and sped off, but at an angle that took it up the street, then into the overgrowth on the side of the road.

I took off running toward him, already aiming at the car for any sign of his escape. As Tony jumped out, I saw he was wounded, bleeding from the neck area. He was armed, though, and raised an unsteady pistol in my direction. I screeched to a halt and took aim with two hands, pretending I was back at the gun range with LC as an impressionable teenager.

Keeping my anger at bay, I unloaded the clip. From habit, I counted down the number of rounds with each trigger squeeze.

Tony was hit dead in the chest by at least three of my shots. He didn't even shoot back. As he fell over, his face wore the same smile I saw when he first came to my rescue. I wished I'd known then that it was all a setup. He would've gotten the box cutter across his throat, saved us all some misery. As I walked over to his body, I saw that he wouldn't be with us much longer.

"I . . . I spared you," Tony said with his dying breath.

I didn't have time to make peace with what I'd just done. Behind me, the men by the van were trying to retreat back inside the house. They were caught between our advancing group, led by Junior, and the one man we'd left on the side of the house. As I ran to join the gun battle, a man for whom we hadn't accounted emerged onto the porch with a small, hooded child in his arms.

My Mariah.

"There she is!" I screamed at Junior just as Si-had shot one of the men poking out from the van.

The man holding Mariah on the porch grabbed a shotgun from inside the doorway. He harshly shoved my blinded daughter back inside, then fired with a loud boom that was sure to carry through the neighborhood and draw attention. Our man went down immediately from the same shotgun that had probably killed my bodyguards.

My daughter wasn't going to be anyone's hostage any longer. As the man on the porch retreated inside, I broke into a full sprint, even though some of the men by the van were still alive and shooting.

"London! Wait!" Junior yelled as I ran by him, dumping the burdensome tool bag. Giving up on reason, my brother was quickly on my heels, firing over my head to give me some cover.

Dash's men by the van saw us quickly gaining ground. One broke and fled toward the backyard, while the other one dropped his gun and threw his hands up.

"Okay! Okay! I give up," he said just as Junior planted a bullet in his forehead, not losing stride as we charged up the stairs to the porch.

My brother caught up to me and passed me. He reached the front door first, planted his large foot firmly, and sent it flying open. He broke almost into a baseball slide just as a blast of shotgun pellets peppered the door frame. Most of them missed Junior, but some caught the forearm he'd raised to cover his face. While still on his back, Junior returned fire blindly into the home, in the direction of the shotgun fire.

"Junior!" I yelled for fear of Mariah being used as a shield.

"Shot high on purpose," he said, grimacing in pain from the rivulets of crimson quickly flowing from his arm. "Go. Quick."

I darted over my brother, hearing the others coming up the stairs behind us. On a table where the dining room place settings should have been, several bricks of coke were stacked beside a scale. Two large black duffel bags lay on the floor, waiting to be filled.

"Mariah! Mommy's here! Mommy's here, baby," I yelled. I could hear muffled cries, followed by a husky voice shushing someone. At least he hadn't gone back into the basement.

Turning a corner brought me to a bedroom with another door on the opposite wall. The creak of floorboards led me through that door and into an old kitchen at the rear of the house.

The tall, scraggly man with the crooked nose had cleaned up, yet I still recognized him. He was the panhandler from that day. He held the shotgun in his right hand as he carried my daughter by her waist under his left arm. Her little legs kicked as they dangled, but that damned hood was still over her face. Behind him was an open door descending into darkness—the basement where Mariah had been held all this time.

"Don't come any closer, bitch," he scoffed.

"Give me my daughter," I said, pointing an empty gun at his head in a bluff. I was so worked up for fear of him doing something to Mariah that I didn't think to take Junior's weapon.

"So you can kill me?" he said, making me wish Mariah's ears were covered, as well as her eyes.

"Don't give her up and that definitely happens."

"Nah. Why in the fuck would I trust a nigger bitch like you? I ain't Tony, all strung over that sweet black 'tang of yours. Throw your gun over here and I don't turn li'l miss into a pincushion."

"Look . . . do you have any kids?" I asked as he slowly backed toward the basement door. I guess his plan was to hole up down there with Mariah as his shield until some more of Dash's people arrived—backup we in no way could contend with.

He placed the shotgun against Mariah's dangling body. I shuddered, knowing what it would do if he pulled the trigger. "Throw it. Now," he said.

I closed my eyes, saying a quick one-word prayer: Please. When I opened them again, he was still standing, prepared to ruthlessly murder my daughter. A pair of hands with a glint of silver between them rose up out of the darkness behind him.

"Okay. I'll do it." I relented, not giving away what I was witnessing. I threw my empty pistol off to his left, knowing his eyes would follow it. At that moment, the shotgun moved clear of Mariah's body and he turned it toward me.

"Bye, bitch," he said with a grin just as Sihad emerged fully from the basement and whipped the taut wire over his head, twisting it tightly around his neck. As the panhandler gagged, he dropped both the shotgun and Mariah to the floor, fighting for his life. With fingers desperately trying to come between wire and flesh, both he and Sihad tumbled down the stairwell into the darkness below.

I could hear thuds and the sounds of a struggle. Then silence. Kicking the shotgun farther away, I ran to my daughter.

"Mommy?" Mariah called out as I swiftly pulled the hood off her head. Her eyes flickered as she adjusted to the sudden light. I couldn't tell just yet if she'd been drugged.

"Shhhh. It's okay. Mommy's gotcha," I said as I rocked with her in my arms.

I could hear feet lumbering up the stairs, unsteady but getting closer. I held on to Mariah tightly as I scooted away from the basement door on my butt. I didn't know who would emerge.

It was Sihad, bruised from the fall and the struggle, but alive.

"How did you . . . ?" I asked.

"Hey. You said they were keeping her in the basement, remember? Figured I'd double back and go in that way. Window was tight, but I didn't go on Weight Watchers for nothin'," he crowed with a cocky, busted-lip smile.

"Thank you," I whispered.

"No need. Just doing my job," he replied.

Junior came into the kitchen, helped along by the remaining member of our group. "Hey. We gotta get word to Pop and get the hell outta here. Now," he urged.

"Mommy? Why are you all dressed alike?" Mariah asked, looking up at all of us.

"'Cause they're Mommy's playmates, and we've been playing hide-and-seek with you. Now you're it," I said, softly kissing her forehead as I sobbed. "You're it, baby."

Harris

57

I checked my phone for the millionth time as LC and I headed to the meeting with Sal Dash. No calls, no texts—nothing about Mariah had come from the assault team. I'd told London to call me as soon as they had news. I still couldn't believe she'd gone out with Junior acting all urban commando, but then again, there were a lot of things I couldn't believe about her lately.

My phone vibrated with a text alert, and I opened it, expecting to see a message about Mariah's rescue. Instead, I saw this on my screen: is he dead? I deleted the text, which had come from an unknown number.

"Any news?" LC asked.

I whipped my head in his direction. His eyes were focused straight ahead now, but what if he'd looked at my phone and saw the text before I erased it? I had no way of knowing what he knew. My heart was pounding as I lied, "No. Just a robo-text from Verizon telling me I'm over my monthly limit."

Mercifully, LC took me at my word and dropped it. He was probably too distracted to give it much thought as we approached the Verrazano-Narrows Bridge heading into Staten Island.

The closer we got to the meeting with Sal Dash, the more I thought about his orders: kill LC and I could have Mariah back, no questions asked. If it got to that point, would I even be able to do it? I prayed we could get my daughter back before I was faced with making that decision. I'd reloaded the gun back at the house, though, just in case. It sat in my jacket pocket now, its presence giving me very little comfort.

LC's phone rang. He kept his conversation brief. "Uh-huh. Uh-huh. I see. I see. Very good. Thank you," he said, his stone-faced expression not giving away any emotions.

"Any news?" I asked, barely giving my father-in-law time to hang up the phone.

"Nope." He was cool, calm, and collected.

I, on the other hand, was nervous enough for both of us. LC had no idea that if we didn't hear something soon, I was going to have to put a bullet in his head to get my daughter back.

I glanced at the two bodyguards seated in the front and realized that if I was going to hit LC, I sure as hell wasn't going to get a better chance than this. There were only three of them in the car with me, and I had six bullets. I wasn't an experienced shooter, but at this range, maybe I could do the job. Just shoot LC and the two men up front when they parked the car, then call Dash to clean up the mess. At least then I'd have my daughter back.

I took a deep breath. Okay, Harris, get it together. You're not going to have to shoot anyone. They're going to call. They're going to call, I repeated like a sort of prayer. I looked down at my phone, willing it to ring. Nothing.

We drove past the entrance to the Verrazano-Narrows Bridge, continuing down the Belt Parkway, going who knows where. No one else in the car seemed concerned about the detour we'd just taken. Apparently I was the only one in the dark.

"Uh . . . why did we just pass the bridge? Staten Island is that way."

"There's been a slight change in plans," LC said, tapping the driver's shoulder. "I decided against meeting in Staten Island, but we're still meeting with Dash. Anyway, before we get there, anything you want to share?"

"Uh . . . no," I answered. "Why?"

"Think carefully about your answer," my father-in-law said, sitting calmly next to me with his hands folded together in his lap.

He advised me to think carefully, but I could barely think straight. How the hell was I going to get myself out of this? I couldn't come up with a lie, so the next best thing was to play dumb.

"I don't understand what you mean," I said with a casual shrug. "We're supposed to be going to see Dash, see what he wants, while Junior and them try to get my daughter back. I trusted you to do that. Otherwise I wouldn't be here. What's going on, LC?"

"You're the father of my grandbaby. Keeping family together is important to me," he stated cryptically. "You can appreciate that, can't you?"

"Absolutely," I answered. This line of questioning and LC's demeanor were making me extremely nervous. I felt the palms of my hands getting damp as the SUV exited the parkway.

"You know, I'm a little hungry. You want something to eat? You hungry?" LC asked me, his mood suddenly switching to a more energetic, animated state. The problem was that when LC mentioned he was hungry, it often meant someone was about to die. I'd learned that the night he took me to the apartment above the fried chicken joint and initiated me into the family business.

I checked my phone again. Still nothing.

"Nah, I'm good," I told him. I could barely hear my own voice above the sound of my pulse pounding in my ears. "I just want to get this meeting over with and go home to my daughter."

"C'mon. Let's grab a bite in Long Island. I know a good Italian place. You'll like it. It's called Frangio's. Ever heard of it?"

My lip started quivering uncontrollably.

"They say it's Sal Dash's favorite eatery, this place Frangio's. You ever been there?" He intentionally stressed the last four words. Obviously, he already knew the answer.

I took a deep breath and wiped my sweaty palms on my lap, prepared to beg for my life if I had to. "LC, I—"

"What was the plan, Harris?" he asked, no longer toying with me.

I lowered my head, heart pumping rapidly as I considered the revolver given to me by Dash. Clearly, LC knew something, and the men seated in front would be ready if I tried anything.

The truth. It might be my only chance for survival.

"The plan was that I kill you and they let Mariah go," I answered in defeat.

"You still gonna kill me?" He pointed at my jacket, almost daring me.

"No. I wouldn't, LC. I swear. It was never my intention."

"Really? So why didn't you tell us about your meeting?" He pointed at the space between us on the back seat. "Go on, now. Take it out. I want to see it again."

"LC, they . . . they showed me a video of Mariah," I said, choking up. "But I couldn't do what they wanted me to. You gotta believe me."

"Take the gun out, Harris," he demanded.

I warily complied, closing my eyes as I pulled the revolver from its hiding spot. Once in the open, I placed it on the seat beside me then pushed it farther away. Then I raised my hands in surrender. A bullet to my head was sure to come next. I should have killed him when I had the chance.

"Put your damn hands down," LC instructed me, sounding disgusted. I listened, but kept my hands tightly gripped on my seat.

The SUV came to a stop. We'd traveled down a worn road riddled with potholes and covered in debris. I looked out the window at the bleak surroundings, which were remote, far away from prying eyes.

Then the doors unlocked. I'd been brought here to die.

"I only did what I had to do. I never wanted to hurt or disrespect you or the family," I said solemnly. "So . . . I guess this is it."

"We're still meeting with Dash," he stated, not taking his probing eyes off me. "Or rather, you are."

"Me? I . . . I don't understand."

"Take your gun and get out," LC ordered.

"LC, I never planned on using it."

"Well, you're going to use it now—if you want to leave here alive."

A wave of panic came over me. Did he expect me to shoot it out with his men?

"Please, please don't kill me," I begged. "I just wanted Mariah back safe."

"Who said anything about killing you? You're my son-in-law, part of my family, right?" he said with only a slight hint of irony in his voice.

"Yes."

"Good. So I need you to prove it, or, as the Italians say, it's time to make your bones."

"What do you want me to do?"

"You'll know when you get there. And while you're doing that, I'm going to follow up on a few things, check on Mariah."

LC motioned toward the door. I still wasn't sure where I stood with LC—did he consider me family or foe now?—but I took the revolver and got out as ordered. I flinched when the bodyguard lowered his window, half expecting him to shoot me. Instead, he instructed me to walk through the overrun parking lot in front of me, toward a building that looked to be abandoned.

"Just knock on the door," he said.

The door of the abandoned building was rusted, but from the flakes on the ground I could tell it had been opened recently. Someone was inside. I took a nervous breath, patting the gun to make sure it was still in my pocket before I knocked.

I was greeted by a well-built white man around my age, probably Italian, if I had to guess. He stepped aside so I could enter. Inside the dimly lit space, two men were leaning against a desk smoking cigars. When they saw me, the white-haired one got up and led me to another door.

"Right this way, Mr. Grant. Mr. Dash is expecting you."

I nearly shit my pants when I realized Sal was there—and LC knew it before he'd sent me into the building. At this point, I was pretty sure I'd been set up. LC had probably made some type of deal with Dash the same way he'd done with Rio. The difference between me and Rio, though, was my sharp lawyer's mind. I had the ability to talk my way out of sticky situations. I just had to figure out a way to talk myself out of this one.

It took me a minute to process what I saw when I opened the door, because it was so far from what I had been expecting. Sal Dash was there, but instead of sitting behind a large desk surrounded by juice-head goons ready to kill me, Sal was in his underwear, tied to a chair in an otherwise empty room.

I walked cautiously toward him, still trying to make sense of what I was seeing. Sal grunted as he tried to free himself with a harsh tug. His chair hopped once, but that was all. Expert knots held the rope that bit into his skin. His face looked like someone had taken out some frustration on it.

I removed his gag. "Hello, Sal," I muttered, feeling cocky all of a sudden.

"Look at this shit. Bastards snatched me when I was going to church service. I'm a family head, Harris! You just don't do something like this to me."

"Just like you don't take a man's child?" I said, taunting him.

Sal stared at me in contempt, until he saw me remove the gun from my jacket. For the first time, I witnessed something less than the supreme confidence he usually displayed. I witnessed fear in his eyes.

"That was overreaching," he offered meekly. "I'll be the first to admit it. But you have to understand. I never intended to hurt your daughter. I wanted LC to think the Mexicans took her, so they'd go to war."

"You used my child to start a war?" I asked, barely able to contain the rage I felt building in my chest.

"My men are weak . . . selfish. I knew if we had to go head to head with LC, they would fall apart under pressure. I needed to do something to weaken LC . . . take his family out of the equation. At least enough where my family could survive. That's all it was."

"Is my daughter okay?" I whispered harshly, gripping the pistol with a new intensity.

"Of course. She's somewhere safe."

I raised the gun.

"Cut me loose," he pleaded, his face now wet with tears. "I'll pay you anything you want. You name it. . . . Don't you see? They're trying to pull you in, make you just like them. But you're not like them, Harris. You're not."

"They didn't pull me in, Sal. You did, when you first visited me back at Georgetown all those years ago, trying to make me into something I wasn't. I see now that I'll never be through with you. I'm done trying to play both sides of the fence." I pressed the gun against the side of his head.

"Please. I'll leave you alone. For good. I swear. Don't you understand this was just business?"

Sal's red face and shaky voice gave me a feeling different from anything I'd ever experienced. I felt incredibly powerful. Never again would I let him push me around.

"Don't become monsters like them," he urged as he closed his eyes.

"They're not monsters. They're my family," I said as I pulled the trigger. "And nobody messes with my family—or our family business."

For a few seconds, I just stood there, a changed man with a smoking gun in his hand. I had done the one thing I was determined never to do. I'd killed a man in cold blood, becoming a murderer just like my father.

I turned away from Sal's lifeless body and walked out of the room. The three men were still there, now joined by LC.

"Is Mariah okay?" I asked, unable to bring myself to look at him.

"Yes," my father-in-law replied. "She's fine."

"And London?"

"She's fine also."

I nodded, thankful that my family was safe, but unable to say anything else. I think part of me was still back in that room with the man I'd just murdered.

For LC, though, this bloody business was nothing new. He continued on like it was just another day at the office. "I have someone I want you to meet, Harris."

He turned toward the older, white-haired man. "Johnny Mazz, this is Harris Grant. Harris, Johnny is a very dear friend and business partner. He also represents the Commission."

From the first time he sought me out in college, Sal had spoken about the five Mafia families of New York and the Commission that ran them. I could always tell that he admired those families and aspired one day for his family to hold a seat on the Commission. And now I was meeting someone from the Commission mere minutes after shooting the man who'd told me about its very existence.

"I'm sorry I didn't have a chance to formally introduce myself," Mazz said in a heavy Brooklyn accent, "but I'm sure you understand. We all needed to focus on the task at hand."

I nodded but said nothing. I was too busy trying to make sense of this scene. Here was my father-in-law, proudly introducing this Mafioso, who didn't seem the least bit bothered by the fact that I'd just killed a made Italian man.

"The Commission is in your debt for removing such a worthless piece of shit like Sal from the earth." Mazz offered me his hand and I took it tentatively.

"I don't understand. You wanted him dead? I thought he was one of your people."

"Sure, he was Italian, but Sal's family wasn't a voting member of the Commission. They were warned specifically not to interfere with LC's business."

So, LC had the protection of the Mafia, and he was apparently very friendly with a high-ranking member. I was the family lawyer, but obviously there were some things LC still saw fit to hide from me.

LC continued the explanation where Mazz had left off. "That's why Sal was trying to manipulate us and the Mexicans. If he could get us to kill each other off, then the Commission couldn't say shit if he moved in on our territory. And because of the amount of money he'd make, the five families would have no choice but to give him a seat at the table."

"But LC brought this to our attention, and thanks to your help, we no longer have that problem." He reached out his hand again, and this time I shook it with more confidence.

Mazz said, "By the way, your father was a good friend and a good man."

"That he was," LC echoed.

"You knew about my father?" I asked, turning my attention to LC.

"Sure did. Did you think I was going to let you marry London and not know every minute detail about you? It wasn't until I found out you were his son that I was convinced you had the right stuff to marry a Duncan."

I shook my head. "I don't know what you're talking about. My old man was a scumbag."

"No, your father was a good man," Johnny explained. "It was Sal who was the scumbag. That's why we had him killed. I know you want to get to your daughter right now, but when you have a chance, I'll tell you all about your father."

I looked back at the door, behind which lay Sal's corpse.

Good riddance, you son of a bitch. I guess the next time we meet will be in hell.

Epilogue:

Orlando

The backyard of our compound was packed with more than two hundred people helping to celebrate Mariah's birthday. I was standing near the doorway to the main house with Pop, observing the festivities as we shared a couple of cold ones.

It was a little over three months since the war with Alejandro had ended, and our family had just begun to recover. Pop was still uneasy having all these people at our house, despite the fact we had more security than the President of the United States, and the guests were all confined to the backyard. It was his opinion that our recent battles with Sal Dash and Alejandro had exposed us in ways we weren't prepared for and that most of our family couldn't comprehend. Although we'd come out on top, Pop reminded me constantly that Vinnie Dash's whereabouts were still unknown. He was also concerned that once the shock of Miguel's death wore off, Alejandro might reignite the war between us.

What concerned him the most was that we could never be sure if the violent nature of Uncle Lou's death and Mariah's kidnapping had drawn the attention of law enforcement. Truth is, only time would tell, and that made the old man very uncomfortable.

"You know we have a lot of rebuilding to do," Pop commented with a bit of weariness apparent in his tone. "Sooner or later someone is gonna come gunning for us."

"So I take it you don't plan on going to Florida anymore?" I asked.

"If you don't mind me sticking around, I kinda want to see how things play out. You've turned into quite a man, son, but these are trying times, and there are still some things you're going to need to learn. I'd like to stick around and teach them to you."

The fact that he wanted to stay didn't surprise me. What did surprise me was that he still planned to hand things over to me someday. I had expected him to announce some changes that included removing me from my spot at the top.

"I can't think of anyone I'd rather learn from, Pop."

He nodded, raising his beer. "To the family."

I joined his toast, sipping my beer as I looked out at the crowd and thought about the work that lay ahead.

We still needed to appoint four lieutenants to replace Pablo and Uncle Lou and to cover the slice of Dash's territory the Commission had given us. We also needed to get on steady footing with a major distributor from areas beyond the U.S. Until we had a new pipeline, we were vulnerable. What good were we to the Commission or anyone else if we didn't have the quality product they desired?

"Maybe we should go in the house and talk this thing out."

"Pop, Dash is gone, and we've got a meeting with your man Lee on Monday about distribution. For at least one day, can you savor the moment and think positive thoughts? Relax and enjoy your granddaughter's birthday party," I requested of my father.

"You're right." He looked over at Mariah and London with a smile. Harris was taking pictures of them in silly poses, showing off their catlike faces, courtesy of the face painter we'd hired for the party.

Just watching them interact made me think of Ruby and the fact that she was carrying our unborn child. I hadn't seen her since she disappeared from the protective custody of my men three months ago, and I really missed her. I had hired several private investigators to find her, without any luck.

"Look at them, son. After all that's happened, who would've thought they'd come together like this as a family? I guess the baby helped. . . . I still can't believe London's pregnant again."

"I just hope its Harris's baby," I replied. "Because if that baby comes out with blue eyes and straight hair, we're all gonna have to restrain Mr. Harris Grant from committing his second murder and killing your daughter."

"Didn't you just tell me to think positively?" LC shook his head, but I'm sure he was a lot more concerned about the parentage of his unborn grandchild than he wanted to admit. "Come on. Rio and Paris are finally here. Let's take that family picture your mother wanted."

We headed over toward my mother, who was handing out plates for the buffet.

"What about Junior?" I asked. "Aren't we gonna wait for him?"

"No, your mother has him running some errand. He probably won't be back until tonight."

I peeked over at the old man, but he purposely avoided making eye contact. We both knew Junior would never miss Mariah's party unless it was something important, and a simple errand wasn't that important. My father was hiding something.

"Pop, is there something I should know?"

LC stopped abruptly, just far enough away so my mother couldn't hear him. "Leave it alone, son. You know how she can get when she's on a mission."

I took his advice and dropped the subject. I loved my mother, but everyone knew she could be a real bitch if you got in the way of one of her motherly missions. If it concerned the family business, I'd find out about it soon enough.

My mother gathered everyone together for our photo, and the photographer began arranging everyone. Of course, Paris made sure she was in the middle—until Momma put a monkey wrench in her plans.

"London, I want you and Paris to switch places."

"Huh? Why? I'm good right here, Ma," Paris protested.

"No, you're not. I said move." My mother put a hand on Paris's shoulder to nudge her out of the way.

"But why? She's good right next to her husband." Paris rolled her eyes in London's direction. London just smiled and flicked her hand at Paris like she was shooing a fly out of the way. The more things change, the more they stay the same. These two had been going at it like this for years, and I sure didn't see it ending anytime soon.

"Because your sister is pregnant, and I want all our family members present to be in the photo, including the baby in her belly. Now move, girl."

Paris and Rio exchanged a glance, communicating something in that "twin telepathy" they seemed to have. He shrugged, and Paris turned to my father.

"Daddy, that's not fair," she whined.

As hard as he was in the streets, my father was like a puppy dog around Momma. It was obvious by now that Momma had an attitude, and when she gave the old man the eye, he folded like a tent. He'd just recently gotten out of the dog house for sending Rio out to California, so Paris was on her own with this one.

"Paris," he said, "just do as your mother says. When you get pregnant, you can be in the front of the picture, okay?"

"When I get pregnant?" She laughed and gave Rio another look. This time she spoke to him out loud. "They just don't know, do they?"

Rio winked at her. "Well, like I been sayin', ain't no better time than the present to drop the bomb and school 'em. Besides, you said you were gonna tell 'em today anyway."

"Tell us what?" My father was starting to sound a little agitated.

Paris smirked at London as she lifted up her unusually loose sweater to expose a small, round-

ing belly. She rubbed it in a slow circle and announced, "I'm pregnant."

"Oh, Paris, no." My mother's hand flew to her
mouth. She shook her head in protest. The rest
of us were stunned into silence.

It took a while, but my father asked the question we'd all been thinking. "Who's the father?"

Paris stared at him, looking genuinely taken
aback by his question. I guess she thought her
announcement was going to be cause for cel-
ebration, but judging from my father's growing
anger, the news definitely didn't make him feel
all warm and fuzzy.

"Who's the goddamn father?" he asked, louder
this time.

Rio chimed in like a comedian at a game show.
He placed his fist near his mouth like he was
holding a microphone. "Now, that's the million-
dollar question. Who is Paris's baby daddy?
Well, behind door number one there's the newly
elected congressman's dead son, Trevor."

Whom, I suspect, she killed, I thought.

"And behind door number two there's the
West Coast pharmaceutical distributor's dead
son, Miguel."

Whom, I might add, she definitely killed.

"Place your bets, ladies and gentlemen. We'll
find out in about six months who the winners
are, but for the record, my money's on the Mexican."

Rio was about to continue his comedy routine, until Pops, Momma, and Paris all said, "Shut up, Rio!" in unison.

"Paris, my office now!" LC stomped off toward the house without waiting for a response.

Momma, on the other hand, was still staring at Paris like she'd brought home the Plague. "You heard your father. Now, get—"

"Junior!" Mariah spotted my brother and ran over to him. He lifted her up with one arm, kissing her cheek as he handed her the present he held in his other hand.

My mother pointed at the house, making sure Paris was headed in that direction, and then walked over to Junior. He placed Mariah down so she could open her present then walked about twenty feet away from the group with my mother. I'd stopped paying attention to them and was gossiping about Paris's pregnancy with Rio, London, and Harris when my mother called my name.

I gave Junior a pound. "Hey there, bro, where you been?"

His mood seemed grim. "I was down in Philly taking care of something for Momma."

"And?"

"Orlando, I don't know how to tell you this. . . ."

He just stopped speaking, and my mother had to continue for him. "We've found Vinnie Dash."

I turned my attention back to Junior. "That's great. Wait until Pop hears this. Did you take care of him?"

"Couldn't. He's got too much protection. If I took him out, it would bring a lot of heat down on us that we don't need."

"Protection? Who's backing him?" I asked. Vinnie was a man with no home. There had to be a couple hundred guys out there looking for him—and that was just the Italians.

"Ma, that doesn't make any sense. Who the hell would protect him? He's got all kinds of money on his head."

My mother handed me a picture as she spoke. "He's being protected by the Jamaicans . . . and the mother of your unborn child. It seems Miss Ruby gets around."

I looked down at the photo of Ruby, her belly round with my child, all hugged up with Vinnie Dash. Son of a bitch!

To be continued in The Family Business 2: Extended Family.

Discussion Questions

1. Who would you have chosen to lead the family?
2. If you could be any member of the family, who would it be? Whose personality is most like yours?
3. When did you realize the Duncans were more than meets the eye?
4. Did you like the idea of Chippy naming her children after cities she wanted to visit?
5. What were your thoughts about Paris and London's relationship?
6. Orlando once paid Maria $10,000 for night of pleasure. Do you think a night with anyone is worth that much money?
7. What did you think of Orlando and his relationship with Ruby?
8. Was Junior stupid for not wanting a larger leadership role?
9. Was LC homophobic? Did he treat Rio differently than his other children?
10. Was Paris misunderstood, or a true black widow?

11. How long did it take you to figure out the secret behind LC's car?
12. Did you think LC was going to kill Paris? Should he have?
13. Was London wrong for sleeping with Tony? Was Mariah's kidnapping her fault?
14. Was Orlando wrong for disobeying LC and sending Paris to L.A.?
15. What would you have done if you were Alejandro and your child was killed?
16. Were you surprised by the Italians' involvement?
17. What did you think of Harris' family ties to Sal Dash?
18. Do you think LC ever planned on giving up leadership of the family?
19. What were your feelings about Vegas? Would you like to see more of him in the future?
20. Whose baby do you think Paris is carrying, Miguel's or Trevor's?
21. Are you looking forward to the second installment of The Family Business?

Coming September 2013

Prologue

"Dammit, Harris, can you slow down a little bit?" London Grant said to her husband as he led her through the dimly lit showroom full of exotic cars at Duncan Motors. They were on their way to the back of the building, along the dark corridors of offices, headed for the boardroom.

"Come on, London. We're already running late," Harris said with a sigh. He had tried to convince his wife, who was due to give birth to their second child any day now, to stay home. Her pregnancy had been difficult, and the last place she needed to be was at an emergency board meeting where tensions were likely to be running high. London refused to be left out, arguing that she had a responsibility as a stockholder and a member of the Duncan Motors board of directors to attend. Harris had given in simply to avoid another argument. He did, however, suspect that her insistence on being there had more to do with her being nosey than any real sense of responsibility or duty to the company. She wasn't about to miss a meeting when she knew all of her siblings would be there.

Sure enough, when they entered the room, Harris saw that almost all of the other Duncan siblings were in place at the table. He nodded to London's brothers, Rio and Junior, as he led his wife around the table and helped her into her seat, purposely avoiding the seat next to Paris. Like London, she was about to pop, and if their sibling rivalry wasn't already fierce enough, pregnancy was just making it worse. It was best to keep those two sisters at a distance.

Lavernius Duncan, or L.C. as he liked to be called, stood at the head of the table with his wife, Chippy, seated next to him. An imposing figure in his mid sixties, L.C. was the founder of Duncan Motors. Although he had recently handed over the title of CEO to one of his sons, L.C. was still the chairman of the board, and there was no doubt about who was in charge in this room. As he scanned the table, his eyes fell disapprovingly on his youngest daughter, Paris, who quickly removed her feet from the table and sat up straight. L.C. was known to have an explosive temper, and as irritated as he looked already, she did not want to anger him further.

When L.C.'s gaze rested on an empty chair at the table, Junior, the oldest child, shared a knowing glance with Harris. Conspicuous in his absence was the man who had summoned them all to this meeting, the company's new CEO, Orlando Duncan.

"Where's Orlando?" the elder Duncan barked.

The room fell silent until Rio, the youngest son and twin to Paris, said, "He went to get something out of his lab, Pop. He said to tell you he'd be here in a minute."

Rio's explanation did not help L.C.'s mood. "What's he doing in his lab?" he snapped. "Is that where he's been the past few weeks? He's supposed to be running this company, not dissecting frogs."

Rio shrugged, slumping back in his chair. "You gotta talk to him about that, Pop. I'm just relaying the message."

L.C. started grumbling something under his breath. It was obvious that he was not happy about Orlando calling an emergency meeting in the middle of the night and then not being on time.

Chippy spoke up for her son. "You're the one who wanted them all to have specialties outside their jobs with the company," she reminded L.C. "You know him. He's probably got some experiment running that needs to be checked on every couple of hours. He'll be here soon."

L.C. looked at Chippy and his posture relaxed a little, signaling a shift in his attitude. She'd always had that effect on him. Besides, she wasn't wrong about what she said. L.C. was the one who'd always pushed his kids to hone their interests and abilities no matter what they were. Each child was expected to have an expertise outside of the car business, so that they could fall back on them if need be. In Orlando's case, he held a master's degree in chemistry, along with a pharmacist's license.

Just then, Orlando strode into the room still wearing his lab coat. He closed the door behind him and checked to be sure it was locked.

"Finally," Paris huffed.

"I know, I know. Sorry I'm late," Orlando apologized, looking directly at his father.

L.C. took his seat and folded his arms across his chest, but even the stern expression couldn't wipe the excited grin off of Orlando's face.

"Well, I'm sure you're all wondering why I called this meeting tonight," Orlando started in right away, placing his briefcase and a small brown paper bag on the table in front of him.

"No joke," Paris said. "I mean, if you haven't noticed, I'm not exactly in the best condition to be coming to no late night meetings." She placed both hands over her swollen belly and frowned at her brother. Across the table, London rolled her eyes, and Harris put his hand on London's arm as a silent reminder not to take Paris's bait.

Orlando ignored the drama playing out between his pregnant sisters. "I suppose I could have waited until next month's meeting, but

I wanted you all to hear the good news right away."

L.C. leaned back in his chair. "Okay then, son. Let's have it. What's the good news?"

Orlando's grin spread into a huge smile. "I've done it, Pop. I've fucking done it! After all these years I've finally done it!" His eyes darted from one family member to the next, but all he got back were confused stares. Standing there in his lab coat with a wild look in his eyes, Orlando came across like some kind of mad scientist, and no one quite knew how to process any of this.

As usual, Paris was the first one to speak up. "Yo, O, you been sniffing that shit you makin' over at the lab? Your ass is talkin' real crazy. Keep it up and I might have to check your ass into Creedmoor for a psychic evaluation." She gave him the universal sign for crazy, twirling her index finger at the side of her head.

Paris's joke broke the awkward silence at the table. Even Chippy couldn't help but laugh.

Orlando was not deterred, though. "I'm not crazy, Paris. Am I, Rio?" He tilted his head in his younger brother's direction, and all eyes turned to Rio.

Rio and Paris were usually the least mature of the Duncan clan, but this time Rio sat up straight in his chair, articulating his message clearly and professionally. "No, O, you are not crazy. Far from it." Then he looked at his father and said, "What Orlando is about to do is make us all filthy fucking rich."

"We're already rich," Paris spat skeptically. Clearly she didn't like her twin brother taking anyone else's side.

"No, little sister, we are nigger rich," Orlando said firmly then turned his attention back to L.C. "I'm about to make us Donald Trump rich, Bill Gates rich . . . Warren Buffet rich. I'm talking about billionaire rich."

Orlando wasn't normally one to exaggerate, so his pronouncement stunned even Paris into silence for a second. Finally L.C. spoke up. "Son, what the hell are you talking about?"

Orlando looked over at Junior and asked, "You got that thing on?"

Junior nodded. As the head of the family's security, Junior had outfitted the boardroom and his father's office with electronic jamming devices to be sure that all boardroom conversations remained private. The devices were so powerful that even the cell phones of the board members were disabled when the jammers were on.

Orlando's insistence on tight security at that moment changed the whole tone of the meeting. It let everyone know that the business at hand had nothing to do with their automobile distributorship. He was about to talk about the Duncan family's dirty little secret—one they'd worked hard to keep hidden from both law enforcement and the general public. The Duncans weren't just successful car dealers. They also ran one of the nation's largest illegal narcotics operations on the East Coast.

Orlando stood in front of his family, purposely hesitating for a moment as he enjoyed the expressions of confusion and anticipation on their faces. For him today was like Christmas Day, and he was Santa Claus about to give them the biggest Christmas present of all. He glanced over at his mother, who looked at him with love in her eyes, just like always. She was his biggest supporter, reinforcing in him the idea that he could do anything if he put his mind to it. His father, on the other hand, was not as easily impressed. For the first time in his life, though, Orlando wasn't worried about that, because once he finished his presentation, he was sure L.C. Duncan would be kissing his ass.

Orlando spoke directly to his father. "For the last thirty years we've been the ultimate middle man, distributing other people's product around the eastern United States through our dealerships and transport businesses. Now, don't get me wrong, we've made a lot of money. Distribution is a good business and we're good at it, but wouldn't it be nice if we didn't have to pay for the product we distribute? Wouldn't it be nice if we ran not only the distribution side of the business but the manufacturing and production side as well, Pop?"

The two of them stared at each other for a minute, and it was as if no one else in the room dared to breathe—until a smile crept across L.C.'s face and he nodded his head.

"You got my attention, son. What exactly do you have in mind?"

"This!" Orlando picked up the paper bag he'd carried into the room and emptied its contents onto the boardroom table. At least a hundred red M&Ms came sprawling across the table. "Ladies and gentlemen of the Duncan family, I give you H.E.A.T."

LC stared at the M&Ms and frowned. "What the hell is this, some kind of joke?"

"I ain't complaining. I been craving M&Ms all week." Paris reached out to pick up a handful, but she'd barely closed her hand around the candies before Rio grabbed her wrist.

"Don't eat that!" he yelled, squeezing tight.

Paris yanked back her arm. "What the fuck is wrong with you?"

"Those aren't M&Ms," Rio said.

"Then what the fuck are they?" Paris snapped.

"Orlando, what the hell is going on?" L.C. demanded. He picked up a handful of the candy lookalikes then dropped them on the table. "What is this crap?"

"I call it H.E.A.T., Pop." Orlando held one in his hand. "It's the new crack. No, actually, it's better than crack. It's extremely potent synthetic pheromones and endorphins laced with morphine, and it's gonna make us wealthy beyond your wildest dreams."

Ever the practical one, Harris gave his brother-in-law a cynical look. "Excuse me if I sound doubtful, but . . . better than crack? How is that possible? And how about you explain it in a way us non-scientists can understand?"

"Harris is right. What makes these things so special?" L.C. asked.

Their skepticism did nothing to dampen Orlando's excitement. "It's a high no user has ever seen," he said, practically vibrating with energy. "The drug takes them to the same place of exhilaration that crack does for about an hour—but it doesn't cause the physical addiction or withdrawal. The worst that happens is a mental craving along the lines of marijuana. To make it simple, they can't get enough of this stuff."

"Who's 'they'?" Harris asked, and this time Rio jumped in to answer.

"He gave me five hundred of these things, and I gave half of them to the club dealers to give away last Friday. The next day dealers were buying them wholesale, five dollars a pill with a retail price of ten bucks, and they were begging me for more before the end of the night. Now the wholesale price is ten dollars a pill, and demand is so high that if I want I can raise the price at any time."

As the family's flamboyant party boy, Rio was well suited to his position as head of marketing and promotions. L.C might have had issues with his son's homosexuality, but he couldn't deny that Rio had his finger on the pulse of New York's nightlife. Rio knew which drugs were in high demand and made sure the Duncans' products got into the right hands in and around the clubs. L.C. listened to Rio's explanation with interest.

"We can barely keep up with demand," Rio continued. "I must have sold five thousand already, and that's being conservative. I'm telling you, these little red M&Ms are a gold mine."

Harris leaned forward in his chair, his doubt giving way to the dollar signs in his eyes. "What's the manufacturing cost?"

"Right now about a buck a pill, but once we gear up production I can get it to about thirty-five cents," Orlando told him.

Harris reached down into his briefcase and pulled out a calculator. He punched in some numbers then stared at the results, his eyebrows coming together in confusion. His fingers flew across the keys to recalculate. When his second attempt produced the same number, he shouted, "Holy shit!" and showed the screen to L.C.

L.C. glanced at the numbers then did a double take, removing the calculator from Harris's hand. "Is that yearly?"

Harris shook his head. "That's monthly, using just our domestic network numbers. If we go outside the network, you can triple, possibly even quadruple that number. And that's not including overseas."

L.C. sat back in his chair, stroking his goatee as he contemplated all of the information that had been presented to him. It wasn't the type of thing that happened often, but he actually looked impressed.

"Have you tested for side effects?" London questioned. Her specialty was nursing. "Synthetic drugs usually have side effects."

Orlando had been ready for her question. "Yes, extensively. There are no side effects that we can see other than the user sleeping for long periods after consecutive use. Like I said before, it's not physically addictive." He opened his briefcase and handed her a folder. She seemed satisfied to sit back and skim through his lab documents.

"Pop, it's the ultimate recreational drug with no side effects," Orlando said, continuing his pitch. "The yuppies can use it all weekend long and with a good night's sleep, go to work on Monday feeling fine."

L.C. turned to Harris. As the family's lawyer, he had a practical side that L.C. appreciated. L.C. liked to hear Harris's opinions even when it came to their activities that fell well outside of the law. "Okay, Mr. Grant. What are your thoughts?"

"You saw the numbers, L.C., and numbers don't lie. If Orlando and Rio are anywhere close to being correct about demand and production cost, this is a no-brainer. We can't afford not to be involved. There's too much money at stake," Harris replied without a moment's hesitation.

"How much money we talking about, Harris?" Junior asked.

"We could make our first billion within a year, and that's just in the US market." Harris smiled as his legal mind went into overdrive. "Smart thing to do is set up a factory outside the U.S. Buy a small South American pharmaceutical company under a shell corp to do all the manufacturing. We can do it here for a while, but once this thing goes national, we're going to want to put some distance and corporations between it and us. We might want to bring in some of your Cuban and Colombian friends as fronts to give us some cover, L.C. We're also going to need quite a few legitimate companies to launder the amount of new cash we're gonna pull in."

Junior whistled. "A billion dollars. Damn, that's a lot of bread."

"No, that's a lot of shopping," Paris interjected, dancing in her chair. She raised her hand and Rio high-fived her with a laugh.

"That's enough out of you two." L.C. reprimanded them then turned his attention to his older daughter. "London, anything in that report that we should be worried about?"

"Nothing that I can see, Daddy. He's done a pretty through job and all the proper tests. From the looks of it, Orlando's right. He's created the perfect drug."

L.C. nodded. "You've done good here, Orlando. Real good. I'm proud of you, son."

Orlando was beaming. "Thanks, Pop."

L.C. looked around the room at his family, smiling for the first time since he'd entered the room. His vision of their future was suddenly much brighter, and he was eager to get right to work.

"Well," he started, "I say we go forward with this new H.E.A.T. venture. Harris, you start putting together the corporations and the legal protection we'll need. I'm thinking we should buy a couple of big rig dealerships in the Midwest and down South to launder some of this money. Oh, and set up a meeting with some of the law enforcement folks we have on payroll. Probably time some of them got new cars."

"I'm on it, L.C.," Harris replied.

"Orlando, you gear up manufacturing on a small scale for now, until Harris can buy us a pharmaceutical company south of the border. Junior, put together a security plan. If this takes off, there are going to be more people than normal coming after us. When they do, I want them to know that the Duncans are not to be played with. Also, I want Orlando's lab to have twenty-four-hour armed guards."

"What about me, Pop?" Rio sounded annoyed. His club activities had been an important part of the test run for H.E.A.T., but now he felt like he was about to get pushed to the side once again. His father always had a way of making him feel like a second-class citizen because of his sexuality, and he was getting more than a little sick of it.

The two Duncan men locked eyes for a second and everyone expected the worst, but L.C. surprised them all by saying, "I didn't forget you, Rio. I want you to go on a little road trip to our club down in South Beach. See if you get the same response down there that you got up here. Personally, I'd like to start distribution outside of the Northeast, away from our normal base of operation."

L.C. glanced around the room. "Any objections before I close the meeting?"

A lone dissenting voice came from the most unlikely source. "Yes, I have an objection. I have a big objection."